Business Before Pleasure

"And what about my land you so desperately need? Are you here to bargain for that?"

Alana winced at the harsh note in his voice. She stiffened and stalked angrily toward the door.

Raine was swift, blocking her exit. "I'm sorry, Alana. That was a low blow. I don't usually kick opponents when they're down."

She looked up at him, feeling the heat from his body, wanting nothing more than to wrap her arms around him, feeling his strength and drawing on that strength. "Are we opponents?" She raised her eyebrows. "I hoped we could be friends."

His hands settled on her shoulders. "You are a vice president of Hudson Enterprises. I own Bradburn International. We compete for the same contracts, the same money. We both want to be the biggest and best. Wouldn't you say that makes us opponents?"

"I suppose," she murmured, her eyes tracing the tanned column of his throat, imagining planting a kiss right at the base. "Couldn't we ignore business and be friends?" She looked up, her eyes gleaming.

"We can be many things, but we'll never be just friends."

His hands roamed from her shoulders to her arms and back to cup her face. The fire in his eyes mesmerized her, the low timbre of his voice seductive.

He pulled her toward him . . .

CATCH UP ON THE BEST IN CONTEMPORARY FICTION
FROM ZEBRA BOOKS!

LOVE AFFAIR (2181, $4.50)
by Syrell Rogovin Leahy

A poignant, supremely romantic story of an innocent young woman with a tragic past on her own in New York, and the seasoned newspaper reporter who vows to protect her from the harsh truths of the big city with his experience — and his love.

ROOMMATES (2156, $4.50)
by Katherine Stone

No one could have prepared Carrie for the monumental changes she would face when she met her new circle of friends at Stanford University. For once their lives intertwined and became woven into the tapestry of the times, they would never be the same.

MARITAL AFFAIRS (2033, $4.50)
by Sharleen Cooper Cohen

Everything the golden couple Liza and Jason Greene touched was charmed — except their marriage. And when Jason's thirst for glory led him to infidelity, Liza struck back in the only way possible.

RICH IS BEST (1924, $4.50)
by Julie Ellis

From Palm Springs to Paris, from Monte Carlo to New York City, wealthy and powerful Diane Carstairs plays a ruthless game, living a life on the edge between danger and decadence. But when caught in a battle for the unobtainable, she gambles with the only thing she owns that she cannot control — her heart.

THE FLOWER GARDEN (1396, $3.95)
by Margaret Pemberton

Born and bred in the opulent world of political high society, Nancy Leigh flees from her politician husband to the exotic island of Madeira. Irresistibly drawn to the arms of Ramon Sanford, the son of her father's deadliest enemy, Nancy is forced to make a dangerous choice between her family's honor and her heart's most fervent desire!

Available wherever paperbacks are sold, or order direct from the Publisher. Send cover price plus 50¢ per copy for mailing and handling to Zebra Books, Dept. 138 , 475 Park Avenue South, New York, N.Y. 10016. Residents of New York, New Jersey and Pennsylvania must include sales tax. DO NOT SEND CASH.

THE LION'S SHARE

JULIA KENT

PINNACLE BOOKS
WINDSOR PUBLISHING CORP.

PINNACLE BOOKS

are published by

Windsor Publishing Corp.
475 Park Avenue South
New York, NY 10016

First printing: December, 1988

Printed in the United States of America

Chapter One

Phillip Hudson placed his hands on the polished surface of the walnut conference table and leaned forward looming over his board of directors like a storm cloud, his massive shoulders blocking their view of Diamond Head. Silver hair stylishly cut, a charcoal suit custom made by the best tailor in Hong Kong, a white silk shirt and conservative burgundy tie belied the ruthless, tyrannical dictator determined to get his way. "I want the Aloha Shores project started and I want it started immediately." He spoke slowly and deliberately in a voice as hard as granite, steely grey eyes shadowed by bushy eyebrows, daring anyone to contradict him. When no one spoke, he straightened, a complacent look on his face as he crossed his arms over his chest. "It's settled. We start construction immediately."

Alana Jordan leaned back in her chair, absently running a hand over her ebony hair pulled into a knot at her nape. Violet eyes, ivory skin and delicate features gave her a fragile look, but she had proved her toughness to more than one unsuspecting businessman. A mass of contradictions, she was mysterious and open, sensuous and innocent, intelligent yet naive. Few men had bothered to probe below the beautiful, sophisticated surface, regretting the day they thought her a piece of fluff eager for their masculine attention. Alana readily acknowledged to herself that she didn't encourage anyone to explore the depths of her character. Self-contained, her emotions were camouflaged by amethyst eyes that could look right through a person and a practiced expression effectively masking her thoughts. Alana stifled a sigh, knowing Phillip's penchant for attempting to intimidate and bully the board. It made for marathon meetings. She had started in the management training program right after graduate school, and after long hours, hard work, and more determination than she had thought possible, at thirty-two, she was a vice president and on the board of directors. She knew she deserved it, but sometimes wondered if her abilities were the sole reason she had risen as quickly as she had. Phillip had become her mentor when she had presented a proposal for a condominium complex on the Big Island. Just about the time she was named vice president for the research and development division she and Phillip had become lovers. Coincidence or Phillip's master plan? Her violet eyes darkened momentarily before clearing and returning to the business at hand. Her gaze rested on the stubborn set to Phillip's jaw. Phillip's commanding personality made him a man people either hated or loved. She was one of the latter, but it was hard to remember that this was the same man who had whispered words of love to her just last night.

Phillip's forehead was crisscrossed with frown lines, his tanned skin leathery from a disregard for the intensity of the tropical sun. At fifty-four he had the energy of a man half his age. Aloha Shores was his pet project, one Phillip and Alana had developed together. She had to voice her concerns since no one else seemed inclined to speak. Meeting his gaze with a direct one of her own, her voice was low pitched but firm. "Nothing is settled. We can't start work on a project of that magnitude without access to the ocean."

His gaze would have withered a lesser person. "We can start any time *I* say we start."

She didn't flinch from his hostile glare. "This project is the biggest we've ever undertaken in the development division. Unless the majority agree to begin construction, the project stays on the drawing boards." She held her breath, waiting for the explosion that was as inevitable as the sun rising every morning.

"So what are we waiting for?" he demanded, waving one arm to encompass the table, a deep red creeping up his neck and into his face.

"You can't bully us into voting for something that could ruin Hudson Enterprises." A deep baritone voice from the far end of the table commanded attention. "The shareholders didn't elect us to this board so that we could spend money unwisely. If you wanted sole authority, you shouldn't have taken the company public." Dan Asuka leaned forward and tapped his finger on the paper in front of him. "It would be foolhardy to start building a resort worth millions of dollars without owning that ocean access."

"We own all of it but one damn piece," Phillip maintained stubbornly, his deep voice rumbling around the room.

"A very important little piece," another director added. "That land cuts the complex in two. Without it we have two separate resorts and neither of them have ocean access. A resort development in Hawaii without access to the ocean is like a car without a steering wheel. It won't work."

Phillip grunted, calming down only slightly and slowly sitting down. "We'll get the land."

Alana watched Phillip carefully. Although his last heart attack had been five years ago, the frustration of this project was taking its toll on his health.

"You've been saying that for three years," Ben Adams muttered, tossing his pen down and leaning back in his chair. "Ever

9

since we started this project, you've said we would get that land, but it is still in Bradburn's possession."

Phillip's fist hammered the table, causing several people to jump. "If that damned real estate agent hadn't been such an asshole, we'd own that property. He told the bastard I wanted it! If the jerk had kept his mouth shut, we wouldn't be in this bind."

"The fact remains. We don't own the land." Alana fingered the black silk bow at her throat. "No land, no resort."

Phillip focused his wrath on her. "Whose side are you on?" he demanded, then took a deep breath, and with a lightening quick change of mood, he smiled and murmured softly, "You and I developed that project. Don't you want to see it come to life?"

Alana adjusted to his abrupt change of mood. Her voice wary, wondering what he was up to now, she said, "I'd be a fool to say I wouldn't but I would be doing a disservice to the shareholders if I demanded that we go ahead with the project now and jeopardize the entire division." She held his gaze, detecting the admiration reflected in his gray eyes. The respect in his gaze warmed her heart and gave her the confidence to continue. She leaned forward and clasped her hands in front of her, studying her manicured nails for a moment before speaking. "I want the company to prosper, and if you look at this situation objectively, our credibility in the business world would take a beating if we went ahead. Our stock would take a dive." Alana knew she had the other directors' backing on that point. Every one of them had substantial shares of Hudson stock in their portfolios. No one wanted to take a loss on their investment.

"Phillip," Dan spoke, choosing each word very carefully. "This is the biggest project the division has ever undertaken. The other divisions can't carry the loss if we fail. We have to think of the total corporation, not just one division."

Phillip's mood changed abruptly. "Afraid some of those Hawaiian boys of yours might lose their jobs, huh?" he sneered, not waiting for a reply, barely flicking a glance at the angry color staining Dan's teak skin. "I know what the consequences are." He glowered at no one in particular. "I also know that every day we delay in building, the cost goes up."

"My father is right." Hilary Cummings spoke up for the first time. As soon as all eyes were focused on her she continued, "If we delay much longer and interest rates climb even one per cent, we could be adding millions to the final cost of this project. It'll take twice as long to recover our losses." Icy blue eyes scanned the table.

Alana looked at the other woman for a long moment, trying to decide if she should oppose father and daughter. Hilary returned Alana's stare, her classic features smooth, her shoulder length hair perfectly coiffed in a smooth twist. Her pristine white blouse was buttoned to the throat, the severe lines of her royal blue suit making her look even colder and more remote than Alana knew her to be.

Phillip's daughters were as different as fire and ice. Melanie used her position as Phillip's daughter to snare men, while Hilary froze when someone looked as if they might touch her. Hilary took her job as comptroller seriously while the activity in Melanie's office in the public relations department had little to do with business. Melanie went through men like some women went through hair styles while Hilary had been married to her present husband for ten years. Hilary was thirty-eight and looked older. Melanie was thirty-three and looked twenty-five. Alana had never seen Hilary smile, but she had seen Melanie raise a man's blood pressure with one dazzling look. It was only a matter of time before Melanie would demand her share of attention.

Alana continued with her objections. "If this project fails, Hudson Enterprises will be vulnerable to a hostile take over or

11

bankruptcy. We need Bradburn's land or another suitable location for the resort or the project is dead."

"The feasibility studies showed there was no more suitable land for this project." Hilary's words were clipped, but then she paused, a sly look on her face as she glanced first at Alana and then her father. "We could scrap the project, cut our losses, and start on the dude ranch on the Big Island."

Alana's heart sank. The dude ranch was Hilary's project. Nothing would give Phillip's daughter more pleasure than to dump the resort Alana had helped developed.

"No! I want that complex built." Phillip's face was grim, white lines of stress and pain etching his mouth. He pounded the table again, venting his frustration. "The man's a damn fool. I'm willing to pay him ten times what that land is worth."

Alana saw him wince slightly as beads of perspiration dotted his forehead. Phillip wouldn't welcome her concern, but it was difficult to watch the man she loved in pain. Her life revolved around Phillip and Hudson Enterprises. She couldn't imagine life without either one of them.

"But he doesn't want to sell," Dan muttered, running his hand through thick black hair, exasperation sharpening his usually mellow voice. "Until we get the land, the project is at a standstill."

Phillip's piercing gaze swept around the table, his voice hard, his face implacable. "We'll put it to a vote."

"And if we vote to table the project until we have the land, will you stop badgering us about it?" Alana asked.

Phillip was silent for a moment. "I haven't much choice, but I must warn you that I will do everything in my power to sway your opinions." He gave them all a smile as deadly as a cobra's bite.

"It's a good thing our jobs don't depend on a favorable vote." Alana's voice was dry as one fine brow quirked. Although some of the directors were executives of the company, there were enough members from other corporations to keep the board from being overpowered by Phillip's authority.

Phillip gave her a long searching look, then murmured, "I wouldn't say that."

Alana was aware that all eyes in the room were on her, making her say, "What *would* you say, Phillip?" She wondered how many of the board members knew that she and Phillip were lovers. She hoped their affair had been discreet enough to keep the gossip to a minimum. When he didn't reply immediately, she said, "Are you saying that if we don't vote for construction of a project that's doomed to failure without a vital piece of property, you'll use your power to get us off the board or send us away to work on an obscure project?"

"There are some of us who would never be sent away," taunted a feminine voice at the other end of the table.

Alana groaned inwardly. Phillip's other daughter demanded her share of attention. Melanie Hudson Adams Steinberg Shawnessey had turned more than one board meeting into a circus. At the age of thirty-three, she had the body and face of a centerfold. Jade eyes, red hair that tumbled around her shoulders, and her generous curves made for a lethal combination. Melanie had refined the art of seduction in the certain knowledge that she was every man's fantasy, fulfilling as many of those fantasies as possible. Out of the corner of her eye Alana could see Melanie leaning toward Dan, the thrust of her lush breasts straining against the confines of her tailored scarlet suit jacket.

"No one is going to be sent away or kicked off the board," Phillip blustered. He looked offended that Alana would even think such a thing. "I promised I wouldn't threaten any of my employees, and I meant it. I always keep my promises."

She met his gaze and didn't answer. She didn't have to. He knew the answer to that one. His promise to ask his wife for a divorce several months ago was as yet unfulfilled. Not that she had been the one to broach the subject. She was attracted to

13

Phillip, and even loved him, but she wasn't sure she wanted to be married to him. Nevertheless, he had charmed her with glowing promises about their life together, while he continued taking his wife to the society events that a man of his position was expected to attend, and when he left Alana's bed he went back to the house he shared with Betty. It was one of the aspects of their relationship that bothered her a great deal, but she didn't want to destroy his marrage either.

Phillip looked away from Alana and searched the faces of the other board members. When no one met his piercing gaze, he sighed heavily. "If I can get Bradburn to sell the land, will you agree to start work on the project?"

"How are you going to do that?" Dan asked, his voice dry as he leaned back in his chair.

Phillip rubbed his chin, his eyes turning to slate. "I'll come up with something."

"Phillip, please remember we have a lawsuit pending on the electronics firm you wanted to buy. You've been accused of intimidating the management. Don't do anything illegal," warned Robert Somers, the corporate lawyer, pushing his horn rimmed glasses firmly into place.

"I'm no fool," Phillip retorted, pushing himself out of his chair. When he walked over to the scale model of the project, he reached into his pocket and quickly put his hand to his mouth before running his hand over the complex of buildings. Alana thought of all the times he had run his hands over her body. Phillip was a wonderful mentor and lover. She wasn't blind to his faults but he had taught her more about business than she could ever learn from textbooks, and his lessons in love had made her aware of her own sexuality.

His hand stopped at the top of the bluff and he traced a finger down the diagonal path to the peninsula and beach below. "Just this small piece of land and Aloha Shores will be a reality. Exciting, isn't it? Condominiums, hotels, a convention center, golf courses, lagoons, world class tennis courts, shopping centers, helipad. Everything the affluent tourist could want, right at their finger tips." He lifted his head and his voice was hard. "I want ideas on how to get Bradburn to part with that land."

Melanie's soft voice broke the tense silence. "I think we should appeal to his sense of loyalty to the islands. After all, what's good for Hudson Enterprises is good for Hawaii." She flashed a wide smile at Jeff Marino, her boss in public relations.

"Melanie, Bradburn is loyal to no one but himself. That's an assinine idea!" He silenced any further remarks she might make with his harsh words and a quelling look.

Several board members shifted in their plush chairs when Phillip strode back to the head of the table and picked up a sheaf of papers, tossing them into the air. All eyes were on the fluttering paper rather than the creator of the storm as Phillip's voice boomed across the room like rolling thunder. "You tell me to get the land, but not one of you assholes has a goddamm idea how the hell to get it! Hudson Enterprises pays you damn good money to think. I want some ideas and I want them now." His gaze narrowed on Alana. "Ms. Jordan. You developed this project. I want an idea from you." He pinned her with his gaze. "Now," he growled.

Alana inwardly fumed and fought the color that threatened to flood her cheeks, but then she reminded herself that this was a classic move of Phillip's. Leave it to Phillip to bluster his way out of a corner. She had outmaneuvered him more than once. She met his glower with a smile. "Since we aren't the military and we can't just take over the land, perhaps we could try another tactic. You're the only one who's really talked to him, Phillip. One of us could try negotiating a reasonable settlement with Bradburn. One of us might succeed where you've been ... unsuccessful." Her chin lifted as she allowed her words to sink in.

He was quick to retaliate. "Who would you suggest, Alana?

15

Yourself? Melanie? I suppose one of you could offer him something that I'm not equipped to do." The suggestive tone of his voice and the smoky grey eyes that raked her body made her skin crawl.

Melanie murmured in a low voice, "I'll be glad to try and convince Raine Bradburn to sell the land to us."

"I thought Dan or Robert would be the most likely to present a package Bradburn might accept," Alana countered, her voice calm. She would never let anyone see how Phillip's words wounded her. Violet eyes darkened to amethyst. "Dan has known Bradburn for a long time. They went to school together and even played football together. Maybe he could find out what Raine would settle for, and Robert is one of the finest negotiators in the United States. Remember the settlement he was able to get with the canning companies in Alaska just before the salmon spawning? If it hadn't been for Robert, the foods division would have had a major loss."

Phillip gave her a withering look. "So you think one of these men could succeed when I couldn't?"

Alana shrugged slim shoulders and picked up her pen, tapping it on the sheet of paper in front of her. "What do we have to lose? Putting this project on hold for a few weeks won't cost nearly as much as if we go ahead without the land and lose everything." Her eyes reflected her pride as her gaze strayed to the model of the project. The complex would be her crowning achievement, her credibility as an executive in the business world would be established beyond a doubt.

"I think Alana is right," Dan said, rubbing one finger along his jaw. "I can give it a try. Maybe he'll at least tell us what he wants for the land. If I don't get anywhere, Robert could give it a try. Why don't we meet again next week. We'll report on our progress." He paused, leaning back in his chair.

"Maybe he'd sell for a percentage of the profits from the

project," Alana murmured, glancing at Phillip through lowered lashes.

"He gets no interest in the complex at all! Nothing!" Phillip thundered. Both hands slashed the air before striking the table with a resounding thud like a judge's gavel sounding the final decree. He took a deep breath and Alana saw him wince, raise his hand to his chest and then drop it quickly. "I see no reason to discuss this further. We'll meet again Monday, and I want some action on this. Meeting adjourned." He whirled around and stalked out of the room without a backward glance.

Phillip paced around the penthouse of Hudson Towers. The hotel consisted of three towers of luxury suites on beachfront property at Waikiki. The penthouse was used exclusively by Hudson Enterprises for entertaining guests and clients. White plush carpeting and creamy walls gave it an open, airy feeling. Overstuffed polished cotton cushions of oyster and lemon covered the chairs and couches. Glass topped ratan tables held huge crystal vases of fresh flowers, the vivid tropical blossoms brilliant splashes of color in the living room. Two walls were floor to ceiling glass, revealing a breathtaking view of Diamond Head, the ocean, and Waikiki. At the moment, there was only one thing on Phillip's mind. He glanced at his gold Rolex. Where was she? Maybe she wouldn't show up. He had been rough on her at the board meeting, and Alana was stubborn enough to show him how angry she was. It was one of the things that attracted him to her. She stood up to him like no one else did. He checked the Dom Perignon chilling in the silver bucket. Perfect. He checked his watch again. He had cancelled two meetings for this. She'd better show up. He was booked solid with meetings for the next two days and nights and Betty, his wife, had filled the weekend with social commitments he had to attend. He wouldn't tell Alana he couldn't see her until next week. She'd get that wounded look in her eyes, and he would feel guilty. He couldn't help it if he was married to one woman and loved another one.

He heard the click of the door and whirled around, a wide smile on his face when Alana appeared in the doorway. "Hi, honey. I was beginning to wonder if you'd show up."

She dropped her pigskin briefcase by the door. "A hand delivered invitation from the chairman of the board is difficult to refuse." Alana stepped into the room, her gaze scanning the room. "Why are we meeting here?"

"Why not?" He crossed the room to take her into his arms. He felt her resistance. "It's not a business meeting, Alana."

"I gathered that much." She tried to pull out of his arms, but he held on to her.

He nuzzled her neck. She smelled so good. She wore a light, lemony fragrance that drove him crazy. "Ease up, Alana." He kissed the column of her throat.

"How can you be so rotten to me in a board meeting and then expect me to make love to you an hour later?" she demanded, her hands pressed against his chest.

"That is business, this is personal. One has nothing to do with the other." He pulled the comb from her hair and ran his hands through the silky black curtain.

"I can't turn my emotions on and off as quickly as you can." She broke loose and stepped toward the windows. "I love you, Phillip, but when you start bullying me in board meetings I want to walk out. It's degrading."

"It's business." He stood behind her, his hands on her shoulders, gently massaging the tense muscles. "I have to be in control at all times in those meetings. If I show any weakness, someone is certain to use that against me." He pulled her back against him, wrapping his arms around her waist and resting his chin on top of her head. "You take it too personally."

18

"You're not as hard on anyone else as you are on me," she said in a small voice.

He smiled as his hands moved up to unbutton her jacket and slip it from her shoulders. "I'm not having an affair with any of them. No one would ever suspect we were lovers."

She turned to him, tugging off his tie. "Sometimes I have difficulty remembering that we are."

He led her back to the couch, pushed her down gently and poured her a glass of champagne. "I love you, Alana. That's one thing I never want you to forget."

She sipped her champagne, Phillip's gaze on her moist lips. His body ached for her. He took the glass from her lifeless hands. His lips moved over hers, his tongue seeking the interior of her mouth. His hands worked on the buttons of her blouse, pushing it from her shoulders. His lips trailed over her shoulders as he pressed her into the cushions, removing her bra and tossing it aside.

His mouth covered a swollen tip of her breast and she arched toward him. Phillip felt himself drowning in a passion and need for this woman, but he fought for control. He wouldn't take her until she felt the same consuming need. His tongue played with her breasts, tormenting and teasing until her hands clutched the back of his neck and pressed his mouth against her. Phillip smiled as he obliged her.

Phillip rolled off Alana and knelt beside her, his hand sliding up her skirt to caress her inner thigh. He pulled off her remaining clothes, bending to kiss her flushed body.

When he felt his control slipping, he stood and stripped off his clothes, his body covering hers. Her skin was silky and smooth, the taste of her body filling his mind with desire. Her body was warm and willing under him, welcoming him with a matching desire. Conscious thought fled as he felt the burning hunger of his body. His hands roamed her body as if he could never get enough of her. He entered her and his control snapped like a raging fire. He felt her response and the low moan from deep in her throat. Her arms and legs were wrapped around him as he muttered her name over and over, feeling like he was rushing through a dark tunnel before being catapulted into blinding light, soaring higher and higher before the bliss of release and gentle reentry into reality.

Alana touched his cheek with her lips. "I love you, Phillip."

"And I love you, Alana. Someday . . ."

She pressed her fingers to her lips. "Don't make promises you can't keep. Let's just take it a day at a time."

"I'd rather take it a night at a time," he growled, kissing her with an intensity that surprised him, hurt that she didn't want him to make a commitment to her.

"Any time," Alana sighed, her eyes closed.

Chapter Two

Hilary stalked into her office, slamming the door behind her without a word to her secretary. She tossed her notes from the board meeting onto her desk before turning to the view of the mountains, her arms crossed over her chest, her face grim. Her father had often sought Hilary's advice about key projects. Finally she had felt a closeness to her father she had craved all her life, but Alana Jordan had changed all that. Since he had promoted Alana to vice president, he didn't have time for Hilary. It wasn't fair! She was Phillip's daughter, Alana Jordan an employee.

Hilary's arms dropped to her sides, her shoulders sagging. She had noticed the way her father looked at Alana. He wanted Alana for more than her business acumen.

Dropping onto the white leather chair, Hilary stared at her notes from the meeting. She had agreed with her father, and yet, he had listened to Alana. Hilary had been replaced as her father's sounding board, and she didn't like it one little bit.

Picking up her telephone, she quickly punched out a number and waited for someone to pick up the other receiver. "Marco? It's Hilary Cummings."

"Hello, Mrs. Cummings. What's it going to be today? The ponies?"

"I don't think so." She pulled her calculator closer. "How about the big fight?"

"I didn't think you bet on boxing," he said with a chuckle.

"I feel like being adventurous. What are the odds on the defender?"

"Three to one to repeat for the title."

Hilary punched numbers into her calculator. "Put ten grand on him for me."

"Gotcha. Anything else? How about the Super Bowl?"

Hilary tapped her chin. "What are the odds on that?"

"Defending champions favored by three."

"Put ten grand on the challengers." Hilary felt better already. There was something about beating the odds that gave her a thrill. "I'll talk to you on Monday, Marco." She hung up and sat back, a smile softening her features. She could make a lot of money this weekend.

Melanie sauntered back to her office, a smile firmly in place, hiding her frustration. There just didn't seem to be any way she could win Phillip's approval. He didn't care. He never had. She closed her office door and paced around the desk. No matter how good her ideas were, he wouldn't even listen. When he had suggested she serve on the board, she had been thrilled, certain that it meant he had finally realized she was an intelligent member of the family. Yet he continued to treat her like an empty-headed teenager. He gave her little responsibility, while Hilary was made comptroller. And now they had both been replaced by Alana Jordan.

Melanie smoothed her skirt, and pushed a button on the panel next to her telephone. "Chad, would you come in here?"

Melanie's assistant knocked once and entered her office. He

was tall, blond, bronzed, and good looking. "How did the board meeting go?"

"Father was in a foul mood. We're meeting again on Monday." She sauntered around the room as Chad settled into a chair.

"Anything I can do to help?" His gaze followed her around the room.

She leaned against the door, flipping the lock with a deft movement. "Yes, I think you can." She regarded him through heavy lids. "Do you think I'm attractive?"

Chad's gaze was warm. "Very."

"How do you feel about mixing business with pleasure?" Melanie gave him a dazzling smile. If her father didn't care about her, there were plenty of other men who did.

"What did you have in mind?" His gaze raked her body before meeting her glittering gaze.

"We need to develop an idea to pry some land from Raine Bradburn." She straightened and strolled toward Chad.

"And the pleasure part?" he murmured, tilting his head back to look up at her.

"I've always thought the best ideas come when a person is completely relaxed." She leaned over him, her hands on his shoulders, her lips hovering inches from his.

Chad swallowed hard. "I, ah, don't feel very relaxed right now."

"But you will," she crooned, stroking the back of his neck with one hand. She traced his lips with her tongue.

He closed his eyes, opening his mouth to her invading tongue. His hand curled around her neck, pulling her closer.

Melanie slipped off his tie and slowly unbuttoned his shirt, sliding her hand over his taut skin. Her pulse raced. The first time with a man was always exciting. One never knew quite what to expect.

Chad suddenly pushed her back, jumping to his feet. His breath was ragged. He pulled Melanie into his arms, his mouth capturing hers while his fingers worked on the buttons of her

23

jacket. Tossing it aside, he took a step back and slipped her camisole over her head, freeing her breasts to his touch. He stopped, a puzzled look on his face. "Are you sure you want to do this? Here?"

"I wouldn't have locked the door if I didn't," Melanie murmured, pushing his shirt off his shoulders. She nipped his neck.

All restraint gone, Chad fumbled with the zipper on her skirt, letting it fall to the floor as he ran his hands over her lush curves, stripping off her remaining clothing.

Melanie expertly unbuckled his belt and ran a fingernail down his zipper. "Do you want me, Chad?" she murmured.

"Since the day you interviewed me," he muttered, his voice thick, cupping a breast in each hand.

She loosened his slacks and pushed them off, surprised and delighted that he wore no briefs. Her gaze raked his body. He was fantastic. A moan escaped Melanie's lips as Chad tugged at a nipple. She felt desire warm her body.

They fell to their knees, hands probing, tongues dueling. Melanie was on her back, Chad covering her body with kisses. He hovered over her, his hand stroking her body. "A real red head," he murmured, his hand stopping between her thighs.

Melanie pulled him down, desire raging, but he resisted. His mouth followed his fingers, teasing and tempting until Melanie shuddered. Taking the initiative, she pushed against him and hovered over him, her hands on his shoulders. Straddling him, she gave a satisfied smile as he plunged inside of her, moving with an ever quickening rhythm. Melanie threw her head back, a low growl coming from her throat.

Chad's fingers continued to probe, finding the spot that made her shudder and move faster until they were both spent.

Collapsing on his well muscled chest, Melanie closed her eyes. Chad was good. Very good. He deserved a raise.

* * *

Stepping out of the air-conditioned hotel, the hot afternoon air immediately engulfed Alana. Phillip had left a half hour earlier, and now it was her turn. She wished they didn't have to be so careful but understood the need for it. It didn't make her feel any less guilty. She stood still for a moment, turning her head in the direction of the trade winds, lifting her chin and letting the breeze caress her face. She loved the warmth, thankful once again that she had chosen Hawaii instead of Michigan, New York, or North Dakota. She savored the caressing heat of the sun while trying to ignore the sounds of snarled traffic. The scorching pavement burned through the thin soles of her Gucci shoes as she threaded her way through a bus load of Japanese tourists taking pictures of Waikiki Beach before finding a cab to take her home.

She ducked into the lobby of Sunset Towers and paused at the security desk. "How's your daughter doing, Frank?" She greeted the uniformed man behind the desk with a smile.

He returned her smile, his bronzed leathery face crinkling like used tissue paper. "The doctor says she'll be walking without crutches in a couple of weeks. She really loves the art supplies you sent to her." He reached into the desk and pulled out a large manila envelope, opening it carefully. "She drew this for you and told me to give it to you as a thank you."

Alana looked at the watercolor painting of a young Hawaiian girl doing the hula at the base of a cascading waterfall, her arms raised gracefully over her head, her body swaying to unheard music. Flowers were tucked into her flowing black hair and a pink lei adorned her neck, the brilliant purple of her dress in contrast to the green mountainside. There was an ethereal quality about it that caused a lump in her throat. "This is beautiful, Frank. Tell her I'll hang it in a place of honor."

He sat up a little straighter. "She'll like that."

Alana waved and strode toward the elevators.

Sunset Towers was a cluster of five high rise apartment buildings that shared a common entrance. They also shared underground parking, a health club, swimming pool, tennis courts and social center. The ground level boasted a small grocery store, several boutiques, a sporting goods store, a deli, and a good restaurant. The focus of the center of the complex was a manicured garden, the perfect spot to entertain guests or just relax. This was the first project Alana had developed for Hudson Enterprises, and it held a special place in her heart. She had picked out her apartment before it was built and was the first tenant to move in.

She rubbed the back of her neck with her free hand. God, she was tired and sticky. She couldn't wait to change her clothes and get out and run and then jump into the pool. Her key was in one hand and as she opened the door she dropped her attache case and Sarah's painting on the small glass and brass table in the foyer. Her jacket was tossed on the chair next to it. Unbuttoning her blouse and kicking off her shoes, she padded across the foyer and sank her toes into the sand carpeting.

"Are you that anxious to have me make love to you again?" came a teasing voice from the far end of the living room.

Startled, Alana jumped and then visibly relaxed, a soft smile curving her lips. Phillip Hudson was sitting on her sofa, his dark suit a contrast to the beige overstuffed couch. Copper, brown and rust pillows were tossed on the other end of the couch. His feet were propped on the brass and oak coffee table.

Alana's smile turned into a grin. "Sounds like a marvelous way to end the day." She laughed at his comical leer before disappearing into the kitchen. She poured two glasses of iced tea and sauntered back into the living room, handing one glass to Phillip. "I didn't expect to see you again this afternoon." Her tone was dry as she raised her glass to her lips.

Phillip raised his glass in a salute. "I couldn't stay away.

Besides, I wanted to talk to you about the project and I forgot about it before." He gave her a satisfied smile that quickly turned to frustration. "I want Aloha Shores built."

"I know." Alana curled up in a chair and rubbed the muscles of her neck. She gave Phillip a level look. "I didn't voice my objections to make everyone think we weren't having an affair. I meant what I said."

"We both want it built. Why do you have to make people think about the negative side?" A determined look crossed his face as he took a deep swallow of his drink.

"Because you refuse to acknowledge it." Alana was tired of arguing. She stretched her arms over her head. "Why did you come here?" she asked, stifling a yawn.

"Why do you think?" The hunger in his voice unmistakable.

Alana swirled the ice in her glass. "You're insatiable." She paused. "Phillip, do we have any future together?" Amethyst eyes met a smoky grey gaze.

He leaned forward, rubbing his forehead with one hand. "No one can predict the future," he murmured, not answering her directly. "Are you unhappy with our relationship?"

"No, of course not." She paused. "Well, maybe a little. I wish we could go out in public, like other couples do. It would be nice just to go to a restaurant together." She tried to hide the wistful note in her voice.

"My affairs have always been discreet," he said, a wary look in his eyes. "I have to maintain a certain image in the community. As long as Betty is my wife, she's the only one seen with me in public."

Alana was silent for a moment before saying slowly, "I care about you too much to settle for the remnants of your life." She took a deep breath, meeting his gaze. "Maybe we should stop seeing each other before too many people get hurt."

He looked at her in surprise. "You're not interested anymore?"

"I didn't say that." She took a sip of iced tea.

"What are you saying?" His tone of voice was demanding, insistent.

"I love you," she murmured, not meeting his gaze. She had known from the beginning that an intimate relationship with Phillip Hudson would mean getting hurt.

"Honey, I'm just as involved as you are." He put down his glass and got to his feet.

"You are also involved in a long term marriage." She took another swallow of her tea, forcing it down passed the lump in her throat.

"I married Betty for the money and social position she could give me. Her money started my empire." He waved a hand through the air. "This building wouldn't have been possible if I hadn't married her and gotten started in real estate. She gave me two children and the best years of her life. I can't just dump her."

"But you can dump me when you get tired of me," Alana said with a long sign, finishing her tea.

"Don't worry, Alana. Nothing and no one is going to break us up." He put a hand on either arm of her chair.

"Phillip, I've never had an affair with a married man before, and it bothers me. I hate it when you leave me and go home to your wife. I hate seeing your picture with her at a premiere or charity event, and then I feel guilty when we make love because you belong to someone else. I try to put myself in her position, and I think I'd die if my husband was having an affair." Alana had finally admitted aloud what had been bothering her for a long time. Her conscience bothered her more than she would have thought possible. Leaving the hotel today feeling like a criminal had proven that.

"I'm sure Betty would appreciate your concern," he mocked, "but we haven't slept together ..."

"Don't say that!" Her eyes flashed. "It's the oldest line in history. Don't patronize me!"

Phillip stared at her then said very seriously, "I would never patronize you. I can't give up what we have together. We're fantastic in bed, and we generate more good ideas for the company than any six other people."

"Do we have to go to bed together to generate business for Hudson Enterprises?" She tilted her head to one side.

"Honey, I'd go to bed with you even if you never did anything more than answer the telephone." His hand touched her shoulder and moved down her open blouse, tracing the line of her bra.

"So it's just my body you want." His touch warmed her skin.

"We share more than most married people I know." He hooked a finger in the edge of her bra and pulled it down to expose her breast.

It was difficult to think as he rubbed his thumb over the tender nipple. "What do we share?" She took a deep breath. "A love of power? Lust?"

"Can't think of a better combination." He bent to flick his tongue over her nipple and then stood up, pulling off his suit coat and dropping it to the floor.

Alana was filled with anticipation and frustration. He'd make love to her, and they'd never finish this conversation. "There has to be more than that. And I'm tired of the intrigue and lies. I can't even admit that I have a lover!" She stared up at him, pain in her eyes. "You and Betty made the front page this morning."

"Betty chaired that benefit last night," he said, as if it meant nothing. His eyes narrowed. "You were there with Griff! Why did you go with him, anyhow? He's nothing but a boat bum." Phillip unbuttoned his shirt and tossed it aside. For his age he had an impressive physique. Not quite as muscular as a younger

29

man, but good enough to make Alana's heart quicken at the sight of his bronzed chest.

Unwilling to let him see how he affected her, she lashed out at him. "Are you jealous of a man twenty years younger than you with so much money he doesn't ever have to work? Or are you just possessive?"

"Did you let him make love to you?" Phillip demanded, his hands on her shoulders.

Alana met his gaze with a determined one of her own. "You don't own me, Phillip. It's really none of your business if I go to bed with a different man every night. How do I know you don't leave my bed and sleep with your wife?"

Phillip's mouth thinned. "That was a low blow." Like quicksilver, his mood changed. He chuckled as he slid one hand inside her blouse. "Where did you learn to be so headstrong and independent?"

"From the master," Alana sighed, leaning into his caress and lifting her face so he could kiss her.

"Bitch." Phillip teased her lips with his tongue, tangling a hand in the silken curtain of her hair.

As he caressed her, Alana spoke, regret in her voice. "Phillip, this isn't going to work."

"You are a wonderful lover," he muttered, his tongue tracing the shell of her ear.

"This won't solve anything." She struggled to slip from his grip.

"I don't give a damn." He pulled her into the bedroom, his voice husky.

"We have to talk." She balked, trying to pry his fingers from her arm.

"Later." He pushed the blouse from her shoulders. His fierce look turned to fire as his mouth touched her shoulder. "You have such beautiful skin."

Alana's head went back, her eyes closed. "You're just intrigued because I'm the only person in the islands who doesn't have a tan."

"Like fine porcelain." His lips trailed from one shoulder to the other. He removed her bra and tossed it aside. "You smell like sunshine." His mouth left a trail of kisses from her shoulder to the hollow of her throat and then to her ear. All the while his hands were busy undressing her until she stood before him naked. He leaned back to gaze at her. "Damn, but I can't get enough of you." Desire thickened his voice as he pushed her back onto the bed and hurriedly stripped off his own clothes, never taking his eyes off her. "You want me, too."

"And if I say no?" Alana murmured, a defiant glitter in her eyes.

He leaned over her, parting her thighs with his hands, his tongue invading her. When she arched involuntarily, he looked up, triumph shining in his eyes. "You want me just as much as I want you, Alana. That's all that counts."

As Phillip moved up her body, his mouth hungrily suckling her breasts, she tried to feel and not think. She wanted more than just a physical relationship.

Phillip loomed over her, his hands on either side of her head. "Where the hell are you?" he demanded. "Are you wishing you were with your younger lover?"

She stared at him, eyes flashing.

Crimson color flooded his face. "Were you making love to Griff last night?" One hand gripped her chin, forcing her to look at him.

"Were you making love to your wife last night?" She met his heated gaze, refusing to be intimidated.

Phillip dropped his full weight on top of her, clasping her hands above her head. "My wife is my business!"

"My life is my business!" Her voice rose as she struggled to free herself from his grasp. "I'll do as I damn well please. You don't own me, Phillip Hudson!'' She had never seen Phillip in a mood like this before.

"I'll show you I'm better than any young stud!" He ignored her protests, shoving her legs apart with one knee and entering her forcefully, penetrating deeper and deeper until he shuddered and collapsed on top of her, his breath coming in short gasps.

Alana felt violated by his disregard for her feelings. She was furious for being so powerless and unable to control the situation. She was enraged that Phillip brushed aside her protests as unimportant while he satisfied himself. She pushed him away, jumped out of bed and stalked into the bathroom, locking the door behind her.

She turned on the shower to drown out the sound of Phillip knocking on the door. "Alana, honey. I'm sorry." Phillip rattled the door knob. "It's just that you turn me on and I can't help myself."

"You never even considered my feelings!"

"I'm sorry, Alana." He paused. "Open the door." His voice rose so she could hear him clearly, even over the sound of running water.

"No." Alana closed her eyes and clenched her fists.

"Open the door or I'll knock it down." He pounded on it.

"I'll call the police. How would it look for the CEO of Hudson Enterprises to be caught in his vice president's bedroom?" Tears streamed down her face.

"You wouldn't be a vice president if you did a stupid thing like that!" he bellowed, pounding on the door.

"Get out of here, Phillip!" Alana stepped into the shower and stood under the pulsing water, drowning out Phillip's words.

Alana finished showering, cautiously opening the bathroom door and peering into the bedroom. Phillip's clothing was gone. She wrapped a towel around her body and explored the rest of her apartment. She was alone. Padding back into the bedroom, she braided her hair in a single plait down her back, pulled on shorts, a shirt, and her running shoes.

A run through Ala Moana Park and Magic Island did little to relax her. Usually the rhythmic murmur of the surf and trade winds rustling the leaves of the palm trees had a calming effect, but not today. She concentrated on the blend of turquoise ocean and cobalt sky, the chirp of tiny birds at her feet, the heady scent of plumeria, the gnarled roots of banyan trees, and the joyful shouts of children playing in the sand. Nothing worked, not even running to the point of exhaustion. All she accomplished was a strained calf muscle. Cooling down and walking back to her apartment, confusion clouded her mind. Phillip could be the most charming, irresistible, fascinating man in the world, but after today, she wasn't sure she wanted to see him again.

When Alana reached her door, she stood open-mouthed, gaping at the huge arrangement of tropical flowers. A long box rested in the foliage. It hadn't taken Phillip long to make amends, she thought dryly, struggling to get the arrangement through the door. Putting it in the middle of the coffee table, she lifted the box out of the arrangement before flopping onto the sofa and staring at the multihued bird-of-paradise, scarlet anthuriums, pink hibiscus, yellow lilies, and purple bougainvillea.

She opened the box, a smile tugging reluctant lips. Five strands of tiny ivory pikake flowers were woven into a lei. She put it over her head and held the intoxicatingly perfumed blossoms to her nose, inhaling deeply of the jasmine scent. Phillip knew she loved these flowers. She reached for the card, opening it with trembling fingers.

YOU WON'T LET ME BUY YOU JEWELS,
BUT YOU CAN'T REFUSE THIS LEI.
I'M SORRY. PLEASE FORGIVE ME.

Was he really sorry for what he had done? She frowned,

tugging on the end of her braid. Jumping to her feet, she stretched and inhaled the intoxicating scent again.

Phillip settled back in his limousine, wondering if Alana had received her flowers. He had paid enough for quick delivery. Alana had probably gone jogging after he left her apartment. He wasn't really sorry for what had happened. It was her own fault, sitting there with her blouse open. What did she expect him to do? He might be older than that bastard, Griff, but he had more money and power. And he had Alana. A smug look settled on his face. It was time to get rid of Betty. She was drinking too much these days anyhow. He wanted to improve his image, and Alana fit his plans perfectly. She was young, intelligent, beautiful, and sexy as hell. He had seen the way other men at the club looked at Alana. They all wanted to take her to bed. Only *he* had succeeded where others failed.

Phillip gripped his chest. Damn heart. He had been as strong as any stud until his heart attack. Damn nuisance. He stuck a nitro tablet under his tongue, slowly counting to fifty. The pain subsided. He'd give Betty the house and anything else she wanted. She could continue her bridge games and her charity functions. Hell, she'd never miss him. Thoughts of Alana's smooth taut skin heated his loins. She could make a man forget everything. He meant to have her, binding her to him so completely that she couldn't escape. He wanted her, and if he had to marry her, so be it.

As the limousine pulled through the gates and up the long drive to the house, excitement coursed through Phillip. He'd tell Betty he wanted a divorce, and then he'd go back to Alana. She'd be putty in his hands after the flowers and the note. As soon as the car stopped, he hopped out, lengthening his stride as he approached the door. He threw it open, bellowing as he walked over the threshold. "Betty! Where are you? I want to talk to you!"

"Mrs. Hudson isn't home, sir." Leonard calmly closed the door, his black bow tie and crisp white shirt immaculate. Although slight of stature, he was not intimidated by his boss, showing respect but never cowering. He looked up now, his face inscrutable. "She said she would return at six."

Phillip stared for a moment into the weathered Japanese face. "Where did she go?" he demanded, whirling around and stalking into the living room.

"Said she had some special shopping to do." Leonard followed him, pouring him a martini and handing him a cigar.

Phillip greedily accepted both. "Shouldn't have these, but, what the hell, a man has to take charge of his own destiny." He took a gulp of the cocktail and lit the cigar.

"As you say, sir." Leonard inclined his head and left the room.

Phillip settled into his favorite chair and put his feet up, staring out the open window at the magnificent view of the Pacific Ocean. From his mountain top home he could look down on Waikiki and out over the ocean. He could see the top of the Hudson Building, brilliant in the late afternoon sun.

He downed three drinks, placed phone calls to New York, San Francisco, and Hong Kong, smoked the cigar, and ate a bowl of Macadamia nuts before Betty came home.

"Hello, Phillip." Her voice was soft. "What are you doing home so early?"

"We have to talk." He reached for the pitcher of martinis.

She took the pitcher out of his hand, pouring the clear liquid into a glass.

There was no easy way of saying it. He took a deep breath. "I want a divorce."

Shattering glass followed a moment of deadly silence.

Chapter Three

"A divorce? Oh, Phillip, you don't mean it." Betty looked at her husband in disbelief, her voice anguished, her face ashen.

"I mean it, Betty." Phillip took a drink, puffing on his cigar, ill at ease. He wasn't sure this was what he really wanted to do, but if he didn't he knew he'd lose Alana, and he didn't want to do that. "What do we have in common? Nothing."

"We have this house, thirty-five years of living together. Hilary. Melanie." Her hands twisted, the diamonds on both hands flashing in the lamp light. Her pale blue silk dress rustled as she wandered around the room. Coming to a stop in front of Phillip's chair, she looked down at him, tears glistening in her eyes. "I just can't believe it."

"We should have done this a long time ago." Phillip couldn't meet her gaze.

She backed away and dropped into a chair. "We love each other," she said with a sobbing plea in her voice.

Phillip rubbed his temple. This was more difficult than he imagined it would be. "Our marriage is boring! There's no excitement, no fun!" In her prime, Betty had been a beautiful woman. It had been a pleasure seducing her. Betty was aging gracefully, her blond hair softly framing her oval face, her green eyes still bright, her classic features adding dignity, but she reminded Phillip of his own mortality. He wanted a younger, more vibrant woman. He wanted Alana.

"Phillip, how can you say that? I love you. I've always been here for you." Her face was pale, her eyes huge.

He made an impatient sound. "Maybe you should have been more independent. Our marriage has been over for a long time. It's time to make it legal."

She buried her head in her hands and then looked up, a stricken look in her eyes. "Is there someone else?" she paused, frowning. "I've heard rumors about you and Alana Jordan. Is that why you want a divorce? She has nothing to offer a man like you."

Like hell she doesn't, Phillip thought, stung by Betty's words. So she suspected his interest in Alana. He answered to no one. "Why can't you just accept this? We've led separate lives for a long time. It can't be a surprise to you."

She raised her head, wiping at a cheek with the back of her hand. "Why do you want a divorce now if you've been unhappy for a long time?"

"I'm not getting any younger," he said, bored with the conversation. "I've spent my entire adult life tied to you. I want my freedom." He saw her flinch, then continued, "I want young women, and I want everyone to see them!"

"Why? To prove you're not getting old?" Her voice was bitter as she clenched her hands together in her lap.

Phillip got to his feet, swayed slightly and took a deep breath. He'd be damned if he'd take a pill now. "I'm not old!"

"Are you all right, Phillip?" Betty was on her feet and by his side. "Can I get you anything?" When he shook his head, she said with real concern, "Who would take care of you if you had an attack?"

"I don't give a damn!" he bellowed. He stomped over to the window, looking over the water, his back rigid.

She wrapped her hands around her waist, her head bowed. "Please don't walk out on me."

He strode over to her and grasped her shoulders, shaking her until she finally looked up at him. The stricken look on her face caused a twinge of guilt. "We haven't shared a bed in a long time! I don't want to spend the rest of my life with you! I want a divorce and I want it now. I'm going to Mexico!" He released her, resting his hands on his hips. "You can have the house and anything else you want, but nothing will convince me to stay here another night."

He strode out of the room and took the steps to the second floor two at a time. He felt wonderful. Free. He couldn't wait to tell Alana. She'd make a great wife. Every other man on Oahu would be jealous. He headed for his suite of rooms, grabbed a suitcase and threw in just the clothes he'd need for Mexico. He heard the click of the door closing and spun around. "What do you want?" he growled, a wary look on his face. Betty hadn't been in his room in a long time.

She walked slowly into Phillip's bedroom. "It's not my fault we haven't slept together."

Phillip's eyes narrowed as Betty approached him, her hips gently swaying. She stood in front of him, a pleading look in her eyes. "We were always good together, weren't we?"

"Sure." He wondered what she was up to.

Betty freed Phillip's shirt from his slacks and slipped her hands underneath, gently massaging the taut muscles of his back. "No one else knows you as well as I do, Phillip." She unbuttoned his shirt and pushed it off.

Phillip steeled himself to her touch. He wanted Alana, not Betty.

Flicking her tongue over his male nipples, she tugged on one and then the other.

"Stop that!" Phillip began to weaken, his hands on her shoulders.

Betty's hands ran up and down his spine before reaching for his belt.

Phillip grabbed her hands. "No."

"Yes." Betty loosened his slacks and pushed them over his hips. She pushed him back onto the bed, her hands never stopping as she caressed and teased him.

"You know me too well," he muttered as Betty stood and quickly stripped off her own clothes.

"Yes, Phillip. I know you very well." She leaned over him, her mouth trailing kisses from his chest, down the narrowing of hair to his stomach and lower. "I know exactly what you like." She took him in her mouth, working her magic until he reached for her and pulled her on top of him.

In one swift movement he turned her onto her back and entered her, thrusting deeper and deeper until he was spent. Rolling onto his back, he flung his arm over his eyes. When he could speak, he said in a weary voice, "This won't change anything."

Betty sat up and looked down at him, hope fading from her eyes. "I love you." She slipped off the bed, softly closing the door behind her.

It was dark when Betty finally stirred. She couldn't believe Phillip had actually asked for a divorce. Divorce. She'd be ruined. As the wife of the CEO of Hudson Enterprises she commanded power and attention. As the divorced wife of Phillip Hudson she was nothing. She'd be as useless as yesterday's coffee grounds. She had seen it happen to too many of her friends.

Pushing herself to her feet, she went down the stairs, heading for the bar and taking a long look at the Baccarat decanter before she picked it up. Grabbing a glass with her other hand, she walked around the room, her head spinning with the implications of a divorce from one of the most influential men in the islands. Wandering out onto the lanai, she sank into a chair, pouring vodka into the glass and emptying it with one long swallow. She poured another generous portion, draining it as well. She stared at the twinkling lights of boats cruising off Waikiki. The liquor did nothing to block out Phillip's words. She abandoned the glass and drank straight from the decanter. Women got old and men matured. Old men wanted young women. Young men wanted young women. No one wanted old women. She wiped at the tears streaming down her cheeks. Betty took a long pull of vodka, the clear liquid dribbling down her chin. Her friends would murmur insincere sympathies and scratch her from their guest lists. Her children would shrug and go about their own lives, after all, they worked for Hudson Enterprises. She drained the bottle. Dropping it to the floor, she leaned back against the cushions and closed her eyes.

When Betty came to she rubbed her eyes and tried to focus on her watch, but it was too dark. She pushed herself to her feet, staggered into the house and stumbled into the den. Collapsing into the leather chair by the antique rolltop desk, tears moistened her cheeks again. She ran a trembling hand over the scarred surface of the desk. Phillip treasured this desk more than anything in the world. She grabbed some paper and a pen, and after writing for a few minutes, she dropped the pen and staggered into the living room. Reaching blindly for another bottle, she wove her way through the house, bumping into door frames, falling over chairs, and knocking priceless porcelain to the floor without a backward glance.

When she entered the garage she paused, taking a long drink. She squinted at the row of cars. The antique Porsche. Phillip loved his Porsche. She reached for the keys on the rack by the door, knocking other sets to the ground. Phillip. Alcohol couldn't dull the pain of rejection. She had invested the best years of her life in him, and now he wanted to get rid of her.

Vodka dribbled down her chin and onto her dress as she took another drink, opened the garage door and fumbled for the latch on the car. How did you start this damn thing? She managed to get the key into the ignition and start the car. She liked the loud noise. Taking another drink, she put the bottle on the seat next to her, patted it as if it were a pet, and jammed the car into gear, screeching out of the garage and going around the curve of the driveway on two wheels.

A big grin spread over her face. Serve the bastard right if she dented his precious car. At the end of the drive, she slammed on the brakes, took a long pull on the bottle that had spilled all over the calfskin seat, turned the wheel sharply to the right and pressed the accelerator to the floor. Who the hell cared about her? No one. Tears blurred her vision as she swerved to avoid oncoming headlights. The blaring of a horn didn't register as she sobbed, her hands clenching the steering wheel, wishing it was Phillip's neck. She hated him. She hated herself for loving him.

Careening around one curve, she turned the wheel to the right just in time to avoid hitting a van. She found herself on the lookout above the Halona Blow Hole. Skidding to a halt, she searched for the bottle of vodka, found it empty and tossed it out the window. Staring into the black ocean one thought burned in her mind. It was the reason she had taken Phillip's car in the first place. Maneuvering the car into position, she groped for the headlight switch, plunging her into total darkness. The rumble of the engine and the roaring thunder of waves crashing on the rocks below the cliff were the only sounds filtering through her numbed mind.

Her lips twisted. The son of a bitch. His image appeared in front of the hood, mocking and taunting her. She had humbled herself and he didn't care. Damn him! Her face contorted and her eyes filled with rage and pain as her foot pressed the accelerator to the floor. With the shrill squeal of rubber, the car crashed through the protective barrier. Floating through the air, Betty closed her eyes, a smile on her lips. The image of Phillip's taunting face was gone.

Her brain was too fuzzy to register panic or shock as the car smashed against the rocks at the bottom of the cliff, her body tossed out of the car like a rag doll just before a ball of fire engulfed the crumpled vehicle.

Phillip sat in his office, staring at the unread papers on his desk and then at his Rolex. He had given Alana enough time to appreciate the flowers. He had been surprised when Betty seduced him. It was true she knew him better than any woman, but it was time for a change. He relished the look on Alana's face when he told her the news, especially when he said they would marry. Alana would be just the right adornment for him. A satisfied look crossed his face. He called Lew. "Meet me in front in five minutes." He wondered if he should take another gift to Alana. What if she had another man in her apartment. The thought of her with other men filled him with rage. He'd make sure that she was his and his alone as quickly as possible. He wanted exclusive rights. He telephoned a jeweler who owed him a favor.

"Harry, I want your finest sapphire and diamond necklace, wrapped and ready to be picked up in fifteen minutes." There was a pause and then Phillip said, "Great! I want matching earrings and a ring delivered to my office next week. Better toss in a bracelet, too." Alana would never accept expensive gifts from him before, but once she was his wife, he'd smother her in jewelry. He could flaunt his wealth on her gorgeous body.

Hurrying down to the waiting-limousine, he settled into the back seat after directing Lew to the jewelry store. He had just poured a cocktail when the soft electronic ring of his telephone interrupted pleasant thoughts of a naked Alana in the back seat with him. Picking up the receiver, he barked into the mouth-piece, "Hudson here."

"Father, you have to get here as fast as possible."

He hardly recognized Melanie's voice. "Why?" he demanded, scowling.

"Father, hurry. The policy want to talk to you."

He heard her sob. She never called him father. "The police? What are they doing at the house? What the hell is going on?"

"I'm not at the house. I'm ..." There was a long pause and she said, "At the lookout above Halona Blow Hole. Mother's ... dead. I ... I don't know what happened ... the police said she drove your Porsche ... off the cliff. She ... was thrown from the car before ... it exploded." She was sobbing now. "She's dead." The line went dead.

Phillip held the receiver in his hand, staring straight ahead. Betty drove his Porsche off the cliff? Betty dead. Had their marriage really meant that much to her? She couldn't have been despondent enough about his demand for a divorce to kill herself ... could she? He buried his head in his hands, trying to grasp the reality of Betty's death. After thirty-five years of marriage, he'd never talk to her, see her again. He hadn't meant for this to happen. He just wanted to be free. He sat up and took a deep breath, the pain in his chest making him gasp. He slipped a nitroglycerin pill under his tongue, the pain easing. Phillip pushed a button and the glass partition slid down between the driver and the rear seat. "Head up to Halona Lookout," he said, his voice cracking slightly. "Make it as fast as possible."

He had to think. If Betty had been drinking, he wanted to make certain no empty bottles were found. He wouldn't have the Hudson name plastered on every paper in the islands with talk of drunken driving. Scandal had a way of affecting stock values, and shareholders might get nervous. Damn! Now he'd have to wait to tell Alana about the divorce. He caught himself.

No divorce. No one would ever know about the bitter scene with Betty. He grudgingly admitted to himself he didn't want anyone speculating that he might have been the cause of Betty's drastic solution to his demand of a divorce. His public image as a family man and pillar of the community would not only be tarnished, it would be destroyed. He thought about Betty. He would make certain her death was handled with dignity. It was the least he could do.

When the big car pulled into the parking lot, the police were already there, red and blue lights casting an eerie glow over the cluster of people standing on the edge of the cliff. A tow truck with a search light pointed toward the inky blackness of the sea was backed up to the guard rail, the grinding of winches and chains heard above the crash of the waves and the shouts of rescue workers.

Phillip sat and stared out the window for a moment. He'd rather face a hostile board of directors than the scene of Betty's death. If there was anything left to identify, he would have to do it. The thought of seeing Betty's crushed body made his stomach churn. No one should have to die like that. Had she suffered? The thought sent a chill through his body. Pulling himself out of the car he reluctantly headed toward the uniformed men crowded around the guard rail.

Melanie came rushing toward him, throwing her arms around his neck and sobbing. "Daddy! Daddy! What are we going to do?"

"The first thing you're going to do is pull yourself together, Melanie." His voice was low so only she could hear it as he put his arms around her. "Do you want your picture on the front page of the newspaper and on the local television news programs with mascara running down your cheeks?" Phillip handed her an ivory handkerchief. "Clean your face and act like a Hudson."

"How can you talk about the Hudson image when paramedics are hauling mother's body up from the bottom of a cliff!" Her eyes narrowed, her voice laced with bitterness. "You're a cold blooded, heartless bastard." She whirled around and stalked toward her car.

Phillip opened his mouth to call her back, but snapped it shut as she disappeared into the darkness. She had never understood the need for a dignified public image. He turned back to the activity on the edge of the bluff. The most logical reason for the accident was that Betty had been drinking and had driven off the edge of the cliff in a drunken stupor. In his own mind that didn't explain why she was in his Porsche when she never, ever drove that car. When a familiar yellow car squealed around the corner and lurched to a stop, his stomach twisted. How the hell did that weasel of a reporter get here so quickly?

Putting on his most intimidating frown, he stalked over to the battered yellow car and loomed over the short young man struggling to get out with his tape recorder and note book. "What are you doing here, Dudley?" He looked in distaste at the orange, blue, and purple shirt and red shorts worn by the slight man.

"I heard the call on the police radio. You're news, Mr. Hudson. A story like this will get me a promotion." He grabbed a stubby pencil from his back pocket. "Care to make a statement? Was it an accident? Suicide? Murder?"

Phillip felt like tossing the cocky young man over the cliff, but forced himself to say calmly, "I haven't talked to the police yet. I don't know what happened. My wife will be sadly missed by the people of Hawaii." He turned around and walked toward the bluff.

"Don't you think it's strange that your wife accidentally drove off the end of a parking lot when she knew every inch of this island? How do you explain that?" Dudley probed, hurrying to keep up with Phillip's long step.

Phillip remained silent. He had never allowed anyone to drive that car. What had possessed her to do so tonight?

A tall, well-built, dark haired man approached Phillip. He was dressed in chino slacks and a cotton shirt, with a police I.D. clipped to the pocket of his shirt. He held out his right hand. "Mr. Hudson? I'm Detective Maxwell." After shaking hands, he pulled out a notebook and a pen. "Do you have any idea why your wife was up here tonight?"

"Are you certain it's Betty?" Phillip frowned. He still couldn't believe she might be dead.

"The car is registered to you. We won't be sure it's your wife until you make a positive identification." He paused, his rugged features softening slightly. "She was thrown out of the car before it exploded."

Phillip flinched. "If it is Betty's body, then I don't know what to say. She never drove that car." He waved a hand in the direction of the men working around the truck. "How long before they bring . . . the body up?"

"Soon."

"Do you suspect foul play?" Dudley asked eagerly, shoving his tape recorder into the policeman's face.

Phillip sent the reporter a withering look. "Could I talk to you in private, detective?"

"Certainly." Dan looked at the crestfallen reporter. "You might want to go talk to the rescue team. They can tell you how they're retrieving the body."

Dudley shuddered slightly. "As long as I don't have to look at it. Blood makes me sick."

Phillip turned and walked away. He rubbed the back of his neck and closed his eyes for a moment, deciding how to approach Detective Maxwell. He chose his words carefully. "If that woman is my wife, we're going to have a problem." He paused. "Betty was an alcoholic. She was a respected member of society, serving on the boards of more charities than I can

47

name right now. I would hate to have her reputation ruined. I can't bring her back, but I can assure she receives the respect she deserves." Phillip meant what he said. It was too late to undo the hurt he had inflicted on her, but he could assure she was buried with dignity. He took a deep breath. "She may have come up here to think. We had . . . ah, an argument earlier this evening. She may have been drinking."

"There were twenty foot skid marks," Dan said, looking in his notebook. "And an empty vodka bottle was found in the ditch."

"The bottle may have been thrown out the window of any car," Phillip muttered. "Even if it was Betty's, it'll only prove she had been drinking. I would like to see this officially listed as a tragic accident rather than a drunken error in judgment."

"I can't promise, Mr. Hudson, but I will try to do whatever I can. She helped our benefit program many times."

Both men turned at the shouts of the rescue workers. Hurrying to the edge of the cliff, they watched as a body bag was hoisted over the edge.

"Will you identify the body, Mr. Hudson?" Dan asked softly.

Phillip nodded, never lifting his gaze from the bag. Of all the difficult things he had had to do in his life, nothing compared to this. He braced himself for the shock, but he couldn't have imagined what it would be like. It was Betty. A bloodied, broken image of his wife. He nodded his head and turned away, fighting the nausea that threatened to overwhelm him. The guilt he felt for his harsh words and rejection of her would stay with him for the rest of his life.

He blinked rapidly, rubbing a hand over his eyes. "If you don't mind, Detective Maxwell, I'd like to go home now. I need to notify the rest of my family." Phillip trudged toward the car, his shoulders sagging, his head bent. He felt old for the first time in his life.

"It was mother, wasn't it?" Melanie asked, falling into step beside him, tears streaming down her face.

"Yes." His voice was heavy.

"Are you going to call Hilary?"

"Yes."

"Do you know why she did it?" Melanie asked, her voice cracking.

"No." He took a deep shuddering breath. "I'll never forget tonight. Never!" He desperately needed to be alone. "I'll see you at home."

Dudley stopped Phillip just as he was getting into his car. "Mr. Hudson, is it possible that your wife committed suicide?"

"No!" he exploded. "I'll sue you and your newspaper if you even suggest such a thing." Phillip slammed the door. "Get me out of here, Lew."

"The house on Koko Head or Sunset Towers?"

"Koko Head. I only go to Sunset Towers on business."

"Yes, sir." The men exchanged a long look. "Shall I pick up the package at the jewelers after dropping you off?"

"Yes." Phillip's thoughts turned to his home. What if Betty had meant to drive off that cliff? Had she been capable of taking her own life?

He was surprised to see Melanie pacing back and forth in the living room, her red hair fanned out around her face when he entered the living room. "It's about time you got here!" She faced her father, her hands on her hips.

Phillip rubbed a hand over his eyes. "Have you called Hilary?"

"That's your responsibility, not mine!" Melanie stood in front of him, blocking his path to the bar. "Mother left a note before she drove off that cliff! She killed herself—because of you!" She spat the words at him, her jade eyes narrowed.

Phillip's face turned ashen.

Melanie's face was flushed, sparks in her eyes, her voice bitter. "You demanded a divorce. You wanted your freedom! You as good as killed her!"

Phillip winced as her words struck a nerve. He picked up the telephone. "It was an accident." He wiped his face with a hand and punched out some numbers. Turning his back on Melanie's stormy face he said, "Hilary. It's your father. There's been an accident. Could you come up to the house?" When there was silence for a moment, he gritted his teeth. "Get your ass up here right now if you know what's good for you. I don't care if Chandler and Mitchell are both having crises." He slammed the receiver down and swore under his breath.

Pouring some cognac into a snifter, he returned to the living room, trying to get comfortable on one of Betty's antique English settee's. "Did the note say anything else?"

Melanie was silent for a long moment and then said, "You demanded a divorce and she couldn't bear the pain and humiliation. She may have been drunk, but she knew what she was doing. She drove off that cliff deliberately. In your favorite car."

He sipped his drink, letting the fiery liquid settle in his stomach. "I can replace a car, but there's nothing I can do to bring Betty back."

"The only person who really understood me is gone." Melanie buried her face in her hands and sobbed. "She loved me, really loved me. You never had time for me, but mother did. She was the one who listened to me, was there for me, cared about me." She lifted her tear stained face, green eyes glittering. "And it's because of you she's gone."

Phillip took a deep breath. "She's gone, Melanie. Nothing either of us can say or do will bring her back."

Before Melanie could answer, the front door opened and slammed shut.

"What's going on?" Hilary demanded as she stalked into the room, glancing at her sister before staring at Phillip.

Phillip regarded his older daughter for a moment. "Want a drink?"

"Am I going to need it?" she replied.

"I think so." He waited until she had poured whiskey into a glass and walked back into the room. "Your mother drove off the cliff at Halona Cove."

The color drained from her already pale face. "She's ..."

"Dead."

The harsh word made her flinch. "God." Hilary slumped onto a chair, taking a long drink. "How? Why?"

"She had been drinking." Phillip's face was grim.

"Because our father had just demanded a divorce!" Melanie snapped.

"A divorce?" Hilary looked blankly from one to the other.

"I wanted my freedom," Phillip said with a shrug. "I never thought she would take it that hard."

Hilary's shoulders sagged as she stared into her drink. "I can't believe it. Mother gone."

"Ladies, we have to present a united front to the press. We will tell them that your mother didn't drive that car very often and hit the accelerator instead of the brake. If anyone wants to know why she was up there, we'll say she loved the spot and went up there often to think." He looked right at Melanie. "No other information. Anyone starts prying, you refer them to me."

Melanie met his gaze. "The public may never know what happened to mother, but we'll know and we'll never forget."

Chapter Four

Phillip had just completed a call to the funeral home when the alarm on his watch made him swear under his breath. He took a vial of pills out of his pocket. Damn nuisance. One heart attack and the doctors had you hooked. Take these pills, take that medication, exercise, don't smoke, don't drink, don't get excited. How was he supposed to run a company and not get excited? When was he supposed to exercise? In the middle of a board meeting? He gulped the pills and washed them down with a bottle of beer he took from the small refrigerator concealed in a wall of books. No one said he had to take them with water.

Phillip headed back into the living room. "Did you call Chandler?" he asked Hilary.

"He was very upset." She sat back on the white leather couch.

"He's always upset about something," Phillip grumbled, pouring a cup of coffee from the silver pot on the coffee table.

"Chandler is a fine, sensitive man." Hilary raised her chin. "Something you wouldn't know anything about."

"Thank the Lord," Phillip sneered, putting down his coffee cup and pulling a cigar from his pocket.

"Aren't you supposed to stop smoking?" Melanie said, looking at his cigar with distaste.

"An occasional cigar isn't going to hurt me." Phillip puffed on the cigar, a cloud of blue smoke circling his head.

"Fine." Melanie settled back in her chair, crossing her arms in front of her. "Kill yourself. See if we care. Then we inherit everything, and we can do what we want with your precious money and the company."

"Don't count on it." He leaned back and closed his eyes, thinking about Alana. She made him feel young again.

Both girls looked at him oddly. "Who else would inherit the company and your estate?" Hilary finally said.

"Not that lazy son of yours." Phillip opened his eyes, his gaze hard as he looked right at her. "You've spoiled him, Hilary. Mitchell is twenty-one years old and hasn't done an honest day's work in his life. He spends most of his time on the beach." Mitchell was one of Phillip's greatest disappointments in life. When his grandson was born, Phillip had such great plans for him, but Hilary had indulged Mitch's every whim.

"He's young. Let him have fun." Hilary's look was defensive. "If you want him to work, why don't you give him a job at Hudson Enterprises?"

"Because the kid wants to start out as vice president." His voice was dry. He puffed on the cigar for a few moments before saying, "He won't get a dime of my money until he realizes he'll have to earn it." His dream of having a grandson run Hudson Enterprises had disappeared long ago.

Melanie looked at her father and tilted her head to one side. "Who will inherit your stock and your estate if not your two devoted daughters?"

Phillip looked from one daughter to the other, prepared for their disapproval. "My new wife."

Melanie and Hilary gaped at Phillip. "Your new wife?" they said in unison.

Phillip nodded, putting his feet on the glass coffee table and puffing contentedly on his cigar. He hadn't meant to tell them quite like this, and he sure as hell hoped that Alana would say yes. Of course she would. No woman in her right mind would refuse the offer he would make her. And he knew she loved him.

"Mother isn't even in her grave yet and you're talking about getting married?" Melanie demanded. "How can you be so callous?" She looked at him in disgust, "You're not planning to marry Alana Jordan, are you?"

He put down his cigar and settled back in his chair before nodding his head, surprised that Melanie had figured it out so easily. Betty had mentioned rumors about Alana, too. How many others guessed they were lovers? The entire island would know soon enough. "I'm going to marry her just as soon as I can."

His daughters stared at him in disbelief.

"She fights you every inch of the way in board meetings," Hilary said with a frown. "She's hardly your style." She smoothed her navy linen skirt before looking up at him.

"She's younger than I am!" Melanie shuddered.

"She's intelligent, beautiful, and terrific in bed. She deserves my money more than either of you." He would make sure they got something, but not his entire fortune. Alana would put it to better use than either of his daughters.

"You're senile!" Hilary sneered, looking down her nose at him. "You'll be judged incompetent."

Phillip ignored her words. "It'll do you good to live on an equal footing with the rest of the world. You've had the benefits of my money for long enough. Too long. Neither one of you deserves the company or my estate."

"What about mother's money?" Melanie interrupted.

"Everything goes to me." His voice was harsh.

"Mother had a will." Melanie's eyes glowed with triumph. "It's in a safe place. She had money you didn't know about.

She set up trust funds for Hilary and me a long time ago. She also split her stock between us."

Phillip's eyes narrowed. Where did Betty get money to set up trust funds? He tried to remember how much stock had been put in her name when the company had gone public. It couldn't be more than five percent. "She wasn't smart enough to pull something like that."

"No?" Melanie laughed in his face, her eyes glittering. "There may be quite a few things you never knew about mother."

"We'll see about that." He gripped her arm. "Get me that will."

She stood her ground. "You'll see it at her lawyer's office."

"How come I never knew about this?" Hilary demanded, jumping to her feet.

Melanie twisted out of Phillip's grasp and confronted her sister. Her lips curled. "You never gave a damn about mother. You've been too busy with your career and the roulette wheel."

"You haven't exactly been a model daughter yourself." Hilary's gaze flicked over Melanie's halter topped sundress and disheveled hair.

"Maybe not," Melanie conceded, "but at least I cared about her. We talked every day."

"I always meant to call ..." Hilary said sadly, sitting down again. "Now it's too late."

Phillip rubbed the back of his neck, uncomfortable as he tried to deal with the emotions of his daughters. He hadn't been involved enough in their lives when they were growing up to understand either one of them, and he didn't have the time or energy to worry about it now. "We have a funeral to organize and a statement to prepare for the press." He gave them a hard look. "Remember: if anyone asks, your mother's death was an accident. Understood? And, Melanie, I want that note she left in a sealed envelope on my desk Monday morning."

Her eyes glittered mutinously like emeralds as she held his gaze.

His voice was as cold and hard as steel. "Monday morning." He was still in charge, and his children better realize it.

"I'll see you rot in hell first," Melanie muttered under her breath as she stalked out of the room.

Hilary trudged up the marble steps to her living room, her shoulders sagging. It was after two in the morning. Soft lights shadowed the contemporary living room decorated in hues of white with smoked glass accessories. The floor to ceiling doors that led to the garden terrace were closed. The penthouse was quiet.

"How are you doing, Hilary?" Chandler spoke from one corner of the white silk couch.

"I can't believe my mother is dead." She dropped her purse on a chair and headed for the bar. "Father said she accidently drove off that lookout, but from the little Melanie said, there's much more to it." She took a long swallow of scotch.

"You think someone killed her?" he said, following her to the bar. Chandler Cummings was a distinguished looking man in his mid forties. Almost six feet tall, a trim body, clean shaven, neatly trimmed brown hair, and soft brown eyes gave him the look of an aristocrat, which he was, but he had lost the family fortune before marrying Hilary. His pale blue silk pajamas were covered with a navy silk robe, matching navy leather slippers on his feet.

Hilary shook her head. "Suicide." She emptied her glass. "Father had asked for a divorce. Rather than face the humiliation, she drove his car off the cliff." She blinked the tears from her eyes. Guilt weighed her down. She had been trying so hard to gain her father's approval that she had neglected her mother. Maybe her mother wouldn't have felt so lonely if Hilary had been closer to her; if she'd known Hilary wouldn't desert her even if Phillip did.

"Why would Phillip want a divorce?" He leaned against the bar, his arms across his chest.

A harsh laugh escaped her lips. "The age old reason. Another woman."

Chandler shook his head. "Your father has had affairs for years. What makes this one different?"

"He wants to marry this one." Hilary buried her head in her hands. "I can't believe it. My mother is dead and my father's going to marry a woman younger than his daughters!"

Chandler walked around the bar and pulled Hilary into his arms, silently holding her until she stopped sobbing. "Who's causing all this trouble?"

Hilary sniffed and pulled away from him. "Alana Jordan."

Chandler let out a low whistle. "Classy lady."

"She's turned my father against me, caused my mother's death, and is going to be my stepmother. Some class!" Her scornful voice filled the room. "Father is going to marry her as soon as possible."

Chandler's eyebrows lifted. "Your mother's death was rather ... convenient, wasn't it?"

Hilary raised her eyebrows. "You think *she* killed my mother?" She refilled her own glass and offered one to Chandler.

He shrugged. "I don't know enough about her to even guess at that, but maybe the idea of Phillip's power and money made her greedy and anxious."

Hilary drained her glass, a thoughtful look on her face. "Possibly. Father seemed genuinely shocked, but things always work out the way Phillip Hudson wants them to. Obviously he wants to marry Alana, so he will." Her eyes clouded. "Mother dead. It doesn't seem possible." She turned a stricken face to her husband. "I never told her how much she meant to me." Fresh tears slipped down her cheeks.

Chandler took her into his arms again. "Your mother understood, Hilary." He rubbed her back.

Hilary looked up at Chandler, a pleading look on her face. "Make love to me."

He pulled away slightly, a wary look in his eyes.

She took his hand and pulled him toward her bedroom.

"Are you sure, Hilary?"

She closed the door behind them, gesturing toward her canopied bed. "If it will make you feel better, I'll turn off the lights while you get into bed." Chandler never made love with the lights on. He said it was more romantic in the dark, but Hilary felt it was because he didn't like to look at her.

A resigned sigh escaped Chandler's lips as he slipped off his robe and climbed into Hilary's bed.

Hilary turned off the lights and stepped out of her clothes. She reached for Chandler. "You might start by taking off your pajamas," she said.

He did as she asked, pulling her into his arms. He kissed her cheek.

"I might as well tell you the rest of the news," Hilary said, trying to get comfortable in Chandler's embrace. She felt his tension, but didn't know how to ease it. "My father is changing his will. He's going to leave the company and his estate to Alana."

Chandler gasped. "He's not going to leave anything to you or Mitchell?"

"No. He said Mitchell is spoiled enough and Mel and I don't deserve any money." She started to cry again, reliving her father's words. "But at least Mother left us some money and her Hudson stock."

He patted her shoulder. "We'll be fine."

"As long as I keep working and Phillip Hudson stays alive,"

Hilary muttered. "Make love to me, Chandler." She didn't want to talk, she wanted comfort, and she wanted to forget what had happened.

He took a deep breath and began to kiss and stroke her with an impersonal touch that left her cold.

Hilary tried to respond, tried to feel the emotions she had read about so often, but nothing happened. She was on her back, her arms at her sides while Chandler's hands explored her body with the touch of a doctor instead of a lover. She tried one of the techniques she had read about, fantasizing about someone else making love to her, but her heart didn't race, her breath didn't quicken, and she was unmoved.

Chandler tried. She gave him credit for that. He did all the right things. He kissed her, he stroked her, and then he was on top of her.

She spread her legs and closed her eyes, feeling nothing at all when he entered her, just wishing he would hurry up.

He pumped vigorously for what seemed like an eternity and then rolled off of her.

Hilary stared into the darkness, her breathing even, feeling unmoved and unloved. Her first husband, Mitch's father, had mocked her for being frigid, blaming his affairs on her cold and remote attitude toward sex. He had been right. Her relationship with Chandler proved it. She flicked the light switch and avoided looking at her husband. She couldn't bear to see the disgust in his eyes.

"Good night, Chandler."

"Good night, Hilary." He picked up his pajamas, robe, and slippers and left the room.

Hilary hurried into her bathroom and took a long, hot shower before returning to bed. How could sex get so many people into so much trouble? Like her father, for instance. If it weren't sex, would he have been so hot to divorce his wife and m a woman young enough to be his daughter? She doubted it.

Somehow she had to prove to him that Alana was just after his money. Maybe Melanie would help. Between the two of them they should be able to make him see the truth. Alana Jordan couldn't be as perfect as she appeared to be.

She stared at the flowers on the canopy for a long time before turning out the light and falling into a restless sleep.

Melanie flopped onto her bed, looking at her reflection in the mirrors above it, and knew sleep would elude her. Drawn to the red lacquered trunk in the corner of the room, she knelt beside it, opening it slowly. It contained the memories of her youth, the time of her life when she so desperately tried to gain the approval of her charismatic father. She pulled out a worn photo album and leaned against the trunk, the album in her lap.

The picture when she won her first award for diving made her smile. Her mother had been so proud of her. Her father had never even seen her dive. Melanie blinked back the tears. She smiled at the picture of the four of them taken the Christmas Melanie was eight. She was looking up at her father with adoring eyes, while he looked bored and uncomfortable. Hilary was the mirror image of their mother with her blond hair and blue eyes, while Melanie looked like Uncle Ralph with her wild red hair and fair skin. There was the picture of her dressed for her first date. Mother had taken the photo. Father had been in Japan on business. She grinned. He had been livid when he returned and discovered that Melanie had stayed out all night. At last she had found a way to get his attention and she used it shamelessly throughout high school. Her graduation picture, with her head barely visible above the leis. Her mother had taken Melanie on a trip to California. Father was too busy to go, and after she turned eighteen, he didn't care what she did. She had lost him.

She snapped the book shut, tears clouding her vision. Her mother was the only person who had loved her, cared what happened to her, really understood her, and now she was gone. It was her father's fault. She pulled a crumpled note from her pocket, smoothing it out over the scrap book. Her mother had committed suicide because she couldn't stand the humiliation of a divorce. Phillip Hudson had killed the only person who had loved Melanie as surely as if he had pushed her off that cliff. If it hadn't been for Alana Jordan, he never would have asked for a divorce. Melanie knew of his other affairs, but Alana was the first one he wanted to marry. It was up to Melanie to prove that Alana wasn't worth marrying even if it was too late to bring back her mother. She owed that much to her mother.

Wiping at the tears with the back of her hand, she put the note in the back of her album. Phillip Hudson would pay for what he had done.

Melanie replaced the album, spying her childhood teddy bear. Pulling it out, she crawled into bed and hugged it tightly, crying herself to sleep.

Chapter Five

Alana sat at her desk and stared out the window, her chin resting on the palm of her hand, her violet blouse matching the color of her troubled eyes. The other hand fingered a button on the skirt of her white linen suit. The azure sky and aquamarine water beckoned, and she cursed her inability to concentrate on business. Phillip had buried his wife three days ago. The newspapers said it was an accident, an error in judgment. But what if she had killed herself because Phillip had asked her for a divorce? Then she, Alana Jordan, was indirectly responsible for her death. She sighed and leaned back in her chair, picking up a pencil and tapping it against her chin. Only Phillip could tell her what really happened.

She leaned forward, scanning the diagrams and blueprints in front of her, making notes on a legal pad, determined to put it out of her mind. She was interrupted by the door opening at the same time her intercom buzzed.

Her head turned to the door. Phillip stood there, a wide smile on his face as her secretary's voice said, "Mr. Hudson is on his way in to see you."

Her gaze never leaving Phillip's face, she punched a button on the console. "Thanks, Leilani, he's already in."

Phillip softly closed the door behind him and leaned against it, his arms crossed over his chest. "Good morning, Alana. You're more beautiful than ever."

Alana blinked and sat back in her chair. "Good morning, Phillip." She paused, her voice dry. "It's been a long time since you've come to my office."

"Much too long." He slowly advanced across the room. "But a man in my position does have an image to maintain." Phillip rested his weight on his hands as he leaned over her desk. Desire flared in his eyes. "I've missed you."

Her body warmed under the heat of his gaze. "I've missed you, too. It seems longer than a week."

"It's been forever." He walked around the corner of the desk. "Have lunch with me today."

"Phillip, don't you think it's a little soon after . . . well, after Betty's death to be seen together?" When he reached out his hands to her, she put her cold fingers in his warm hands.

"You're my vice president. It'll be a business lunch." His smile made her heart skip a beat. "In fact, it is a business lunch. We're meeting Raine Bradburn."

Alana jumped to her feet, pulling her hands from his grasp. "Raine Bradburn? You're kidding! How come I'm going along? How did you arrange a meeting with him? I thought he wouldn't even talk to you!"

Phillip laughed then gave her a sheepish look. "He doesn't know that I'm meeting him. He thinks he's meeting with you to discuss plans for the Diamond Head Invitational Race."

Alana felt her stomach drop to her toes. "He's not part of that committee."

"He is now. I talked to Wyatt. He thought it was an excellent idea to have Bradburn on the committee since he's won the race for the last three years." His chin jutted forward, his eyes turned to flint. "I'm going to win this year. He's not going to make a fool of me again. We've got several months to practice on tuneup races and with the new boat, custom sails and you navigating, I can't lose."

Phillip's desire to beat Raine Bradburn was obsessive. Alana often wondered what had caused the intense rivalry between the two men, but Phillip always evaded answering her questions with kisses. "It's not the end of the world if you don't beat Raine. He's got a fast boat and he's an excellent skipper."

"I've got a fast boat, too, and I'm a better skipper." He crossed his arms over his chest. "Bradburn loves to gloat."

"I've never seen him gloat." Alana frowned. Phillip was a terrible winner, gloating to the point of being obnoxious. "When has he done that?"

"Every time he beats me." Phillip's lips twisted. "This time I'm going to win. I'm going to win that damn race, *and* I'm going to get that land."

His face revealed a bitter hatred so intense that Alana flinched. But as quickly as it came, it disappeared and he smiled at her, his eyes twinkling. "At least this gives us an opportunity to talk to him."

"How am I going to organize a race with you there? He'll never discuss the race when we start talking about Aloha Shores. In fact, when he sees both of us, he'll probably turn around and leave the restaurant." She shook her head. "It won't work."

"That's a chance we'll have to take. He never returns my calls, but if we meet in a public restaurant, he'll have to be civilized." He smiled, his hands on her shoulders, gently massaging them. "Come on, honey. Loosen up. Turn on the charm for Bradburn. He's always been a sucker for a pretty face. Maybe you'll be able to get through to him. Tonight we'll celebrate. Both the land and my freedom."

Alana searched his face as his words sank in. "You want me to charm Bradburn so you can get the land?" She was incredulous. "Would you use me like that?"

"It's not like I'm asking you to go to bed with him," he

65

muttered. Possessiveness tinged his voice and his grip. "You're *my* woman."

She slipped from his grasp and moved around the desk. "I'm my own person, Phillip." She met his look with a hard one of her own. "You don't own me."

"You wouldn't be sorry if you were mine." His voice was as soft as a caress, his eyes warm with desire.

She resisted the invitation she saw in his gaze. As much as she loved him, she wouldn't let him dominate her completely. "Accept me as an equal, and I'll consider it." She slipped her arms into her suit jacket, running a hand over the side of her head to smooth her hair into the knot at her nape.

"It's hard to think of you as equal when all I want to do is take you to bed and make love to you. Let's get this lunch over and go back to your place." He took a step toward her.

She took a step backward. "It seems disrespectful. Betty's only been gone a few days."

"You've been my mistress for six months. Betty's gone and nothing can bring her back. I want you and you want me." His arms came around her. "I've missed you, honey." His lips touched hers.

Her arms went around him and she buried her head in his shoulder, drawing comfort from the strength of his body. She had needed his reassurance that nothing had really changed between them since his wife's death. He still wanted her. She relaxed against him, tilting her head back to meet his lips with a hunger that left them both breathless.

"We'd better get out of here before I make love to you right now," Phillip muttered. He kissed her once more and released her.

Alana smiled. Phillip cared about her. He wanted to be with her. She picked up her Louis Vuitton purse and walked toward the door. "I hope this works." She looked over her shoulder. "Where are we eating?"

"Pierre's."

Alana grinned. "Nice touch. Gourmet dining. Busy enough that he can't make a scene and yet intimate enough that we can talk without being overheard." Her smile widened. "If you're doing that for lunch with Bradburn, what are your plans for tonight?"

"Honey, just be prepared to be swept off your feet!" His breath was warm on her ear just before they opened the door and walked out.

Pierre's was one of Alana's favorite restaurants, but she doubted if circumstances would allow her to enjoy her food. From the determined set of Phillip's jaw and his silence on the drive to the restaurant, she knew it was going to be difficult.

Walking into the lobby was like walking back in time. Soft Hawaiian music played in the background as a tawny skinned young woman with waist length black hair greeted them with a smile, placing a fragrant lei around their necks. "Aloha. Welcome to Pierre's." Her voice was soft and lyrical. Phillip gave his name and she smiled. "Follow me, please." Alana smiled as Phillip appreciated the view of the woman's thigh exposed by the slit in her aqua silk sarong as they followed her through the main floor of the restaurant. Each bamboo table was covered with a different color of the rainbow. One wall was open to the beach and ocean beyond. Diners could sit inside under the thatched roof or out on the patio under the protection of swaying palm trees. A waterfall in one corner of the dining room sent water winding through a manmade stream that wandered through the room, inviting guests to view the tropical fish swimming past. Phillip and Alana crossed a small foot bridge and followed the hostess outside to a table set off to one side.

Raine Bradburn was already there, drumming his fingers on the red cloth. When he looked up and saw Phillip the animosity between them was almost tangible. Neither man spoke. "Hello,

Raine." Alana felt someone had to start. "Thank you for accepting this invitation on such short notice."

He got to his feet, towering over Alana and inches taller than Phillip. Alana admitted to herself that he was an impressive man. A navy double breasted yacht club blazer covered broad shoulders. The pale blue silk shirt looked custom made, as did the burgundy silk tie. Grey slacks hugged muscular thighs. He was everything any woman would dream about from his wavy black hair and handsome features to his compelling blue eyes and vigorous body. Being one of the wealthiest bachelors in the islands didn't hurt either.

"Please, stay." Alana's heart skipped a beat as her gaze locked with the angry blue depths of Raine's. "We really do need to discuss the race."

His deep voice was laced with cynicism. "And the land?"

"And the land," she acknowledged, wishing Phillip would say something. She took a chair next to Raine. When Phillip took the chair opposite Raine, she felt like a referee or bait between two lions. She relaxed only slightly when Raine sat down and leaned back.

Eyes the color of an angry sea roved over her, examining every inch. Alana felt like she was under a microscope. Willing herself to remain calm, she met his gaze coolly when he finally raised his eyes, her hands clenched in her lap. "Using a woman to bait the trap? I've always said no one should ever underestimate you, Hudson."

"Now, listen, Bradburn, we're here to negotiate. And Alana does need to talk to you about the race." Phillip leaned forward, one arm on the table.

Alana watched Phillip trying not to bristle. She wondered if he was just a little afraid of the younger, more powerful man.

"It's amazing, isn't it, how I just got appointed to the committee?" His voice was dry as one brow quirked. He leaned back in the chair putting one hand in the pocket of his slacks.

"Not so amazing when you realize that Wyatt is commodore," Alana said with a knowing smile. "He's so disorganized. It's a shame he was elected."

"Politics beats ability sometimes," Raine said without a smile, his gaze never leaving her face.

Alana stared back, the strangest sensation growing in the pit of her stomach. When she had first come to Hawaii and started crewing at the yacht club, she had noticed Raine, but his aloof manner didn't encourage friendship. When her family had lived in Florida, sailing was her favorite sport. After her parents' death, it became a release from the stresses of her life. She had never been quite so aware of Raine Bradburn, the man, before today. An electricity, an awareness she had never experienced sparked between them. Perhaps because of the negotiations. Whatever it was, it was a potent force, one she didn't like but felt compelled to examine a little closer.

When Phillip ordered a drink for himself, Alana ordered iced tea. Phillip looked across the table at his adversary. "Are you open to any offers on the land on Maui?"

Raine swirled the ice in his drink. His gaze returned to Alana. The heated look made her heart race and her nipples respond. She was grateful for the jacket that covered her chest. Then she was angry. Did he think she was part of the deal? Phillip could jump off the Pali Lookout if he thought she was going to charm this man.

"What are you offering?" His eyes never left Alana's face.

"What do you want for that land, Bradburn?" Phillip's voice was hard.

He nodded in Alana's direction. "Her."

Alana blanched, the only outward sign of her shock. Twin flags of color tinged her cheeks as the impact of his words sunk in. In all the years she had seen him around the club, she had never known him to be deliberately cruel. Was this his way of evening the odds and getting back at Phillip? She glanced at

69

the older man. He was enjoying himself! She wondered how much he'd enjoy it if she threw herself into Raine's arms and walked out with him! As much as she would have liked to tell both men to go to hell, she searched for an answer to Raine's insult that wouldn't endanger a deal for the property. Phillip deserved a lesson as well. She swung her gaze to Raine.

Her amethyst eyes turned the color of the sky at twilight. Her voice was as smooth as the ocean appeared to be in the distance and just as deadly below the surface. "I'm flattered to think that I'm worth millions, Raine. You must've been admiring me from a distance all these years, too shy to ask me out. It's too bad we've wasted all this time because of your timidity. Perhaps Phillip wouldn't mind sharing me." She turned her lethal smile on Phillip. "Time sharing is popular these days, right?"

Raine released a low chuckle, his eyes shining with reluctant admiration. The shocked look on Phillip's face pleased him, too. "Nice, Alana. Very nice. You put us both in our place with a few well chosen words." He glanced at Phillip. "Do you realize what an asset you have in this woman?"

"I'm learning more all the time," Phillip said, his voice dry as he took a long drink.

Alana took advantage of Raine's good humor. "There must be something that you'd like in exchange for that land."

"It's possible." His expression gave nothing away. "What are you offering?"

Before Alana could reply a waitress came to take their order. The young woman's obvious attention to the two men would have been funny if Alana hadn't wanted to talk business. When the woman dropped her pen on the floor and stooped to pick it up, Alana almost groaned out loud. The expressions on Raine and Phillip made her grit her teeth.

Regaining control of her temper and her urge to dump a glass of water over both men, she looked at Raine. "You like to make money just as much as Phillip does. Aloha Shores is going to be a big money maker. A wise investor could make millions."

"But no one will make a cent without my land." He raised his glass to her, his features calm while his eyes were alive with interest. "Looks like a draw."

"Not necessarily." Phillip looked into his empty glass, unaware of the long look between Alana and Raine. "You could lease the land to us." He swallowed hard and took a deep breath. "And if we give you a percentage of the profits, you'd make money with no effort."

"I don't want a percentage of the project's profits." Raine broke eye contact with Alana and waited until Phillip looked up at him. His voice was rock hard. "I want an interest in Hudson Enterprises."

Phillip's back stiffened and his face was grim as he growled, "I'm going against my better judgment just offering you an interest in the project, but that's as far as I'll go to get that damn land. You'll never have an interest in my company, not as long as I have anything to say about it."

When Phillip's face turned a motley purple, Alana put a restraining hand on his arm. If he threatened Raine, Hudson Enterprises would never have a chance of negotiating for that land. She had felt a glimmer of hope when Raine didn't stalk out of the restaurant, but Phillip could destroy the opportunity by lashing out in anger. "Phillip, please." Her voice was low but intense.

Phillip shook it off, his eyes narrowed to slits as he leaned forward, one fist clenched on the table, his eyes riveted on his adversary. His voice was unyielding as he said, "A long term lease and five percent interest in Aloha Shores. That's my final offer."

Raine's face was just as unrelenting. His eyes darkened to midnight blue, a threat of steel in his deep voice. "The only offer I'll even consider is fifteen percent of Hudson Enterprises, and even if you offered it, I might not accept." He took a sip of the drink in his hand, looking every inch the powerful business tycoon that he was.

Alana had to admire him for his ability to stand up to Phillip's attempts at intimidation. A lesser man would have shown signs of discomfort or awe. She admitted to herself that she admired more than his business acumen, but then she quickly dismissed the thought. Instinctively she knew that even a mild flirtation with a man like Raine Bradburn could only lead to trouble.

"That's the damndest thing I've ever heard!" Silverware clattered as Phillip's fist hit the table.

Aware that Phillip's theatrics drew the attention of other diners, Alana spoke before Phillip could continue. "That's a big price to pay for one piece of land." Amethyst eyes met sapphire ones and Alana felt a tingle run down her spine. The odd sensation made her uneasy, making her bristle even more at the blatant interest reflected in his eyes.

"It's a very valuable piece of land," he countered, one dark brow quirking.

"Is there room for negotiation?" Alana asked, her voice husky for no apparent reason.

"Sell the land you own that surrounds mine to Bradburn International." He tossed back his head and finished the last of his drink.

"And let you build the resort?" Phillip bellowed. "You'll rot in hell before you'll ever own one rock of my land."

"Then there's nothing more to discuss." Raine stood and dropped his napkin on the table. "My regrets at not eating lunch, but I have another commitment that will be much more pleasant." The innuendo in his voice left little to the imagination. Alana wondered what kind of woman attracted him. At the club he was always surrounded by beautiful women, but she couldn't remember one particular woman at his side.

Alana was surprised when Raine stopped and turned to look at her. "I'll give you a call about plans for the race." His voice was hard and cynical when he said, "If you ever decide to part company with your, er, escort, let me know. I could use someone like you in my company."

Phillip jumped to his feet, blocking Raine's exit. "I'll get that land from you, Bradburn, if it's the last thing I do."

"Don't threaten me, Hudson." Raine's face was carved in granite. "You'll regret it."

"I never say anything I don't mean." The two men faced each other in deadly silence for one tense minute.

Then Raine pushed the older man aside and stalked out of the restaurant without a backward glance.

Alana was frightened by Phillip's expression. "By the time I get through with him, he'll wish he had never heard of the Hudson name," Phillip muttered. When he saw the fear on Alana's face, his mood shifted abruptly. "Come on, Alana. We might as well eat." He smiled at her and held out her chair. "We'll start celebrating early."

Alana was thrown off by his quicksilver change in mood. She was still shaking inside from the confrontation between the two men. "Phillip, I'm not hungry anymore." She put her napkin on the table. "Could we just leave?"

"No." He picked up his fork and knife and began cutting his steak. "If we leave now, it'll look like Raine got the best of me." He stabbed a large chunk of red meat and popped it into his mouth. "Lyle Montgomery and Henry Lu are at a table right behind you. I don't want them to know that I need something from Bradburn. They'd bid on that land themselves just because I want it." He pointed at the crab salad in front of Alana. "Eat. You'll need your strength for tonight." He paused and then said in a low voice. "Wear something sexy for me, will you? We're going out on the town."

She was silent for a moment. "Phillip, I don't think we should go out yet."

"Damn it, Alana. Stop acting like a reluctant virgin. Let's get on with our lives. People are going to have to know about us sooner or later." He bit into another chunk of steak. "I'll pick you up at eight."

Afterwards they drove back to the office in silence, each involved in their own thoughts. All afternoon Alana tried to think of a compromise between Phillip and Raine, but nothing seemed suitable. It was almost dark when finally giving up, she went home, kicked off her shoes and collapsed in a chair.

She needed to run. Glancing at the grandfather clock in one corner of the living room, she figured she had enough time for a quick run before showering and dressing for her date with Phillip. Slipping out of her clothes and pulling on shorts and a shirt, she pulled out the combs in her hair and tied it up in a pony tail.

Alana started running as soon as she hit the street. There were plenty of people around and she wasn't afraid to run at night. Ala Moana Boulevard bustled with tourists and natives alike. She crossed the Ala Wai Canal and headed for the park, setting a fast pace for herself. Nearly breathless, she slowed down slightly as she circled the park. The lighted tennis courts were all in use. Other joggers sped past her as she kept pace with two race walkers. She turned toward the ocean, the soft rhythm of the surf on one side and the rustle of palm leaves on the other. This section of the beach was still crowded as people swam and picnicked on the warm evening. It was one of the things she liked most about Hawaii. People spent as much time outdoors as they possibly could. Several runners going in the opposite direction nodded and said hello.

Beginning to finally relax and clear her mind, she headed for Magic Island, being careful to avoid the roots of banyon trees. Tiny birds fluttered around her feet. She lifted her face to the gentle trade wind and looked out over the ocean, stopping to watch the moon begin its journey across the sky. The huge white sphere hovered on the horizon, spilling a milky path across the dark ocean. Alana felt as if she could walk on that silvery path and touch the moon. The serenity of her surroundings calmed her nerves and soothed the fire in the pit of her stomach.

She stretched her arms over her head and was about to run again, but something stopped her. She stood very still and turned away from the ocean, looking into the darkness of the park.

She heard it again. It sounded like a moan. Should she investigate or run as fast as she could? Peering into the shadows, she couldn't see anyone. The moan came again. She looked around for other runners, but there was no one in sight. When she saw someone crawl from behind a tree, she made up her mind. If someone needed help, she couldn't walk away.

Still cautious, she inched toward the shadow hunched against the tree. "Are you all right?" she asked, her voice little more than a whisper.

"If I was all right, do you think I'd be crawling around on my hands and knees?" a familiar voice growled.

"Raine Bradburn?" She ran forward, leaning over the shadowy figure.

He leaned his head back and closed his eyes. "God, just what I need. Did Hudson send you to finish the job or just to get my name on that goddamned piece of paper?"

Alana didn't know what he was talking about. She bent down and peered into his face, frowning. "My God! What happened?"

"I tripped," he mocked, his words muffled by a bruised and bleeding mouth.

Alana was on her knees. "Is anything broken? Can you walk?"

Raine glared at her with the one eye that wasn't swollen shut. "Please. Don't let me keep you."

She reached in his jacket pocket for a handkerchief and dabbed at the gash on his cheek. "You're going to need stitches in this."

"Get away from me," he snarled, pushing her away with one arm, wincing as he did it. "I'll kill the bastard for this."

She touched his side and when he winced, she sat back on her heels. It didn't take a genius to figure out what had happened. "Who beat you up?"

Even with his injuries she couldn't mistake the anger in his voice. "I'm wise to your little scheme. You play the angel of mercy figuring that I'll be so grateful I'll sign over the land, right?"

"What are you talking about?" she demanded, wondering if she really wanted to know the truth. What had he said when she had first seen him? Something about Phillip. "Who beat you up? And why?"

"Can't you guess?" His words were bitter.

Alana stiffened. "Phillip is many things, but he'd never resort to violence."

He regarded her skeptically with his one good eye, his voice soft. "You're incredibly naive." Then his voice hardened and he muttered as he struggled to get to his feet. "Either that, or you're a very good liar."

She met his gaze with a steady one of her own. "I don't lie. And I don't believe Phillip did this to you." She doubted that Phillip could physically beat up a man in such good physical condition.

"There are ways of doing it without getting your hands dirty, Alana Jordan." He winced as he grabbed the tree trunk to pull himself up. "I've got to get out of here."

"You need to go to the hospital and have your face stitched up." She jumped to her feet and took a step toward him.

"No hospital." He tried to stand on his own, swayed, and fell back against the tree, a sheen of perspiration covering his face.

"Let me help you." Alana reached out one arm to him.

He tried to push her hand away, but couldn't raise his arm. "No. Get the hell out of here."

She could be just as stubborn as the injured man at her side. "Stop trying to bully me. You're not in any condition to order anyone around. I'm not going anywhere without you. If you won't let me help you, I'll go back to the boulevard and flag down the police." She stood her ground, her hands on her hips. "Think of the headlines you'll cause. Wait until they hear about it at the club. Saved by a woman!"

Raine glared at her. "You won't call the police. You might get your boss in trouble." He pushed himself away from the tree and tried to stand again, only to fall back once more. "So is Hudson your lover?"

Alana felt like punching him herself, but ignored his question and put his good arm around her shoulder and steadied him before starting the long walk back to the boulevard.

"Just get me to a cab. I'll go home."

"Easier said than done," she muttered, having all she could do to stay on her feet as he leaned heavily on her. He should see a doctor, but Alana knew he'd never agree. She couldn't take him to her apartment, Phillip would be there. She'd see that he got home safely, and then he was on his own. He didn't want her help and she would be more than happy to relinquish his care to someone else.

Chapter Six

Alana was worn out by the time they reached the busy boulevard. She eased him onto a park bench and then collapsed next to him, her legs rubbery and her arms like lead weights at her sides. Perspiration dripped into her eyes but she didn't have the strength to wipe it away. She gasped for air, for the first time in her life fully understanding complete physical exhaustion. The term dead weight had new meaning to her. "Did the muggers take your wallet?" she managed to ask between breaths.

Raine gave her a dark look. "I wasn't mugged." He said each word distinctly. "And there's a money clip in my left pocket."

She reached into his pocket and felt the clip with bills in it, struggling to get it out. She had been in awkward situations before, but sitting on a park bench on a busy street with her hand in a man's pocket was ludicrous. She would have laughed if it didn't take so much energy.

"Don't stop now," he murmured, his good eye closed.

"I should leave you here," she retorted, seeing a cab and standing in the street to stop it. Running shorts and a shirt plastered to her body almost caused an accident.

79

When it screeched to a halt, she opened the door, returning to help Raine into the back seat. He proceeded to pass out. At the look on the cabbie's face, she smiled as sweetly as possible, "This is my boy friend. He's a harmless drunk. Really."

She suddenly realized Raine hadn't told her where he lived. "Go toward Diamond Head," she instructed the curious driver, guessing that Raine Bradburn might live in the area. When the driver's attention was focused on the highway, she searched Raine's jacket and found his driver's license. Thankful that she had guessed correctly, she gave the driver the exact address.

She looked anxiously at Raine. They were almost through Waikiki and he hadn't stirred. How was she going to get him into his house? Keys. She needed keys. She checked his left pocket. Allowing herself a small smile of victory as her fingers closed round a key ring, she gently nudged Raine as the car climbed Diamond Head Road. Large iron gates loomed ahead. She shook him again. "Raine! What's the combination to your gate security?" She hoped it was similar to other estates in the area.

He grunted and mumbled, "Thirty-six, twenty-four, thirty-six."

She wrinkled her nose. "That's disgusting."

"But memorable." He struggled to sit up, groaning and holding his ribs, trying to open his one good eye. "The intercom is in the left wall. Punch out the numbers and the gate will open." He leaned back, sweat beading on his forehead and upper lip.

Alana scrambled out of the car, punched the buttons, and hopped back into the car. When the car wound its way up a tree lined drive toward a house, Alana roused Raine. She barely noticed the subtle lighting of the spectacular house and yard as she paid the driver, gave him a generous tip, and dragged Raine out of the car. She breathed a sigh of relief when the tail lights of the car faded in the darkness. Draping Raine's arm over her shoulder, she began the laborious journey up three series of steps before reaching the double oak doors. No one answered her persistent ringing of the doorbell, so she struggled with Raine's key ring while she sagged under the burden of his weight, wondering which key would open the door and which key would probably set off the alarm system and alert God knows how many people. She didn't need the publicity any more than Raine did. Taking the key that looked most like a house key, she slipped it into the lock, closing her eyes in relief when the door opened and no alarms sounded.

"Raine, you're home." She dragged him across the threshold and slammed the door shut behind them, looking around the massive foyer. "Any alarms to shut off?"

"In kitchen," he muttered. "One minute. Blue button." He tried to stand on his own but swayed and would have fallen if Alana hadn't caught him.

"I've got to get that button. Try to stay on your feet." She backed him up against the door, gave him one quick look, and hurried through the house looking for the kitchen. Finding it, she scanned the walls and doors until she found the control panel, pushed the blue button and let out a long breath. At least they wouldn't have the police swarming all over the place.

She retraced her steps, groaning when she entered the foyer. Raine was sprawled out on the floor. Kneeling next to him, she shook him roughly. "Raine!" When he opened his eye, she hovered over him. "Can you stand?"

"No problem."

It took her ten minutes to get him on his feet. "Where's your bedroom?" She had to talk between breaths, exhausted from the effort of getting the big man on his feet. If his room was on the second floor he could sleep in the gently tinkling fountain in the far corner of the foyer for all she cared.

"Is that a proposition?" he managed to say, his voice muffled.

81

"Yeah, right. You'd be a lot of fun tonight!" At least he had retained his sense of humor.

"Down hall. Last door."

Dragging him into the bedroom, she had no time or energy to appreciate her surroundings. Her feet sank into plush navy blue carpeting, making it difficult to maneuver Raine across the room. "Why couldn't you have hardwood floors?" she muttered.

The thirty feet across the room seemed like thirty miles as she stumbled toward the king sized bed. Lowering him onto the edge of the bed, she collapsed next to him, gasping for air. Keeping an eye on his slumped body, she rubbed her aching shoulders and stretched her arms, then got to work. She eased the torn and bloody jacket from his shoulders and dropped it on the floor. Pulling the heavy navy and red striped antique satin bed spread out from under him, she helped him lie down, holding her breath when he let out a low moan. "Raine?" He didn't answer, and she knew he had passed out again. Concerned about the extent of his injuries, she considered calling a doctor, but discarded the idea for the time being. Calling a doctor at this time of the night would be asking for trouble, for Raine and for herself. How would she explain her presence in his house? And what if Phillip was responsible for this? She didn't want to think about it. She slipped his tie from his neck and carefully unbuttoned his ruined shirt. Even bruised and battered he had a magnificent chest. Alana gave herself a hard mental shake. Thoughts like that would only create more problems. Since the custom-made silk shirt was beyond repair, she found a small scissors in one of the drawers of the massive walnut headboard and cut the shirt off of him. She scanned the floor to ceiling unit behind the bed. Shelves contained everything from the latest spy thriller to Shakespeare to business manuals and nautical guides. Her gaze returned to Raine. The man had eclectic tastes.

The gash on the side of his face was still bleeding. She needed to get him cleaned up and disinfect the wounds. Padding through the huge room, she stepped into a gigantic walk in closet. There were two doors at the far end. Turning to the left she found herself in a state-of-the-art exercise room, gleaming chrome throwing off a bright reflection in the wall of mirrors. Retracing her steps, she tried the other door, walking into a luxurious bathroom. One wall had ten-foot high sliding doors that opened to the sea. Mirrors covered the other walls. Her eyes were drawn to a tub large enough for six people. The dark blue tub rested in the middle of a raised platform, illuminated by indirect lighting, giving it a soft romantic look. Crossing the white marble floor, she peered into the tub shaking her head. Alana could only imagine what Raine did in that tub. She checked out the circular shower at the far end of the room, looking at it longingly. She'd give anything for a shower right now, but Raine's needs came first. Rummaging through the bank of drawers beneath the double marble sinks, she finally found antiseptic, bandages, and towels. Returning to the bedroom, she gazed down at Raine for a moment before she began her task.

After cleaning up Raine's face, she found some ice in the wet bar at the opposite end of the room, wrapped it in a towel and put it on his eye. Her hands on her hips, she looked down at him, a frown wrinkling her brow. There was no way around it. She had to do it. Taking a deep breath, she slipped off his shoes and socks and then tackled the buckle of his belt. Her hands trembled as Alana pulled Raine's slacks down over his flat stomach, slim hips and powerful thighs, her gaze roaming freely over taut skin bronzed by the tropical sun, the hair on his arms and legs bleached almost white. Even while he was unconscious, there was a vitality about him, a controlled power that was extremely seductive. She couldn't resist running her fingertips up a powerful thigh. He was in much better shape

than Phillip. That thought brought her back to reality. She was
supposed to be with Phillip right now! She had forgotten! Covering Raine with the pale blue satin sheet, she grabbed the
phone behind Raine's head. Punching out the numbers, she
tapped her foot as the phone rang and rang. Why didn't the
answering service pick up the call when Phillip didn't answer?
Where was he? Maybe he was at her place. Halfway through
dialing she stopped. What would she tell him? Sorry, Phillip,
I'm at Raine's house in his bedroom. And her conscience
wouldn't let her abandon Raine when he was unconscious and
might need help.

Alana slowly put the phone back down. She'd just have to
stay until she was sure that Raine could take care of himself or
until one of his staff could take over. Phillip would be furious.
She'd worry about it later. Checking on Raine, she was reas-
sured when his breathing was normal and the bleeding had
stopped. There wasn't much more she could do except wait.
Looking down at her own clothes as she stopped to pick up
Raine's, she made a face. Her shirt and shorts were stained
with his blood. Her thoughts turned to the decadent tub. One
more glance at Raine told her that he wasn't going anywhere
and she headed for the bathroom.

Turning on all the gold faucets, she pulled her shirt over her
head and pulled off her shorts, dumping them into one of the
sinks and filling the bowl with water. She sank into the tub,
closed her eyes and breathed a heartfelt sigh of relief. Her
muscles ached from dragging Raine around. Her mind was
numb from the questions bombarding her from all sides, and
she was emotionally drained. Freeing her mind of all thoughts,
she relaxed completely, finally stirring when she found herself
slipping under water.

Stepping out of the tub and grabbing a thick towel from the
heated rack, she wrapped it around her and padded around the
room. Raine had to have a robe somewhere. She pushed on a

button next to one of the mirrors and stepped back as it slid silently behind another mirror. She walked into the small room, gazing at the neatly stocked shelves of bed linens and towels. A red silk kimono and navy velour robe hung on hooks next to the door. She chose the kimono and wrapped it around herself. It fit. Which one of Raine's women had worn it last? What did she care? She wasn't one of them. Washing her clothes as best she could, she carried them out onto the lanai that ran the length of the house. Spreading her clothes over a chair, she settled into a cushioned lounge and released a heartfelt sigh. Looking one way she viewed dark ocean and a sky that glittered with stars, but with a turn of her head the lights of Waikiki and Honolulu spread a jeweled cloak before her.

Alana's stomach reminded her that she hadn't eaten since a slice of papaya for breakfast. She was starving and figured Raine owed her at least a meal for her efforts of his behalf. She smiled as she pushed herself to her feet. Exploring Raine's house would prove to be interesting. Maybe she'd discover more about the man behind the granite facade.

The living room was open and spacious, two walls of glass doors and windows spilling light out onto the lanai and lighted swimming pool. A huge seascape dominated one wall, and another one was prominently displayed above the marble fireplace. Alana took a closer look. They were original oils done by her friend, Jade. Polished hardwood floors bordered oriental rugs. Conversation centers were clustered around the room. At one end a sofa of pale blue and coral formed a semicircle with a wing backed chair of soft coral. An antique captain's brandy decantor and bronze statue of a native casting his net into the water sat on two small marble tables in front of the sofa. A magnificent glass topped ship's wheel coffee table dominated the center of the room, surrounded by blue and coral striped overstuffed chairs. A four foot high bronze statue of King Kamehameha stood watch next to the fire place. An oak wet bar with glass top glowed in the soft light. In another area was an oversized, blue velvet chair positioned to look out over the water. A weathered oak table cluttered with books and papers was next to it. Alana smiled softly. Raine's favorite spot. She knew it immediately. As she wandered around the room, she picked up a koa wood carving to examine it more closely. She had expected to find a cold, formal house but found a welcoming warmth instead. A step up took her into the dining room, a pleasant room with a brass, glass, and teak dining table and caned chairs. Ferns and broad leafed plants added color to the house.

She wandered back into the foyer, really looking at the fountain, the chandelier sparkling in the two story entry, and the spiral staircase at the far end. She checked the polished floor, thankful that it was unmarked by Raine's blood.

Alana ended up in the kitchen, gazing around in satisfaction. Copper kettles hung around the center island. Teak cabinets and a terra cotta floor gave it an air of warmth and coziness. Opening the refrigerator, she wondered if she should awaken Raine to eat but decided against it. She'd take some juice and water in to him. For herself, she had an omelet, a muffin that tasted homemade, and a glass of iced tea.

She returned to Raine's room with a tray, putting it next to the bed. Looking at the control panel behind Raine's head, she wondered which button turned off the lights and what all the other buttons were for. Rubbing her hands together and chuckling softly, she peered down at the panel and pushed the first one. A panel slid open on the wall opposite the bed and the television turned on. She hit the button again and the panel closed. Curious now, and seeing that the noise hadn't disturbed Raine, Alana settled down to discover the technique that made this sleeping giant the most eligible bachelor in the islands. The stories that circulated around the club about his exploits with women were legend. She had never thought one man could possibly have time for what they credited to him, but now she wondered.

Grinning like a child who just opened a full cookie jar, she pushed the next button. Drapes silently covered the wall of windows overlooking the lanai. Pushing it again, the drapes parted once again. Chuckling, she pushed the next button. The mellow sound of a piano and violins filled the room. She felt like she was in the middle of a concert hall. A plush, romantic music hall. Leaving the music on, she tried the next button. The glass doors slid open, the gentle rhythm of the surf a subtle addition to the romance. This guy knew how to create atmosphere, Alana thought, wondering which button would produce the champagne. Pushing the next button, the indirect lighting dimmed until the room was in soft violet and blue shadows. Wow! His reputation was well deserved. What wonders did the rest of the house have? She hadn't scratched the surface of the buttons in the mirrored bathroom. Pushing another button, another door opened next to the bed and a tray slid out with a bottle of chilled champagne and two fluted crystal glasses. He hadn't disappointed her. The champagne and glasses disappeared.

Not bad, Alana thought, looking at one last button. What could it be for? Her finger itched. She couldn't begin to imagine anything else that could possibly add to this bewitching scene. When she finally tried it, she heard a soft whirring sound and looked up, gasping as the ceiling parted and she stared into the stars. Never would she have imagined a bedroom like this. It was the most blatantly romantic room she had ever been in. Her gaze drifted to the man on the bed. How could someone who appeared to be so hard and cold have a room like this? How did he treat the women in his life? Did he have any lasting relationships? She shook her head. It didn't make any difference to her. She would see that he was taken care of and then leave. He would only add another complication to her life. She looked around one more time. She had thought herself sophisticated, but Raine Bradburn was way out of her league.

Closing the roof, she turned off the music and curled up on the chaise at the far end of the room, staring at Raine until her eyes were too heavy to stay open.

Raine groaned when he awoke and tried to move. Alana was awake instantly. He looked at her through his one good eye, his voice thick. "Usually when I wake up my women are next to me in bed, not curled up halfway across the room." What was Alana Jordan doing in his bedroom?

Alana gave him a dry look, her hands on her hips. "Usually when I wake up the man next to me doesn't look like he got bashed in the face with a surf board."

"Touche." He winced when Alana touched his face, turning away from her. His memory was returning with a vengeance. Alana's boss had had him beaten up. "Leave me alone."

"Grouchy this morning, are we?" she taunted, holding the good side of his face with one hand and lifting the dressing she had put on the gash with the other. "Are you always like this?"

"You'll never know," he muttered as he tried to sit up, every muscle in his body protesting the action.

"You'd better believe it." She slipped another pillow behind him, stopping as their faces were inches apart. Putting some distance between them she finally said, "I hope you're going to see a doctor about those ribs and the cut on your face."

"I'll be fine." Perspiration covered his face as he closed his eyes. He had a monstrous headache.

"Sure, and I'm the queen of England." She paused, concern in her voice as a frown puckered her forehead. "Is there someone who can take care of you today?" She glanced at the digital clock on his control panel.

"My housekeeper comes in about nine." His good eye remained closed and the other was swollen shut. He lifted a hand to his face. His lips were puffy and his jaw was tender. He felt like hell, and having a woman hovering over him made it even worse. His ego was as battered as his body.

"Can you eat anything?" Alana picked up the tray from the night before.

"Can you cook anything?" he muttered, opening his good eye.

She shook her head in disgust and dropped the tray back on the nightstand. "Am I ever sorry I bothered to take the time to help you last night. I should have left you in the park!" She whirled around and headed for the doors leading to the lanai.

"Hey! Wait a minute." The effort exhausted him. It had been a long time since he had felt so helpless and it wasn't a pleasant feeling. He didn't believe for one minute that Alana Jordan just happened to be jogging through the park and heard him groan. How could he have been so stupid to agree to a meeting in the park. Alone. It was an obvious set up and he had fallen for it.

He looked at the clock. Alana had stayed the night. While he was passed out, she was probably snooping around. All his important papers were in the safe, but she was a smart woman. He could only imagine what she had discovered while he was sleeping. His gaze strayed to Alana as she returned to the bedroom with her clothes in her hand. She was beautiful, even through one eye at eight in the morning. Beautiful but dangerous.

"I'm going to get dressed and then I'm out of here."

"I suppose you want me to thank you for helping me last night," he grumbled, forcing himself to sit up in bed, wincing at the pain.

"I wouldn't think of it." Her chin lifted.

"So what do you want?" he demanded. "Did Hudson send

you to mop up after the beating thinking I'd be so grateful that I'd give you my land?"

"You already threw that accusation at me." She gave him a weary look. "Can't you come up with anything better than that?"

He was silent for a moment and then sneered, "Is Phillip offering me your ... services?" If he had felt better, he just might be tempted.

She stiffened and then whirled around, her hands on her hips, her eyes flashing. "I helped you last night in the same manner I would've helped any human being in trouble. Nothing more. Nothing less. I won't even dignify your last remark with an answer. And believe me, if I should ever stumble over your carcass again, I'll leave it for the birds." She stomped off to the bathroom, slamming the door behind her.

Raine waited for her to return, wondering if he might have misjudged her. It was possible but not probable. Alana Jordan worked for Phillip Hudson. They were obviously lovers. No, Hudson wanted his land, and he'd stop at nothing to get it. Alana Jordan was involved right up to her pretty little neck.

She stalked back into the bedroom, dressed in her running clothes, her hair pulled into a pony tail. She looked young, fresh, and infinitely appealing.

Raine steeled himself to her beauty. "Hey, wait. How are you going to get home?" he asked as she headed for the door, not even looking his way. The least he could do is offer to give her cab fare.

"On my own two feet." She stood at the door, turning to glare at him.

"Do you live close by?" He frowned slightly and peered at her with one eye. Maybe she'd moved in with Hudson now that his wife was dead.

"What do you care?" She turned the knob.

He tossed back the sheet and tried to get his legs over the

side of the bed, wincing as he did so. He felt as battered as the bronze sculpture of the old sailor above his head. "Wait."

"For what? Another blast from your sarcastic tongue? Just stay in bed and wait for your housekeeper. I'm sure she'll be glad to take care of you." She pointed to the phone behind his head. "Or use your handy little speed dialing to call one of your girl friends. I'm sure they'd love to spend the day in bed with you."

Raine grunted and lay down again, pulling the sheet back over his body. "Thanks."

"Don't mention it." She paused, speaking slowly. "In fact, don't ever mention it again."

"Hudson might get mad?" he sneered, touching his hand to his jaw.

"I'll get mad! I don't want to be reminded about what a jerk I was for helping you last night!" She slammed the door behind her.

Melanie settled back in the limousine, smiling at the man pouring her a glass of champagne. "I'm impressed, Charles. I never thought of you as the champagne type." She took the proffered glass.

"There are many things about me you don't know, Melanie." Charles Reese raised his glass to hers and took a sip.

Charles was short, pudgy in an endearing sort of way, had a round face, and a fringe of silver hair. Melanie didn't care what he looked like. He was a powerful man and she needed him. "I know you're an investment banker in New York and you're a director for other companies as well as Hudson Enterprises." She paused. "You probably have a wife and several kiddies waiting at home for you."

"Only one child." He put the glass down, hazel eyes focused on Melanie's face.

Melanie put her empty glass next to his. "Charles, what's your opinion of Alana Jordan?"

"She's a beautiful, intelligent woman who craves power as much as Phillip does." He sat back and rubbed his chin. "Why?"

"What are the chances of an outside corporation taking over Hudson Enterprises?" she murmured, moving closer to him.

"Impossible as long as Phillip controls the major block of stock." His gaze was speculative. "Why all the questions?"

"Just wondering." She paused, her hand moving to his shoulder. "Could someone with less stock cause trouble?" One finger traced a line from the collar of his shirt to his ear.

"I suppose." He smiled at her. "What's going through that devious mind of yours, Melanie?"

She returned his smile. "I'm looking for a way to get Alana Jordan out of my father's life, professionally and personally. Would you help me?"

"I'll try, but it won't be easy. Your father usually gets whatever he wants, and it's obvious he want Alana Jordan."

"We'll just have to change his mind, won't we?" Melanie felt better already. Charles had a soothing effect on her. What kind of lover would he be? Her finger traced the outline of his ear. "Would you like a guided tour of the island?"

His hand rested on her thigh. "I've seen the pineapple fields."

"Not like this you haven't," Melanie murmured, leaning forward. "Lew, Mr. Reese would like the grand tour." She pushed a button and the smoked glass slid between the front and back seats.

Melanie turned the full force of her sensuality on Charles. She wound her arms around his neck, meeting his hungry mouth with a curiosity that quickly turned to passion.

His tongue explored the moistness of her mouth, while his hand moved under her skirt to stroke her thigh.

She loosened his tie, flicked open his shirt and slipped her hand inside.

Charles released her lips, nibbled at her neck, and pulled her panty hose and shoes off.

She buried her face in the soft grey hair on his chest. He pushed her gently backward onto the leather seat. He tugged at her skirt and Melanie lifted her hips, expected him to pull it off, but he didn't. It was soon bunched at her waist.

He was on his knees, his hands and mouth massaging and licking her ankles, her calves, the back of her knees.

Melanie squirmed, her breasts aching.

Charles moved higher, stroking and kissing her inner thigh, urging her legs apart. One finger twirled her soft, curly hair, his mouth tormenting her until she arched her back. He spread the soft lips, his tongue doing incredible things to her.

Her eyes closed, she gave herself up to his ministrations, writhing and twisting, her breath coming in short gasps. She felt as if she were plunging into the depths of the ocean, floating without a sense of time or space, then exploding into the air before floating back to earth. The sensation startled Melanie. Charles wasn't much to look at, but he certainly knew how to turn a woman on. Melanie struggled to sit up, a frown on her face. "You never touched ... I didn't ..."

"Later, Melanie, my dear. Later." He smiled down at her before he began to arouse her once again.

Chapter Seven

Phillip paced around his massive mahogany desk, barely glancing at the ocean or the mountains. He stopped behind one of the black leather chairs opposite his desk and gripped the back. Damn heart! He reached into the pocket of his jacket and popped a pill under his tongue. When the pain subsided, he stepped up into the intimate conference area, dropping onto the grey leather sofa. The indirect lighting, smoked glass and chrome were meant to relax business associates, but at the moment the affect was lost on Phillip. He wanted to storm into Alana's office and demand an explanation, yet he knew if he did that, she would give him that icy stare and tell him her life was her own. She would withdraw, effectively closing him out. He could scream until he was hoarse, but she would remain silent, a look of disdain on her face, never denying his accusations or justifying her actions. She'd just sit and stare at him, totally in control.

Phillip got to his feet and wandered into the larger, more impersonal conference area. The lighting was stronger, the table large enough to accommodate eight chairs, and a wet bar was hidden along one wall. Next to the bar was the door to his dressing room and bathroom. He reached for the coffee pot and poured a cup of coffee, returning to his desk. He wanted Alana. Nothing would stop him from owning her, body and soul.

He knew she was in her office. He planned his attack very carefully. When he was ready, he drained the cup and headed for her office, a look of satisfaction on his face. Without knocking, he entered her office. "Good morning, Alana."

She glanced up, startled, then wary. "Good morning, Phillip." She paused only slightly. "I'm sorry about last night."

He held up a hand and smiled ruefully. He had her off balance and that's what he wanted. "You don't owe me any explanations, although I was looking forward to our evening together."

"I had an emergency." She spoke softly, her expression unreadable.

He held up a hand again. "I trust you, Alana." About as far as I can throw you, he thought. He gave her a hopeful look. "What are your plans for this evening?"

"I have to work late. We need the specifications for the project in Kona. We can't wait much longer." She picked up a sheaf of papers and held them out to him.

"I have a meeting that will probably last until seven. How about if we meet in the lobby at seven-thirty? You have to eat." He gave her the smile that was guaranteed to charm her right into his bed. He wanted Alana and he would do anything to get her.

He had known her long enough to know that shrug. She didn't know what to think about his reaction to the broken date. "Sure. Seven-thirty will be fine."

Phillip courted Alana for thirty days. He sent so many flowers that her apartment looked like a greenhouse. He visited her office at least two or three times a day. The company was buzzing with rumors about their relationship. Phillip wanted people to know they were seeing each other. He might as well have a billboard made with their names plastered on it.

Alana didn't want to accept the expensive gifts he showered on her, but he insisted, looking hurt when she tried to give them back. He was so thoughtful and charming that Alana didn't have the heart to hurt him, so she accepted the gifts and wore them when he requested it.

Melanie and Hilary cornered Phillip after a meeting late one afternoon.

"Father, you're making a fool of yourself over Alana Jordan," Hilary muttered, standing in front of his desk, her hands clasped in front of her. Outwardly she looked cool and composed in a rose linen suit with a floral print blouse, but inwardly her stomach lurched and she felt her heart racing. "Everyone is talking about it."

He shrugged. "Let them talk. Who cares?"

"We care," Melanie said, her voice firm. She jammed her hands into the pockets of her aqua gathered silk skirt. A white batiste cotton blouse was cinched at the waist with an aqua alligator belt. She stared at her matching alligator shoes for a moment before saying, "She only wants your money."

"So do you," he said, leaning back in his chair.

"But we're your children." Hilary took a deep breath. "How well do you really know her?"

"Well enough." He cocked his head to one side. "Is there something you want to tell me?"

Melanie and Hilary exchanged glances. "She was down at the yacht club yesterday. I saw her talking to Griff." Hilary watched her father's expression carefully. She had hit a nerve. "Griff had his arm around her. You're not the only one interested in her."

His mouth thinned. "All the more reason to marry her."

"How can you say that!" Melanie erupted. "Do you think she'll be less interested after marrying you?"

"She damn well better be!" he said between clenched teeth, his hand curled into a fist.

"She's a fortune hunter," Hilary argued. "Don't do anything hasty. Wait a few months."

"I'm not a young man, Hilary. I don't have the luxury of time. I want Alana Jordan, and I'm going to have her."

"So keep her as a mistress." Melanie leaned forward, her hands on his desk. "An affair is one thing. Marriage is something different."

Phillip nodded. "Marriage means she's mine."

Hilary paced around the office. "You're making a big mistake. She doesn't really care about you. All she wants is the power and money you represent."

"You may be right, but that's my concern, not yours." Phillip stood up.

"It is our concern." Melanie met her father's intimidating look. "Because of Alana Jordan our mother is dead and our father is making an ass out of himself over a woman younger than his daughters."

"The fact that I'm changing my will wouldn't have anything to do with your feelings, would it?"

Hilary's head snapped back. "Of course it does! But as long as you're alive, it's irrelevant. We're concerned about you."

"Don't bother." He waved a hand through the air. "I know exactly what I'm doing. I've got work to do." He sat down, dismissing them with a look.

The women exchanged a look, shrugged and walked out of the room.

Late one Friday afternoon, Phillip left a message with Leilani cancelling his dinner date with Alana.

Alana didn't really mind. She was bone tired after a busy week and looked forward to a quiet night at home. Awakened out of a deep sleep, she heard the key in the door. Struggling to open her eyes, she groaned when she saw it was five in the morning. Phillip walked into the room with a huge smile on his face. He leaned over her and kissed her deeply. "Wake up, honey."

"What are you doing here at this hour?" She snuggled back into her pillow.

"We're going on a little trip." His hand stroked her silky hair.

"Tomorrow." She buried her head deeper.

"Now. It's a surprise." He pulled back the sheets and gazed at her slim body.

Alana stretched and yawned. "Where would we be going at five in the morning?"

"You'll see." He took her hands and pulled her from the bed. "Get dressed." He pointed toward the bathroom. "There's a new dress in there that I want you to wear."

"A dress? At five in the morning?" Her look was wary. He was definitely up to something. "What's going on?"

He threw back his head and laughed. "If I told you, it wouldn't be a surprise."

"Hmmmmm." She padded into the bathroom and her eyes widened. Hanging on a hook in the bathroom was an exquisite confection of a dress. The pearly irredescent quality of the gossamer fabric gave it an ethereal quality. The delicate fabric was gathered at the shoulders and held in place by pearl clips. The bodice was fitted with a deep V in the front. Seed pearls were scattered in a random pattern on the full tea length skirt. On the floor next to the dress were strappy sandals to match the dress. The finest French silk lingerie was nestled in a bed of tissue. Alana looked at the name on the box, letting out a low whistle. It was one of the most exclusive boutiques in Honolulu.

She quickly showered and dressed, the feel of the silk on her body bringing a smile to her lips. She didn't know what the surprise was, but she was eager to find out. She walked into the living room, stopping when she stood in front of Phillip. "Thank you for the dress. It's beautiful."

He got to his feet and kissed her lightly, holding both of her hands in his. "You look lovely, just like I thought you would." He led her toward the door. "Now, it's time to go."

Alana held back. "Do I need to take anything with me? My brief case? Other clothes?"

"Nothing." He chuckled at her bewildered look. "I guarantee this will be a happy surprise."

She shrugged her shoulders and followed him. Why not? Phillip was obviously happy and relaxed, the dress was fantastic, and she liked surprises, especially good ones.

The limousine pulled away from her apartment and headed for the Lunalilo Freeway. Phillip poured champagne into two glasses and raised his to her. "To us."

She gave him a puzzled look and returned the toast. "Where are we going, Phillip?" She was really curious now. Champagne at five in the morning, an expensive dress. What next?

"To the airport." He reached over and kissed her gently, his hand tracing the outline of the dress from her shoulder to the valley between her breasts. "I hope I can wait." He chuckled again, his grey eyes twinkling with laughter.

His excitement was contagious. "Where are we flying at this time of the morning? Why are we drinking champagne? Why did you buy me this dress?"

"You'll see." He nibbled at her ear lobe, then sat up, snapping his fingers. "I knew I forgot something." He opened a drawer and took out a large, black velvet box. Handing it to her he said, "Open it."

Alana looked at it for a long moment then slowly opened it, her eyes widening at the glittering jewels nestled on black satin. A stunning circle of diamonds held a pendant with three large pear shaped diamonds surrounded by gold. A matching bracelet formed a smaller circle in the box and pear shaped diamond earring studs were in the center. Alana could only guess at the worth of the jewelry in her hand. "Oh, Phillip. I can't accept this."

"Of course you can." He took the box from her shaking hands and clasped the necklace around her neck. "It's part of the surprise."

"But—"

"No arguments." He brushed her shoulder with his lips. "You'll spoil the surprise." He kissed the inside of her wrist and fastened the bracelet, then put the earrings on her ears. "Beautiful jewels for a beautiful lady."

"Thank you." Holding out her glass she said, "Might as well sit back and enjoy the surprise."

"Now you're beginning to get the idea." He filled both their glasses and settled back in the seat, his hand on her thigh.

It didn't take long before they were at the airport and boarding Phillip's jet. Once they were settled in the luxurious salon, the plane took off. Alana had flown on the company plane so many times it was almost a second home, the rich browns, copper, and sand making it seem more like a living room than an airplane. A brown leather love seat was on one side and two brown, copper, and beige striped chairs were on the other with a teak coffee table between them. Sand colored carpeting deadened the sound of the engines. A conference table was behind the seating area with chairs for eight people. Behind the conference area was a well-equipped bathroom and bedroom. When they could take off their seat belts, she stood up and yawned, taking the steps toward the galley kitchen and pouring two mugs of coffee. "Which island are we going to?"

"The Big Island."

"Why?" She handed Phillip one of the steaming mugs of coffee.

101

"You'll just have to wait and see." He leaned back, a smug smile on his face, watching her over the rim of his cup.

Alana sat in one of the chairs across from him, returning his smile. "So far it's been lovely."

"It'll get better." He paused, a look of uncertainty crossing his face so briefly that if Alana hadn't been looking at him so intently, she would have missed it. Phillip pulled an envelope from his jacket. "I just have one request. Will you sign this?"

She looked at him warily. "What could you possibly want me to sign at six in the morning?"

He put his mug on the table, leaning forward and adjusting the knot of his tie. It was a sure sign that he was ill at ease. It was a few minutes before he said in a low voice, "It's a prenuptual agreement."

She stared at him, her mouth gaping. "A what?" She couldn't have heard him right. It had to be the altitude.

"I want this trip to be a surprise." He cleared his throat, looking at the table between them. "If you sign this, I'll know that you really care about me and not just my money."

"You already know that." She frowned. He sounded like a little boy asking for an important favor. "Why would I sign a prenuptual agreement when we're not even getting married?"

"Please, just do it for me."

She grabbed the envelope from his hand and pulled out the single sheet of paper, trying to read it in the dim light. It was short and simple. If they married and divorced, she'd get a settlement. No percent of money made during the marriage, no claims to his personal fortune, no security of stock in Hudson Enterprises. She raised her head and studied him for a long time. She had none of those things now, so what difference would it make? She scribbled her name across the bottom, Phillip signed it, and Michael, Phillip's personal secretary witnessed it.

When they landed, another limousine was waiting for them.

Alana looked around. "Hilo? Our next project is at the other end of the island."

"This is a special project," Phillip murmured, enjoying her curiosity.

It was early morning when they entered Wailuku River Park. "Phillip, what are we doing in a park?"

"Getting married."

He said it so matter-of-factly that it took several seconds for the words to sink in. "Married? In a park? Us?"

"Yes to all three." He beamed at her, happiness settling on his features, making him more handsome than Alana had ever seen him.

"That's why you had me sign that agreement!" She shook her head. "You didn't have to do that, you know."

"I know." The car came to a smooth stop at the path leading to Rainbow Falls. Phillip jumped out and escorted a bemused Alana up the stone path. A minister and three Hawaiian men waited. One of the men had a guitar and the others carried leis. The fragrant maile and ginger lei was for Phillip, and the lei of delicate white rosebuds and carnations was for Alana.

Alana was impressed that Phillip had gone to so much trouble to set up the surprise. A lot of thought and money had gone into the planning of it. She touched the diamonds at her throat, felt the rustle of silk against her body. Phillip must love her very much to do all this for her. Alana let herself get caught up in the romance of the moment. The sun caught the spray and mist from the tumbling water of the falls, surrounding them with rainbows. Alana regarded it as a good omen.

Her eyes widened when Phillip put a ring on her finger. The rays of the sun picked up the facets of the circle of diamonds that surrounded the stone in the center.

* * *

Deep melodious voices sang romantic ballads. Alana looked up at Phillip. "We're really married."

"Yes." The others drifted away. "You're Mrs. Phillip Hudson. My wife."

She closed her eyes and lifted her face to accept his kiss. "Is this the end of the surprise?" she murmured long moments later.

"Only the beginning." He took her hand and led her down a narrow trail toward a secluded area. Place settings of crystal goblets and bone china rested on a white damask cloth spread over the green velvet grass. A bucket filled with ice and a bottle of champagne awaited them.

"Oh, Phillip. How beautiful." She gave him a hug and approached the cloth, dropping to her knees and motioning for him to join her. "What's under these silver covers?"

Phillip followed, his gaze on her happy face. He bent to kiss her, his hand on her cheek. When she returned his kiss, he was at her side. Feathering kisses down her jaw and over her shoulder, his hand slipped under the hem of her dress and snaked up her thigh. "I want you, Alana."

"What if someone walks through here?" she murmured, pulling back slightly, her voice teasing.

Phillip eased her onto her back, his hand dipping into the low bodice and cupping one breast. "The park is closed until we leave and Michael is standing guard at the falls."

"You thought of everything." She returned his smile as his hand teased and caressed.

He reached in back of her and released the zipper of her dress, pulling the garment off of her body. He quickly dispensed with the rest of her clothing, bending over her naked body as he loosened his tie.

Alana watched him shrug off his clothes, reminded of Raine's muscular body. He had no place in her mind on her wedding day. She gave herself up to Phillip, turning her face to accept his kiss.

Neither of them gave a thought to their surroundings as his lips began a thorough investigation of her body. His hands followed his lips, stirring her blood.

Alana responded to his touch, her hands making an exploration of her own. She kneaded the muscles of his shoulders and back, pulling him closer, feeling him quiver with desire.

His mouth was on her breast, gently tugging the tip into a taut peak.

She arched against him, opening her body and heart to Phillip. She loved him and now he was her husband. They moved together, the fire of desire burning between them. When Alana cried out in ecstasy, Phillip growled, "You're mine, Alana. Body and soul."

The intensity of his words startled Alana, but she quickly dismissed it. She was his wife now. He was entitled to feel possessive. She closed her eyes and drifted back to earth in the shelter of Phillip's arms.

Melanie and Hilary were in their mother's suite of rooms sorting through a lifetime of memories. Betty had saved every school paper, every newspaper clipping mentioning the Hudson's, every greeting card she had received, and every special costume worn by either daughter throughout their years of dance lessons, riding lessons, swimming lessons, and tennis lessons.

Melanie held up a well worn child's riding habit. "I remember this. You cried for two days when mother said you had outgrown it and needed a new one."

Hilary chuckled, a faded racing swim suit hanging from one

finger. "And I remember the days when you were so modest, you were embarrassed to wear this."

A rueful look crossed Melanie's face. "That was a lifetime ago."

Hilary opened another box and pulled out a photograph. "My graduation picture." She touched it and sighed. "A year later I was married and had a child."

"You and Billy never had a chance," Melanie muttered, putting the children's clothes back in the carton.

"It was a disaster from the beginning." Hilary shook her head. "When Phillip Hudson held a shotgun to your head and demanded you marry his pregnant daughter, you did what he said, but that didn't mean you had to like it."

"And Billy took off for the mainland after Mitch was born." Melanie had a thoughtful look on her face. "I can't imagine why father wouldn't put Mitchell in his will."

"He's right when he says I spoil Mitch, but he's my son. I was little more than a child when he was born, and by the time I married Chandler, I didn't want any more children." She wrinkled her nose. "Chandler's not the fatherly type."

"Neither was our father," Melanie said. "Mother made up for his indifference." She sat down in the middle of the floor. "She loved us, Hilary." Her face crumpled.

Hilary tried to swallow past the lump in her throat. "Yes."

"She was always there for us." Melanie wiped her wet cheeks.

"I wish I would have told her I loved her." Hilary let the tears flow.

Melanie was silent for a few moments. "I can't believe father actually married Alana. Even after we asked him to wait!"

Hilary took a deep breath and dried her eyes before picking up a black velvet jewelry case. "If mother hadn't died, he still would have married her after the divorce. When he makes up his mind to do something, nothing stops him."

"And he wanted to marry Alana Jordan." Melanie's voice was hard. "Mother's dead because of Alana and our father."

Hilary flipped open the jewel case. "We can't let them get away with this, Mel. Somehow we have to discredit her in father's eyes, make him see the truth." She lifted a diamond and emerald necklace from the case. Betty didn't believe in putting any of her jewelry in a safe deposit box. A sly smile touched her lips. "This matches your eyes perfectly." She tossed it onto Melanie's lap.

The women exchanged a look. "It's dishonest," Melanie murmured, scrambling to her feet and pulling another velvet box from the shelf.

"I'm sure mother would want us to have it." Hilary clipped a gold and sapphire bracelet to her wrist.

Melanie opened the box, sapphire and diamond earrings in the palm of her hand. "Here. These match the bracelet."

Hilary picked them up, frowning. "How can we get rid of Alana?"

A cunning look settled on Melanie's face. "Maybe if he discovered she was having an affair, he'd toss her out. I heard them arguing one day when I went to his office. Remember the look on his face when we mentioned Griff?"

"Yes. He married her that week!"

"So we'll just have to make sure they get divorced."

Hilary was thoughtful. "We can start planting the seeds of doubt. Subtly of course." If Alana was out of their lives, he would change his will again. He would have to leave everything to his children. She leaned back. They needed insurance, just in case Alana could talk her way out of being unfaithful. "What do we really know about her?" Hilary said.

"Not much," Melanie admitted.

"I think it's time to find out." Hilary stood up. "We can start with the personnel files. She might have been a hooker working her way through school."

Melanie grinned. "Or maybe she posed for men's magazines to pay her tuition." She rubbed her hands together. "If we can't get him jealous enough to kick her out, we'll expose her for what she really is, and daddy will have to dump her."

Hilary nodded. "We'll have to hire a private investigator to dig into her past."

"I know the perfect man for the job," Melanie said, getting to her feet. "As soon as we finish with mother's things, I'll give him a call." She looked at her sister. "Are you going to Johnson's cocktail party tonight?"

Hilary nodded. "They had commissioned Chandler to do their family portrait. I'm anxious to see the finished result."

"Photographer of the elite," Melanie mocked. "Do you think he would have obtained that position without marrying a Hudson?"

"I doubt it," Hilary retorted with a shrug. "Even with his commissions, we couldn't live on what he makes. We need the Hudson money."

"Don't we all," Melanie murmured.

Melanie leaned on the ledge gazing sightlessly over the ocean. The Aloha Tower seemed a strange place to meet, but then Arty Jones was a strange man. As she stared out at the ocean from the tenth floor balcony, she found it difficult to believe that the tower had once been the tallest building on the island.

A short stocky man in black shorts, red Hawaiian print shirt, white canvas hat, black socks, loafers, and a camera slung around his neck approached her and leaned on the railing. After glancing in her direction, he raised the camera to his face. "Nice day."

"Lovely." Melanie opened her purse, looked around, and

handed him an envelope. "I want you to find out anything you can about the woman in the picture."

He took the envelope and opened it, whistling through his teeth. "Good looking broad."

"My stepmother," Melanie muttered between clenched teeth. "Her personnel file is in there, too. No one seems to know much about her background."

"This'll cost you." He slipped the envelope into the camera case.

"It'll be worth it." Alana's past was too sketchy not to hold some unsavory secrets. Melanie's eyes glittered. Alana would pay for her part in killing Melanie's mother. "Will you do it?"

He grunted. "My usual fee."

She pulled out another envelope. "Five thousand in cash. The balance when you bring concrete evidence of her 'questionable' past."

"And if she's clean?" He lowered the camera and took the second envelope, checked the contents, and slipped it into the camera bag.

"I'm sure you'll come up with something," she murmured, her voice dry. "My unlisted number is on a card in the envelope with the cash. Check in with me every day."

"In a hurry, huh?"

Melanie was silent for a moment. "Yes." She wanted Alana humiliated, without a husband, home, job, or money. It was a beginning.

"I'll call tomorrow night." He drifted off toward a crowd of people waiting for the elevator.

Hilary stood at Chandler's side. Her dress of fuschia raw silk reached to mid calf. The sash emphasized her small waist, and the princess neckline was perfect for the teardrop diamond necklace she wore. She reached for a glass of champagne being offered by the tuxedoed waiter then leaned toward Chandler. "We've got to find father. Remember what I told you."

"I'm not an imbecile, Hilary." He straightened his burgundy paisley tie, the diamond in the ring of his little finger catching the light. "How do you like the portraits?" He nodded in the direction of the living room. Over an ornate white and gold fireplace was a huge portrait of the Johnson family.

Hilary studied it for a moment. "It's very nice, Chandler."

"That's all? Very nice?" He pulled on the lapel of his charcoal suit. "It's a masterpiece."

She caught a glimpse of her father. Alana wasn't with him. "Come on," she muttered. "We've got work to do."

Standing in front of her father, she smiled. "Hello, father. Where's Alana?"

"She went to powder her nose." Phillip flicked a glance in Chandler's direction. "Nice snap shot of the family," he said, nodding in the direction of the portrait.

Chandler bristled, but Hilary scowled at him before her face cleared and she said in a soft voice, "Do you have a new crew member on your boat, daddy?"

He shook his head, sipping a martini, searching the crowd of faces. "Why?"

"No reason. I just saw Alana at the club with Griff, and I wondered if he was crewing for you."

Phillip's gaze bore into Hilary, his voice harsh. "You saw her? When?"

"A couple of days ago. In the evening." Hilary met his gaze with wide blue eyes. "I've seen her with other men who sail with you. I just assumed you knew."

Hilary glared at Chandler.

"I don't know why you even bothered telling your father," he said. "Just because she's married doesn't mean she can't go out to lunch or dinner with a man. I'm sure when I saw her at La Bistro the other day, it was a business luncheon."

Hilary watched the red creep into Phillip's face. She saw Alana over Phillip's shoulder. "Who's Alana talking to? I've never seen him before."

Phillip whirled around, his mouth grim. "I don't know, but I'm going to find out." He strode off toward the young man and Alana.

Chapter Eight

Entering Phillip's outer office, Alana nodded to his private secretary, Michael. "Is Phillip busy? I need to talk to him for a moment." There was something wrong with going through a secretary to speak to your own husband, Alana thought darkly. She had her own suspicions, but so far, she hadn't been able to prove a thing. Six months of marriage to Phillip had taught her to be cautious.

"I'll let him know you're here." He reached for the phone, murmured few words and said, "Go right in, Mrs. Hudson."

"Thank you, Michael." She opened the door and walked into Phillip's opulent office. "Phillip, I'm going down to the boat. I want to check the loran and make sure the new charts we ordered came in. I'll look at the food supply, too, and order anything we need." She stood in front of him, her arms crossed over her chest.

He looked up, frowning, "Why now?"

"We've got a big race in a few days, and since I'm chairing the race committee, I've got to make sure everything is ready."

"How are the plans coming for the condos on the Big Island?"

"Slowly." She rubbed the back of her neck. "Another volcano eruption is predicted. Pele seems to be disrupting everything."

"You don't believe in that mumbo jumbo about the fire goddess, do you?"

"It doesn't make any difference what I believe. The superstitions surrounding that land have been handed down for generations. The people working on the project are the ones who are frightened. I thought I'd fly over next week and see for myself if there's anything that can be done."

"Good idea," he said too quickly, looking at Alana. "Wednesday?"

She nodded. Why did he seem so anxious for her to leave? "I probably won't be back in the office today."

"Is the banquet all set? And the awards?" he asked, rubbing his hands together.

She gave him a dry look. "You'd love to have your name on that trophy again, wouldn't you?"

Determination gripped his face. "When Bradburn won five years ago, I swore I'd get that trophy back. He's won every year since. It's my turn now. With the new sails, new boat, and the crew we have, he doesn't stand a chance. You're the best navigator and downwind helmsman in the islands. We can't lose."

"Thanks for the compliment." She was surprised he'd give her a compliment about anything these days. "We've got a good chance."

"We're going to win, Alana. You can bet on that." His fist hit the desk, making Alana jump. He winced.

"Phillip, have you been taking your medicine?"

"Of course," he grumbled. "Michael nags me as much as you do." He waved a hand toward the door. "I'll see you at home."

"What time do you expect to get home?" she asked as she put her hand on the door knob.

"Why?" His gaze bore into her.

Alana took a deep breath, meeting his suspicious look with one of her own. "So I can tell Helene when we'll be eating."

"Tell her eight o'clock." His eyes narrowed.

She managed to smile. "If you get out of here early, come on down to the club. We can have a drink before dinner." She'd play his little game.

He leaned back in his chair. "I'm making out a new will."

Her brows quirked. "Oh?"

"I thought you'd like to know what I'm going to change." He paused, frowning. "Aren't you curious about how much you'll inherit if I die?"

She gave him an impatient look. "We've only been married six months. I don't think you'll ever die, but if and when you do, I'm sure I'll survive."

"You mean you're not curious about who'll inherit Hudson Enterprises and my personal fortune?" he prodded.

"You'll tell me when you're good and ready."

"You know me too well." He picked up some papers on his desk. "I'm just going over the papers now. All I need to do is sign them." He rubbed the side of his jaw. "Melanie and Hilary won't survive if I leave them nothing. 'Course I don't owe them anything. Hell, they don't deserve a cent. Neither does that spoiled, lazy grandson of mine." A hard look entered his eyes. "You could be a very wealthy widow. Would you like that?"

"That is a stupid question that doesn't deserve an answer," she shot back, her hands on her hips. "Why this hang up about your money?"

"Without it, I'm just another old man. With it, I have power, status, authority." He returned her glare. "And you."

Alana wanted to add ruthless to his description of himself, but kept silent. "Phillip, I have a few errands to run before going to the club. You play your little games. I'll see you later." She closed the door before he could answer her.

Alana's first stop was to the Ala Moana Shopping Center. She needed a couple of new swimsuits and picked up several for Jeremy. She also saw some gaudy shorts and shirts that he'd love. The brighter, the better. She was about to turn away when she saw a man's reflection in the glass. She had seen that face before. Not that it was an outstanding face, but she recognized it. Where had she seen it?

Wandering into a boutique to look at the handbags, she glanced around. The man was in the next aisle looking at women's scarves. In a department store, she tried on sunglasses and looked in the mirror. He was examining the binoculars. Taking the escalator to the next floor she glanced at the jewelry. He had a watch in his hand. Recognition hit her as images from the past six months filtered through her mind. He was the same man she had seen when she ran in the morning, the same one she had seen whenever she was out of Phillip's sight! Damn! Phillip was having her followed!

A fierce, determined look crossed her face, and then she forced her expression to relax as if she hadn't a care in the world, wandering through several stores as she planned her strategy. Sauntering into a clothing store on the lower level, she said "Hi, Sandy. How's it going?"

"Just fine, Alana. How's the bride?" The tall blond woman smiled, the gold bracelets on her wrist jingling as she patted Alana's arm.

"Fine." What a lie that was. "I'm looking for a skirt. White." She looked at the racks and grabbed a couple of skirts, lowering her voice and looking over her shoulder. "Sandy, I know this sounds funny, but I think someone is following me."

"I'll call the police." Sandy took a step toward the telephone.

"No!" She restrained the woman with a hand on her arm. "I can lose him if you'll let me out the back door." She peered

116

around a display rack of jewelry. He was outside, looking at the display in the window.

"Certainly, Alana, but are you sure I shouldn't call the police. That new husband of yours would be real upset if anything happened to you."

"I'm sure, Sandy." The woman went to the back of the store and into the fitting room. Sandy took the clothes from Alana and unlocked the back door.

"You're sure this is what you want to do?"

"Very sure," Alana muttered.

Alana hurried out of the store and toward her car, heading back to Waikiki. She parked her car across the street from Hudson Towers, the same hotel Phillip had taken her to while he was married to Betty.

Several minutes later Phillip's limousine pulled up and Phillip jumped out of the car, hurrying into the hotel. Alana's heart sank. Her suspicions might be true.

Fifteen minutes later a stunning blond sauntered into the hotel. She was wearing a strapless red sundress that hugged her curves.

Alana had to know. She scrambled out of the car and followed the woman, keeping her sunglasses on and hoping no one would recognize her.

The woman pushed the button for the penthouse, and Alana knew her worst fears were true. Phillip was unfaithful. She had thought he loved her, and had hoped her love would be enough for him. It obviously hadn't been. It made her sick to think they had just made love that morning and now he was meeting someone else ... in the same hotel room!

She stayed in the elevator, out of sight. When she heard Phillip answer the door and call the other woman darling, she punched the button for the lobby, closing her eyes against the tears that threatened to spill down her cheeks.

What was she going to do? Who could she talk to? She had planned to visit Jeremy and Thomas. That's exactly what she would do.

She hurried out onto the street, keeping her emotions under tight control, heading her Mercedes coupe toward the freeway and Sunset Beach. Taking the six-lane highway northwest she sped toward Wahiawa and the Schofield plateau. Bipassing the Wahiawa itself she barely glanced at the pineapple and sugar-cane fields, anxious to get to her destination. The beauty of the mountain ranges and Oahu's highest peak, Kaala, were lost on her. She was angry. Furious. She could not live with a man who didn't trust her and then was unfaithful himself. Perhaps his jealousy had just been a cover for his own infidelity. The thought made her sick.

Passing Haleiwa anticipation replaced anger. The vivid blue of the ocean and the endless ribbon of white sand worked its magic on her troubled soul. Just past Waimea she took a sharp left turning onto a road that was little more than a track through a stand of trees. She stopped in the shelter of the trees, took a deep breath and continued on her way.

The familiar bungelow came into sight and she allowed herself a wide smile. She stopped the car and scrambled out. Grabbing the presents for Jeremy, she hurried up the path toward the house. Though it was little more than a cottage, she felt more at ease in this home than she did in Phillip's mansion. Maybe it was the warmth, the caring atmosphere.

She scanned the beach. Her eyes lit up when she saw him. "Jeremy!" she called out. A tall man lithely jumped to his feet and came running toward her. Alana wanted to cry when she saw him. He was over six feet with sun bleached hair, a golden tan, a body like a modern Adonis, features more handsome than male models, a winning smile and the mind of a child. A promising young man frozen in time. He'd always be seven years old.

"Lani!" he called, his deep voice reaching into her heart and squeezing it. "Am I glad to see you!" He grabbed her in a bear hug and twirled her around. There was nothing wrong with his strength. He gave her a big kiss and then set her down. "Did you bring me a present?" he asked, eyeing the packages he had crushed between them.

"Nope. These are for Thomas." She teased him and reached up to tossle his hair.

"Aw, Lani. I like presents, too." He pretended to pout and then grinned widely. "You brought me something. I know you did. You always do."

"You're too smart for me," she said with a smile, handing him the packages.

"Oh, wow." He peered into a bag and held up the vivid shorts and shirts. "Look," he pointed to bright splotches of color. "Red. Green." He paused frowning. "Yellow!" he said with triumph in his voice.

"That's right!" She gave him a hug. "Where's Thomas?"

The young man was busy digging through the bag. "He's in the house. Making lunch. We're having peanut butter and jelly sandwiches." He looked disappointed. "Just clothes!"

Alana pretended to be surprised. "I thought you'd like the clothes."

"I do, Lani." He stuffed the clothes back in the bags.

"What do you say to your sister, Jeremy?" came a rumbling voice from the porch.

"Thank you, Lani," he said, a wide grin splitting his face. "I'm glad you're here. I've missed you."

"I've missed you, too, Jeremy." She smiled, her voice soft, "If you go look in the car, I'll bet you'll find one more package."

He let out a whoop and dropping the bags of clothes he ran

down the path. Alana watched him go with the same bittersweet feelings she always had regarding her brother. How could he be so handsome and look so normal and not grow mentally? She kept reminding herself it was a miracle he was alive. They had been a normal family until one spring day when Alana was twelve and Jeremy was nine. The four of them had gone to the mountains outside of Denver for a vacation. Alana remembered as if it were yesterday. They were almost home when a car ran them off the road. Both parents were killed instantly, Jeremy was in a coma for months and she had a multitude of broken bones. The authorities didn't tell her much about the accident. Her father had been an undercover policeman and someone had found out he was going to testify in an important trial. The newspapers had said the entire family was killed. The documents her father had died protecting were never found. Jeremy and Alana were moved to Hawaii and given new identities, Jeremy's beloved teddy bear the only thing they were allowed to keep from their old life. Jeremy remembered nothing when he emerged from the coma, but Alana lived with the memory of the accident and knowledge that if the wrong people found out who she was and that Jeremy was her brother, they might be killed. Sometimes she wondered if she could still identify the driver of that car given the chance.

"How has he been, Thomas?" she asked, watching her brother open the car door. Thomas and his wife, Shirley, had been assigned to look after Alana and her brother after the accident. Shirley had died three years before of cancer, but Thomas remained with Jeremy. Alana was grateful for that. Thomas looked like he could be Jeremy's father. He had the same athletic build, blond hair, and blue eyes. They made quite an impressive team.

"He's been begging me to show him how to surf. We went down to the Bonzai Pipeline the other day and I was telling him about it. He's been singing along with those tapes you got him." He watched the young man take a long box out of the back seat of the car. "You got him a keyboard?"

Alana nodded. "Since he likes music so much, I thought he might enjoy it. Of course, you'll have to put up with all the sounds it can make."

"I'll just put in my ear plugs," he said with a laugh, his hands on his hips.

"Do you think it would be wise to teach him to surf?" She bit her bottom lip.

Thomas shrugged broad shoulders. "We can give it a try. It would be something for him to do. See if we can stretch his mind a little more."

Alana didn't know what she would have done without Thomas. He was a companion, friend, and guard for Jeremy. Alana looked at his huge hands. She had no doubt that he could kill a man with those hands if he chose to. He was also patient and gentle with Jeremy. He had taught Jeremy to do many things that the doctors said would be impossible.

"Want me to get a surfboard for him?" Thomas asked as Jeremy came running toward them, his face glowing.

"Sure. Just let me know how much it is." Alana wanted Jeremy to have anything he wanted. She just wished she could give him the one thing he needed the most. His mind.

"Lani! Part of a piano. Where's the rest of it?" He turned the keyboard upside down. "How does this work?" He punched the keys and nothing happened.

"Come on, Jeremy," she said, taking his hand. "I'll show you how it works. It'll make all kinds of neat sounds. You can make up your own songs."

"Wow! What kinds of sounds does it make?"

Alana laughed. "You'll drive Thomas nuts."

"I can't drive, Lani." He frowned.

"It's just an expression, Jeremy." Thomas's voice was calm.

"She means that with all the sounds you can make, I'll cover my ears."

Jeremy was silent for a moment and then grinned. "I'll drive you nuts," he repeated. He repeated it one more time and stomped up the steps into the house, muttering the phrase over and over.

"I think he likes the idea of you covering your ears," Alana said with a smile as she and Thomas followed Jeremy into the house.

"I'm sure he does. He'll use that phrase all week."

"Sorry about that." She laughed.

"I'll remind you about it when I order a surfboard for me, too," he retorted, holding the door for her.

"It's only fair. Can't have you both out on the water on one board. It'll sink."

"What will sink?" Jeremy said as they came through the open doorway.

"Oh, just another surprise." Alana dropped her purse on the rattan sofa.

"I love surprises." He plopped down on the sofa and patted the cushion next to him. "Sit here, Lani. Show me how to do this."

Alana sat down next to him as Thomas went into the kitchen. "I'll make a sandwich for you, Alana."

A sigh escaped her lips. "I can't stay that long."

Jeremy pulled on her sleeve. "Show me, Lani. Please."

Alana explained the keyboard to Jeremy. When she left Thomas would have to explain it many more times before Jeremy would remember.

Jeremy's head was bent as he punched the keys. Alana wandered into the kitchen. The bleached oak floors, oriental rugs, high beamed ceiling, and yellow and white overstuffed rattan furniture in the living area gave the little house a light, airy feeling. The kitchen reflected that feeling.

Thomas looked at the shadows under Alana's eyes, the bleak look in her eyes. "How's the marriage going?"

"You haven't told Jeremy, have you?" she asked, leaning one hip against the counter.

He shook his head, cutting Jeremy's sandwich. "He should know about it."

"No." Her voice was more forceful than she meant it to be. "No," she said again more quietly. "He wouldn't understand."

"You haven't answered my question." He glanced at her.

She chewed on a fingernail. "Phillip doesn't trust me. He had me followed."

"You weren't followed out here, were you?" He was instantly alert.

She shook her head. "I lost him at the mall." She paused. "Phillip's having an affair."

"Does he think you've got a lover, too?"

The bluntness of his question made her color. "I suppose. He makes accusations that aren't true. I've never given him reason to doubt me, but today I found out for sure that he's unfaithful. We've only been married six months." She rubbed her neck and accepted the glass of iced tea he held out to her. "So much for love . . ."

"Have you told him about Jeremy?" he asked, watching her intently.

Her gaze rested on her brother, a soft smile on her lips, sorrow in her eyes. "No. Phillip wouldn't understand. Jeremy is happy here. Remember what happened when I tried to keep him in Honolulu?"

Thomas groaned. "Women were all over him like leeches. They didn't care if he had no mind at all. They just wanted his body. He didn't know what was going on."

"I don't want that happening again. I don't want his world disrupted. God knows it's small enough, but he's content."

"We're going to go to the Falls tomorrow. Jeremy is such a

handsome dude that he draws attention just by walking down the street with that million dollar smile on his face." Thomas looked at the man sitting on the floor. "What a waste."

"I try not to think about that." Alana stood up. "Jeremy, I have to go now."

His bright eyes clouded. "Oh, Lani. You just got here."

"I've got to get back to work. I'll try to get to see you next week. Be good for Thomas."

"I always am. Right, Thomas?" He looked at the older man expectantly.

"Most of the time, Jeremy. Except when you don't eat your broccoli."

Jeremy made a face. "I hate that green stuff. Lani, tell Thomas that I don't have to eat that yucky stuff."

Alana laughed. "Sorry, Jeremy, but I agree with Thomas. You need to eat your vegetables." It was heartbreaking telling a grown man that he needed to eat his vegetables. She certainly couldn't tell him he needed to eat to grow big and strong. Left in the real world, he'd have women tripping over each other just to say hello. This was the best world for Jeremy. Small, uncomplicated, safe. She would never let anything happen to him. "Bye, Jeremy."

He scrambled to his feet, towering over her. "Bye, Lani." He gave her a hug and a kiss. "I love you."

"I love you, too, Jeremy." She felt tears prick at her eyes. Blinking quickly, she said, "I'll see you next week."

"I'll miss you." He gave her another hug and looked at the keyboard. "Thomas, show me how to do this. I want to make more sounds."

Thomas and Alana exchanged a look. "You play with him. I'll call tomorrow." Alana called every day. "Bye, sport." She tousled Jeremy's hair and walked out, willing herself not to cry.

* * *

On the ride back to Waikiki, she put an upbeat, rock tape on and turned up the volume. She took the curves expertly, a red blur on the landscape. Checking the digital clock on the dash, she increased her speed. She had to get to the club and do a million things before getting home by eight. Phillip would show up demanding to know where she had been while *he* was the one having an affair. Her thoughts turned to a safe subject, the race. It was a Friday night start with the finish sometime Saturday followed by a party on Saturday night when the trophies would be given out.

Fortunate enough to find a parking spot, she hurried toward the club, pulling out her key card and pushing it into the slot. When the door buzzed she pulled the heavy wooden door open, relaxing immediately as she entered the calm interior. Her heels clicked on the slate floor in the near empty club. She waved to the woman tending bar, the woman's bottled blond hair a riot of curls that stuck out in every direction. It was difficult to see her eyes under the heavy bangs and thick makeup. If it was up to the women members, she would have been fired, but with her mini skirts and half buttoned blouses, the men outnumbered the women's vote. The club lush was in residence, perched on the end bar stool, holding her head up with one hand.

Alana headed for the women's locker room. She looked out over the docks from the open vista of the lounge. Not much activity on a Tuesday. Once in the locker room, she quickly changed out of her silk dress and pulled on pink shorts and a pink and white striped tank top. Pushing her feet into thongs, she slammed the locker door and twirled the key. The soft flip flop of her feet in the sandals were the only sound as she made her way outside, breathing deeply and lifting her face to the sun.

When she reached the boat, she jumped on board, unlocked it, and scrambled below. Phillip thought this new, high tech boat would beat everyone, but Alana had her doubts. Phillip was the one who took the wheel most of the time, and he was an inattentive helmsman.

Her first task was to slather herself with sunscreen. She didn't know why Jeremy was blessed with skin that tanned to deep mahogany, but all she ever got from the sun was a severe burn. She checked the lockers for food. They would race with a crew of eight. Seven hungry men and Alana. She'd need to order food for at least three meals plus sandwiches. Her favorite store would fill her order, deliver the groceries, and put everything away.

She saw the package of new charts on the chart table. Then she flipped the switches for the electronics, checking calculations. She went on deck and checked the instrumentation there. It still wasn't exactly the way she wanted it. Making a mental note to talk to Hardy, she finished her inspection and headed back to the club.

Now she had to talk to the chef about the banquet Saturday night, the head of the race committee about keeping the stats of the racing yachts, and the club manager about extra bartenders on Friday and Saturday. Sailors were a thirsty lot, and if they had to wait too long for a drink, they could get unruly.

As she headed toward Koko Head, she finally had to face the issue she had avoided all afternoon. She had to confront Phillip and she didn't look forward to it one little bit.

Chapter Nine

Phillip heard Alana coming up the stairs. His face was grim as he shifted his weight in the peach silk chair in Alana's suite. He had been sitting there waiting for her for over an hour.

"Hello, Phillip." She looked at him in surprise.

"Where the hell have you been?" he demanded, his hands clenched in fists on the delicate arms of the chair.

"I had some shopping to do and I went to the club." She dumped the packages on the chair next to him and walked toward her bedroom. She glanced at her watch. "It's not even seven o'clock. I told you I'd be home before eight."

"You didn't get to the club until after two. Where were you from eleven until two thirty?" His voice boomed behind her as his frame filled the doorway between her sitting room and her bedroom.

Alana whirled around, anger flaring in her eyes. "You want the truth? You were too willing to have me out of the way for the afternoon. On a hunch I went to Hudson Towers."

"What the hell were you doing there?" he bellowed, wondering if she knew what he was doing there. He didn't have long to wait.

"I followed a cute little blonde up to the penthouse." Her

hands were on her hips, her face was grim. "You opened the door for her! The same place you took me when you were married to Betty! We've only been married six months. Why did you have to betray me?"

"It meant nothing," he muttered. "I don't even remember her name." This wasn't what he wanted to discuss. "What did you do after leaving the hotel? Who were you with? How do I know you weren't with someone in the same hotel?" he retorted, his eyes as dark as thunder clouds. If Hilary hadn't told him about seeing Alana with other men, she might have fooled him with this self-righteous act, but he knew better.

She walked to the other side of the room and picked up her hair brush before turning to face him. "Just because you can't be faithful, don't think everyone else is on your level."

"I demand to know where you were today." His glower should have caused her to cringe, but she refused to be intimidated, infuriating him further.

Brushing past him, she marched into the sitting room, pulling the pins from her hair and brushing it until it crackled. "I left the office at 9:51 am. I walked to my car. Let's see. That took approximately two minutes. Then I went to the Ala Moana Mall." She pointed to the bags on the chair. "I needed a couple of swimsuits." She brushed her hair again. "I left the mall at approximately 11:47." Her voice was laced with sarcasm. She tossed the brush onto a table. "I spent the next forty-five minutes at Hudson Towers, much to my disgust." Her eyes burned with indignation.

"I know you were at Ala Moana until 11. I want to know where you were until you got to the club at 2:30." He took a step toward her, menace in his eyes.

"I wasn't under the bed listening, if that's bothering you." Alana's chin lifted, her gaze defiant.

His eyes narrowed, his mouth thinned. "My man lost you when you went into a little boutique. You knew he was following you, didn't you!" When she didn't answer, he shouted, "Didn't you?"

"Yes!" She didn't flinch from the fury in his face. "You're a rich man, Phillip Hudson. I thought it could be a kidnapper. How the hell was I supposed to know you hired him!"

"Where were you!" he bellowed, taking another step toward her, gripping her shoulders and shaking her. He had to know if Hilary was right. His affairs meant nothing, but he didn't know about Alana.

"You're the one who cheated on me, Phillip. I'll be damned if I'll tell you where I was!"

"I want to know, damn it. I demand to know." He grabbed her wrist and twisted it behind her back, his features contorted in rage, his voice thundering over her. Blind fury made him brutal.

Alana's silence and refusal to cry out made him angrier. "If you don't have anything to hide, why won't you tell me."

A knock at the door silenced him. "What is it?" he muttered, not releasing Alana.

A slight cough was followed by a deep voice. "You wanted the mileage on Mrs. Hudson's car, Mr. Hudson."

Alana's eyes blazed, her voice filled with contempt. "You bastard!"

"Yes," he said in a clear voice. "What's the mileage?" When the man told him, Phillip gave Alana a triumphant sneer. "Thank you, Leonard." He paused. "Now. Tell me where you were this afternoon. There shouldn't be more than fifteen or twenty miles on your car. Where the hell were you?"

"I wouldn't tell you now if my life depended on it." She lifted her chin and stood perfectly still, withdrawing from him completely.

That inflamed him further. Jealousy ripped through his body. "Have you been seeing Griff?" he demanded, tightening his grip on her arm. "Or are there other lovers in your life?"

"Takes one to know one, is that your motto?" she mocked. "You're the one with the lovers."

He grabbed her chin in a vice-like grip, forcing her to look at him. "Tell me!" His face was red, his eyes burning through her. The thought of another man touching her made him wild. He knew it was a double standard, but he didn't care. He was in command.

Alana lifted her free arm. Using all her strength she drove her elbow into his stomach, freeing herself from his grip. She darted behind the chair, putting some distance between them and eyeing the door that now seemed a mile away.

Coughing, and doubled over, he held a hand to his stomach. "You'll pay for this, damn it!" No woman was going to degrade him! He straightened and walked toward her, his fist over his head, fierce rage contorting his features.

"Get out of here, Phillip, before you do something you'll regret." Her gaze darted around the room.

"I never regret anything I do. I'm not senile. I know what's going on behind my back." He took another step toward her, lunging for her, but she sidestepped him and made her move, sprinting toward the door. Anticipating her direction, Phillip got there first, grabbing her arm in a vice-like grip. "Griff. And God knows how many others. You're nothing but a whore!"

"And you're a bastard! It's okay for you to cheat on me, but you'll make sure I don't do the same thing. You disgust me!"

"I won't be made a fool of on this island." His face was mottled with red, hatred in his eyes as he raised his hand. He had never hit a woman before, but he relished the thought right now.

"You'd better make this your best shot, because you won't get another," she said, her voice deathly quiet, her eyes burning into his.

Phillip's eyes narrowed as his grip tightened. "No one threatens me. Ever." She stiffened just before he hit her with the back of his hand, the force of the blow jerking her head violently to one side, the edge of his diamond ring cutting her face.

Stunned, Alana stumbled sideways, her hand to her cheek. Phillip was in a blind rage, capable of anything. Scrambling around behind a table, her words were slurred. "Get out of here!" He came at her with his fist raised. She picked up a Stueben paper weight, throwing it at his head. He ducked and the crystal hit a mirror, shards of splintering glass exploding into the room.

Phillip stood between her and the door, an ugly sneer on his face. His senses were alert, his eyes never leaving her face. He took off his jacket and tossed it aside. His tie followed his jacket and he began to unbutton his shirt. "I'll show you what happens to people who cheat on me." An evil look twisted his mouth. He would make her pay for being unfaithful. No man would ever want her when he got through with her.

Alana picked up a lamp, yanking the cord out of the socket. "Go away until you calm down. Remember your heart."

"Damn my heart. I'm not the doddering old fool you think I am!" He seized her arm. She knocked it away with the lamp. He was thrown off balance. She was stronger than he thought. He relished the challenge, everything forgotten except his need for revenge.

Just as she reached the door, he grabbed a fist full of her hair with one hand and hit the side of her head with the other. She stumbled and fell.

Phillip towered over her, a vicious look in his eyes as he ripped off his shirt. He sneered at her. "Where are all your lovers now, you whore!"

Alana remained silent. She inched away from him, but before she could scramble to her feet he was on top of her, straddling her hips.

Her nails left a scarlet path along his cheek.

Phillip pounded her with his fist.

Alana retaliated with a blow to his chest.

Phillip threw back his head and laughed, the evil sound chilling. "You can't hurt me. You're nothing but a slut! You think you're going to hurt me?" He grasped the neck of her shirt and yanked it, ripping it from top to bottom. He tore off her bra. "How many other men have looked at you like this?" He slapped her face when she remained silent. "No one is going to get the chance again."

He relaxed for just a moment. Alana clutched a bronze statue on the table to her right, slamming it into Phillip's groin. When he doubled over in agony, Alana shoved him off of her, scrambled to her feet, and ran.

Alana ran along the driveway, heading for the protection of the trees and undergrowth alongside the road. Alana ducked into the shrubbery as every light on the property suddenly blazed. Heedless of the branches that tore at her skin, she crawled deeper into the few remaining shadows, Phillip's angry threats making her shudder. Gasping for air, she curled into a tight ball, forcing her mind to function. If she tried to go out through the gates, Phillip would nab her immediately. The alarm system surrounding the estate had been activated. It was as difficult to get out undetected as it was to get in. There was only one way out and even that would be risky. It meant dodging closed circuit television monitors and sensors as well as swimming among the rocks in complete darkness. But there was no other option.

Alana took a deep breath. Her face throbbed. Deep cuts on her arms and legs stung. She tasted blood. Her cotton shirt was little more than tatters on her back, scratches crisscrossing her exposed chest. Stumbling to her feet, she concentrated on putting one foot in front of the other, skirting the house, tennis courts, swimming pool, and guest house.

Dropping to her knees for the last hundred feet, she crawled down a long forgotten path to the sea. Overgrown with vines and bushes, it seemed to take her forever. The sensors were just ahead. She dropped to her stomach, her breath coming in short gasps. Sweat covered her body, the salt stinging her wounds. She was still for a moment, listening and waiting. Phillip was on the bluff. Leonard was with him. Their voices carried on the night air.

"Where the hell is she?" Phillip's voice was harsh.

"She's got to be here. There's no way she can leave the grounds without us knowing about it." Leonard's usually calm voice was grim. "Think she'd be stupid enough to try the sea?"

"If she does, she'll be smashed on the rocks." Phillip grunted. "Which is nothing less than what she deserves." There was silence and then Phillip said, "I'm going to shower. Let me know if you find her."

The men's voices faded in the night. Alana closed her eyes and remained still for a few more minutes. Phillip preferred her dead. It was the impetus she needed to succeed. It was time someone thwarted Phillip Hudson.

Inching her way along the path, it seemed like hours before she passed the sensors and could crawl once again. The sand irritated her cut and bruised palms and knees, but determination drove her on. Water lapped her hands. Slipping into the ocean, Alana wanted to scream in agony. The salt water burned every scratch and cut. Her face felt like it was going to explode. Her vision was hazy in one eye and the other was swollen shut. She plodded on, stopping when she reached the finger of rocks, stripping off the tattered remains of her clothing. She bobbed in the water for several minutes, the exertion of freeing herself from the dead weight of her clothes making her wonder if the effort had been worthwhile. Alana had never been so exhausted in her entire life.

She let the current carry her to the right, floating along, fighting the darkness that threatened to engulf her. All sense of time ceased in her battle for survival. A crescent of sand beckoned her. Too weary to care where she was, she headed for the shore, concentrating on pushing one arm through the water and then the other. Her legs fluttered uselessly. Salt water blurred the little vision she had. Riding a final wave into shore, she stumbled and fell, crawling along the wet sand. Dogs barked. Someone shouted. Alana welcomed the darkness spreading over her like a gigantic ink spot.

A deep voice tried to penetrate her numbed mind before she retreated into unconsciousness.

Alana tried to open her eyes, but only one worked sufficiently enough to focus on her surroundings. It wasn't a hospital room and thank God she wasn't in Phillip's house, but where was she? Gingerly she raised one arm and touched her face. One eye was swollen shut, her lips felt three times as big as normal, her jaw ached, and her whole body felt like she had been tossed over a cliff.

"You're awake."

Alana knew that voice. She groaned and closed her eye. "I don't believe it. I'm in the middle of a nightmare."

"One good turn deserves another," Raine said, mockery in his voice. "At least I won't run off in a huff."

"It was your beach?" she muttered, her eye still closed.

"Yes."

She heard him pull a chair next to the bed.

"Did Hudson do this to you?" She heard the controlled anger in his low voice.

She opened her eye, reliving the nightmare. "Thanks for helping me."

He leaned forward, his elbows on his knees, his face grim. "Answer me, Alana."

She was silent for a long time. Telling him was like admitting she had made a monumental mistake six months ago, but then the whole world would know soon enough. She refused to live with a man who would rob her of her self respect. "Yes. It was Phillip."

"The bastard." The hatred in his voice made her cringe.

She struggled to get up, but the effort made her head explode. She put a hand to her temple. "You can't call him anything that I haven't said to myself a hundred times."

Raine's hands were gentle as he pushed her back. "Take it from the voice of experience. Your head is going to hurt for a couple of days. I'll get you some aspirin and more ice for your eye." He paused. "Can you eat anything?"

"I'll take a steak just as soon as I can open my mouth," she murmured.

"You should see a doctor." There was concern in his voice.

Alana tried to laugh, focusing on his face as best she could. "This conversation sounds like a rerun. I don't want a doctor."

"I figured as much, but I had a doctor examine you last night anyway. Nothing is broken, just badly bruised." He stood up, looking down at her, controlled fury in his voice. He turned around and said over his shoulder, "I'll get the aspirin and ice."

Alana watched him disappear into the bathroom and then closed her eyes. Her head hurt. She didn't want to think about who cleaned her wounds and put her to bed. She must have been a sight when she washed up on the beach, wearing little more than bruises and scratches.

Reliving those horrifying hours made her flesh crawl. Marriage to Phillip had been the biggest mistake of her life. She had no one to blame but herself. Warning signs regarding Phillip's possessiveness and jealousy had been everywhere, but his infidelity was the ultimate humiliation. How had Betty put up with it for all those years? Alana had been the mistress and the wife, neither situation making her feel very proud of herself. Well, she had paid the price, she thought with a sigh. Phillip would make her look like she married the poor grieving widower for his money. A scheming witch. She'd have to find another job, but where? Phillip's influence reached from London to Hong Kong.

Jeremy! Oh, God! What would she do about Jeremy? Tears trickled down her cheeks, but she was too weary to wipe them away.

"Tears?" Raine's chiding voice broke through her misery. "I thought you were tougher than that, Alana." He sat down and helped her sit up, giving her the aspirin and a glass of water. When she collapsed back on the pillow, he put an ice pack on her eye. His touch was surprisingly gentle. "What are you going to do now?"

"What time is it?" she asked, holding the ice in place.

He frowned, glancing at his gold Rolex. "Eight o'clock. Why?"

"The first thing I have to do is call the office and let them know I won't be in today." She opened her one good eye. "Could I use your phone?"

He eased himself off the bed and settled into the chair, facing her, his arms crossed over his chest. Even through one eye he looked disgustingly handsome. His eyes matched the azure polo shirt stretched across broad shoulders. White tennis shorts exposed strong, tanned legs. His vitality made Alana feel even worse. She closed her eye, but that didn't shut out the fresh scent of his after shave or the timbre of his voice. "Do you know how long you've been out?"

She opened her eye, her gaze wary. "I don't think I want to know."

"Twenty-four hours. It's eight o'clock at night."

"A whole day lost," she muttered.

"Want to talk about it?" Raine's voice penetrated her weariness.

"Not really." She plucked at the cool sheet with trembling fingers. The fight had been humiliating enough without discussing it.

"Do you talk to anyone, Alana?" he asked quietly. "Is there anyone you can confide in?"

She thought about it for a moment, frowning slightly, but the movement sent a pain shooting through her cheek. "What an odd question." She answered it honestly. Jade was the closest friend she had, but there were aspects of her life that Jade knew nothing about. The death of her parents had forced her to be self-reliant and self-contained. "There isn't anyone. I prefer it that way."

"Hmmmmm." He stroked his chin with a strong hand, his eyes shuttered. "Kindred souls, Alana. You and I."

Their eyes met and held. He seemed to delve into her very soul while she wanted to drown in the deep blue pools of his eyes. Alana was the first to break contact.

"Don't be ridiculous. We hate each other," she protested.

"There's a fine line between love and hate."

"I'm married to another man." It was ludicrous reasoning, but it was all she had for a defense. It was so hard to think when her head hurt and Raine sat beside her. It had to be her exhausted state that caused her to be so attuned to him, so aware of every emotion that flickered in those bottomless blue eyes, so conscious of the controlled strength, the perception with which he could read her as no man had.

"The man who beat you up." Anger burned in his eyes. "Why did he do it, Alana?"

137

It surprised her to realize he was genuinely concerned. She raised one arm and looked at her bruised wrist.

He smoothed a strand of hair from her forehead. "Tell me what happened."

His touched was soothing. She finally spoke, softly, each word pulled from her heart. "Phillip didn't trust me. He had me followed. When I realized it, I was furious, so I ditched the guy. Phillip demanded to know where I had been, so I told him part of it. I caught him meeting a blonde at the Hudson Towers. He has two standards, one for him and one for me. He wanted to know where else I had been. He didn't even bother to apologize for what he had done. He even had Leonard keep track of the mileage on my car! I refused to justify his accusations. Phillip got mad."

"Obviously." His voice was dry. He leaned back. "So where were you that you wouldn't tell him?"

She gave him a dark look. "If you think I'm going to tell you, we're not as attuned to each other as you seem to think." She had the feeling Raine would understand about Jeremy and treat him with respect. Fatigue dulled her voice. "It's not important where I was. The issue was betrayal and trust."

"So you took a beating on the principle of the matter?" His voice was incredulous. "You're a strong woman, Alana."

She tried to yawn, but it hurt too much, so she snuggled deeper into the pillow. "Not so strong ..." She was asleep before he could answer.

He pulled the sheet up to her chin and carefully removed the ice bag. He settled into the chair, watching her sleep, fierce determination hardening his features as he gazed at her battered face. "Phillip Hudson will pay for this."

Chapter Ten

Melanie sauntered through Sea Life Park, stopping to watch the sea lions. When a man stopped beside her, she glanced at his outrageous outfit and chuckled. "Arty, you'd blend in better if you dressed a little more conservatively."

He smoothed the red, yellow, and black print shirt over his stomach. Purple shorts touched his knobby knees. He pulled his straw hat further down on his forehead. "Look around, Ms. Hudson. I fit in better than you do in your designer dress and Cartier jewelry."

Melanie gazed at the tourists and then at her own chic jade linen suit, white silk blouse and twenty-four karat jewelry. "Touche."

Arty pulled a large manila envelope from his camera bag. "This is all I could dig up on Alana Jordan Hudson. I think you're wasting your money. Her background is spotless." He paused. "In fact, it's too clean. There are some chunks of time where she didn't exist."

Melanie pushed her gold rimmed aviator sunglasses on top of her head, her eyes sparkling with excitement. "I knew it! She's hiding something. Dig deeper, Arty."

He shrugged and put his camera back in the bag. "I'll try. What's the big deal anyway?"

"I want to destroy her like she destroyed my mother.'

Arty regarded her for a long moment. "I'll call you tomorrow night." He paused. "I'll need more money. Cash. The people I'm working with only deal in cash."

Melanie opened her alligator bag and pulled out an envelope. "Here's another five thousand. I expect to see results."

"I can't make up evidence," he protested.

Her gaze was hard. "People do it all the time. It just has to look legitimate."

He rubbed a chubby hand across his eyes. "For that kind of work, I'll need another ten grand. Quality work doesn't come cheap."

"I'll see that you have your money tomorrow." She pushed her sunglasses back onto her face. "I'll meet you at noon in front of the statue of King Kamehameha." Melanie turned and walked away.

Hilary replaced the receiver of the telephone and strolled out onto the terrace, sinking into one of the lounge chairs. She had lost thirty thousand dollars in three days. Not that she couldn't get it back. One week she had won fifty thousand, another week seventy-five thousand. She just seemed to be on a losing streak at the moment. Her luck had to change. Getting Alana out of her father's life would be the turning point. She'd bet on it.

"Hello, Hilary." Chandler joined her, walking toward the bar. "How about a cocktail before we go out?"

"Sounds wonderful." She sat up and smoothed the full skirt of her black and white striped dress. The bodice had a slight scoop, just enough to show off her black coral and ivory necklace and earrings. She had designed the jewlery herself, pleased with the finished results of black polished square cut coral outlined in ivory. Hilary studied the toes of her white calfskin pumps. "What can we do to get Phillip to give Mitchell a job at Hudson Enterprises?"

Chandler handed her a crystal goblet. "We?" He settled into a chair across from her, smoothing a crease in his white slacks. "Phillip barely says hello to me. I don't have any influence at all. You're the one he listens to."

Hilary took a sip of her drink. "He used to listen to me until Alana interfered. Now he seldom comes to my office and never asks my advice." She frowned. "I can't decide if I hate father more because he ignores me and drove mother to her death, or if I hate Alana because she's got him so befuddled he doesn't know what he's doing anymore."

"If that's the case, why don't you simply send Mitchell to the personnel office, make a couple of discreet phone calls, and slip him into a position where he won't have any contact with his grandfather. Phillip can't possibly keep track of all his employees."

Hilary brightened. "That's an excellent idea!" She took another sip. "Now I just have to convince Mitch that he should work instead of going to the beach every day."

Chandler picked a speck of lint from his navy linen jacket. "You've got no one to blame but yourself. You've spoiled him."

"If one more person says that to me, I'm going to scream," she muttered between clenched teeth. "I can't go back and do it over again, so I just have to live with it, and quite honestly, I don't regret one thing I've done for him!" She glared at Chandler. "He's been with me longer than you have."

"True." One brow quirked as he sipped his drink. "Why do you keep me around?"

"Probably because it's convenient." She held out her empty glass. "The investigator Melanie hired still hasn't found anything we can use against Alana." Hilary crossed her ankles.

"Alana wasn't at work today. It's the first time she's ever missed work."

"Maybe morning sickness," Chandler mocked.

"God! That would be the final straw. First a stepmother younger than Melanie, and then a baby!" Her face mirrored her disgust. "We'd better put a few more doubts in father's head." A sly smile curved her lips. "Think how he'd react if she was pregnant and he wasn't sure the baby was his."

Chandler pulled Hilary to her feet. "Margo is the perfect person to spread a little gossip. She'll be at the party tonight. We'll just have to make sure she hears us talking, won't we?" He glanced at his watch. "We'd better go. I don't want to be late."

Hilary groaned inwardly. Chandler was never late for anything. Just once she wished . . .

Alana awoke to light peeking through vertical blinds. Gingerly she touched her lips and cheek. Not quite as swollen. She pushed back the wrinkled sheet, frowning at her scratched legs and bruised knees. No wonder she was stiff. Alana pushed herself upright, dangling her legs over the edge of the bed, examining the cuts on her arms and the palms of her hands. A long sleeved blouse and slacks would cover the physical evidence of Phillip's fury, but the emotional devastation would be more difficult to deal with. She could never forgive him for using brutal strength against her. She eased herself out of bed, swaying slightly. A deep breath sent a sharp pain through her chest. Moving from one piece of furniture to another, she made her way into the bathroom. Flicking on the light, she stared at her reflection, unwilling and unable to believe that the swollen, purple and black face staring back at her was actually her face. One eye was open wide, the other was a bloodshot slit surrounded by purple and black. She flinched when she touched the cut along her cheekbone. Alana's hand trembled as she pushed it through tangled and matted hair, sticky from the salt water. The bleak eyes couldn't be hers!

Gingerly unbuttoning Raine's pajamas and slipping them off, she stepped into the shower, the water stinging at first but then soothing her tired muscles and her weary soul.

Toweling her hair wore her out. She avoided the mirror, putting the pajamas back on until she found something else to wear. Stepping out of the bathroom, she was surprised to see Raine sprawled on the love seat. A tray of food was on the table in front of him. He took a sip of coffee. "I thought you might be hungry by now." He waved a hand over the tray.

Alana looked at the tempting food. "I'm starved." Using furniture for support she made her way across the room, glad that Raine didn't jump up to help her. She'd feel stiffled if he were too solicitous.

"Feeling better?" he asked, his eyes narrowed as he watched her slow progress.

"Much." She sank onto the rocking chair, taking a deep breath before she tackled her hair. She winced as she raised her arm.

Raine gently took the brush from her hand and got to his feet, walking behind her. "Relax. I'll do it." His touch was gentle as he smoothed her hair.

"You'll spoil me." She reached for a warm blueberry muffin, pinched off a bite and put it in her mouth, chewing carefully.

"I doubt it. You wouldn't let anyone take that much control of your life." He smoothed a strand of hair from her cheek.

"Could you please be less astute about me?" She took another bite of the muffin.

His low chuckle sent a tremor down her spine. "What are you going to do now? You're not going back to that ass, are you?" He finished brushing her hair and tossed the brush on the love seat. He poured a cup of coffee for each of them.

"One thing I learned early in life. I never make the same mistake twice. It'll mean my job and public humiliation, but he'll never get the chance to touch me again," she said, her face grim. "I'll kill him first."

He raised his brows. "What's your first move?"

Alana was silent for a moment, leaning back in her chair. "First I have to have some clothes to wear."

His gaze roved over her feminine curves encased in his pajamas. He grinned and pointed to a chest of drawers. "Look in there."

Curious, Alana got to her feet and shuffled over to the built-in dresser. Women's clothing of all colors, shapes, and sizes spilled out. Searching for something to wear, she pulled out the skimpiest string bikini she had ever seen. Holding it up by a finger, she said, "Who would wear this?"

"She didn't wear it for long," was his smooth reply.

Alana pulled out a pair of bright red shorts and a white tank top that she thought would fit. Nothing else looked appropriate to wear out of the bedroom.

He approached her, leaning against the chest with one shoulder and hip. "Now you have clothes. What's next?"

Alana shrugged, walking away from him and staring out the windows. It was a beautiful view. "I'll go back to Phillip's house."

"Isn't it your home, too?"

"No," her voice was sad. "it's never been mine."

"Then what."

He was so close to her she could feel his warmth, drawing on his strength. Taking a deep breath, she said, "I'll pack my clothes and move back into my apartment. Then I'll look for a job. Phillip, being the kind soul that he is, will kick me out of the office so fast, I won't have time to clean out my desk."

"You could work for me."

144

Alana laughed. "I value my life," she muttered. "Work for you? That'd be like treason."

He dug his hands into the pockets of his shorts, rocking back and forth on bare feet. "What do you care what Hudson thinks?"

"I'd . . . better get dressed and go."

"I'll drive you. We'll take a roundabout way and you can walk up the drive. No one will ever know." He quirked a brow, a smile lighting his face.

She frowned. "Did you ever tell anyone about the night I helped you home?"

Raine shook his head. "No one knows about that except for us." His hand came out and he touched her cheek. "What Hudson did to me was bad enough, but I could kill him for doing this to you. I'll be in my office downstairs when you're ready to leave."

Alana stared at the door for a long time, unwilling and unable to sort through the conflicting emotions buzzing through her. Picking up the shorts and shirt she headed back into the bathroom. Looking in the mirror, she groaned. These must be children's sizes. Padding back into the bedroom, she rummaged through the drawer again but found nothing more suitable. The T-shirt fit like a second skin, the white color leaving little to the imagination. The shorts were cut so high that they exposed more than they covered. It was the best she could do, and hopefully, no one would see her when she went into Phillip's house. Slowly making her way downstairs, she ignored the protests from her body. She found Raine's office and knocked. "I'm ready."

She colored as his gaze traveled leisurely over the swell of her breasts then lower to follow the length of her long legs.

He covered the distance between them. His finger trailed along her shoulder and then followed the curve of the T-shirt to the hollow between her breasts.

Alana's hands went to his chest of their own volition. She felt the strength of his heart beat, the warmth of his body.

He bent to touch his lips to her temple. His mouth gently touched her tender lips, easing her mouth open and exploring the sweetness of the interior. His hand cupped one breast, his thumb slowly circling the nipple.

Alana's hands went around Raine's waist, her fingers enjoying the taut strength of his back, the heat of his body through his shirt warming her to the very core of her being. His breath quickened as she kneaded the muscles of his back. Conscious thought disappeared as she lost herself in the touch, the scent, the sensations he was arousing. His hand wandered from her breast down to her waist and hip, slipping under her shorts to cup her closer to him.

Feeling his arousal, she knew it matched her own as liquid fire spread through her veins. She had never felt like this before. Ever. Raine was solid, vital, strong, unlike Phillip.

The thought of Phillip brought her back to reality with a power of a gale force wind. Phillip. She was still married. She pushed her hands against Raine's chest. "I can't do this," she murmured. "Not now. Not after what happened . . ."

Raine fought to steady his breathing. His hands were gentle on her shoulders as he held her away from him. "I'm sorry. I didn't mean for that to happen."

She met his gaze with real regret. "I know." Taking a deep breath, she said, "Let's go."

Walking out to his garage, Alana looked at the silver Lamborghini. "Now that will really be inconspicuous." Her voice was dry. She pointed to the black car next to it. "Or the Rolls. No one will notice me getting out of that car."

Raine laughed. He pointed to a dusty white compact car. "Is that more to your liking?"

She grinned back. "I didn't say anything about liking. I said inconspicuous."

They got in and Raine started the car. They didn't exchange a word as Raine took the side streets and circling around from the other side, stopped the car a block from Phillip Huson's mansion. He turned to Alana, giving her a card from his pocket. "This is my private number. You can reach me any time of the day or night. If you need help, call me."

She gave him a slight smile, tucking the card into her shoe. "Thanks. For everything."

She felt Raine's gaze on her back as she walked up the hill. She stopped at the gate, punching numbers into the control panel and then walked up the long driveway.

Phillip waited until he made sure Alana was in her suite. He was torn between begging her forgiveness and beating her again. She had been missing for over a day. Where the hell could she have disappeared to? Was another man protecting her? He felt the rage begin to build again, trying desperately to smother it.

He opened the door to her sitting room. She was standing by the window dressed in white cotton slacks and a pink cotton pullover. Alana whirled around when she heard him.

Phillip stood in the doorway. "Where have you been?" he demanded, a scowl on his face.

"If you take one step toward me, Phillip Hudson, I swear that I will call the police and press charges against you."

"You wouldn't dare." He jammed his hands into the pockets of his black pin striped suit. He wasn't sure if she was bluffing or not.

"You bet I would. How would that look in the papers? Wife of six months accuses husband of beating her. You think that publicity would be good for you?" She pointed a finger at her eye. "How do you think this will look in color? On the front

147

page? Do you think the police might wonder if your first wife really died accidently?''

She wasn't bluffing, and looking at her bruises made him feel quilty about losing his temper and hitting her, but he didn't handle guilt very well. He was angry when he said, "Don't threaten me, Alana. You're still my wife.''

She took a deep breath, her hands clenched at her sides. "Not for long, Phillip. I'm getting a divorce.''

"The hell you are!" He roared like a wounded animal, waving his hands in the air. He didn't want a divorce. He loved Alana. How could he have let his temper get so out of control? Had his affair really upset her that much? "I'll contest it. I'll get the best lawyers in the country. You'll be an old lady before you'll be free!''

Alana gave him a cold look. "You destroyed my self-respect when you beat me, Phillip. You don't trust me out of your sight, and yet, you think it's okay for you to be unfaithful to me. I can't live like that.'' She raised her hands into the air and let them fall to her sides.

"You married me for better or worse,'' he muttered, taking a step into the room.

"Well, I've had enough of the worse and I don't care to stick around for the better,'' she answered, her head held high.

He gazed at her bruised and swollen face. Had he really beaten the woman he adored? He didn't remember much about their argument except for an overwhelming rage. "I'm sorry I lost my temper.''

"Apologizing won't change the facts.'' Her gaze met his. "Are you willing to let me live my own life without accounting for every minute I'm out of your sight, and will you promise not to have sex with other women?''

Phillip was silent. Alana was so damned beautiful. He had seen the look men gave her. She was young and desirable. Could he trust her? Could he be faithful to one woman?

"I thought not," Alana muttered when he didn't reply.

There had to be a way to keep her. "You won't get a thing," he warned, watching her closely. "You signed that prenuptial agreement. If you divorce me, you lose everything."

"All of this means more to you than it does to me. I don't give a damn about any of it."

He had one option left. "What about your job?" His eyes narrowed as he crossed his arms over his chest.

"What about it?" she asked, her eyes wary.

He had her now. He didn't care what it took to keep her bound to him. "If you divorce me, I decide whether you're out on the street or you stay. You can be replaced."

"I can also get another job. You're not the only employer in the islands." She crossed to the closet and pulled out a suitcase.

"I'll see to it that no one will hire you," he ground out, following her and standing in the doorway. "You'll be without a job and without money. I'll see you crawling back to me for mercy."

"Only in your dreams, Phillip. I'll never crawl. You of all people should know that." She opened a lingerie drawer and dumped the contents into the bag.

Phillip bristled as she watched his movements warily. He didn't want her to fear him. He was afraid to touch her. "You're a beautiful woman, Alana. You weave this magic, like a golden chain. I thought by marrying you I'd break that chain, but it didn't work. It only tightened." His face was grim as he said the words unwillingly.

She was silent for a moment, her eyes smarting from unshed tears. "You were too possessive, Phillip. You couldn't trust me." She grabbed several dresses and dropped them into the bag.

"I still can't," he admitted grudgingly. He tried once more to make her change her mind. "I'll see you crushed if you leave me."

"A waste of energy, Phillip. I can always leave the islands," she said. Shoes followed the dresses. She got out a smaller case. She went into the bathroom and collected her cosmetics.

"I'll haunt you, wherever you go." He raised his voice as he followed her around, feeling helpless and frustrated.

"That's your problem." She brushed past him and stalked back into the sitting room.

"I'll make a deal with you," he finally said, pacing around her sitting room. "We've got an important board meeting in the morning with some sensitive negotiations. And there's the race this weekend." He paused. "With you navigating and on the helm downwind, I'll win. I'll beat that son of a bitch Bradburn." They faced each other. "Stay until after the race and I won't contest the divorce."

Alana crossed to her desk, opening the drawer and pulling things out, throwing them into her brief case, stopping to look at him for a long moment. "The race means that much to you?"

"Yes," he ground out. "If I can't have you, at least I can have the satisfaction of beating Bradburn."

"I'll race, but I won't stay here."

"You have to stay." He took a step toward her, a pleading note in his voice.

"Don't touch me, Phillip," Alana warned, her hand wrapping around a letter opener.

He backed off, his shoulders sagging. "Okay. That'll be part of the deal. I won't touch you, you won't go to a lawyer until I win that race."

She snapped her briefcase shut. "I'll be at the board meeting and I'll race on your damn boat, but on Monday I file for divorce."

"Think about it for a while," he said, his voice soft. "Don't make a decision you might regret. I really am sorry, Alana. I don't know what came over me." He shrugged. "It won't happen again. And I won't go to bed with anyone but you. I promise."

She opened another drawer and pulled out velvet boxes of jewelry. "Don't make promises you can't keep. Jealousy doesn't disappear that easily. The next time I didn't explain my actions or you saw me talking to a man, you'd react exactly the same way. The next time an attractive woman makes a play for you, you'll have sex with her. Nothing will change."

Alana thrust the jewelry box into his hands. "I wouldn't want to be accused of stealing these."

He looked at them in dismay. "But I bought them for you. They're yours." He didn't understand her bitterness. "What am I going to do with them?" He had never seen her so cold.

"Give them to one of your lovers, like you tried to buy me when I was your mistress." She twisted the wedding ring from her finger and threw it at him. "I don't want anything that might remind me of you."

Phillip was incredibly hurt by her anger. "I said I was sorry. What more do you want?"

"Nothing," she snapped. Scorn filled her eyes. "Send the rest of my things to my apartment."

"Give me two weeks to try to change your mind," he pleaded.

"Monday." Her voice was firm.

"But you'll race?"

"It's against my better judgement, but I'll race," she muttered. "Now get out of my room," she said, her voice soft, her jaw clenched.

Phillip had had enough. No woman was going to order him around in his own home. Being nice hadn't dented Alana's resolve to divorce him. Anger boiled through him. "I'll leave your room, Alana, my sweet, but by the time I get through with you, there isn't a man on this island who would go near you, not even your lovers."

"Don't be too sure about that," she retorted, her voice silky.

"You can threaten all you want, Phillip, but a woman has a way of making a man forget about threats and deals."

Phillip's face went scarlet, his fists clenched at his sides. "Damn you! You deserved exactly what you got!" He turned around and slammed the door behind him.

Chapter Eleven

Melanie looked up from her desk at the soft knock on the door just before it opened. Her face lit up. "Charles!"

He closed the door and leaned against it. "I thought we might have a . . . talk before the board meeting." Regret tinged his voice. "I have to get back to New York. My plane leaves at three."

Melanie tossed her pen on the desk and leaned back in her chair. "I'm going to miss you." It was true, she thought suddenly. She would miss him. It came as a shock. She never missed the men in her life, not even her ex-husbands.

"I'm going to miss you, too." He approached her. "I won't be back until the next board meeting."

"Three months is a long time," she murmured, her gaze drawn to his eyes. It was the first time she had ever met a powerful, wealthy man who could be kind and gentle. Charles aroused feelings in Melanie that were new and different. She felt special when she was with him. He also made her feel vulnerable, and that feeling she didn't like at all. When you were vulnerable it meant you cared about that person, and caring meant getting hurt.

He stood beside her then reached down to flick open the

pearl button on her black wrap dress. "Did you wear this dress on purpose?" he asked, pulling her to her feet.

Melanie smiled. "I hoped you'd see me before you had to leave." She eased his jacket off. "Better lock the door."

"I already did." He bent to strip off her hose as she kicked off her shoes. Charles ran his hands over her lush curves as she took off the rest of his clothes. He buried his face in her breasts, letting out a long sigh before he sat down in her chair.

Melanie stared at him perplexed.

"Come here," he murmured.

When she was going to sit on his lap, he shook his head. "Straddle me."

A seductive smile crossed her face. "Charles, you never cease to amaze me." She sat down facing him, feeling his instant desire and relishing it. Her fingers twirled the hair on his chest.

"I amaze myself sometimes," he said with a chuckle, lifting her breasts in his hands and flicking his tongue over the hard tips.

He entered her, but instead of the rhythm she knew so well, he was still.

Melanie gave him a puzzled look. "Not yet, darling," he murmured. "I want to feel you around me. I want to savor every moment. It has to last so long." His lips fastened on one breast, gently tugging until Melanie moaned.

She wrapped her hands around his neck, pulling him closer.

His hands caressed her thighs, his fingers tangling in the soft hair before he reached her pleasure point and gently massaged it.

Melanie pressed herself closer to him, her mouth fusing with his, her tongue seeking his as her body shuddered. She didn't care if Charles did want to savor every moment. She was ready and eager for him.

He moved inside of her, his hands on her buttocks, urging her closer.

She threw her head back, her hands gripping his shoulders as she gave herself up to the pleasure of release. Her blood boiled, her pulse raced, and coherent thought disappeared as she felt them step off a cliff and soar through the air, riding the air currents, dipping and swaying, incredibly free.

Long moments later they stirred. Charles ran his hand down her back. "Every time you sit in this chair, remember me."

Melanie chuckled. "And every time I ride in the limo, sleep in my bed, take a shower, and swim in my pool."

He kissed the tip of each rosy breast. "We'd better get dressed. The board meeting started five minutes ago."

Hilary glanced around the board room. Several members were already there, reviewing their notes, having a cup of coffee, talking among themselves. She approached Dan Asuka. "Have any luck with Raine Bradburn?" she asked.

He shook his head. "We talked about everything else, but when I mentioned the land, he shut up. Said he didn't want to ruin our friendship over some rock and dirt."

Hilary frowned. "If he feels that way, why doesn't he just sell it? It doesn't sound like he has any feeling for that piece of land."

"He doesn't, but he knows your father wants it. That makes it very valuable in his eyes." Dan sipped his coffee.

Robert Somers joined the group. "Is money the issue?"

Dan snorted. "Are you kidding? The guy has more money than he knows what to do with!"

Hilary was silent. It would be a coup for her to get that land when all the others failed, but how was she going to do that? Raine Bradburn was as stubborn as her father.

Robert looked at Dan, his face thoughtful. "If it's not money, then it must be some sort of personal vendetta with Phillip."

"Of course it is," Dan agreed quickly. "Too bad we don't know what it is. It would make our negotiations easier."

Phillip arrived and the meeting began.

Hilary gave Melanie a speculative look when she and Charles arrived late. Melanie glowed and Charles looked quite pleased with himself. Hilary wondered what was going on, and then decided she was better off not knowing.

Phillip glowered at Melanie. "What the hell do you think you're doing coming late to a board meeting?" His voice thundered across the room.

Melanie's gaze glittered. "Charles and I met in the hall. We had some business to discuss."

"I'll bet," Phillip sneered, then glanced at Charles.

Hilary stared at her father in the tense atmosphere. He was in a foul mood. What had set him off this time?

Charles returned Phillip's gaze. "Just because you don't respect Melanie, doesn't mean other people feel the same way. You should listen to some of her ideas. You might be pleasantly surprised."

Hilary looked at her sister. Melanie was blushing! Hilary hadn't seen that look on her sister's face in years. She and Charles must be having an affair. Hilary looked at Charles with renewed interest. Melanie could have her pick of any man on the island. What did she see in Charles? He was shorter than Melanie, overweight, and getting bald. It didn't make sense.

"I'd be surprised, all right," Phillip muttered, bringing Hilary's thoughts back to the meeting. He raised his hands and dropped them on the table. "Do something useful and get me a cup of coffee, Melanie!"

Melanie sent him a withering gaze before doing as he asked. She sauntered over to Phillip and put the cup down in front of him. "Here, father dear. The caffeine will either calm you down or do you in."

An audible gasp echoed in the stony silence.

Hilary straightened the jacket of her pale blue raw silk suit before fingering the strand of perfectly matched pearls around her neck. She waited for Phillip to erupt.

"If you don't shut up, I'll throw you out!" Phillip glared at Melanie. "Why did I ever suggest you for this board? I thought you'd learn something. Women have no place in business!"

"It's a good thing all the women in this room are related to you or you'd have a lawsuit on your hands for a sexist remark like that," Hilary murmured, her icy gaze meeting Phillip's steely one. "And don't forget, we have stock in this company, too. You need our vote."

"And I wished to hell I didn't," Phillip muttered under his breath.

Hilary strained to hear the words, sitting back in satisfaction. He did need his daughters, and when they proved Alana was nothing more than a fortune hunter, he'd need them even more.

"Now, what's been done about Bradburn?" He looked at Dan. "Did you have any luck?"

"No." He tapped a pen on the yellow paper in front of him. "But he said something odd. He said he didn't like the way you negotiated, and he wouldn't sell to you for any amount of money. Do you know what he was talking about?"

Hilary gauged Phillip's reaction, wondering what her father had done to Bradburn. If she could only get close to him, find out what he'd take for that land. If she got the land, her father would have to take her seriously as a businesswoman. He might even begin to seek her opinion again.

Phillip shuffled through the papers in front of him. "I haven't the vaguest idea what he meant. I know he's a very stubborn man, but then, so am I." He sat back. "Robert, are you ready to try?"

Hilary watched Phillip twist the huge gold ring on his finger. He was hiding something. "Why don't you let me try?" Hilary asked. "I've drawn up a few charts and tables that might sway him." She stood and handed a copy to Phillip. "Money isn't the answer, but maybe we could work on an exchange of land. We give him the right-of-way to the highway from his ranch on the Big Island in exchange for this parcel of land."

Phillip grunted and looked at the paper in front of him. "What's your idea, Robert?"

Robert pushed his glasses up the bridge of his nose. "I've got some contacts. I'll see what he would be willing to settle for. The land exchange idea is a good one." He looked at Phillip.

"Interesting." His glance flicked to Alana, derision and anger in his voice. "What do you think? You're the head of the real estate division."

"I hate to give up that right-of-way Hilary suggested, but what about the land near Kapaa on Kauai? It isn't suited for our future plans, but maybe he'd take it in exchange." She watched Robert made a notation on the paper in front of him. "I think Bradburn owns a section of the adjoining land. It's at least worth a try."

Phillip grunted in reluctant admiration. "Try it, Somers." Phillip stood up. "That's all for today. I want results. It's dragged on for too long." He turned and walked out of the room, leaving a stunned board.

Hilary glanced at her watch. Usually these meetings lasted all morning, but this one was over in less than an hour. There was an entire agenda they hadn't touched. Many of the directors had to return to their own businesses after today's session. Phillip was up to something . . .

"The first boats will start at 1600. A class will start every fifteen minutes after that. You have copies of the racecourse. We start off Waikiki, round Diamond Head, cross the Molokai

Channel, round the buoy off Molokai, and return to finish off Diamond Head. The Race Committee will be there to take times and finish you." She looked at her notes. "Winds are predicted to be twenty to twenty-five knots out of the northeast. Seas ten to fifteen feet." She paused. "Except in the channel." Everyone laughed. The Molokai Channel was notorious for confused seas and strong currents. Alana looked around, the adrenalin already flowing. She loved racing. When she saw Raine, her heart skipped a beat and their eyes met for one moment before she looked away. It was too difficult to concentrate when he looked at her with those sapphire eyes. "Any questions?"

"What about position reports?" The commodore looked at her, waiting for her answer.

It figured he'd ask that question. He never knew where he was on land. Put him out on the water and he could end up in Tahiti. "Every three hours. I know that's closer together than we've had in the past, but we want to make sure everyone comes back to enjoy the banquet tomorrow night." There was a nod of agreement, all those remembering the past year when a boat broke up in the channel and one crew member lost his life. She gathered up her papers. "Good luck and smooth sailing!" Skippers from other boats stopped to talk, but Raine disappeared. It was just as well. She had enough to worry about without any more complications.

Alana was gathering her notes when she noticed Phillip and Raine at one end of the bar, Melanie and Hilary trying to pull Phillip away. Phillip's face was crimson and Raine's stance was stiff and unyielding. She hurried over to them.

Phillip gulped down his scotch, slamming the glass on the bar. "Damn you, Bradburn! Why the hell won't you sell? You can't use that land for anything."

Hilary grabbed her father's arm. "Come on. This isn't the place to discuss business."

Melanie looked up at Raine. "You don't want to cause a scene, do you?"

Raine ignored Melanie as his glance flicked over Alana, his gaze touching on each bruise she had tried to carefully hide with makeup. His voice was grim. "I don't care about the land. I won't sell to a bastard like you and see you make money from it."

Phillip pulled away from Hilary and jabbed a finger against Raine's chest. "You'll be sorry."

"Don't threaten me, Hudson." His gaze was rock hard as he grabbed Phillip's wrist in a vicelike grip. Melanie and Hilary stepped back, fear on their faces. "I could kill you for what you've done." He pushed Phillip away, turned around and stalked toward the dock.

The three women stared at the fury on Phillip's face.

"Come on, Phillip. Let's get on the boat." Alana's voice was soft. She really didn't care if he stood here forever, but people were openly staring at them.

"Leave me alone." He ordered another drink and turned his back on her.

Hilary sat down next to him. "Don't worry, we'll get that land. I don't know how, but we'll do it."

Phillip scowled. "Murder would be too good for that man. Why does he have to be so stubborn?"

Hilary sent a triumphant smile in Alana's direction. Alana left them alone and Melanie headed for the pool.

Alana turned toward the dock. The waterfront was a kaleidoscope of color as sailors carried food and equipment to the boats. Outrigger canoes headed down the channel and out into the ocean to practice for their races. Power boats cruised the harbor, spectators looking at the sailboats. People lined the shore, fishing or just watching the boats.

Alana tossed her duffel bag on the deck of Phillip's boat and jumped on board.

"Hi, Alana. How was the skipper's meeting?" One of the crew, Sandy, a tanned, blond young man with no neck looked up from the line he was coiling.

"Short and sweet. Everyone knows the course. Nothing's changed from last year except position reports every three hours." She didn't mention the confrontation between Raine and Phillip. She scrambled below reaching for her duffel bag as the young man handed it to her. "If the wind stays over twenty knots we're going to fly. With a good start we could be the first boat to finish."

"We have to do better than that," Phillip muttered coming down the ladder. "With our rating we have to give every damn boat time. We'll have to be first to finish by eleven minutes. That's the only reason you're still around." His hand clamped on her shoulder as he whirled her around. "If I didn't think I needed you to win this race, you would have been out of my life, my house, and my company." His eyes were cold steel. "Just remember that. When the race is over, so are we."

What had caused his change in attitude? When she had left his house, he was asking for a second chance. "We were finished long before the race," she murmured, refusing to tell him that he was hurting her. "I can survive, Phillip Hudson, without you or your job."

"We'll see," his voice was low, his expression murderous. "I'll see you on your knees before this is finished."

"Never. You'll burn in hell before you'll break me." She met his gaze with a heated one of her own.

Phillip was about to say something else when another crew member climbed down the ladder into the cabin. He squeezed her shoulder and pushed her slightly. "Make me some coffee," he demanded. "I'm going into the club for a few minutes." He never looked back as he climbed the ladder and disappeared.

Alana rubbed her shoulder and stared at the ladder.

"You okay, Mrs. Hudson?" a worried young voice asked.

Alana focused on the concerned face of the newest member of their crew. "It's Alana, Peter. There's no room for formality on a boat." She dropped her arm and turned to the galley, taking Phillip's coffee pot and filling it with water.

"Okay." He paused, looking at his feet. "Alana."

"That wasn't so bad, was it?" she asked, returning his shy smile.

"No." He rubbed his hands on the sides of his multicolored shorts. "Do you want me to make his coffee? I heard Mr. Hudson ask for some."

Alana shook her head and opened a storage locker, taking a can of coffee out and opening it. "I'll do it. We'll need gallons of it tonight to stay awake." She lit the gimbaled stove and put the coffee pot on the burner. "Check the battery and make sure it's charged, okay?"

"Sure thing, Mrs. Hud . . . Alana." He hurried off to do as she asked.

Alana felt suddenly old and weary. What had happened to those days when you eagerly charged into the day, anticipating new and exciting adventures. Alana closed her eyes, the excitement about the race draining out of her as she heard Phillip on the deck bellowing orders. She never should have agreed to race with him.

Phillip growled. "Alana! Get me a scotch! Then get these instruments going!" He grabbed the wheel as she appeared with his drink. "Let's get the hell out of here!"

It was going to be a very long night, Alana said to herself as she released a spring line and lightly jumped back on board.

Raine leaned forward, his arms on the wheel as he checked the compass. He looked up as *Retribution* powered down the canal and headed for the open sea. Alana moved lithely around the deck, coiling lines and checking instruments. She never glanced his way. Raine stared until the high tech, yellow yacht was out of sight. What the hell was she doing on Hudsosn's boat? Alana had told him that she was leaving Hudson, but here she was, racing with him. Raine hadn't heard any rumors of a divorce, either, and that would certainly make the headlines. An odd sense of disappointment weighed him down. Had she decided that the power and wealth of Phillip Hudson were worth the beatings and degradation? He had misjudged her strength of character. Raine frowned and clenched the wheel. The woman had gotten under his skin, against his will. The harder he fought the attraction the stronger it became. Just his luck. Of all the women who had passed through his life, he was drawn to the wife of his hated adversary. She felt the electricity between them, too. He was sure of it.

"Hey, skipper! Ready to cast off?" His tactician, Jake, stuck his head out of the cabin.

"Ready." Raine's face took on a grim determination. He would beat Hudson and his new boat. He'd convince Alana that she was better off without that bastard. After that, he wasn't sure. Did he love her? He scoffed at his own thoughts as he eased the big black boat away from the dock. He didn't believe in love. He was intrigued by her, attracted to her physically, and wanted to know what thoughts she hid behind those violet eyes. An image of her washed up on his beach dominated his mind. That beautiful ivory skin had been covered with cuts and bruises. She had been helpless. Tender, protective feelings he didn't know he possessed sprang from nowhere. Damn it. He wanted to shield her from pain, from misery, from Phillip Hudson.

"We've got an hour before our start," Jake said, breaking into Raine's thoughts. "Let's head downwind and try out the new spinnaker. I want to see what kind of speed we're going to get from it."

"Right." Raine tried to concentrate on Jake's words, wishing Alana were here beside him. Maybe if he just made love to her, he'd get her out of his system.

"Bradburn! Fall off! There's a canoe crossing the channel!"

Jake's harsh words brought him back to reality. He had a race to win.

Melanie reclined on the lounge next to the pool at the club, her well oiled body glistening in the sun, the white of her bikini a perfect foil for her golden skin. She watched her father's boat head out into the harbor. Her mouth thinned. He had been married to Alana for six months, Melanie's mother long forgotten. But Melanie hadn't forgotten her. She went to the cemetary every week to talk things over with her mother. She had even told her about Charles. Her mother would have understood.

"Hi, Melanie." Hilary dropped into the chair next to her sister. "Father made a spectacle of himself in the bar, didn't he?"

"No more than usual." Melanie didn't even open her eyes. "Why do you suppose he even approached Raine? I thought he was going to let Robert handle the negotiations."

"He probably ruined Robert's chances now." Hilary sighed. "When is that detective going to give us something on Alana? They've been married six months and we haven't done a thing." She chuckled. "Well, almost nothing." She told Melanie about the cocktail party. "Father was livid."

Melanie smiled. "Wonderful. Maybe we won't need anything on Alana. Father will do it for us." She paused. "Of course, unless he divorces her, it won't change his will." She opened her eyes. "Do you think he really cut us out?"

Hilary frowned. "I don't know. Anything is possible. He's been in a terrible mood lately. What do you suppose is bothering him?"

"I hope it's Alana." Melanie turned over and settled down. "Let's hope we'll be finished with both of them soon."

"We should be so lucky." Hilary stood up. "I'm going into the bar. Let me know if you hear anything good from that detective."

Chapter Twelve

"Get the main up!" Phillip shouted, his hands gripping the wheel.

As crew members scrambled to hoist the sail, Phillip winced, slipped a nitro pill under his tongue and took a deep breath. When the pain eased, he drained the glass of scotch he found next to him. He didn't remember asking for it, but he could use it.

He felt anger and frustration return when he thought of Raine Bradburn's arrogant, stubborn refusal to sell his land. Phillip was certain Bradburn knew about the plans Hudson Enterprises had for that long before they were made public. He wondered how long Bradburn had owned that land. He would have someone look into it Monday morning. There had to be a way to get to him.

His gaze narrowed as Alana disappeared down the hatch. He had seen the interest in Bradburn's eyes whenever he looked at Alana. Hell, he had offered her to him this morning. The guy should have jumped at the chance instead of looking at Phillip with murder in his eyes.

And then there was Alana. He turned the wheel of the boat sharply to avoid hitting a canoe, swearing at the young man for his incompetence. Phillip took a deep breath. He didn't understand Alana. He had apologized for losing his temper and hitting her. Why was she being so stubborn? Probably because of that blonde at the hotel. She couldn't possibily know about his offer to Bradburn. She was bluffing with this divorce thing, but he had called her bluff. When she discovered the power he would still have over her even if she left him, she would come crawling back. If they divorced, it would be his decision, not hers. He controlled their lives. She wouldn't tell *him* what to do! "Damn it, Jack! Trim the jib! It looks like hell!" Couldn't anyone do anything right?

Alana returned to the cockpit. "We're going to have a tough time through the channel. With these winds it will be lumpy."

"I already knew that," he said sarcastically. "We'll carry a chute, and make some time on Bradburn." He rubbed his forehead. "I shouldn't have had that last drink. I've got a splitting headache." He squinted at the shoreline. The buildings looked like they had halos. He tried to focus on the compass, but the numbers blurred. "Get me a different pair of sun glasses." He ripped off the pair he had on, tossing them at Alana. He had trouble concentrating. He gripped the wheel harder, bellowing orders to the crew. He felt like hell, but he wasn't going to drop out of the race. He was determined to beat Raine Bradburn, no matter what the cost.

Going below, Alana found a spare pair of glasses and handed them to one of the crew scurrying up the ladder. "Give these to Phillip."

"Alana!" Phillip barked. What was she doing hiding in the cabin?

She poked her head up through the hatch. "What do you want, Phillip?"

Her patronizing tone of voice made him clench his teeth. "I want to know exactly what course we're going to sail. Are you ready to set the timer? I want a stop watch going, too." He would beat Bradburn right from the start. He slipped another nitroglycerin pill under his tongue.

"Everything is ready for the ten minute gun. When we get out to the starting line, I'll check my figures and set a course. Everything is under control."

Phillip didn't answer, waiting for the pain to ease. It was a hell of a time for his heart to act up. Probably just the tension of the start of the race.

From the time the ten minute gun went off, Phillip focused all his energy into outmaneuvering Raine for the best position along the starting line.

Alana stood in the hatch, checking her watch and the other boats in their division. "Head for the other end of the starting line," she yelled.

"No!" Phillip continued on his course. "Bradburn is here. We'll cover him!"

"No, you won't," Alana argued. "He's in a better position. He'll send us across the line early."

Phillip ignored Alana's advice. He wondered why she was sabatoging his effort to beat Raine. "We're in good position to keep him off the line."

"Not with this course."

Phillip glared at her. "This is my boat, and we'll do as I say!"

"Fall off!" the foredeck man yelled from the bow. "There's a boat dead ahead with right of way!"

"Damn it! Why wasn't someone watching!" He spun the wheel, missing a collision by inches.

"Watch where you're going, Hudson!" the other skipper screamed.

"You saw me coming. Why didn't you change course?" Phillip demanded.

"I was on starboard tack, you fool!" His last words were muffled by the flapping of sails and grinding of winches.

Phillip was livid. The exchange had cost them precious seconds as they approached the starting line. Raine slipped over the line ahead of them. Phillip stared at the black transom of Bradburn's boat. "Damn it! Trim that main. Watch the jib! Get on the high side. Alana! Check our course." He took another pill, but the pain in his chest only eased slightly. He wouldn't think about it. He forced himself to focus on the black yacht ahead of them.

Trying to catch the sleek vessel, the crew wore themselves out, changing sails, tacking, trimming, doing everything Phillip demanded. When Raine tacked, they tacked. When he changed sails, they changed sails, dogging his every move. Phillip wondered if Bradburn was playing with them. They narrowed the gap when Raine's genoa blew out and his crew scrambled to change it. The two boats were side by side.

"I'm going to beat you, Bradburn," Phillip bellowed, his words traveling across the water.

"Like hell you are," Raine shot back, his face grim as he barked out an order and inched ahead of Phillip.

Phillip put another pill under his tongue. The pain was getting worse, his head felt like it was going to blow off his shoulders, and the change of sunglasses hadn't changed the halos. He muttered under his breath, adjusting his course slightly.

The boats remained in sight of each other as the sun set, Phillip trying everything he could to make his boat go faster than Raine's. He focused his energies into beating Raine, ignoring his body's protests. They would inch ahead and Phillip would crow with delight, certain of victory, but then Raine would take the lead, and Phillip called his crew every vile name he could utter. Grim lines of pain were etched on his face, but he wouldn't give in. He had waited for this race for too long to quit now. If he couldn't get Bradburn's land, at least he could get that trophy back.

Pete brought sandwiches on deck, but Phillip didn't touch his. The thought of food nauseated him.

Alana gave him a strange look, but he didn't acknowledge it. He had no energy for anything but racing. It was an effort to speak. His face felt hot. Perspiration dripped down his back and chest. His left arm felt numb from clutching the wheel. A heavy weight pressed down on his chest.

"Aren't you hungry?"

He shook his head. "Touch of sea sickness, I guess."

"You never get sea sick," she chided.

"So it's just a touch of the flu then," he grumbled. "Don't bother me!"

Alana went below.

Phillip tried to wipe the sweat from his forehead, but his arm wouldn't move. He began to panic. He remembered his last heart attack. He felt like the nightmare had returned. He tried to focus on the other boat, but couldn't.

Phillip gasped. It felt like a steel band was tightening around his chest. He was dizzy and lightheaded. He fumbled for a nitro pill, but couldn't open the box. He squinted at the compass, but it was blurred. He clutched the wheel so he wouldn't fall. No sound came out when he opened his mouth to call for help. Gasping for air, he tried to yell, then blacked out.

It was time to call in a position report. Alana was checking the chart when the boat lurched and she was tossed backward into the bulkhead. Rubbing her bruised ribs, she heard the commotion on the deck and scrambled up the ladder.

Phillip was slumped over the wheel, the boat rolling violently in the high seas. Every time the huge sails emptied and filled with air, there was a loud whack, the boat shuddered and pitched, water pouring over the deck.

Alana was stunned. What had happened? What was wrong

with Phillip? "Phillip!" she yelled. There was no reponse. "Phillip!" she called again. The boat lurched and she caught herself before she tumbled back into the cabin.

The crew had glanced at Phillip when the boat surged out of control, too shocked to do anything but hang on to the life lines so they wouldn't be dumped into the ocean.

The boat tossed about like a bobbing cork. Alana crawled across the cockpit and yelled, "Someone help me!"

Two crew men finally reacted, scrambling back into the cockpit. They pulled him away from the wheel and laid him down.

Alana looked around wildly, pushing wet hair from her eyes. A wave washed over them. "Mack, take the wheel!" She bent over Phillip, feeling helpless as she touched his cold face. Had Phillip had another heart attack? "Does anyone know CPR?"

One man was by her side, gently moving her out of the way. "Get the sails down!"

Alana heard Mack's words, but her attention was focused on Phillip.

Her eyes never left Phillip's ashen face. "Pete get on the radio and call the Coast Guard for help. Give them our location." She rattled off the numbers, thankful that she had just looked at the chart. "Tell them about Phillip." Her own heart thumped wildly. Time crawled. Someone brought dry towels and a blanket on deck. Alana covered Phillip.

The engine was turned on and the boat headed back toward Honolulu, the crew silently watching the efforts of the man kneeling over Phillip.

The boat surfed over the waves. Alana was numb. Phillip had just been barking out orders, and now . . .

Pete shouted from the cabin. "The Coast Guard is on its way." It wasn't long before they heard a helicopter coming toward them, a powerful spot light scanning the ocean.

Alana forced herself to think. "The other boats are monitoring sixteen. Tell them the Coast Guard is here and everything is under control. They should continue with the race." It would serve no purpose to have other boats drop out because of their problem.

The helicopter hovered over them, giving instructions over the radio. They lowered a paramedic who quickly assessed Phillip's condition and then lowered a litter. The man turned to Alana as Phillip was hoisted into the helicopter. "It doesn't look good. No vital signs. I'd let you come with us, but it'll waste precious time."

"Please, just help Phillip. I'll be okay."

"We'll have the police meet you at the dock to escort you to the hospital."

Alana nodded and watched until the helicoper disappeared. She sat huddled in the cockpit, her arms drawn around her legs, staring into the night.

"Can I get you anything?" Peter asked quietly.

She shook her head. Questions bombarded her. Questions without answers. Conflicting emotions warred within her. Phillip could be dead. And though she had wanted him out of her life, she hadn't wanted it this way. Had this race meant so much to Phillip that he'd risk his life for it?

The lights of Waikiki twinkled and beckoned as they plowed through the water toward the harbor. Alana drew on her inner store of strength as they approached the dock. No matter what she felt for Phillip, she would handle herself with dignity, and no matter what happened to him, she was still his wife.

As soon as they docked, she jumped off the boat. A policeman was there and hurried her toward a squad car. "How is he?" she asked.

The policeman shook his head. "I don't know. The doctor's are working on him."

"Have his daughters been notified?" she asked.

"Yes. They're on the way to the hospital, too."

Facing Melanie and Hilary was on the bottom of her list of

things she wanted to do, but Phillip was their father. When the police car pulled up to the emergency entrance, Alana scrambled out and hurried into the hospital.

Melanie saw Alana approach the waiting room. Melanie wore a spotless white sundress, delicate sandals, and ivory jewlery. Her hair tumbled about her shoulders. She was totally in control, allowing herself a slight smile of satisfaction at Alana's appearance. Her stepmother was pale, her eyes slightly glazed, her hair unkempt, and her clothes wet and rumpled.

"It's all your fault," Melanie muttered as soon as the nurse left the room. Her eyes burned into Alana. "You never should have allowed him to race."

"Be realistic," Alana said as she slumped into a chair and rubbed her neck. "No one ever tells your father what to do. You know that."

"Why didn't you come on the helicopter with him? It's not going to do much for your image, taking so long to get here." Hilary sniffed and looked down her nose at Alana. She smoothed the fine cotton of her ivory and black skirt.

Alana rubbed her temples, remaining silent.

Melanie wanted to prick Alana's self-control. "Well, the least you could do is cry," she taunted. "Your husband could be dying. Don't you care?" She stood over Alana, her hands splayed over her hips, her scarlet fingernails like drops of blood against the white of her dress.

"He's your father. I notice neither of you are crying either," Alana retorted.

Melanie leaned forward, hatred in her voice and eyes. Alana put her on the defensive, and she didn't like it. Her mother was dead because of Alana. This younger woman had no right slipping into their lives and disrupting everything Hilary and Melanie deserved. "If anything happens to my father, you're going

174

to pay for it. He wouldn't have been out on that race course if it weren't for you."

"Melanie, he wanted to beat Raine Bradburn. Nothing would have stopped him from racing. Now, nothing's going to happen to your father. He's determined to live. He won't die unless he decides he wants to." Alana rubbed her eyes.

Hilary shuddered. Her voice broke when she said, "Daddy always had a tremendous will to live. I can't believe he's critically ill."

"I can't believe it either," Alana murmured. "Could we please put our personal differences aside and concentrate on Phillip's well-being?"

Melanie stiffened. Alana had caused her mother to commit suicide and convinced her father to marry her. How could Melanie ever put those thoughts out of her mind?

"Mrs. Hudson?" A masculine voice made them all turn toward the doorway.

Alana looked at the doctor's face. "Phillip didn't make it." She closed her eyes for a moment and then opened them.

"I'm sorry, we did everything we could, but it wasn't enough."

"It was his heart, wasn't it?" Hilary said, a sob in her voice.

The doctor looked at Alana. "Was he complaining about chest pains?"

"My father had a heart condition," Melanie answered before Alana could open her mouth. Tears slipped down her cheeks.

Hilary's face crumbled. "Father dead. It's impossible. He's probably just faking it, waiting to see what we're going to do." She looked at the doctor for a moment, her eyes glassy. "This is a trick, right? He's going to come walking out here, swearing and blustering."

"No, he won't," the doctor said as gently as possible. "He's gone."

He looked at Alana. "Had he been complaining about chest pains?" He sat down in the chair next to Alana.

Melanie watched them from lowered lashes, waiting to hear what Alana would say. How would Alana explain to the physican that Phillip was ill but insisted on racing and she hadn't done anything to stop him?

Alana frowned. "He was popping nitro pills like candy, but then we were racing and he was under a lot of stress." She paused. "He felt nauseated. Said it was sea sickness or the flu. He even complained about halos around everything." Her gaze focused on the doctor, her soft voice making Melanie's hands curl into fists. "It was his heart, wasn't it?"

He seemed to choose his words carefully. "His heart ceased functioning. I think we need to do an autopsy to clarify just what caused his heart to stop beating."

"What does that mean?" Hilary said, her eyes narrowing, her gaze jumping between the doctor and Alana. A linen handkerchief was clutched in her hand.

"It sounds like you're not certain he died of ... natural causes," Melanie murmured, her teary gaze settling on Alana.

"We don't know yet," the doctor finally said. "That's what we intend to find out. In light of what you've just told me, we need to be positive of the cause of death." He jammed his hands into the pockets of his lab coat. His eyes were on Alana. "As his wife and next of kin we need your permission to do the autopsy."

Alana was silent for a moment. "Can I see him first?"

"If you'll wait for just a moment, Mrs. Hudson. I'll send in a nurse when you can see him." Melanie thought he looked relieved to get out of the room.

Alana looked at Hilary and then Melanie. "Do you want to see your father?"

Hilary got to her feet, swayed slightly, and sat down again. She shook her head. "I don't think so. I can't bear the thought

176

of seeing him like that." She touched her eyes with her handkerchief. "First mother, and now father. Both of them gone. It's so hard to believe." She looked up at Melanie. "We're alone now."

"Yes." Melanie lifted her chin, her expression hard as she looked at Alana. "I'll stay with my sister. I prefer to remember my father vital and alive." She turned her back on Alana and sat down next to Hilary.

Alana steeled herself to walk into the room a few minutes later. She didn't know what she expected, but she was shocked when she stared at the steely look of grim determination carved on his face. She expected him to open his eyes and demand to know what was going on. He would be furious to discover that they had pulled out of the race when they were doing so well. She reached out to touch him and stopped, her hand dropping to her side.

Tears slipped down her cheeks. "I'll never forget you, Phillip. I remember when you became my mentor." Her voice was soft. "You tried to bully me into agreeing with your ideas, but you admired it when I stood up to you and challenged your opinions." She smoothed the sheet with a shaking hand. "I remember the first time we made love. You were so caring, so romantic. I didn't want to fall in love with you, but I did. You were such a charismatic person. You could charm and cajole anyone into what you wanted before they even knew you had done it." Tears ran unheeded down her cheeks. "I'll always remember our wedding. You were so wonderful, so filled with love and laughter. We had some good times, Phillip. What happened to those feelings? Where did we lose them?" She bent over and kissed his cheek. "Good-bye, Phillip. If only . . ." her voice trailed off. Regrets and recriminations were useless now.

She turned away and walked toward the door, looking back

one more time before squaring her shoulders and leaving the room. When the nurse gave her the forms to sign, she did so automatically. There were funeral arrangements to be made. People to be notified. Hudson Enterprises would have to issue a statement immediately to calm panicky shareholders and let them know everything would continue to run as expected until a new CEO could be elected. When the press heard about Phillip's death, it would be worldwide news and Alana would have to deal with endless questions and interviews. She wanted to go home, get some sleep, and gather her thoughts before facing inquisitive reporters.

Returning to the waiting room, she looked for Hilary and Melanie but they had disappeared. It didn't take her long to find them. It was four o'clock in the morning, but the lobby was filled with reporters, television cameras, and curiosity seekers. Hilary and Melanie were being interviewed and Alana could only guess at what they were saying, none of it complimentary to their stepmother. Out of the corner of her eye Alana saw Dudley closing in on her, followed closely by a television cameraman, an eyewitness team, and the island's hottest television news reporter.

"Mrs. Hudson. Could we have a statement from you about your husband's death?" Three microphones were shoved under her nose. Bright lights made her squint.

"Come on, Mrs. Hudson. We know he's dead. What's the cause?"

"Was he really out on a boat when the doctor told him not to race?"

"Did you really encourage him to race when you knew it would kill him?"

"Are you going to inherit the Hudson fortune or will it all go to his children?"

The questions were fired at her from all directions. She was in no condition to answer them coherently, but if she walked away it would look like she had something to hide. With as much dignity as possible at four in the morning, looking like she had run a marathon in record time, she looked from one reporter to the next and when they were all silent, she said, "There will be a statement issued in the morning regarding Phillip Hudson's death. Your questions will be answered at that time. And now, if you'll excuse me, I have a funeral to prepare for." The crowd separated as she walked out of the hospital, her head held high. She climbed into a squad car waiting to take her home, surprised when they stopped at the gates to the big white house on the bluff. She couldn't tell the officer to turn around and take her back into Honolulu. She'd have to stay here tonight. She hated this house.

Not bothering to wake the housekeeper or her husband, Alana wandered around the mansion. It was strange. Phillip was gone and yet his presence echoed through the silent rooms. What would happen now? Had Phillip changed his will? Who would inherit the Hudson fortune? Melanie and Hilary? Possibly. And what had he done about her? Their marital troubles had only come to a head in the past week. Not long enough to do much. Phillip was planning on a divorce, he hadn't planned on dying. One thing was certain. She didn't want to stay in this house. She shuddered when she thought of living here with Phillip's ghost haunting her every step. Walking into Phillip's den, she collapsed in his worn black leather chair, sifting through the clutter on his desk, deciding what matters needed immediate attention and what could wait until a new CEO was chosen. She got to her feet and stood beneath the huge portrait of him, painted twenty years earlier. It was a portrait of a man in his prime, filled with confidence, optimism, and arrogance. The quality of the work was a reflection of his power and wealth. It showed a man in control of everything around him. Except his own mortality, Alana thought with a sigh.

Phillip Hudson may be dead, but he'd never let any of them forget him. He would reach from the grave to influence and manipulate. It was as inevitable as the sun casting its first golden rays into the gloomy room.

Chapter Thirteen

Hilary smoothed a strand of hair behind her ear as the limousine stopped in front of the glass and steel office building. She picked a piece of lint from the tucked bodice of her Italian black silk dress. A single strand of matched pearls circled her neck. She tugged black gloves over her stubby fingers with their bitten nails. How wise of Alana to hold a memorial service for Phillip in the auditorium of corporate headquarters, she thought cynically, her eyes cold. Anyone else might have chosen a church, but knowing Phillip and his dislike for anything religious or emotional, Alana had followed his instructions and had his body cremated and his ashes scattered over Diamond Head. Anyone would think she was the grieving widow. Hilary gave an unlady like snort and reached for the bottle in a drawer of the car. A quick nip and she was ready. The chauffeur opened the door. A memorial service was expected, she supposed, her head high, her back ramrod stiff as she walked through the maze of reporters, cameras, and popping flash bulbs, the wide brim of her hat shadowing the mockery in her eyes. Phillip was an international personality. And she was his daughter. No one could change that. She thought about her mother's funeral six months earlier. It had been so different. She had felt so different. Her mother's death had devastated her, but this time, she felt strangely remote, separated from the empty feeling and loneliness she had experienced at her mother's funeral. It was almost a relief to have Phillip gone. She had tried so hard to win his approval, and now it didn't matter anymore. She was free from his domination and criticism.

Her mind turned to the corporation. Speculation regarding his successor had caused the stock to drop five points. A special board meeting was to be held the day after the memorial service. Hilary would do anything to assure that Alana wasn't given Phillip's power, not even temporarily. The very thought made Hilary furious. Giving that tramp control of Hudson Enterprises would be like treason! Her lips thinned. If it was the last thing she did, she would make certain that Alana was off the board and out of Hudson Enterprises. All the directors were in town for the service and the meeting. She'd have to make a few phone calls that evening.

Hilary entered the familiar building, accepting condolences from the staff as she made her way toward the auditorium. Phillip had discarded his daughter in favor of the younger Alana, but now Hilary was getting the attention, not Phillip and not Alana. As she murmured the proper words, she thought about visiting Zacary's and calling her favorite bookie. Her father had never approved of her gambling, but now he was gone. She could do whatever she wanted to, and he coudn't stop her.

Hilary climbed the marble steps and stopped just inside the double smoked glass doors. Alana had a flare for the dramatic, she thought, clutching her black pigskin purse. A trio of musicians in the balcony played classical selections. Phillip was a patron of the arts. What a joke! He gave them money and slept through every opera, symphony, and play he attended. Her gaze was drawn to the stage. The huge portrait of a younger Phillip that hung in the library of his home was draped in black. Tasteful arrangements of flowers stood on either side of the portrait.

A podium on the right side, the familiar Hudson logo on the front, was surrounded by more flowers. Five black leather wingbacked chairs were set at an angle to the rows of seats. Hilary settled into one, her feet firmly on the floor. Oh, what she wouldn't do for a sip from the silver bottle in her purse. She was the first of the grieving family to arrive. Grieving. Ha! Melanie hated Phillip, too, and Hilary was certain that Alana had only enticed her father and tricked him into marrying her because of his power, position, and money. Good reasons for a little nobody looking for success.

From her position in the front of the room, Hilary watched Alana's entrance, irritation growing into fury. People were fawning over her stepmother, a woman who had spent only months with Phillip Hudson, while Hilary was his flesh and blood! Alana was gracious to everyone, accepting their condolences with a dignity that made Hilary boil. Alana's black suit looked like an original, her only jewelry a cameo at the neck of her ivory blouse. Her hair was pulled back from her face in a French twist. What was she saying to David Jones? Probably using the opportunity to try to secure his vote. A tight smile touched her lips. David had already assured Hilary he would vote against Alana. Alana proceeded toward the front. Her stepmother! The thought made her stomach churn. She was six years younger than Hilary. Phillip must've been crazy to marry her. God! She needed a drink.

Alana sat down next to Hilary. "Hello, Hilary. I'm glad you chose to come today."

Hilary muttered between clenched teeth, staring straight ahead. "Phillip Hudson was my father. I have more right to be here than you do. Melanie and I should have planned this, not you."

Alana smoothed her skirt. "I tried to contact both of you. Chandler didn't know where you were and Melanie refused to talk to me." She paused, her voice firm. "And as Phillip's widow, it's certainly not out of place for me to make the arrangements."

Hilary gave her a disgusted look. "You think you're so important, but you'll be sorry you ever got involved with my father or this company." She turned away from Alana and watched the auditorium fill with employees and business associates of her father.

Melanie struck a pose in the doorway, Charles Reese next to her. All she lacked, Hilary thought, was a trumpet to announce her arrival. She marveled at the way Melanie could look so sexy while in mourning. Her black shantung sheath hugged every curve. Diamonds twinkled from her neck, ears, fingers, and wrists as she sauntered down the aisle, Charles taking a seat in the front row reserved for the directors.

Melanie settled into the chair on Hilary's right. "I don't know why *she* gets to talk and we don't," Melanie muttered to Hilary loud enough so Alana could overhear.

Alana shrugged, her voice cool. "You can say anything you want to. Be my guest."

"Thank you," Melanie murmured, pulling a sheet of paper from her black calfskin purse. "I intend to do just that."

Hilary stared at her sister. "You're going to speak?"

"Why not? Phillip Hudson was my father." She looked at her notes, whispering to Hilary. "Don't worry, Hilary, I won't tell them what I really think about his death."

"Just remember, anything said today will appear in newspapers from New York to Hong Kong." She looked out at the interested spectators, wishing she was in front of a roulette wheel instead of this audience.

Melanie nodded toward the two vacant chairs and said to Alana, "Who else is going to get up and lie about father?"

"Robert Somers will speak for the board and Howard Putting is going to speak on behalf of the arts council."

Hilary turned to Alana. "I'm going to say something, too."

184

She didn't know exactly what she would say, but she wasn't going to be the only one on the stage who didn't add to Phillip's eulogy.

The music faded into the background and Alana got to her feet. Hilary despised Alana, attempting to hide her contempt behind a cool facade, but it wasn't easy. Alana thought she was so wonderful, handling the service with dignity and grace. What a farce! The admiration on the faces of the people in attendance was disgusting. Couldn't they see it was all an act? All Alana wanted was Phillip's money.

When the service was over, the three women walked out, stopping to talk to people along the way. Hilary couldn't believe so many people wanted to talk to Alana. They gave Hilary and Melanie little more than a cursory hand shake, mumbling a few words of sympathy. Alana got the lion's share of attention. Hilary finally stalked out, getting into the waiting limousine without a backward glance. "Take me home, Leonard." Her voice was brittle, but she didn't care. She just wanted to get out. She needed a drink.

"Are the others coming?" he asked, bending down to speak before closing the door.

"I don't give a damn if they chase us all the way down Kapiolani Boulevard. Take me home." She rarely swore, considering it undignified and vulgar, but the situation called for it.

He was about to close the door when Melanie hurried out, her heels clicking on the cement. "Oh, Leonard. I'm glad you're still here." She gave him a helpless shrug before she settled into the back seat next to her sister. "You don't mind, do you, Hilary?"

"As long as Alana isn't with you, I don't mind at all," she muttered. "Let's go, Leonard." She leaned forward and pulled out a crystal decanter, pouring the amber liquid into two glasses.

She handed one to Melanie and raised the other one in her hand. "Let's drink to the downfall of Alana, shall we?"

"Definitely." Melanie sipped the scotch. "Mother killed herself because of that woman. Father has paid for his sins. It's her turn now."

Hilary nodded. "We've got to get enough votes to assure that she doesn't become CEO tomorrow."

"I think we can count on Charles," Melanie said. "Any others?"

"David Jones doesn't like Alana." Hilary sipped her drink. "That makes four of us. Where does Jeff Morino stand?"

"I'm not sure." Melanie sighed. "We need five votes to kill a vote in her favor."

"She needs five votes, too," Hilary murmured. "Ben Adams is really conservative. I'd be surprised if he voted for a woman. We might make it." Her face was grim. "I want to see her out of Hudson Enterprises and out of our lives!"

"I'll drink to that," Melanie agreed, taking another sip.

Alana wearied of the glowing, kind comments. Phillip Hudson had turned from devil to saint with the cease of a heart beat. Hilary and Melanie had slipped out immediately after the service, leaving Alana to deal with reporters, business associates concerned about the future of Hudson Enterprses, curiosity seekers, and employees. When the last of the guests left the auditorium, she took a deep breath, staring at the imposing portrait of Phillip. With a sense of relief she turned her back on it and walked out.

Alana left the building, suddenly restless. The evening stretched ahead, long and lonely. She didn't want to think about the board meeting the next day, and she didn't want to go to Phillip's house and face the hours of tedious work waiting for her there. Sorting through the files in his study would take days.

Her apartment seemed too confining. She drove through Waikiki but decided against shopping. Her face had become too familiar during the last week. Driving aimlessly along the ocean, her mind was numb.

An hour later she found herself in front of the gates to Raine Bradburn's house. Lines creased her forehead. How had she ended up here? She stared at the gate. Several times she put her car in gear and started to leave, only to turn off the engine each time. Finally she slipped out of the car and approached the intercom. She pressed a button and waited. A woman's voice answered. Alana hoped it was his housekeper. "This is Alana Hudson. I'd like to talk to Mr. Bradburn if he's available."

There was a long pause and then the woman said, "Mr. Bradburn will be happy to see you. Please drive in." When the wrought iron gates opened, Alana clenched the leather steering wheel with both hands. It was crazy. Stupid. Foolhardy. Raine Bradburn was trouble. He'd devour her and spit out the pieces. He was Phillip's enemy. She couldn't stop thinking about him. She drove through the gates.

Parking her car in front of the house, Alana got out and stared at the coral two story house. The windows were golden in the late afternoon sun. Raine opened the door and stepped outside. Neither of them moved. Alana clutched her purse in both hands, drinking in the sight of him. White shorts settled on slim hips, his powerful legs bare. A red polo shirt stretched across broad shoulders, tapering to his waist. His hands rested on his hips as he waited for her to make the first move. The sight of him soothed and excited her at the same time. She didn't understand it, her mind too weary to analyze it. Slowly, hesitantly, she started toward him. His dark gaze never left her face. "Ah, hello, Raine." The words seemed to come from someone else.

"Hello, Alana." His shuttered expression gave nothing away.

He stood aside and opened the door. "I'm surprised to see you."

She closed her eyes for a moment, then took a deep breath, her forehead creased, her gaze troubled as she looked up at him. "I'm surprised to be here."

He touched her elbow and guided her into the bright airy living room, settling her into an overstuffed chair. He headed for the bar. "Would you like something to drink?"

"Just lemonade if you have it." She stared out the wall of windows, looking at the ocean and watching the clouds turn lavender and pink from the setting sun.

"Nothing stronger?" he asked, putting two glasses on the bar and opening a small refrigerator.

She shook her head, still not looking at him. "I'm trying to clear my head, not muddle it any further."

"Ah, yes. A wealthy widow needs a clear head." He dropped ice cubes into one glass and poured lemonade into it.

Her head turned. She watched him pull out a bottle of beer, open it and pour it into a glass. "Try not to say it with such contempt," she said, her voice dry, rubbing her temple with her fingertips.

"I'll try." He moved back into the room and handed her the glass with the lemonade. Their fingers touched and gazes locked. His eyes darkened to indigo, boring into her, making her feel vulnerable and exposed. It scared her. She dropped her gaze and broke the spell.

"Alana, why did you come to see me?" He sprawled in a chair directly across from her, watching her over the rim of his glass.

She clutched her glass with both hands, looking at the ice cubes. "I've been trying to figure that one out myself." A horrified look crossed her face. "I didn't interrupt anything, did I?"

His voice was dry as he said, "There are no naked girls

188

running around the house and grounds, if that's what you mean. I was catching up on some paper work. Nothing that can't wait."

Alana relaxed. She was quiet for a moment, trying to collect her thoughts. She spoke slowly, as if each word was difficult to say. "I needed to talk about everything that's happened, and there's no one who would understand it . . . except you."

One dark brow quirked. "Oh? What do you want to talk about? Phillip? His charming daughters? Hudson Enterprises? My land?"

He wasn't making this easy for her. She didn't blame him. Putting her glass on the coffee table, she pushed herself to her feet, her shoulders sagging. "It was a dumb idea. I'm sorry. I shouldn't have come here."

He stood and face her, his hands on her shoulders. "It wasn't a dumb idea. It's been a tough week for you."

She searched his face for a touch of compassion. Seeing it flicker in his eyes, she shifted away from his grasp, walking across the room and digging her hands into the pockets of her skirt. "It's been one of the worst weeks in my life." She thought about the auto accident that claimed her parents' lives and froze Jeremy's mind. "I survived before. I'll do it again."

"But you don't have to do it alone." He was behind her, so close that she could feel the warmth of his breath tickle her hair.

"Yes, I do. I've been alone most of my life." It was difficult to hide the desolation when she was so exhausted.

"You had Phillip." His voice hardened slightly.

Alana uttered a bitter laugh. "Like I said. I've been alone. You knew Phillip."

"Maybe he loved you." He ground out the words.

Alana was silent for a long moment, feeling the anger in him without looking at him. "Loved me?" She turned to face him. "Perhaps in the beginning Phillip thought he loved me, but I don't think Phillip was capable of loving anyone but himself." Her face mirrored her disgust. "I wasn't the only woman he was involved with during his marriage, but for some reason known only to Phillip, he decided he wanted to marry me. Probably wanted to keep my brain in the corporation. Of course, our marrage didn't stop his affairs, it just assured him that I'd be available when he wanted me." Her hands clenched at her sides. Her voice was soft as she said, "I'll never know if he married me because he wanted me, or if he just didn't want anyone else to have me." She lifted her chin. "I loved Phillip when I married him. I don't know what went wrong, but we did have some good times together."

Raine leaned back against the open door to the terrace, rubbing his jaw with his hand. "You don't have to justify your marriage to me."

Alana closed her eyes. "But I have to justify it to myself. I thought I loved him." She wandered out onto the terrace, leaning on the rock ledge with both hands, watching the waves lap the silver crescent of sand below them. "Love means trust. You saw the results of Phillip's trust." The wall she had carefully erected over the last several weeks cracked, spilling out her pentup emotions. "I trusted him when I started working for him. I thought he was wonderful. Clever. Powerful. Charming." Her eyes narrowed. "He could be damned charming when he wanted something."

"And ruthless?" Raine offered.

"Yes." She bit out the word. "But there was always a rational reason for whatever he did."

Raine sat on the stone wall, his legs crossed at the ankles, his hands braced on either side. He pinned her with his eyes. "Even having me beat up?"

Her eyes clouded. "He never admitted to that."

"Did you confront him?" He continued to hold her in that dark gaze, drawing her to him like a magnet.

She took a step toward him. "No, never. I guess I was afraid to. Or maybe I didn't have to; I knew the truth." Her eyes were wide. "I can't believe he's dead."

"It was his heart, wasn't it?" The pull of his eyes refused to release her.

"They think so."

"Think?" His gaze drew her closer.

"Yes. They did an autopsy before cremating the body. The doctor wanted to make sure. You don't just write your name on the death certificate of someone as important as Phillip Hudson. You make a name for yourself by investigating the death." Her voice was soft. She was close enough now to see the fan of laugh lines at the outer edges of his eyes, the deep grooves around his mouth, the slight indentation in the middle of his jaw, the fading cut along his cheek. His powerful gaze continued to hold her captive.

"How have his daughters taken all this?" he asked, reaching out a hand to her.

Alana put her small white hand in his large tanned one. The contact was a catalyst. He felt strong and vital. She looked down at his muscular thighs, wondering how it would feel to have them wrapped around her. She blinked and refocused on his question. Pulling her hand from his and feeling instantly alone, she moved away from him, concentrating on a purple hibiscus. It was safer to inhale the scent of the flowers than the tantalyzing scent that seemed uniquely Raine Bradburn. She tried to place the scent, but it eluded her. A touch of lime, a hint of salt air, a fresh vibrant smell. She shook her head, clearing it of the heady aroma. "Melanie and Hilary have disliked me from the time Phillip became my mentor. When I was promoted to vice president and elected to the board the dislike turned to anger. When their mother died and we married, anger escalated into hatred. Now that he's dead . . . it'll mean war."

"Melanie is relatively harmless." He dismissed her with a wave of his hand, watching Alana prowl around the terrace.

"As harmless as a volcano about to erupt." Alana was warm. She unbuttoned the sleeves of her wilting silk blouse and rolled them up. She kicked off her shoes. "Don't underestimate Melanie. She's Phillip's daughter. She learned from the best." Alana frowned, tapping her chin with one finger. "There's a scheming mind hidden behind those sexy eyes."

"And Hilary? The iceberg?" Raine got to his feet, went into the living room and returned with fresh drinks. He handed Alana a glass.

She took a long drink, the cool liquid refreshing. "Hilary is as ruthless as her father." She shuddered. "I think I'd prefer Melanie's devious manner to Hilary's cold ruthlessness." She looked at Raine over the rim of her glass. "She fired an employee because she didn't like the way the woman dressed."

"And you found that employee another job." He leaned against the stone wall, watching her reaction.

She frowned. "How did you know that?"

"Word gets around about things like that. People don't forget when someone takes the time to do something special for them."

"It wasn't that big of a deal." She felt the perspiration trickle down between her breasts. Her panty hose clung to her legs like hot packs. Alana looked longingly at the tempting swimming pool. "The woman was an excellent employee. She would have gotten a job without my help."

"What about your job? How secure is it now that Phillip is gone?"

Her hands on the stone wall, she leaned her head back and closed her eyes, the silk of her blouse taut across her breasts. "Mel and Hilary will try to get me out, but I think the other board members respect my business acumen. I've got enough stock so they have to take me seriously. We're having a special

192

board meeting tomorrow to elect a temporary CEO. I don't see any one person being a strong contender for the position." She took a deep breath. "And then there's Phillip's will. He had the controlling block of stock."

"How's Hudson Enterprises running without the illustrious Phillip Hudson?" He emptied his glass.

"It's hell," she admitted, wandering to the edge of the pool, looking into the dark water. "Chaos. Phillip hoarded his power and authority. I thought I knew what was going on, but it's going to take weeks to figure everything out."

"You might not want to know everything." He stood behind her. She had sensed his presence before he spoke. He pulled the pins from her hair.

She didn't resist. "It's inevitable." Her hair tumbled about her shoulders. Warm, masculine fingers traced the line of her shoulder, leaving a trail of fire through the thin material of her blouse.

"And what about my land you so desperately need? Are you here to bargain for that?"

Alana winced at the harsh note in his voice while his touch was so gentle. Just when she thought he might understand. He didn't trust her any more than Phillip had.

She stiffened and stalked toward the door picking up her jacket as she went.

Raine was swift, blocking her exit. "I'm sorry, Alana. That was a low blow. I don't usually kick opponents when they're already down."

She looked up at him, feeling the heat from his body, wanting nothing more than to wrap her arms around him, feeling his strength and drawing on that strength. "Are we opponents?" A frown creased her brow and her eyes clouded. "I hoped we could be friends."

His hands settled on her shoulders, gently massaging them. "You are a vice president of Hudson Enterprises. I own Bradburn International. We compete for the same contracts, the same money. We both want to be the biggest and best. Wouldn't you say that makes us opponents?"

"I suppose," she murmured, her eyes tracing the tanned column of his throat, imagining planting a kiss right at the base. "Couldn't we ignore business and be friends?" She looked up, her eyes shining. He quickly dashed her hopes.

"We can be many things, but we'll never be just friends." His hands roamed from her shoulders to her arms and back to cup her face. The fire in his eyes mesmerized her, the low timbre of his voice seductive.

He pulled her towards him.

Chapter Fourteen

Raine's lips touched Alana's in a kiss as soft as the trade winds caressing an orchid. He tilted her head up, feathering kisses along her jaw, his lips warm and moist. A deep sigh escaped her lips as she wrapped her arms around his neck, molding her soft curves to fit the hard contours of his. When her mouth opened and she allowed him free access to explore, desire flared in him. He drank as if parched. His hands trailed down her spine. He held her tightly, his need surprising him.

His kiss deepened, their tongues duelling. He held her away from him slightly, his hands lingering on her shoulders. "Are you sure, Alana?" His eyes burned into hers. "I won't be able to stop if we continue."

"Don't stop," she whispered.

His finger traced the line of her blouse from the neck to a button. He took his time unbuttoning first one, and then another, and another. He brushed his hands over her shoulders, the thin material slipping to the floor. He rubbed a thumb over her lacy bra until her nipple was hard and responsive. His breath was ragged when he lifted his head and said, "Open your eyes, Alana."

She gave him a quizzical look. "Why?"

195

"I'm not Phillip. I want you to make sure you know exactly who's kissing you." He'd rather not have her at all than have her thinking he was Phillip.

She pushed away from him. Her breath came in short bursts. She wrapped her arms around her body, turning away from him as she tried to rein in her emotions. "I'm sorry. That never should have happened. I may not have loved Phillip, but I was his wife."

"And you're mourning his loss?" Raine asked, his voice sarcastic, hurt at her withdrawal.

"I respect death." She shivered, bending to retrieve her blouse. Shaking hands made it difficult to put on. She didn't attempt the buttons.

"And as his widow, I should respect you." His voice was hard, his words making her flinch, but he couldn't stop himself. "You're a wealthy widow. Hands off, is that it, Alana? I'm not good enough for you?"

"Don't be silly." She faced him, her eyes flashing. "You make me feel like I'm on a roller coaster. One minute you're sensitive, passionate, the next you're hard, cruel. You're probably too good for me! I haven't had the sexual experience and variety you have. You'd find me very dull!"

He stepped toward her. She stepped back. "Let me be the judge of that." His gaze roamed over her body, watching her nipples respond to the heat of his gaze. He took another step toward her and when she stepped back, she was against the wall.

"No, Raine."

"Yes, Alana," he mocked, reaching out one hand and running his thumb across her trembling lips. "You wanted me just moments ago. I just want to be certain that you know who's making love to you."

Her gaze locked with his. "Phillip never made love to me."

196

Her voice was little more than a whisper. "We had sex. There's a difference."

"He was a fool." He slipped the blouse from her shoulders. He lifted a hand, reaching behind Alana to pluck an orchid. He brushed it along her shoulder, a knowing light in his eyes when she shuddered. "Beautiful skin. Alabaster white." He touched her shoulder with his lips. "Softer than the finest satin." He inhaled deeply. "A scent more seductive than the orchid." He had to have her. With one swift movement he lifted her, long strides taking them around the short wall and into a private courtyard. Raine continued to hold her as he stepped into the room.

Her arms circled his neck as he released her. She slid down the length of his body, their bodies touching from shoulder to thigh, enflaming Raine until he had to imprint his body on hers, staking his claim in a way as ancient as time itself.

One flick of his hand and her bra was on the floor. "I didn't think any woman wore a bra in the islands," he teased, stroking the orchid over each soft mound.

"They do in the board room." Alana's voice was husky as she threw her head back and closed her eyes.

"And in the bedroom?" His voice was ragged, the orchid kissing her erect nipples. It took steely self-control not to follow the orchid with his lips.

"They wear nothing at all," she murmured, straightening and looking at him through desire laden eyes.

"Then you're overdressed for the occasion." He turned her around, his lips exploring the nape of her neck, stringing kisses along each bare shoulder. A moment later her skirt was a pool of black around her ankles. Hose and panties quickly followed. Raine pulled her back against his chest, his hands wrapped around her body, a shuddering sigh escaping his lips. "Open your eyes, Alana."

She did as he asked, stunned at the reflection in the wall of mirrors. Raine was behind her, his hands caressing her lovingly. Her breasts were full and taut, straining for his touch. Her hips arched toward the wayward hand that stroked her thighs with maddening slowness.

"You're a temptress, Alana."

"Oh, God, Raine! Touch me. Kiss me."

"I'll touch you," he murmured, cupping her breasts with his hands. "And I'll kiss you." His tongue flicked along the length of her spine. "But I've waited for this for a long time. I'm going to savor every moment."

Alana turned in his arms, facing him with eyes heavy with need, raising a hand to his cheek. "Two can play this game," she murmured, a sensuous smile curving her lips. She ran her hands down the front of his shirt, raking her nails over his nipples, smiling when he gasped.

"And you said you didn't have experience," he mocked lightly.

"Just survival instincts." She paused, gripping his shoulders. "You're overdressed for this party." She pulled his shirt up and over his head. Wrapping her arms around him, she pressed their bodies together, her flesh pliant against the muscled wall of his chest.

Long dormant feelings sprang to life as Raine inhaled deeply of the feminine scent of her, needing the soft warmth of her body to fuel the fires raging inside of him. He cupped both breasts in his hands, looking at them with fire in his eyes before he lowered his head to leave a moist trail with his tongue. He touched and kissed each one until she quivered all over.

Raine moved his hands down her spine in little circles. Raising her face to his, they met in a kiss that left them both awed and breathless. His tongue explored the moist interior of hers, playing and caressing while his hands fanned the fires he was igniting. "Alana, you're so beautiful."

"Take me, Raine, please." Her voice was an impassioned whisper as she wrapped her hands around his body.

"Not so fast, Alana. We've got all night."

His hand dropped between their bodies, stroking the triangle of dark curly hair between her thighs. Her hands gripped his shoulders. "I don't think I can stand up much longer."

"Me either." He drew an unsteady breath.

Alana fumbled with the snap on his shorts, unzipping them and easing them over his hips. She ran her hands over his chest and hips while her gaze wandered over his body. "Erase the scars Phillip inflicted," she murmured.

Raine regarded her for a long moment. Could he do as she asked? "I'm not Phillip."

"I never thought you were," she answered, reaching out to kiss the cleft in his chin.

He pulled her close, the heat fusing them together. "I want you," he murmured.

"I want you, too." She rained kisses on his chest.

Raine picked her up and carried her to the bed. He stood over her, the heat of his gaze making her breath quicken. He hovered over her, taking the orchid that had dropped to the pillow and brushing it over her shoulders and then between her breasts. He circled each soft mound, his gaze intent. "Your skin is as beautiful as the orchid, Alana. As soft and delicate, too." He trailed it over her stomach and down her thighs, the fire in his eyes following the gentle touch of the flower. After tucking the blossom behind her ear, he kneeled beside her, running one hand over her breasts and down to her narrow waist then continuing down her hip and thigh before returning to her breast. "Beautiful," he said reverently, retracing the path of his hand with his mouth. He blazed a trail of kisses, Alana writhing under his touch. He stretched out beside her, his hands touching, exploring.

Enboldened by his desire, she moved on top of him, her

hands tangling in the crisp hair on his chest. His thumbs circled her breasts, never quite touching the sensitive tips. Alana leaned forward, kneeling over him. "Kiss me, Raine. Make me feel alive!"

Her back arched as he flicked his tongue in maddening circles, ever closer to their quivering prize. His mouth found their target, licking and nipping as Alana gasped. His mouth moved lower, nipping at her stomach, circling her navel with a ring of kisses.

In one swift movement, Alana was on her back and Raine was stroking the length of her body. His mouth followed his hands, finding every pleasure point in her body. He spread her thighs, and she revealed her most intimate secrets as he stroked and caressed. His head moved lower, kissing, licking, nipping, his only thought to please her.

"Oh, God, Raine, please! Please, take me!"

"Soon, Alana, soon," he murmured in a raspy voice. "Touch me, Alana."

He fought for control as she explored his hard body, kissing and tasting, beyond conscious thought. All that mattered was the two of them. She pressed kisses along the strong column of his neck, her hands and mouth finding places that pleased and tormented him. Her mouth trailed down his chest, following the path of hair as it narrowed below his navel. He groaned. She was driving him mad.

Raine's control snapped. He lifted Alana off of him and levered himself on top of her in one movement, entering her with a force he hadn't believed possible. He was catapulted through timeless space, tumbling and turning in a release so great and so encompassing that he felt he was riding the crest of a rainbow, a myriad of colors before his eyes, the passion of red, the spirit of light in yellow, the vibrancy of orange, and the glorious ectascy of blue. The descent was a blend of weightlessness and pleasure. This is what he had been missing all these years. Fulfillment.

Their slick bodies fused and they collapsed, side by side. It was long moments before either of them could speak.

Alana kissed Raine's neck. "Do you make all women feel like this?"

He ran a hand down her arm, his eyes closed, his breathing returning to normal. He looked at her then with a gentle smile, touching her cheek with the back of one hand. "That was very special, Alana."

Tears dampened her face. "It was for me, too."

He kissed away the tears. "Hey, none of that. I can't stand to see a woman cry." He stood up, pulling her with him. "How about a swim to cool off?"

"Like this?" She put her hands on her hips and let her gaze wander over the athletic physique of his body. "No wonder you have no tan lines."

"You don't either," he retorted, running a hand down her waist to her hip.

She wrinkled her nose. "That's because I burn. I learned long ago to use a sunscreen."

"I'm glad. I'd hate to think of that gorgeous body burned." He gave her a quick kiss and took her hand, padding toward the open door. "No one will see us. My housekeeper and her husband have a wing to themselves. The gates are locked and it's dark. No need to fear a burn on that lovely derriere." His hand stroked her, feeling desire stir as he touched her.

"Seems like you've got everything figured out," she said, her voice dry.

"I've got nothing figured out, honey," he said on a sigh, regret and frustration tinging his voice. "I just know I want to be with you tonight. We'll worry about tomorrow when it comes." He led her down the steps into the silky warmth of the water.

"That's a bad attitude." She shook her finger at him. "I have had that attitude and its gotten me into more trouble than I know what to do with." She followed him into the water, stopping when it reached her waist.

"Do you think of me as trouble?" he asked, turning her around so she could lean back against him. He covered her breasts with his hands.

"I think you are probably going to be more trouble than ten Phillip Hudsons." She rubbed against him like a cat wanting someone to pet it. Her voice was husky.

"Good," he murmured as he nibbled on her ear. "I wouldn't like to think that Phillip Hudson had outdone me at anything."

Alana's tinkling laughter echoed across the water. "Next to you, Phillip Hudson was a bumbling schoolboy. Sex was to be endured not enjoyed."

His hand wandered down over her hips, seeking her pleasure point, the warmth of the water and the starlit sky conspiring to bring them both to a new level of sensual awareness. Alana moved restlessly. "I would like to know how you learned the art of making love so well."

"Just relax and enjoy," he told her, running his tongue around the shell of her ear.

They made love again, pulling themselves out of the water as the sounds of the night serenaded them.

The sun tinted the morning sky pink and gold as Alana awakened. For a moment she wondered where she was, and then memories of the previous night flooded her mind. She turned her head, a soft smile on her lips. Raine's hair was tossled and his features relaxed. Sprawled on his back, his arms were thrown over his head. The sheet that had covered them was around his waist. Alana's gaze wandered over his teak chest, craving the warmth and strength she knew awaited her, but she remained still. She thought about the night she had just spent in his arms. It had been the most wonderful, glorious, soul shattering mistake of her life. In one night Raine had torn down the barriers she had erected around her heart. Barriers never endangered by marriage to Phillip. Yes, she had lost temporary control of her life to Phillip, but he had never won her heart, never made her feel so vulnerable, never made the earth move beneath her. She was scared. It was too soon after Phillip. Her confidence was shaky. Raine made her feel things she hadn't known existed. She had to regain control of her life and emotions before she could think of the risks a relationship with Raine would involve. He would demand total commitment, something she had never given to anyone. The very idea terrified her. Commitment meant total honesty and trust, two values she had never found in any man, and the two things she couldn't give.

Carefully getting out of bed so she didn't disturb Raine, she padded around the room, picking up her clothing as she went. She would have been better off never knowing the exquisite joy of being in his arms, of making love with him. After one last, longing glance at Raine, she knew it wasn't true. Raine had awakened a passion in her she never knew existed, changing her life forever. She could never be sorry for that.

Alana drove down the winding drive, hoping that when she tripped the sensor the gates would open. They did and she drove through the quiet streets, her mind reliving the wonders of the previous night. Hawaii awoke with the sun. Joggers loped along the shore, surfers headed for the water, people walked their dogs, and others headed for the beaches and parks, staking their claim to a piece of paradise, at least for the day.

Melanie looked across the massive table at Charles. They had spent the entire night making love and yet he looked fresh and rested, while she felt pleasantly weary. How did he do it? She glanced around at the other directors. Who would be the new CEO? Anyone but Alana, she vowed to herself. Charles had promised to help. He was so kind and gentle, and yet, when she told him how she felt about Alana, a ruthless, hard look entered his eyes. He hadn't become a millionaire by being a pushover. If he could show Melanie a softer side to him, why couldn't her own father have done the same thing? She gave herself a mental shake. It was too late now. Her goal now was to make certain that Alana didn't take Phillip's place of authority.

Robert Somers was the vice chairman and ran the meeting. The first order of business was the election of a temporary CEO, president, and chairman of the board. Robert looked down the long table. "Until Phillip Hudson's will is read, and we know where his stock is going, we'll have to elect temporary officers."

"I think we should elect one person for all three positions," Dan said. "Phillip held those positions and it would make it easier for one person to be the temporary head of the company than to try to work with three people."

"I agree," Jeff said.

"I don't." Charles looked from Dan to Jeff. "Even in a temporary capacity, one person handling everything could really do a lot of damage. We're better off with three people working together."

"I agree with Charles," David Jones added in a clipped English accent. "Let's put different people in those positions and see how they all do. It'll give us a better idea of who we want running the company when we know what Phillip had in his will."

"Unless he left his block of stock to one person," Hilary murmured. "That person could do whatever they wanted to."

"Not necessarily," Melanie answered. "The board would still have the authority to elect someone else to those positions."

Charles smiled and nodded his encouragement.

Melanie continued. "Let's vote for each position. Maybe the same person will get them all." She paused. "And maybe they won't."

Robert nodded. "The first position is chief executive officer. Any nominations?"

"Alana Hudson," Dan said. Jeff seconded the nomination.

"Charles Reese." Melanie's voice was clear and strong. David seconded her nomination.

"Any other nominations?" Robert looked down the table.

"I move the nominations be closed." Ben looked at Robert over the top of his glasses.

"Seconded." Jeff nodded his head.

"Those in favor so indicate." Everyone raised their hand. Robert nodded to his secretary. "Susan will give you each a ballot. Please write down the name of the candidate you wish to vote for as CEO of Hudson Enterprises, keeping in mind that it is a temporary position."

When the ballots were returned to him, he frowned. "The vote is tied. I'll have to break the tie." He took a deep breath, looking from Alana to Charles. "I'll cast my vote for Alana."

Melanie had been holding her breath. She let it out in a hiss. Alana had won that round. Melanie flashed a surprised look at Charles, but he just returned her look with a calm one.

Robert spoke again. "The next office is president."

The process was repeated. The vote was five to three for Ben Adams as president, and then Charles was elected the temporary chairman of the board.

Melanie felt herself glowing with pride when Charles took over the meeting from Robert. She hoped this would mean he would be in Hawaii more often. All the special meetings were fine with her. Charles attended them all.

Charles looked at the other directors. "Until Phillip's will is read, I'd like to know what you think we should do about the projects we have on hold. We've also talked about acquiring several more companies. What do we want our position to be?"

Ben spoke up. "I move we table all projects that haven't been started yet."

"But then we'll look like we're afraid to move without Phillip Hudson," Jeff protested. "It won't look good for our image."

"It's only for a short time," Hilary protested. "The shareholders are panicky enough. I agree with Ben. Let's wait and see what Phillip's will says."

Melanie nodded. "I second his motion. It won't hurt the corporation if we're cautious right now. If we blunder ahead with some of these projects, we could end up looking incompetent." She sought Charles' gaze, warmed by his approval.

"I think we should proceed carefully," Alana said, drawing Melanie's gaze. "Several of these projects will be worthless if we wait much longer."

"Like the Aloha Shores project?" Melanie said, her voice dry.

"That's one of them," Alana said with a nod. "But there are others, and we've talked about taking over another company. That really can't wait."

Charles called for the vote, and with a five to three vote all existing projects were put on hold.

When there was no more immediate business, the meeting was adjourned.

Alana left the Hudson Building and hurried to her apartment, showered and changed into shorts and a shirt, tossed some clothes into a bag and headed for two days of peace, hoping to sort out everything that had happened in the last few days. It was a big responsibility to be the CEO, but until they filled the empty seats on the board, Charles was in control, and his main interest was Melanie! Although she couldn't fault him for running a good meeting, and he was fair, he was still on Melanie and Hilary's side.

Peace. She wondered if she'd ever know peace again. At least she'd have a couple of days to figure out what to say to Raine when she saw him next. If she saw him again. She couldn't decide which was more depressing, not seeing him and knowing she had meant nothing to him or seeing him and knowing she could never be in those arms again. Hudson Enterprises pulled at her, too. Being CEO would mean additional work, and working with Ben was going to mean justifying every decision she made.

Tension drained from her as she pulled into the sandy yard, Jeremy and Thomas waiting for her. "Lani!" Jeremy's happy cry tugged at her heart. He ran toward her, picked her up and twirled her around. "I missed you."

"I missed you too, Jeremy." She returned his hug and smile. When he put her back on the ground she turned to Thomas. There hadn't been time to talk much in the last weeks. They communicated silently. She raised her eyebrows in question, he shook his head. Jeremy was unaware of the publicity surounding his sister. Thomas had made sure that Jeremy hadn't seen any of the pictures in the newspapers.

Thomas stood by her side later that day when Jeremy headed for the surf to show her what he had learned. "How did the memorial service go?"

Alana shaded her eyes with her hand, watching Jeremy's progress. "Okay."

"What about you?" He turned to look at her. "There's something bothering you and it has nothing to do with Phillip Hudson."

"It's something I have to work out for myself." She gave him a quick smile. "Nothing I can't handle. I was elected temporary CEO today. I'll be busier than ever until Phillip's will is read and we know what he did with his shares of stock." Her gaze returned to Jeremy. "Is it safe for him to be out there by himself?"

"He's fine." Thomas patted her shoulder. "He's such a natural athlete, he needed little instruction." He paused. "It's funny. There isn't anything he can't do physically, but mentally and emotionally he's just a little boy."

"Damn!" Alana gave vent to her frustration. "If I ever find out who ran us off the road that day, I'll kill him with my own hands."

"Easy, Alana. It won't do any good. We never did find the key to the safety deposit box, so the documents and identity of the man behind it are lost forever. Forget it. I think you've got other more important things to consider." His shrewd look made her blush.

"You're right." She clapped her hands as Jeremy emerged from the water, looking like a sun drenched Adonis, his golden body glistening with droplets of water. "You were wonderful, Jeremy!" She ran and gave him a hug. "I'm so proud of you."

"Thanks, Lani. I really like this board." He patted it and smiled. "Thank you. Thomas told me you bought it for me." He frowned. "Some day I want to buy something for you."

"Jeremy, just seeing you happy is all I want." She patted his cheek. "You'd better hit the shower and rinse off that salt water."

"Okay." He propped his board against a palm tree and headed for the shower outside the house.

The days passed quickly and Alana was headed back to the city before dawn Monday morning. She was no closer to knowing what to say to Raine, except that a relationship was impossible. Her life was complicated enough. She mourned the loss of what might have been more than she mourned the man who had been her husband. It was unsettling.

* * *

Melanie tapped on Hilary's door and slipped into the office. She strode across the room, her teal silk mantailored dress making her look both feminine and competent. Gold jewelry gleamed at her ears and throat.

Hilary wondered how Melanie managed to look seductive and buinesslike at the same time. Melanie had a flair for the dramatic. It was one of her sister's traits Hilary always admired. She looked down at her tucked poppy red blouse and royal blue suit. She felt dowdy compared to her sister. "Hi, Mel."

Melanie perched on the edge of Hilary's desk. "I just talked to Arty Jones. He can't find a damn thing on Alana!" Melanie's eyes glittered. "How are we going to get her out of our lives now that she's CEO?"

Hilary sat back, silent for a moment. "I can't believe she has a spotless background."

"Part of the problem is that Arty can't find out much about her before she came to the islands. He can't seem to get any information, and it takes time to come up with fake documents, not that they would do us much good now."

"True." Hilary's eyes narrowed. "But we've got to get her out of Hudson Enterprises."

"Maybe we could scare her." Melanie stood and turned toward the windows, staring sightlessly out over the mountains.

"She doesn't scare easily." Hilary sighed. "If we could discredit her before the board, it would weaken her position."

"Father's stock is the key. If we inherit it, we can get her out immediately." Melanie whirled around.

"And if *she* inherits it, we're out," Hilary pointed out, standing up and facing her sister. The thought of Alana controlling the company was too horrible to think about.

"We can't take that chance," Melanie muttered.

"Short of murder, what do you suggest?"

Melanie's hands rested on her hips, a grim look on her face. "I'm not sure yet, but I may have a plan." She paused. "We need to fill those four empty seats on the board with people who will vote with us."

"If we could fill those empty seats with allies . . ." Hilary's voice trailed off.

"We would control the board." Melanie smiled at her sister. "Time to start looking for possible directors."

"I'll ask Chandler if he has any suggestions. He might have some contacts on the mainland. He was in San Fransciso last week."

"And I think I know how we can get Alana out of our lives." Melanie squared her shoulders. "I'll let you know when I'm sure it will work."

"Melanie, you're not going to do anything illegal, are you?" Hilary had been in on some of Melanie's escapades through the years.

"Don't worry, Hilary." Melanie wagged her fingers and disappeared through the door.

Hilary sat down and lifted the receiver, punching a button for speed dialing. Her eyes sparkled, her mouth softened, her features glowed with anticipation. "Hi," she murmured. "What looks good for the weekend?" She pulled her calculator closer.

Chapter Fifteen

Alana sipped her champagne. She had dressed carefully for this cocktail party, ever mindful of her image as Phillip Hudson's widow. Her black silk crepe wraparound dress was secured at her waist with a diamond pin. The diamonds she had returned to Phillip adorned her throat and ears. Since he was dead they were hers now, with no strings attached.

Cocktail parties bored Alana, but since more business was conducted over drinks than over a desk, she forced herself to look interested. This party was special. Lee Taka, owner of half the restaurants and hotels in Hawaii and Japan, was unveiling a new hotel complex. She was curious to see how it compared to Aloha Shores.

She looked around the large room. Lee was known for quality and elegance, and this room reflected both. The floor was covered with swirls of grey and mauve carpeting. One wall was open to the ocean, the opposite one covered with mirrors, reflecting the beach, palm tress and blue sea. Crystal chandeliers cast a muted light on the distinguished guests. Long buffet tables were weighed down with exotic delicacies, ice sculptures of game fish centered on each table. A pianist played Chopin from a white grand piano. The elite of Oahu's society mingled, trading golf scores, sailing stories, and tennis rankings.

Alana wondered what she was doing, pretending to be excited by Tippy Jensen's golf score when she had a company to worry about. She had been able to talk to a stockbroker who told her there was lots of activity in Hudson stock. She wouldn't worry until she knew what Phillip had done with his stock. If he had divided it into small enough chunks, an outsider might be able to put together a hostile takeover.

Ben Adams and his wife approached her. "I hope you weren't upset when I was elected president," he said in a soft voice.

Alana shook her head, smiling. "We work well together, Ben. I think Charles was correct. Right now we're better off with three people. At least I won't be blamed for everything that goes wrong."

He gave her a rueful glance. "Melanie and Hilary won't make it easy for you."

"Don't I know it." She sipped her Perrier.

"Have you had any time for tennis?" Ben's wife, Cindy asked. She was a petite woman in her early thirties, with shoulder-length blond hair, green eyes, a perfect tan, and an easygoing personality. Ben and Cindy had six active children and a sound marriage. Alana envied them.

She looked at Cindy with a smile, wondering how a woman stayed so slender after six children. Her fitted, strapless, white beaded dress was stunning. "I haven't played much lately," Alana admitted.

"I hope you'll be ready for our celebrity tournament. We've got some great players coming to the islands just for the tournament. You'll have to play."

"I'll try." Alana wondered where she'd find time to practice. Maybe three or four in the morning when insomnia kept her awake.

She had just turned from talking to Ben and Cindy when she saw Raine. Taken off guard, Alana stared at him, drinking in the sight of him. He had on a crisp white shirt, red striped tie, and black pinstriped suit tailor made to hug broad shoulders and narrow waist.

He approached her, his face shuttered.

Alana prepared for a scene similar to the ones Phillip subjected to her to, filled with accusations and innuendos, demanding to know where she had been, but then she remembered where she was. He wouldn't draw attention to them. She still squared her shoulders, telling herself she answered to no one.

"Hello, Alana," he said softly, his sapphire eyes stroking her face with an almost physical touch. "You've got to be the most beautiful woman in the world."

Of all the things she expected him to say, that wasn't one of them. She swallowed hard, draining her glass. "Hello." A wary look entered her eyes. What was he up to?

His gaze continued to caress her flushed cheeks and violet eyes, the slight peeling of her nose. "You've been out in the sun."

Her eyes widened. "How did you know that?"

He pointed to her nose, a smile lighting his face. "Not enough sun block."

Alana cleared her throat, looking for someone to come rescue her. His presence was enough to make her want to rip off her clothes and hold him close. "Why are you here?"

"The same reason you are. I wonder if Lee's hotel will compare to the complex you want to build but can't." His voice was soft, but the sarcasm was clear.

"And we both know why," she muttered, glaring at him.

"Have dinner with me later."

Her brows lifted. "Just like that? Have dinner with you? Why? What could we possibly have to discuss, unless you're ready to sell your land."

"I don't want to talk about the land. I want to talk about us." He pinned her with the intensity of his gaze.

How was she going to tell him there was no future for them when she wanted it more than anything in her life? She had to convince herself before she could convince him. "There is no us." Turning, she walked to the open doors of the magnificent ballroom, staring out at the ocean. She took a deep breath. "The night I spent with you was the most exquisite mistake of my life. I'll never forget it, but there is no way we can have any kind of a relationship as long as I'm working for Hudson Enterprises."

"So quit." He leaned one shoulder against the door frame, taking a sip of his drink.

She frowned in disappointment. She had expected better from him. Her voice was dry as she said, "Why don't you quit Bradburn International?"

"I own the company. Why would I want to do that?" He frowned, then faced her, one hand in his pocket.

"I have stock in this company, an important position. Why should I want to quit?" she countered.

He was silent for a moment, rocking back on his heels. A sheepish look crossed his face. "Outdated attitude, huh?"

She nodded, a wistful longing in her eyes. "We can't have a personal relationship, and a business relationship would never work." She shook her head, regret in her voice. "I wish it could be different, but we both know it can't."

A glint of determination flickered in his eyes, but his gaze was hidden as he asked, "How about a business lunch?"

"To discuss the land?" she asked, wary of his motives.

He shrugged. "Possibly."

She was silent for a long moment, then said, "No, Raine. If you really want to sell the land, talk to Dan Asuka or Bob Sommers. It would be better that way."

"It wouldn't be very wise for Phillip Hudson's widow to be

seen with his fiercest competitor, is that it?'' She winced at the bitter tone of his voice.

"It wouldn't be wise for me to see you at all,'' she answered, meeting his fierce glare with an open one. "I needed comfort the other night, and you gave it to me.''

"Is that all it was?'' he demanded, scorn tingling his voice.

"That's all I'm going to let it be:'' Her voice was firm as she looked away. When she looked at him again, there was a pleading note in her voice, begging him to understand. "Please, Raine. I can't handle anything else right now. I need time.''

He nodded slowly. "I can understand that, Alana, but believe me we're not finished.'' In quick strides he grabbed her hand and pulled her outside into the shadows. He kissed her so thoroughly she was breathless when he raised his head. His voice ragged, he muttered, "Something to keep me going until you come to your senses.'' With that, he strode back into the ballroom.

Melanie looked glum. She glanced at her desk calendar. She missed Charles. How could that little man who looked more like a cuddly teddy bear than a powerful banker make her feel so lonely? It had to be the stress of her life these days. Her father's will was to be read in an hour. Had he really written his daughters out of it? Had he given everything to Alana? She sat up, her fist clenched, but then she relaxed slightly. It didn't do any good to worry about it. She'd find out soon enough. There was nothing on her calendar for the rest of the day.

She smiled, pushing the button on her intercom. "Have Chad come in.'' She sat back. Chad was the perfect diversion. She'd forget Charles and Alana.

When Chad entered, she murmured, "Lock the door.''

The soft click echoed in the silent room. Chad approached Melanie.

She stood. "I want you to do something for me."

His eyes crinkled as he smiled. "Anything."

"Make me forget I've got to be at the lawyer's in an hour." She closed her eyes and ran her hands up the lapels of his jacket.

"It'll be a pleasure." His lips touched hers. His hand reached for the zipper of her black and white striped silk dress.

Melanie stepped out of it and pushed the pale blue linen sport coat from Chad's broad shoulders. Impatient, she stripped off her remaining clothes while Chad did the same. Her eyes raked his body. He was perfect. Golden tan, well muscled, blond hair, blue eyes, broad shoulders, and he was at least six inches taller than Charles.

Chad pulled her close, his hands and mouth doing all the right things. He lowered her to the plush carpeting, waiting until she was ready for him.

Melanie tried to respond as enthusiastically as Chad did, but Charles kept getting in the way.

When Chad was breathing normally, she pushed him off and sighed. "I have to get ready to go to the lawyer's."

Chad looked at her, then shrugged and got to his feet, gathering his clothes and quickly putting them on.

Melanie moved a little slower. Why couldn't Charles just be another man in her life? He was married, had a child, and lived in New York! She was crazy for even thinking about him. He certainly wasn't thinking about her!

Alana drummed her fingers on the leather steering wheel, glancing at the digital clock for the fourth time in a minute. Damn! She was going to be late. Traffic along Kalakaua Avenue had come to a complete halt. She would have left the office earlier knowing that Waikiki's streets would be snarled with tourists, but Ben's urgent phone call had held her up.

Gritting her teeth, she inched the Mercedes coupe forward as far as she dared, but the car ahead of her seemed cemented in place. Alana brushed a strand of ebony hair from a blushed cheek, her thoughts as tangled as the traffic. Violet eyes clouded. What was she going to do if she wasn't in Phillip's will? She lifted the curtain of wavy black hair from her nape, wishing she had put it up in a knot at the back of her head. She glanced at her slim gold watch. It matched the time on the car's clock. Melanie and Hilary were probably there, waiting.

Alana jumped when a horn blasted behind her. She swiveled in her seat and glared at the driver of the bus, but he just leaned on the horn again and nudged her rear bumper. Alana tapped her toe on the accelerator. The car ahead of her never moved an inch. She tried to concentrate on the serenity of the cloudless sky and the swaying palm trees, but hotels and shops got in her way. "I thought this was paradise," she muttered to herself, scanning the hotels, shops, and high-rise buildings hiding the ocean view. "I might as well be in Chicago," she said as she hit the heel of her hand against the steering wheel. Then she thought of the icy winds, piles of snow, and sub zero temperatures the weatherman had mentioned earlier in the day. A traffic jam in Hawaii in January was infinitely more agreeable than fighting a blizzard in Chicago. A slight smile tugged at her lips until she remembered the meeting. She might very well be looking for a job after her meeting today, and she could end up in Chicago.

Tossing her head, she grabbed the wheel with both hands and whipped around the car in front of her into the right lane, ignoring the irate driver she cut off. Progressing half a block and then stopping once again, she cursed the people who promoted Hawaii as an island paradise. Tourists were a source of needed income for the islands, but they sure messed up the streets stopping in their rented cars to photograph the sights. Hilary and Melanie were probably already there. This would

217

just antagonize them further. Shifting in the leather seat and rubbing one finger against her pearl grey linen skirt she admitted she'd probably feel the same way if positions were reversed, but it didn't make it any easier to tolerate.

Alana frowned. Had Phillip left everything to them? It was possible. If Phillip thought they couldn't survive without his assistance, he might have left it all to them. And what if he hadn't had time to change his will? He never had trusted her. He might have purposely excluded her. If he had left everything to his daughters, she didn't know how she'd convince the board that she was the best candidate for the permanent position of CEO. Phillip's block of stock would assure her of the job. Her share of stock wasn't enough to influence anyone. If Phillip left his stock to his daughters, they could have enough power to have Alana off the board and out of a job. Perspiration beaded her forehead. No one in the islands would hire Phillip Hudson's widow. They hated Phillip, and his influence reached far beyond the islands. When Phillip Hudson roared, men jumped from New York to Hong Kong. There was Jeremy to consider. How would she take care of him? It was a chilling thought, one she preferred not to think about. Better to think positive. When Hudson Enterprises was hers, Jeremy would have a secure future, and she knew exactly what she would do with the Hudson sisters.

Switching lanes again, she made a left turn on two wheels, six cars slamming on their brakes to avoid a collision. A sharp right and another left and she was almost there.

The thought of Jeremy increased her determination. He was her responsibility and she would see to it that he was taken care of, no matter what kind of job she had to take to pay for his care. The thought of working for Raine niggled in the back of her brain, but she refused to think about it. She had been in that situation before with Phillip and she didn't want to do it again. Besides, he might not have been serious in his offer.

Squeezing into the only available parking space in Waikiki, she ignored the fire hydrant next to the rear bumper as she shut off the engine and took a quick look in the rear view mirror. She had two blocks to walk to the professional building where the law firm of Henry, Judson, and Sims was located and she was late. Gracefully easing her long legs out of the car, she smoothed the skirt of her grey suit before dropping the keys into her Hermes purse of grey calfskin and linen.

The heat of the pavement penetrated the thin soles of her shoes as she hurried toward her destination. The tropical sun burned her neck and shoulders as perspiration trickled between her breasts. There was little chance of trade winds cooling her off with the tall buildings on each side. She stalked passed Gucci's and Cartier's without a glance. The young girl hawking time shares in a condo didn't rate a look. Alana cursed the heat, the clamor of people, and especially Phillip. No one could have guessed her state of mind as she walked down the busy street. More than one head turned to get another look at the sultry, stunning woman, her grace and beauty a potent combination. Alana, as the wife of millionaire Phillip Hudson, had been the focal point of gossip columns since she married the man twice her age, but she attributed the stories to Phillip's power, not her looks or style. It appeared that she had it all, but she knew better. She was strong out of necessity, but she longed to lean on someone else.

A frown marred her delicate features when she saw the cluster of reporters at the entrance to the office building. Someone had slipped the news to the press. At the attorney's insistence, and much to Alana's relief, the reading of Phillip's will was to be confidential among the three women. After living with Phillip, she should have realized that nothing would ever be confidential again. Everything and everyone had a price. Composing her features and taking a deep breath, her step faltered only once when Dudley jumped in front on her. Microphones and tape recorders were thrust into her face.

"Are you gong to be the permanent CEO of Hudson Enterprises?" Art Helani asked, his voice louder than the rest.

Alana clutched her purse, her voice quiet. "Can anyone really replace Phillip Hudson?" That should be noncommittal enough. Phillip had taught her to talk to people without saying anything.

"But Phillip Hudson had a major block of stock. Won't the person inheriting that stock control the company?" Another reporter fired the question as Alana continued to move toward the doors.

Alana was silent for a moment, choosing her words carefully. That was a question she wished she knew the answer to, but it was the reason she was heading for the law offices of Willard Sims right now. "I don't think Phillip ever thought he'd die." She looked directly at the reporter while edging toward the door. "You knew Phillip. Can you imagine him admitting to being mortal?"

At the chuckle of the other reporters, she hoped they would stop their questions, but Lee Dudley scurried around, blocking her path just as she reached for the brass handle on the door. "Come on, Mrs. Hudson, you're avoiding the real question here. Phillip's will is going to be read today. Do you know what it says? Will you get the stock?" He paused. "Maybe Hudson's daughters will get it all." A malicious smile cracked his face. "What would happen to you if they inherited everything? Would you still have a job at Hudson Enterprises?"

Alana knew he was saying aloud what the rest of the island was thinking. "I'm sure my husband did what was best for the company." That was the understatement of the century. Hudson Enterprises had been the center of Phillip's life, and it would probably remain the center of attention even after his death. Phillip was not a man to let a little thing like death stop him from manipulating people.

She reached for the handle and pulled the door open. "Now, if you'll excuse me." She pushed the door into the obnoxious reporter's hands and strolled into the building as if she hadn't a care in the world while her stomach lurched and blood rushed to her head. She paused for a moment, willing the open-air lobby to stop spinning as she fought a wave of nausea. Great! Just what she needed. The reporters would have a field day with a picture of Phillip Hudson's widow getting sick in the lobby of an imposing office building. Two deep breaths eased the light-headedness but did little for the fire in her stomach.

The elevator doors opened and Alana stepped in, touching the button for the tenth floor. She slipped the strap of her purse to her other shoulder and looked above the door, watching as the number for each floor lit up. She had never been in the building before and had never heard Phillip mention the name of the law firm handling his will or even the name of the lawyer. The fact that her husband had chosen a lawyer other than the corporate attorneys or his personal attorney to handle his will was strange. Phillip had always been unpredictable.

The hushed atmosphere of the reception area bespoke elegance and wealth. The view of lush mountains from the window and green plants spaced around the room lent just the right touch of tropical splendor. Calm, sedate, and elegant. The perfect atmosphere for an important law office, one of the most powerful and influential in the state. The executors of Phillip's estate. Alana's knees threatened to buckle. Relax. But who could relax when Phillip Hudson's will was going to be read and no one seemed to know what the manipulating, powerful head of one of the largest holding companies in the States had in mind?

Catching a quick glimpse of herself in the mirrors on the wall opposite the windows, Alana pushed a stray lock of hair from her cheek, wishing she had checked her lipstick. It had not started out to be a good day and had gotten progressively worse. Everything skidded downhill from the time she arrived at the office to a fistful of messages all demanding her immediate attention, a pile of contracts to read and sign, and a shipment of building materials for a new hotel was on the way to Japan instead of Honolulu. She took a quick look at her watch. Damn. She was ten minutes late. A cool, expressionless mask firmly in place, she crossed the room to the receptionist. The expensive brass and glass furnishings in shades of oatmeal, chocolate, and honey impressed her. She paused in front of a walnut desk, the receptionist dressed to compliment the decor in a beige silk dress. No aloha shirts were allowed in this office.

The woman looked up at her with just the right amount of professionalism and friendliness. "May I help you?"

"I'm here to see Willard Sims."

The woman checked her book. "Melanie Hudson?"

Alana lifted her chin. "Mrs. Hudson. Mrs. Phillip Hudson," she answered, a chill in her voice. Mistaking her for Melanie made her skin crawl.

"I'm sorry." Looking flustered, she pushed a button on the console in front of her. "Mr. Sims' secretary will be here in a moment."

It wasn't thirty seconds later that an older version of the receptionist appeared and nodded in Alana's direction. "Mrs. Hudson? Please follow me."

Their footsteps were absorbed by the plush carpeting as they walked down a corridor of closed walnut doors and original art work. When they reached the end of the hall, the secretary knocked softly, opened the door and ushered Alana inside.

Hilary looked up, a cold expression carved on her face. The severe cut of her royal blue suit and stark white blouse made her a formidable opponent, and Alana didn't kid herself. They were opponents. Alana's gaze swept the room. Melanie wasn't here yet. Not much of a surprise. Melanie hadn't been on time to anything as long as Alana had known her. She wondered how long they would have to wait for her to show up.

The office had a magnificent view of Diamond Head. Alana filed the address in her mind for later reference. A prime piece of real estate like this needed good management. She'd have to find out who owned it. Remembering where she was and why she was here, Alana suddenly wished she were out on the water in one of those boats sailing across the turquoise sea instead of here in a law office waiting to hear how Phillip had divided his fortune. Her gaze focused on the portly man standing behind a mammoth oak desk with his back to the wall of windows. He extended a pudgy hand, so she took the necessary steps to finish crossing the room and accepted it. She had to tilt her head down slightly to look him in the eye. "Hello. I'm Alana Hudson." Better clear that up right away, so he didn't make the same mistake his receptionist did.

"Hello, Mrs. Hudson. Willard Sims." His voice held just the right amount of respect and authority as he smiled and gestured to a chair. "Allow me to extend my sympathies at your loss."

"Thank you." Alana wondered just how sympathetic the man would be if he weren't the one handling Phillip's will. As she settled into the chair, she noted the placement. Anyone on this side of the desk had to squint into the bright light pouring into the windows, giving Willard Sims a psychological advantage. Her senses sharpened. She noted the lack of music, making any silence seem uncomfortable. The pungent odor of stale cigar smoke made her wonder if he'd light up after they were all present, another way of dominating the women.

She turned to Hilary. "Hello, Hilary." When Hilary gave her a frosty stare, Alana continued, "It took me longer than I

223

thought to get here from work. I had to find a place to park, and then I had to walk two blocks."

Hilary's classic features and blue eyes reflected a malicious satisfaction. "You should have called me. We could have shared the limo."

Alana gave her a wary look without replying. There was no chance Hilary would share anything with Alana, not even the company limo.

Hilary frowned, absently twirling the three karat diamond on her right hand, turning away from Alana as if she had a dread disease.

Hilary's hatred simmered just beneath the surface, making Alana wonder if she would boil over when the will was read. Or would she have the chance to gloat? Phillip knew how his daughters felt about Alana. She suspected he had actually enjoyed the tension between the three women, possibly even encouraged the hatred. Phillip often manipulated people just to see them squirm.

When Melanie made an entrance several minutes later, Alana was wary, ready for a confrontation with Phillip's youngest daughter, but Melanie barely glanced in her direction. "I'm sorry I was late, but I had a meeting with my assistant that took longer than I anticipated and then traffic was terrible." Her voice was apologetic. "I hope I'm not late."

Melanie gave a slight toss of her head sending her red hair tumbling around her shoulders. Alana wondered how long she had stood in front of a mirror practicing that particular move. Alana's gaze swept over her black and white silk dress, professional yet alluring. Green eyes rimmed in kohl, high cheekbones tinted with blush, lips stained the color of lush strawberries, and ivory earrings all would have looked businesslike on any woman, but on Melanie another dimension was added.

"Father hated it when you were late, Melanie," Hilary muttered.

"He's dead. It doesn't really matter what he thinks anymore." Melanie shrugged and settled into the remaining chair.

"He was your father," Alana said. "You could respect his memory."

"Like he respected my mother's memory by marrying you a month after she died?" Melanie demanded, her voice hard, her eyes glittering.

Willard Sims cleared his throat, wiped the beads of perspiration from his forehead, shuffled through some papers on his desk and said, "Let's begin."

Chapter Sixteen

"Phillip Hudson requested the reading of his will in the presence of the three of you." Willard cleared his throat again, looking at each of the women before he looked down at the papers on his desk and opened one of his desk drawers. "In essence the will is very simple. Phillip wanted a parcel of land that Raine Bradburn owns on Maui. That land is crucial to the resort complex Phillip wanted to build." He paused and adjusted the knot of his burgundy tie. "If Melanie, Hilary, or Alana can prove ownership of the land owned by Raine Bradburn between Maaleaa Bay and Wailea within sixty days of the reading of this will, that person will inherit ninety percent of Phillip's stock in Hudson Enterprises. She will also receive ninety percent of his personal estate. The two remaining women will each receive five percent of the stock and five percent of his personal estate. If none of you own the land in sixty days, you will each receive five percent of Phillip's estate and five percent of his stock. The remaining shares will be sold, all his assets liquidated." He paused. "The money will be used to build and maintain the *Vengeance,* a floating palace Phillip designed to sail around the world seeking exotic pleasure. It will be used by Hudson executives for business entertaining and personal pleasure." The lawyer looked up, scanning the stunned faces before him, putting a tape on the desk and closing the desk drawer. "I know that comes as a surprise to all of you, but Phillip had his reasons for drawing up the will this way. When I finish reading the actual document, I have a video he requested you watch." He cleared his throat and read the complicated document.

Alana was oblivious to the actual words, concentrating on the meaning of what Willard had said. Raine's land. Phillip had been obsessed with that land, but making it the most important stipulation in his will was incomprehensible. If it had been impossible for a man with Phillip's power and tenacity to get it, there wasn't a person alive who could gain title to that land. Hadn't she already tried? The will had erected a steel wall a mile high between Alana and Raine. He'd never believe she knew nothing about this part of Phillip's will, and she wouldn't blame him. Her hopes for a fair share of Hudson Enterprises disappeared as quickly as footsteps in the sand.

A stunned silence settled over the room when Willard Sims finished reading the formal will. He made a neat pile of the papers on his desk then folded his hands over the top of them. He knew Phillip's will was tantamount to igniting a fuse under three kegs of explosives, and he relished the fireworks.

"We should've flushed the bastard's ashes down the toilet," Hilary snarled, her features as harsh as her words. From the tenseness of her jaw to the icy glitter of her eyes, Hilary meant every word she said.

An icy chill slid down Alana's spine, her gaze narrowed, watching the malevolence in her face. Damn, she didn't want to see Melanie or Hilary get their hands on all that money, and if anyone had reason to thwart Phillip's plans, Alana herself had the most reason. Phillip had thrived on conflict, money, and power, determined to control as many lives as possible, so it came as no surprise that even death didn't stop his manipulations. Pitting his daughters against one another and against their hated stepmother was just the kind of thing he would do to prove he held the ultimate power. Alana frowned. Under the circumstances perhaps Hilary's words were the nicest a person could say about Phillip. Why hadn't he given her the stock and divided his personal wealth between his daughters? He knew Alana could run the company. It was what she had been trained to do!

"A boat. A goddamned boat!" Melanie pounded her fist on the arm of the chair. "The son of a bitch will sink millions into a boat and give his own flesh and blood nothing!" Jade eyes glittered with hatred.

"I don't believe it. He wouldn't do this to us. You're lying!" Hilary's voice was shrill as Willard shook his head.

"I have no reason to lie." He tapped the paper on the desk. "It's a signed, legal document."

Hilary gave him a murderous glare. "When the hell did he decide this?"

He leaned back in his chair, picking up a silver pen and tapping it against the opposite palm. "Phillip came to me about a month ago. We discussed possibilities for the disposal of his fortune. He made his demands very clear. I drew up the document and he signed it three weeks ago."

Alana tapped her chin with one finger. "Why would he rush through something as important as his will? We're talking millions of dollars and a major block of stock in a large corporation. Phillip was tough, but even he wouldn't dump his own family on the street without a penny."

"Oh, we'd all have something," Hilary muttered, her gaze raking Alana's face. "Even *you* would have an income, but it doesn't compare to what we would have if it was split between Melanie and me."

Melanie frowned. "Daddy said he was going to leave us without money." She paused. "I'm surprised he meant it."

Alana was silent. It would serve Hilary and Melanie right if she could get that land from Raine. But fat chance! She had told him that he should deal with Robert or Dan, that she didn't want to see him again. Her chances of getting that land were zero.

Hilary rubbed a finger along her jaw. "There must be some mistake, Willard. Our father was a bastard, but even *he* wouldn't do anything like this. It's asinine! I've been involved in the business for years. So has Melanie." Her voice had a cutting edge to it when she said, "He never meant for Alana to have his fortune." She turned arrogant blue eyes in Alana's direction. "There must be a loophole somewhere."

"Please, ladies." Willard interrupted, holding up his hands in a placating gesture.

Alana watched him shuffle his papers again and shift his weight several times before patting his tie three more times. He was grossly overweight, had a florid complexion and a rasping cough. "Phillip Hudson was adamant about this will. He made certain there were no loopholes." He gave all three women a hard look. "There is no way to break this will. You either meet the terms or settle for five percent."

Melanie pointed a condemning finger at Alana. "This never would have happened if you hadn't been his lover. Mother would still be alive and daddy might have been, too."

Hilary focused on Alana, her voice hard, her gaze tough enough to wither a strong man. "We lost our parents and, now, possibly our inheritance because of you!"

Melanie squared her shoulders, her eyes rock hard. "You'll never see one cent of father's money, not if we can prevent it."

Alana's voice was dry as she steeled herself to their accusations. "Raine Bradburn won't sell, so this conversation is pointless. I end up with nothing, so do you." Her look was wry. "Seems to me like we're all in the same boat."

Hilary whirled to look in disgust at Alana, her voice shaking with contempt. "I'd drown before I'd be in the same boat with you."

Melanie's gaze ran contemptuously over Alana's body. "Obviously Phillip wasn't as enamored with you as you thought."

"Unless I get that land from Rain Bradburn." Alana lifted one brow. "I'd have the majority of the stock and Phillip's money." She knew her chances of winning were less than nothing, but she wasn't about to let Phillip's daughters push her around. "When I'm elected permanent CEO, I'll be your boss."

"I'll see you in hell before I'll let you run the company." Melanie said it with such vehemence, Alana shivered. There was a core of steel in Melanie's voice. "I'll stop you, Alana. Any way that I can." Melanie's features were taut. "I'll destroy everything, before I'll let you have it."

Alana met her gaze and held it. "You wouldn't dare destroy the empire your father built."

"Ladies." Willard raised his voice. "Please. I'll play the video now."

No one said a word, as Willard slipped the tape into a player and turned it on. Phillip's image filled the screen. He began to speak. "If you're watching this, I'm dead and my ashes have been scattered over Diamond Head, but if you think you're rid of me, you can put that notion right out of your minds." His eyes were the color of thunder clouds, his voice raspy. Alana waited to have him reach out and grab them. Chills ran up her spine. It was eerie listening to a dead man. "I know I wasn't the best father in the world, but I had a company to run. And now, Hilary and Melanie, you just might find out what it's like to work under pressure where you either succeed or fail. I deliberately made this will so you'd have to work for my money. Melanie, use your brains instead of your body. Stop fooling around with every man in sight long enough to think of a way to get that land. You've got a brain. You can do anything if you set your mind to it. Same goes for you, Hilary. I've seen

231

glimpses of an astute businesswoman in you when you concentrate on work instead of bookies and a bottle. Odds are that neither of you will be able to get that land, but you'll have learned to depend on your own wits instead of my money. Of course, if you invest your percentage wisely, you could live comfortably for the rest of your lives." There was a pause while he shifted position. "And then there's Alana, my wife. Of the three of you, Alana has the most ability to run the company, but I'll be damned if I'll turn over my life's work to someone who sneaks off to meet God knows how many men. Maybe Bradburn was one of them, and you'll be able to get that land, but I doubt it. He won't sell that goddamned land at any price. I had wondered about leaving anything to you, and decided a small percentage was rather like a consolation prize ... consolation for not getting everything you thought you would when you married me." He leaned forward. "Quite honestly, ladies, I thought of giving my entire fortune to the luxury yacht, but Willard persuaded me to leave something to each of you." He sat back and folded his arms over his chest. "You thought you got rid of me when I died. But I intend to haunt all three of you for the rest of your lives." He paused. "How did you like the idea of the boat? Clever, if I do say so myself. *Vengeance.* Has a nice ring to it. Wish I could see your faces right now!" He threw back his head, laughter filling the room before the tape went blank.

The women sat in stunned silence.

Alana was furious. Who the hell did Phillip think he was to manipulate people even after death? She was tempted to refuse to play his silly games, but she wanted control of Hudson Enterprises. She owed it to herself. Controlling Phillip's company would be sweet revenge for the way he tried to control her, for the way he had betrayed her with another woman. God! The man had had no feelings for anyone except himself. "It looks like Phillip has set us all up."

"I'll get that land from Raine Bradburn. No one is going to cheat me out of my inheritance." Hatred, bitterness, and determination made Hilary's voice crack. "I've worked long and hard to take my place on the board of directors. I want that stock *and* the estate."

Alana looked at Willard. "Would we retain our positions with just five percent of the stock?"

He shrugged. "That's up to the share holders. The more stock you own the better your chances."

"And the person with the most proxy votes from absent shareholders gets the most votes," Melanie murmured, and then a sly smile crossed her face as she studied the toe of her ivory shoe. "Of course the bottom line is Raine Bradburn's land."

Alana knew exactly what she was thinking. "Raine Bradburn is just as stubborn as your father was."

"Maybe now that Phillip is gone, he'll change his mind." A cunning look crossed Melanie's face.

"Wishful thinking," Alana muttered.

"Bradburn might be ready to sell," Hilary cut in. "Maybe things aren't so bleak after all." Her voice was spiteful as she turned to Alana. "You'd better start packing. You'll be out of Hudson Enterprises just as soon as I get that land."

Alana tapped a well manicured hand on the arm of her chair, the leather muffling the sound. "It's impossible," Alana finally admitted. "Phillip knew we mortals would never be able to accomplish what the king failed to do."

"I can do it." Hilary's voice hardened, her eyes narrowed.

Alana let out a long breath. That look on Hilary's face was more eloquent than words. She'd let nothing stop her, nothing get in her way.

Melanie looked at Willard. "We could fight it through the courts."

"A waste of time and money," Willard answered, rubbing the bald spot on top of his head.

"You're not the only lawyer in the world," Melanie said, her features grim. "We'll find someone to defend us."

"It would be a costly, lengthy battle," Alana told her. "By the time a decision could be made the deadline would be past. The only winners would be the lawyers."

"I didn't realize you were an attorney, Mrs. Hudson," Willard said, his voice dry.

"It doesn't take a genius to figure that one out," Alana replied, her voice just as dry, meeting his gaze and holding it until he looked away.

Melanie sighed. "Is she right, Willard?"

He shifted in his chair and patted his tie. "Yes. Nothing can change the deadline."

"So, until the sixty days are up, we have our jobs at Hudson," Hilary murmured, frowning. "And we have sixty days to get that land."

"Sixty days before all hell breaks loose." Alana glanced at Willard, seeing the fleeting uncomfortable look cross his face. "He didn't try to tie up our salaries or the stock we own, did he?" she demanded.

When Willard didn't reply, Melanie pushed herself out of the chair, waving a hand through the air. "Daddy was a first class bastard." She picked up her purse and glanced at Willard, her voice bored. "Are we finished with this farce?"

"Not quite. Please sit down." His gaze never quite reached her face as he nodded in the direction of her chair.

She sat down again, and Alana wondered what else Willard could possibly have to say. While he sorted through the papers on his cluttered desk, Alana tilted her head to one side, staring at Melanie. What was it about the woman that turned men's heads? Was it the red hair or the sultry look in her jade eyes? Would Melanie seduce Raine Bradburn into giving her his land? The thought of Raine holding Melanie, making love to her, was like a hand squeezing her heart.

She looked out the great expanse of glass to watch a lone sailboat dip and glide through the turquoise wave. She wished she was out on that boat sailing with Raine, no cares, no worries. It was a lovely fantasy.

Willard cleared his throat, pulling her back to reality. He took a deep breath, looking at each of them. "You must purchase the land specifically mentioned in the will and owned by Raine Bradburn. Nothing less than legal ownership will do."

Hilary shook her head. "Sixty days is ludicrous! How the hell are we supposed to get that land in two months when Phillip couldn't buy, steal, or destroy it?" She jumped to her feet, leaning both arms on the edge of the huge mahogany desk and bent forward, her chin jutting out as she glared at Willard. "How could you agree to set something like this up?" she demanded. "You had to know it couldn't be done."

A deep flush crept from Willard's neck into his face. "Don't threaten me," he said, his voice clipped. "It doesn't make any difference what your father had in mind. It was *his* stock and *his* money." His mouth snapped shut. "My first responsibility is to my client, and that is your father, even in death. I'm doing as he instructed. And for your information, I did try to talk him out of the boat, but it didn't do any good. He never took 'no' for an answer."

Alana made a strangled sound before covering it with a cough. She could just imagine Willard trying to stand up to Phillip. It was no contest.

"Willard, do you know why Phillip would want to set something like this up?" Alana asked gently, her composure firmly in place.

He rubbed his temple with his thumb before leaning back in his chair, a frown drawing his brows together. "I'm not really sure of his motives. He talked about wanting his children to work for his money and what a disappointment his marriage had turned out to be. He was bitter and angry when he came

235

in here." He paused. "The idea of putting all his money into a super yacht seemed to give him perverse pleasure. If he couldn't have what he wanted, he didn't want any of you to have what you wanted, namely his stock and his money."

"Will the company be in trouble if his stock is sold?" Melanie asked.

"No," Willard said. "But it will mean someone else will have the majority of the stock and controlling interest in the company."

"The company won't fold," Alana said with a frown. "We might be working for someone else though."

"That's possible." Willard nodded his head. "Hudson stock is valuable. The company has a good track record. There are quite a few large conglomerates that would like to acquire Hudson Enterprises."

Hilary groaned. "I wonder what other surprises are in store for us."

Melanie gave an unladylike snort. "The biggest surprise of all would be if any of us got that land from a man who hated Phillip as much as Phillip hated him."

Alana was realistic. As much as she wanted the stock that would assure her the position of CEO of Hudson Enterprises, she knew it would be impossible to accomplish because of the time limitations and the feud between Phillip and Raine. Phillip had placed her in a no win situation. Had he known about the attraction between his wife and his enemy? The terms of the will would suggest that he did. If she agreed to see Raine and disclosed the terms of the will, he'd either use the land as blackmail to get her into his bed or he'd doubt that she cared about him, just what his land could give to her. Either way it would destroy any chance for a real relationship. If she didn't see him and didn't make an offer on the land, Melanie and Hilary certainly would, gaining an advantage they would use against her. How was she going to approach him? What could she possibly say to convince him that their personal relationship had nothing to do with obtaining the land? She took a deep breath and exhaled slowly. Phillip had intertwined the land and Hudson Enterprises so thoroughly that it would be a miracle if they all came through this intact. It seemed like Phillip had won again. He controlled Melanie, Hilary, and Alana from the grave, at least for another two months. God only knew what else he had planned.

"We'll be back, Willard, in sixty days with or without a signed contract." Melanie stood and smoothed her skirt.

Hilary lifted her chin. "*I'll* be back in sixty days with the deed."

Willard leaned forward. "I must warn you, Phillip tried hard to make it an impossible task." He paused, tapping a pencil on his copy of the will. "Without the deed, the new chief executive officer of Hudson Enterprises will be the person who buys Phillip Hudson's stock."

Willard sat back in his chair, puffing contentedly on a cigar. He was glad the reading of Phillip Hudson's will was completed. In sixty days the three women would return without the land and he would have to draw up the final papers. Phillip had told him it was an impossible stipulation, and the women had reinforced that feeling. Even after talking to Phillip for hours as they worked on the will, Willard still didn't understand his motivation. He was disappointed in his daughters, and he had refused to even mention his grandson, but he was the most bitter about his marriage. It hadn't been everything he had thought it would be. Were those valid reasons for setting your family up for failure?

Chapter Seventeen

Hilary and Melanie stormed out of Willard's office, leaving Alana behind. Hilary's face was flushed, her hands curled into fists at her sides. Her father had said that he was writing his daughters out of his will, but she hadn't really believed him. And he hadn't written them out completely. They would get a small share even if they didn't get Raine Bradburn's land, but it was nothing compared to the lion's share of the estate. She couldn't understand why her father would give so much power to his worst enemy?

When she was alone in the elevator with Melanie, Hilary muttered, "We have to talk."

Melanie nodded. "It's going to take some time understanding why father made such a will. Do you think he really meant what he said? Did he really think we could get that land?"

"I don't know," Hilary said with a sigh. "I thought he would at least mention Mitch, but he didn't. It was as if he didn't even have a grandchild."

"I don't think he liked the idea of being a grandfather all those years." Melanie watched the numbers light up as they went down to the lobby. "It made him feel old."

"But that's no reason to leave Mitch out of his will!" Hilary shook her head. "That really hurt."

"Not as much as it'll hurt if we don't get that land." Melanie stepped out of the elevator. "I'll meet you at the outdoor bar at the Royal Hawaiian."

"Fine." Hilary strode out of the office building and got into the waiting limousine. It wasn't fair! She deserved her father's money, not the woman he was married to for six months, not that she had any more of a chance of getting that land. Hilary didn't want to share five cents with the woman who had taken her father away from her. She reached for the crystal decanter and remembered her father's words. She replaced it and sat back. There was one thing she could do to ease the tension. She grabbed the telephone. "Jimmy! I want to place a bet. . . ."

Melanie looked up at the pink facade of the Royal Hawaiian Hotel. She liked the stately beauty of the old hotel, relaxing as she sauntered through the well kept gardens. Coconut palms and banyon trees that had offered shade to Hawaiian royalty more than a hundred years ago still rustled in the trade winds. A brilliant profusion of ginger, bird of paradise, and anthurium, as well as yellow, crimson, and purple hibiscus added color to the gardens. Melanie inhaled the fragrant air and stepped into the cool, elegant lobby of the hotel. The Spanish style of stucco arches and tile floors combined with the tropical plants and high ceilings to give a feeling of old world elegance. She looked in several display cases before stepping down into the oceanside bar. Thatched roofs protected the patrons from the hot sun while allowing them to relax in the open air and enjoy the view of the water, surfers, and sun worshipers. Melanie slipped onto the rattan chair and sipped the mai tai Hilary had ordered for her. "These can be lethal," she murmured, settling back and looking at her sister.

"We need something lethal after that visit to Willard Sims' office." Hilary leaned forward. "I can't believe father set up that will."

"Do you suppose we could find a lawyer who could prove he was incompetent when he signed it?" Melanie's gaze narrowed as she stared sightlessly at the azure sky and turquoise ocean. "It would be easier than trying to pry that land from Raine Bradburn."

Hilary shook her head. "It would take too long. While we would be fighting the will, Alana would be trying to get that land." She brushed a strand of hair from her cheek.

"God! I hate that woman!" Melanie's eyes sparked. "If it weren't for her, mother would be alive right now, and we wouldn't have to fight for what is rightfully ours." She wouldn't have minded sharing the Hudson fortune with her sister, but she refused to share it with the woman her father had married. "Father might even be alive if it weren't for Alana."

Hilary sighed. "Our lives would have been so much simpler without Alana."

"The fact remains. She's a part of our lives right now." Melanie closed her eyes. Her mother and father would have been alive if it weren't for her stepmother. She clenched her hands in fists.

"Father paid for his sins," Hilary murmured, her glass to her lips. "Now we have to make certain that Alana doesn't get her hands on the lion's share of his estate."

Melanie opened her eyes and nodded, controlling her anger. "Do you think she might have a chance with Raine?"

"Yes." Hilary's mouth thinned. "I saw them together at Lee Taka's unveiling of his new resort complex. It looked like they were having a rather heated discussion. Then they disappeared. I saw Raine later on and he was alone."

"Do you think they're having an affair?" Melanie asked, eating her pineapple spear.

Hilary shrugged. "She always seems to be so straight, I doubt it, but maybe Arty could follow her and see if she meets him or anyone else."

"It would certainly give her a better shot at getting that land." Melanie rested her chin in the palm of her hand.

"Maybe not." Hilary had a thoughtful look on her face. "It might make it more difficult for her. How would you like to barter your body for rock and sand?"

Melanie grimaced. "No thanks. It's much better with no strings attached."

Hilary grinned. "Exactly. There's a big string attached to this rock."

Melanie chuckled. Hilary could be right. She had been worried about a relationship between Alana and Raine. She had seen the look in Raine's eyes at the club when he had argued with Phillip and Alana had approached them. She had seen that look in many men's eyes. He was definitely interested in Alana. "So we've got as much chance of getting that land as Alana does." She looked at her sister. "What are you going to offer him?"

"I'm not sure yet." She looked at Melanie. "What about you?"

Melanie wasn't about to tell anyone what she was going to do. Obviously, Hilary wasn't either. "I haven't had enough time to figure something out." Melanie finished her drink. "Perhaps there's a way we could get some of the money out of the company before the deadline. You're in finance. Is there any way we could do that?"

Hilary was silent for a moment. "Let me check into it."

Melanie stood up, smoothing her skirt. She had plans to make. She had considered asking Hilary to combine forces to try to get the land, but had decided against it. Hilary might not agree with her methods, and besides, she wanted the company for herself. "Let me know if you come up with anything." She turned and walked away.

Alana marched back to her car, her heels a sharp staccato on the cement, her mind as snarled as the traffic, her temper as blistering as the tropical sun. How could Phillip have done such a stupid thing! Threatening them with the notion of putting millions of dollars into a boat was the craziest thing he had ever done. Her lips thinned, her fists clenched. Phillip had manipulated her for the last time! She wanted Hudson Enterprises just to prove Phillip wrong. She reached her car and jammed the key into the lock.

Alana paused. There had to be other options. Automatically she headed in the direction of the yacht club. Congratulating herself on find a parking place so easily, she hurried toward the heavy oak door and pushed her key card into the slot before slipping inside.

She was furious with Phillip, and yet because he was dead, she couldn't release that anger, or try to reason with him, or even argue her point of view. He was in control, even after death. It was so frustrating! And she was angry with Raine Bradburn for being so stubborn that he wouldn't sell that damned land. All this ... this disgusting matter could have been avoided if Raine had sold the land to Phillip. She squared her shoulders. What was done, was done. She wanted that company out of pride. Phillip had issued a challenge and she would accept it. Now she had to find a way to persuade Raine to sell that damn land to her.

Smoothing her skirt, she walked through the club, her gaze quickly scanning the deserted lounge and the busy docks. Birds searched for crumbs, avoiding the feet of sailors sauntering through the lounge. In the center of the lounge was a pool of clear water fed by an overflowing cupid's urn. Wild orchids, brilliant bougainvillea, plumeria, and ginger surrounded the fountain, the fragrance a constant reminder of paradise. The bar inside was empty except for the wife of one of the richest men in the islands. Even though it was only noon, her eyes were mere slits in a heavily made up face, her speech slightly slurred, not a hair on her bleached head out of place. Alana moved to the opposite end of the bar and slid onto a stool, resting her elbows on the padded railing, her chin propped on her hands as she stared out over docks. The snack bar on the patio was busy. It was Friday. Aloha day. No one worked Friday afternoon. Bronzed, well-muscled young men who couldn't afford a canoe talked earnestly to older men who owned the world class yachts they all sailed on. Maybe she should forget this whole damned business and race tomorrow. The boat was ready even though she hadn't been on it since Phillip's death.

"What would you like, Mrs. Hudson?" Hal asked with a smile as he washed glasses.

"Scotch on the rocks."

One dark brow lifted. "Bad day?"

"Hmmm," she muttered, not elaborating. When the drink was put in front of her, she took a sip then followed it with a long swallow.

Her gaze wandered back over the colorful docks, busy with activity. Sails, splotches of brilliant color against the blue of water and sky, were strewn about as crewmen repaired and rebagged them. Two men dangled from bos'n chairs at the top of eighty foot masts adjusting rigging and yelling instructions to the men below. Men and women scurried back and forth from the parking lot to the docks, looking like ants going to a picnic as they carried grocery bags and coolers, supplies for a race starting that evening. Alana sighed as she took another sip. Life was so complicated. How much easier it would have been if Phillip had just given his children the money and given her the security of a job.

Her gaze focused on the forty-five foot black sloop tied to the dock nearest the club. Raine's yacht. Her eyes narrowed. The only person visible was Raine. She wanted to run to him, seeking sanctuary in the warmth of his embrace, but she couldn't, not now. Phillip had seen to that. And she had aided Phillip by telling Raine to talk to someone else in the firm regarding the land. She had told him she didn't want a personal or professional relationship with him. How was she going to explain her renewed interest?

He was in the cockpit fiddling with the electronics. Sure, he could go racing and enjoy himself, she thought with unusual bitterness. He wasn't in another person's power the way she still was in Phillip's. She drained the glass and zeroed in on the one thing she had to have. Raine's land. How would she ever convince him that the land was business and had nothing to do with their personal relationship when she didn't believe it herself.

Slowly getting to her feet, she closed her eyes for a moment before signing the tab. The dizziness passed. Squaring her shoulders, she strolled through the door and headed for the sleek black boat, nodding and smiling to people she knew as if nothing important were on her mind. She stopped to chat with several sailors, discussing wind and wave conditions, while her mind was focused on Raine Bradburn. The intense heat of the tropical sun made her head pound and scorched her back and shoulders through the fabric of her suit. She put her sun glasses on, took off her jacket and dropped it and her purse on a white wrought iron table and strolled toward the dock. Her air of nonchalance covered the knot in her stomach.

Raine was bent over the instruments, giving her ample time to assess him. Stripped to skimpy black swim trunks, his six foot frame was covered with a sheen of perspiration, his skin glowing like well oiled teak. Her gaze scanned his broad shoulders, the muscles flexing and relaxing smoothly underneath that bronzed skin. Powerful thighs were braced as he adjusted a dial. Her breath quickened as she remembered the feel of those legs, the touch of those fingers, the strength of those arms. She cleared her throat. His head remained bent, the sun absorbed into his dark head. Her hands tingled as she remember the feel of his hair on her fingers.

"Raine, could I talk to you for a few minutes?" She chided herself. She sounded like a nervous teenager instead of an executive of Hudson Enterprises. She had to remember her reason for approaching him. Business, not pleasure.

He grunted, turned a final screw and looked, dark eyes widening, his voice dry. "Why Mrs. Hudson. What a surprise to see you here." His voice was deep and resonant, sending a chill down Alana's spine. "Ah," he said, his eyes narrowing. "The reading of the will was today."

Alana frowned, thrown off by his knowledge of the reading of the will. It seemed like the press wasn't alone in being well informed. "How did you know that?"

"I know lots of things." He leaned back in the cockpit, stretching his arms over his head.

Alana watched the play of muscles in his shoulders, chest, and arms. She forced her mind back to business. Where was he getting his information? Hilary? Not likely. Melanie? A possibility. Someone on the board? The press? She tilted her head to one side, taking a guess and hoping she was wrong. "You probably know as much about the company as I do."

"Probably." His gaze was insolent, making her feel like an insect under a microscope as he examined her carefully from the tips of her Gucci heels to the top of her ebony hair. His attitude had changed since their meeting that morning. It threw her off until she realized why. Raine knew Alana needed his land. "So what do you want to talk to me about?"

Alana's hands settled on her hips, her stance aggressive. He wanted to play games. "Since you're so well informed, you know exactly what I want to talk about."

Reluctant admiration flashed in his eyes. He cocked his head, his gaze steady, regarding her intently for long seconds. "Do you have any other clothes here?"

Startled and wary, she answered slowly, "Why?"

"You're overdressed for sailing." His gaze raked over her again, settling on the thin material covering her breasts. "And other things as well."

She was sure he could see her nipples hardened, but she refused to give him the satisfaction of seeing her squirm under his scrutiny. "Sailing and sex aren't on my calendar today, business is," she replied sharply.

He chuckled softly. "I need to swing this compass before the race tonight. I don't want to talk business until that's corrected." He smiled with a flash of white teeth against tanned skin.

"What's the matter? Isn't it calibrated?" she mocked softly.

"We were hit with a rogue wave in a race last week," he explained. "I don't want to go out on the ocean at midnight with a compass that's off." He leaned down to pick up a small screw driver. "If you want to talk, you'll have to come with me. If not, that's your problem." Before Alana could say anything, Raine disappeared below, leaving her open mouthed.

She whipped around, prepared to stalk off, but when she saw the avid curiosity of so many people, she thought better of it. Picking up her jacket and purse, she sauntered back toward the club. Let them try to figure out what was going on. *She* wasn't going to give them the satisfaction of seeing her embarrassed by Raine. What had happened to the gentle lover? His land and Phillip's will, she thought with regret.

* * *

Alana stepped lightly from the dock to Raine's boat.

"You didn't ask permission to come aboard," a deep voice teased from the cabin. Raine was surprised she had returned. He had purposely been nasty to her. He knew exactly what she wanted from him and it hurt his ego to know the only reason she approached him was because of his land.

"I thought we knew each other well enough to dispense with formalities," she answered, her voice dry.

"You do have a point there. We do know each other well, don't we?" His head appeared in the hatch, his gaze burning a trail from her flip flops up the length of her legs and over her shorts and faded White Sox T-shirt. He wondered what she wore underneath, hoping to discover that for himself. "But perhaps not quite well enough."

"I'd like to keep this strictly business," she said firmly.

"By all means," he answered, thinking that it might be best for both of them, but knowing it was impossible. "Ever calibrate a compass before?"

Her head snapped up. "What do you think?" she returned, her hands on her hips.

"Ah, yes. You were Hudson's right-hand . . . man. He couldn't win a race against an outrigger canoe without you on board. Even after beating you up, he managed to convince you to race with him." He climbed another step, searching her face. What kind of hold had Hudson had over her? Why would an otherwise intelligent woman agree to such a thing?

"We compromised," she said quietly. "I agreed to sail with Phillip for that last race, and he agreed not to contest the divorce." She held his gaze. "I had moved back into my apartment. I was going to file for divorce on Monday."

"But he died." Raine's gaze darkened, his voice clipped. "How convenient." Was it possible she might have killed Phillip? He pushed the thought out of his mind.

The color drained from her face. "Maybe this wasn't such a good idea," she said coldly, turning to leave.

He couldn't let her go. He blocked her path, smiling down at her, a wry look on his face. "I'm sorry. I'll try to behave like a gentleman, but it's difficult when I look at you." What had happened to his iron control?

Alana relented. "Okay. Let's get this yacht out on the water. We've attracted enough attention for one day."

He stepped out into the cockpit and glanced around, pulling his sunglasses from the top of his head and pushing them over his eyes. "This should keep the gossips busy for hours."

Alana cast off lines as Raine maneuvered the yacht out of the slip, jumping on board at the last moment. Coiling the lines, she kept her head averted. His gaze softened as he looked at her. She was everything a man could want. She was beautiful, intelligent, kind, gentle, and caring. He wished . . . he stopped himself. She was also the widow of Phillip Hudson.

As they slowly moved about the harbor, Raine barked out orders and Alana automatically did as he said, handling the yacht with ease. The boat responded to her every touch. He was impressed. After another adjustment, Alana swung the boat around to face Diamond Head. "Raine, how long did it take to have *Black Jack* built?"

"Thinking of having one built just like it so you can try to beat me?" he mocked, looking over his shoulder at her.

She grinned wickedly. "Now that's an idea. I'd better warn you that I'm an excellent sailor."

"Distracting to the competition as well," he murmured, his gaze on her long legs, his fingers itching to touch her.

She chuckled, "Not very distracting when most of the navigating is done from below."

"Did you sail with Phillip often?" he asked, watching her closely. He felt a stab of jealously at the thought of Alana and Phillip together.

She nodded. "He insisted. I'm not sure if it was because I'm a good navigator of if he just wanted to keep an eye on me." A deep sigh escaped her lips. "At least it's one thing I don't have to think about any more."

"Bring the boat about," Raine said, never taking his eyes off of Alana. "You're a strong woman. I can't figure out why you allowed him to dominate you like that? My God, he even beat you." The thought renewed his hatred for Phillip.

Alana's shoulders squared, her voice sharp. "Only once, and you're the only person who knows exactly what happened." She paused. "If people found out about our plans to divorce, they'd react just like you did. They'd suspect me of killing him. His death was too convenient." Her mouth turned down at the corners. "Even in death he's still manipulating me."

He looked at her for another moment then returned to his work. "Come about again," he commanded.

Alana turned the big wheel.

Raine finished what he was doing. It was a strange feeling being close to a woman he thought he knew, while realizing he didn't know her at all. It had never mattered before, but Alana was different. He wanted to know everything about her. He moved around the yacht, hoisting the mainsail and then returning to the cockpit to trim it in.

"We've got time for a little sail," he said, shaking his head when she offered him the wheel. "You're doing fine." He settled back to watch her as she guided the boat out of the harbor and then pointed the bow toward Diamond Head. What was it about her that intrigued him? He knew other women who were just as beautiful, just as intelligent. Some were expert lovers. Why was Alana different from all the other women who had moved through his life?

She threw back her head and smiled.

Rained didn't understand it, but he realized Alana felt the same sense of freedom and challenge when sailing that he did.

He'd like to race against her. It would be a challenge. She scared him. She could be dangerous.

"Have you decided whether I have horns or not?" she mocked, bringing him out of his thoughts.

He grinned. "I was wondering . . ."

Her laughter surprised him. "I was wondering the same thing about you."

"And?" he said.

She tilted her head as she turned the wheel, heading into the waves, "I haven't decided yet."

"Me either." He crossed his arms over the wide expanse of his chest, his gaze drawn to her delectable body. He was restless. He felt the stirring of desire. He wanted to make love to her, feel her body molded to his. Raine stood up and stretched, forcing his mind to focus on the sails instead of Alana.

Alana said in a quiet voice, "Raine, we need to talk." She took a deep breath. "You already know the will was read today. I don't know if you discovered the contents of it or not." When he didn't acknowledge the remark either way, she continued, "Phillip wanted the land you own on Maui so badly that he made it a stipulation in his will." She glanced at him. "I want to buy that land from you, Raine. Name your price."

He was silent for a long time, giving nothing away. He didn't give a damn about the land or Phillip Hudson or the future of Hudson Enterprises, but he did need to work through the feelings Alana stirred in him. When he finally spoke, he knew he might be destroying any chance for a lasting relationship, but he had to try.

"I want you."

Chapter Eighteen

Melanie stood under a palm tree, her heels sinking into the soft earth. She had come to the yacht club after leaving Hilary and saw Alana on Raine's boat. Quickly calling Arty and telling him to meet her on Magic Island, she had hurried out to the point of land, watching the boat through binoculars. She tensed as she looked through the binoculars, her mouth grim. Alana wasn't wasting any time getting to Raine to make a deal for his land. "Go ahead," she murmured. "Give it your best shot, because you won't win."

Arty came up behind her dressed in purple shorts and a black and white flowered shirt. A fishing hat was perched on top of his head. "What was so important?" he asked, taking off his hat and wiping his forehead with a red print handkerchief.

Melanie handed the glasses to him. "Take a look, Arty."

He held the glasses to his face. "I told you, Ms. Hudson. I can't find anything on her, and what difference does it make now if she has a different lover every night? She's a rich widow." He adjusted the binoculars. "I wouldn't mind being invited into her bed myself."

"Arty! You work for me, remember? You even think about going to bed with her and you'll be sorry." Melanie was on her guard.

"Don't worry," he muttered.

"So what are we going to do now?" she asked, taking the glasses from him.

"Bradburn might be the key."

Melanie shot him a quick look. "What do you have on him?"

"When he was twenty, Phillip had him arrested for harassing him. Evidently his father was an accountant for your father. Seems like Bradburn's father found some illegal bookkeeping. Your father had him fired and assured he'd never work again. Broke the man's spirit. He died a couple of years later, when Raine was in college."

Melanie was thoughtful. "That explains why Raine hated him. No wonder he wouldn't sell his land to father."

"And maybe that's why he's sailing with your father's widow. Maybe he knocked off your father and now he's going to get Hudson's wife as well." He crossed his arms over his chest. "He's got the power and money to pull it off."

"Not if we do something about it." She paused and put the glasses to her eyes. "What do you suppose they're talking about?"

"The land." Arty rubbed the back of his neck. "Nothing else is important now. What's next?"

The boat was almost out of sight. Arty had given her an idea. If she couldn't get the land from Raine, perhaps she could guarantee that no one else would either. And she just might be able to take care of Alana in the process. "I want you to follow my stepmother. I want to know what she's doing, who she sees. Report to me every evening." She lowered the glasses, her gaze on the horizon. "My father paid for killing my mother. Now, it's Alana's turn and maybe Raine can help."

"What are you talking about?" he muttered, looking up at her, a speculative gaze in her eyes.

"All in good time, Arty. All in good time."

Hilary had followed Melanie to the yacht club, curious to see what her sister's first move would be. By the time she found a place to park, Melanie had disappeared, so Hilary settled onto a bar stool and had a drink. Her gaze narrowed on Alana walking toward Raine Bradburn's boat. Alana was dressed for sailing.

Hurrying to get a better view, Hilary entered the lounge and sat down, wondering how Alana had managed to get to Raine so quickly. She wished she knew what they were talking about. The land, of course, she thought dryly. Nothing else mattered.

When the boat pulled away from the dock, Hilary moved outside for a better view. Maybe they were lovers, although the expressions on their faces had been anything but friendly.

"Hilary!" Muffy Henderson waddled up to Hilary, her voluminous red and white muumuu stretched over her generous body. Her blue hair was piled on top of her head and ten karats of diamonds twinkled from her chubby fingers. "How are you, darling? I was so sorry to hear about your father."

Turning to the older woman, Hilary nodded. "I'm fine." Her gaze returned to the black boat.

"It didn't take her long to find another sugar daddy, did it?" Muffy said in a low voice.

"She worked for my father," Hilary said in a cold voice. What she thought privately was one thing, but she didn't want others to think the same thing.

"And then she married him." The woman shook her head, her chins wobbling. "So soon after your dear mother's death, too. It just wasn't right."

Hilary agreed with her, but wasn't going to say so.

"Do you think she might have . . . well, you know . . . encouraged the heart attack?" Muffy's hands fluttered. "I mean, she was so much younger than your father ... and now, here she is, out with Raine Bradburn." She sighed. "Now there is a real man. If I were younger, I'd go after him myself."

Hilary stiffened. How many other people felt the same way? Maybe she could make the rumors work for her. Muffy was better than an ad in the newspaper. She forced herself to relax. If she could discredit Alana, Raine might be willing to sell to Hilary. If not, at least she could assure that Alana wouldn't win. "Yes, he is quite a man," Hilary finally said. "I suppose there's always the possibility Alana planned everything."

Muffy leaned forward, her eyes gleaming. "You think so?"

"Why not? Like you said, she was much younger than my father. She knew he had a heart condition. Maybe she encouraged him to race when he should have been taking it easy. He had been under a lot of stress lately." Hilary looked at the other woman, an innocent look on her face. "Do you think the stress of trying to keep up with a younger woman could have contributed to the attack?"

"Oh, I'm sure!" Muffy patted her hair with one hand. "She probably was just too demanding for him. She should have taken better care of him."

"Unless she was after Raine Bradburn all the time. Maybe they planned this together." Hilary was enjoying the conversation now. Muffy was taking in every word. "Raine hated my father. Perhaps this was his way of getting even with him. Have him marry a younger woman, kill him, and then take his widow. What do you think?" Hilary had to hide a smile at Muffy's enthusiasm.

"Oh, yes! It certainly looks that way, doesn't it? Look at them out on Raine's boat, having a good time while she should be in mourning for your father." Muffy paused, lowering her voice. "You don't think they had anything to do with your mother's tragic accident, do you?"

Pain etched Hilary's face. It was a thought that hadn't occurred to her. "I don't know," she said softly. "If Alana was desperate enough to get her hands on my father's millions, I suppose anything is possible."

"I've heard of women like that. They marry wealthy men and then the men die, leaving everything to their widows."

For the first time, Hilary was glad her father had set up his will the way he had. At least Alana wouldn't get it all . . . unless she got Raine's land. Hilary vowed to get that land and see Alana humiliated in the process. "I've got to go, Muffy. It's been nice talking to you." She allowed herself a slight smile as Muffy plodded off in the opposite direction, eager to spread the speculation about Alana's part in Phillip's death.

Alana gripped the wheel so tightly it felt as if her hands were welded to it.

"Don't do this to me."

"Why not? It's the perfect solution," he answered, still in that relaxed position while his gaze remained hidden behind sunglasses.

Alana was grateful for his sunglasses as well as hers. Seeing the mockery in his eyes, so evident behind the silkiness of his voice, would have been her undoing. Her gaze shifted to the large sail, automatically turning the wheel slightly to adjust for a shift in the wind. Was he serious or was he baiting her? She had given herself freely to him once, but now he wanted to buy her body. Her heart caught in her throat. Her body in exchange for rock and dirt! A knot formed in her stomach and it had nothing to do with the motion of the yacht. It would become like her relationship with Phillip. What she had given freely turned into duty. Sex without feeling. She had made that mistake once. Hadn't she learned her lesson? "I can't believe you'd sell the land in exchange for a night with me." The harsh sound of her voice lashed out at him.

Deep laughter mocked her scorn. "Christ, no. You're good, Alana, but that land is worth more than one night with you."

"Bastard," she muttered between clenched teeth. "You're no better than Phillip!"

"Don't ever compare me to Phillip Hudson," he warned, his voice turning harsh. "I know you need that land to control Hudson Enterprises. But I wonder if you are desperate enough to sell your soul for it."

"I want to run the company, and I'm capable of doing so, but I'll be damned if you or any other man will use me or own me ever again!" She bristled at his cynicism. As they approached a lagoon, Alana watched Raine move to take down the sails and drop the anchor, a wary look on her face. Her voice was mocking when she said, "Besides my irresistible body, what else do you want for the land?"

"Ten percent of Hudson stock and your services for as long as I want them. Anytime I want them. And any way." In one quick movement he was behind her, his body inches from hers. He ran his hands down the sides of her body, grasping the edge of her T-shirt and pulling it up over her head. He tossed it aside.

The heat from the sun was nothing compared to the flame licking her nerve endings. A lean finger traced a line from her neck to her shoulder and down her arm to the fingers clenched around the wheel. He slowly pulled the bow of her bikini. The scrap of material joined her T-shit. His lips touched her shoulder, his hands sliding around to cover both breasts, his thumbs rubbing the sensitive tips. He pulled her back against him, making her feel the extent of his desire. His hand caressed her stomach, slipping under the waistband of her shorts, seeking the source of her pleasure. She groaned.

Speech was impossible. He knew exactly what he was doing to both of them, His bare chest against her back, one hand teasing her breasts while the other coaxed a response from her eager body. She fought against succumbing to the pleasure of his touch even as her body leaned into his caress.

She closed her eyes, knowing her nipples were puckered with desire, eager for his touch.

One hand made lazy circles down her spine, reaching her shorts and easing them over her hips.

"Someone will see us," she murmured against his lips.

His tongue slipped between her teeth, drinking as if to quench an unending thirst. "There aren't any boats in this cove."

Alana ran her hands over his chest. "I'll get sun burned."

"I'll cover you with my body." He tugged off her bikini bottom, his hands cupping her buttocks.

Her lips explored his chest, her tongue circling his male nipples. She smiled as he gasped.

He trailed kisses down the length of her body, his hands never stopping. He picked her up and gently laid her on the cushions. Raine knelt beside her, passion in his eyes, his voice, his touch. "I want you, Alana. Any way I can have you."

She was silent. Raine's eyes narrowed. "I told you I love a challenge." His mouth fastened on a nipple, tugging and sucking until Alana squirmed with need.

Raine's tongue left a moist trail between her breasts and over her belly. He pushed her thighs apart, nipping at the sensitive skin before his tongue probed deeper, sending a shudder through her body before she arched and groaned. "Oh, God. Take me, Raine!" Another shudder raked her body. "Please!"

He lifted her hips with his hands, continuing his ministrations as Alana writhed beneath him. Consumed by need, Alana gripped his shoulders.

"You don't play fair." Her voice was breathless, her eyes heavy with desire. Her fingers tangled in the hair on his chest. "Please, Raine. Make love to me."

"I thought you'd never ask," he muttered, quickly stripping off his swim trunks and lowering himself onto her, entering her eager body. He moved slowly, rhythmically, as she wrapped her legs around his body. His tongue outlined her ear, his whispered words increasing her need as one hand covered her breast and the other urged her toward him.

His rhythm quickened and she matched his movements, her hands moving over his back. His mouth found hers, fusing their bodies from head to hip.

She moaned from deep in her throat, locked in a mindless, fierce desire. All she wanted and needed was in her arms. Together they rode the crest of a gigantic wave, soaring ever higher, a tangle of limbs and breathless intimacy, until they reached the crest before gliding back to earth.

Melanie met Fred Henderson in the parking lot of the club. Fred was in his mid-fifties, six feet tall, classic features that aged well, grey wavy hair that gave him a distinguished look, and the body of a man half his age. He was a world class sailor and marathon runner. He had moved to the islands years ago after making a fortune building and leasing shopping centers.

"Hi, Melanie." Fred stopped to talk.

"Hi, Fred." Melanie didn't feel like talking. "How's Muffy?"

"Fat and sassy." He pulled off his sunglasses and let them dangle from the cord around his neck. His gaze was openly admiring. He leaned against his black Ferrari. "You have my sympathies regarding your father."

"Thanks." Melanie began to move away and then stopped. She was discontented and frustrated. Charles was gone and Chad was on Maui for the weekend. Fred might be interested. She took off her sunglasses and twirled them between her fingers. She looked at Fred through lowered lashes. "With both my mother and father gone, I feel so alone." She waited for his answer, so she'd know how to proceed.

"I know what you mean." His gaze rested on the thrust of

her breasts. "Muffy is playing bridge all afternoon. I just dropped her off." He nodded in the direction of the club.

Melanie's heart quickened in anticipation. "What are you going to do this afternoon?"

Fred was silent for a moment. "It's awfully hot. Maybe go for a swim."

Melanie looked around then smiled. "I have a pool. Why don't you come home with me?"

"I don't have a suit," he murmured, watching her carefully.

"It won't be a problem." She looked up at him, the invitation in her eyes.

He accepted the invitation. "Separate cars?"

"That would be best." She pulled her keys from her purse. "I'll meet you there." She glanced at him over her shoulder and hurried to her car.

She had just stripped off her clothes and put on a string bikini when she heard the housekeeper answer the door. Melanie sauntered into the living room and smiled at the desire in Fred's eyes. "Come on out to the pool." She dismissed her housekeeper and led Fred outside.

When they were alone, she turned to him. "Something to drink?"

"A beer." He didn't take his gaze from her body.

She motioned toward a lounge. "Relax." Melanie felt the tension building in her body. This was the perfect way to forget her father and her stepmother. She poured a glass of beer for Fred and took it to him, leaning over his chair, her breasts inches from his face.

His hands curled around her neck, pulling Melanie closer, his lips seeking hers while his fingers untied her bikini. He tilted his head back.

Melanie placed a hand on either arm of the lounge.

Fred's hands cupped her full breasts, his thumbs playing with her taut peaks. "Why me, Melanie?"

"Why not?" she murmured in a husky voice.

His mouth touched first one breast and then the other, giving her infinite pleasure. She threw her head back, giving herself up to the sensation he created as he caressed and kissed her.

She ran her hand through his thick hair, lowering her head under their lips met hungrily. She explored the rich interior of his mouth before he pulled away, his lips leaving a moist trail over her shoulders.

Passion flared. His mouth moved over her stomach.

Melanie stood up, watching him through heavy lids. Slowly she untied her bikini bottom, letting it fall to the ground, delighting in the heat of Fred's gaze.

He stood and slipped out of his shorts and shirt, taking Melanie into his arms and kissing her.

She ran her hands over his shoulders and back. He was fit and trim. She vaguely wondered how such a vital man made love to a woman like Muffy. Melanie leaned into his embrace, feeling his desire. The sun was warm on her head and back, Fred's body radiating warmth wherever he touched her. The sounds of rapid breathing touched her ears.

Fred pushed her gently back onto the lounge, covering her with his body. His hands and mouth moved expertly over her, bringing her to a fevered need for release. The moment of climax had them clinging to each other, moving in an ancient rhythm until they were spent.

Melanie's eyes were closed, her breathing returning to normal. The frustration was gone for the moment, but the ache remained. It just wasn't the same with anyone since Charles. She didn't know why. Fred was just as expert at making love. Chad knew how to please a woman, too. So why was Charles on her mind when another man was making love to her? She would just have to try harder to forget him.

Fred rolled to her side. "Time for that swim now?"

Melanie smiled. Perhaps the rumors about Fred's prowess

were correct. "Sounds good to me." She pushed herself to her feet and looked down at the satisfied smile on Fred's face. "Can I ask you something?"

He nodded. "Anything."

"Would you be interested in a large block of Hudson stock if it were available?"

He blinked, then sat up. "That's an odd question."

"Not really." She walked to the edge of the pool. "I might inherit a lot of Hudson stock. If I do, I'm going to sell it all. I was just wondering if you'd be interested in it."

He stood up, joining her by the pool. "You get the stock and then we'll talk about it." He pulled her back against him, his hands on her breasts. "Right now, I've got more important things on my mind."

Melanie rubbed her back against him. "When do you have to leave?"

"Not for a couple of hours," came his muffled reply as he nuzzled her neck.

"Good." It might take a couple of hours to erase Charles from her mind.

It was late afternoon before Alana and Raine headed back to the harbor.

Alana looked up at the main sail, trimming it slightly. "*Black Jack* is a beauty," she said with a sigh. "I could sail on her forever."

"I've thought of it. With you, it would be even more tempting." He relaxed behind the wheel, his gaze on Alana more than the course he was steering. He meant what he said. Too bad it was wishful thinking to believe they could leave the real world behind and sail away together.

She looked into his eyes. The power of his gaze made her tremble. "I wish life were that simple," she said wistfully.

"It could be, if you let it." He sipped his wine. "Oh, I know the land is a problem. I'd be a fool to deny it."

"It's a wall between us," she said with a sigh, her head on his shoulder.

They watched the sun set in silence. The sun turned the clouds on the horizon to orange and gold, burning a path across the indigo water. The brilliant display of color faded to pink and purple as the sun disappeared like a golden coin in a copper sky. The lights of Honolulu and Waikiki began to twinkle in the dusk, fanning out from the shoreline to the mountains.

"I hate to see the afternoon end," Raine said with regret, turning Alana's face to his and giving her a kiss that left them both breathless.

When Raine took the wheel, Alana climbed onto the cabin top, heading for the bow. She sat in front of the mast, drawing her knees to her chest and wrapping her arms around her legs, watching the lights of Honolulu grow brighter.

Raine watched her, wondering what he was going to do about the land and about Alana. The afternoon had been wonderful. There was something special about her ... but he couldn't begin to discover why until the land no longer came between them. And yet, if he sold it to her, she might decide she never wanted to see him again. He didn't know where he stood with her, and he couldn't ask. There was a nagging doubt in his mind as well. Phillip had beaten her badly. Had she retaliated by killing him, hoping to get his fortune? If they had divorced, Phillip was powerful enough to assure she wouldn't get much. He was worth more dead than alive, even without the land. "Alana, we're coming into the harbor," Raine shouted, not wanting to examine his thoughts any closer.

After securing the boat to the dock, she disappeared below, gathering her clothes.

Raine blocked her exit to the deck. "Alana, wait."

Her shoulders sagged. "There's nothing more to say. You're

not going to sell the land to me unless I'm part of the deal, and I can't agree to that." Her chin lifted higher, fierce pride shining in her eyes.

His face was shuttered. "I might be willing to sell the land for the right price." He didn't give a damn about the land, but he couldn't tell her that. Not now.

Alana was wary. "What is the right price?"

"I'm not sure yet," he frowned. Just how important was it to her? "As long as we're talking business ... Hilary and Melanie will want my land as much as you do. I think I'll see what they're offering."

"I'll top any price they're willing to pay," Alana answered quickly.

"You have the resources to do that?" Raine asked, rubbing the side of his nose with one finger. How far could he push her?

"Yes."

"Even if it involves an affair?" He watched the color recede and then return to her face.

She took a deep breath. "Melanie will probably throw herself at you. If you haven't slept with her yet, she'll be more than willing." Alana paused. "I don't think sex with Hilary would be much fun." She shook her head. "Sex and business are a bad combination. Wouldn't you rather have the money?"

Raine shrugged, rocking back on his heels. "I want to know how much you're willing to risk for that land. How money hungry and power hungry are you, Alana Hudson? Are you willing to risk everything, including your self respect for Phillip's stock?" The thought that she would sell herself to run Hudson Enterprises disappointed him.

"I deserve to be elected CEO. With Phillip's stock I'd have enough shares to assure the election. I worked hard to get where I am, and I won't give it up without a fight!" Her face flamed, her hair tumbling around her shoulders, her eyes the color of spring violets.

"In other words, you're selfish enough to want it all for yourself," he taunted. Was this the same soft, desirable woman he had held in his arms this afternoon?

"Money? Power? Control? You bet I want it all," she answered, her voice firm, her gaze never wavering from his. "Aren't those all the reasons you own Bradburn International? Why should a man be able to fight for money and power but a woman shouldn't?"

Raine took a step and pulled the duffel from her grasp and tossed it onto the settee. His arms encircled her, molding her body to his, his head lowering as his lips crushed hers. Her lips were warm and soft, sending currents of desire spiraling through his body. "Now tell me you care about a parcel of land and an office in Hudson Enterprises," Raine said softly, seeing the indecision in her eyes.

She pushed away from him forcefully. "You bet I still care about it," she spit out.

She turned and walked away from him.

Chapter Nineteen

Hilary swallowed the last of her whiskey and tapped her foot, glancing out the smoked window of the limousine. Where was Leonard? Why didn't the gate open? She had never been refused admittance to Zachary's before. Her face whitened. Just because Phillip was dead they wouldn't cut her off ... would they? She visibly relaxed when Leonard returned to the car.

"Sorry for the delay, Mrs. Cummings. Mr. Chong would like to speak to you when you get to the house." His face was inscrutable.

Frowning, Hilary took a cigarette from the console, lit it with shaking fingers, and inhaled deeply. No doubt Simon wanted his money. Her eyes narrowed as she exhaled a cloud of smoke. The car stopped and her door opened immediately, a uniformed young man offering his gloved hand to her. She took it and stepped out, tilting her head back to look at the impressive building. It was rumored that Simon Chong won the house from Zachary Adams in a card game and named the private casino "Zachary's" as a constant reminder to Zachary Adams of his loss. Turrets and chimneys stretched toward the black sky, golden light pouring from every window of the castle-like mansion. Lanterns outlined the brick walks leading to elaborate gardens as well as massive oak doors. Hilary's gaze focused on the doors, the adrenalin beginning to flow through her body. Gambling was in her blood. Not that she couldn't stop if she didn't want to, she just didn't see a reason to stop. It was too much of a challenge. Too much fun.

The doors opened as she reached the top step. Simon greeted her with a slight bow. His tuxedo fit his slight frame perfectly, the white tucked shirt contrasting sharply with his olive skin, black hair, and black eyes. His ancestors had immigrated to Hawaii from Japan working long, back breaking hours in the sugar cane fields so their children would have a better life. She wondered if this was what they had in mind.

"Good evening, Mrs. Cummings." He nodded at the formally dressed waiter. "Please, have some champagne." When she took a crystal goblet, he waved a hand toward a door off the circular two-story foyer.

Hilary's eyes sparkled in the reflection of the crystal chandelier, her heels clicking on the slate floor as she walked beside Simon. She waited for him to open the door, leading the way into his office. It looked more like a sitting room than an office. Gaudy and overdone as far as Hilary was concerned, but appropriate for the purpose, she supposed. Her feet sank into plush carpeting of ebony, poppy, and white. Scarlet satin draped the windows and French doors leading to a small, private courtyard. Antique tapestries covered the remaining three walls. Simon motioned her toward the red and gold brocade sofa, settling himself in a black leather wing chair.

"I know what you want to discuss," Hilary said, taking a sip of her drink before putting it on a rosewood table inlaid with mother of pearl. She pulled a check out of her purse and handed it to Simon.

"Cash." His teeth bit down on the single word.

Hilary was surprised, the check still in her hand. "Why?" There was a lump in her throat, and she felt color flood her cheeks. Simon had always accepted her checks. She dropped it to the table.

"Phillip Hudson is dead. His will makes it impossible for you to obtain funds from your inheritance. How do I know this check is good?" His eyes narrowed.

Hilary thought of the gaming tables waiting for her, the blood quickening in her veins. Her fingers itched to hold the cards and chips. Gambling was her lover, tempting her and caressing her, bringing her the most incredible satisfaction when she won and leaving her to hope for another chance when she lost. Gambling gave her an emotional high she had never experienced with anything else. When she won, she was on top of the world. "The check is good, I promise." She picked up her glass with hands that shook with anticipation and drained it. "Is my credit good tonight?"

Simon's jet black eyes glittered dangerously. "Ten thousand. No more." He picked up the check from the table, flicking a glance first at it and then at Hilary. "Not until this check clears the bank." Simon stood and nodded to Hilary, a smile on his lips that never reached his eyes. "Good luck tonight."

She heard the mockery in his voice, but her mind was already on other more important things. Hilary stood and hurried out the door, breathing deeply of the scent of leather, exotic flowers, and money. Zachary's was the most exclusive club in the islands, known only to those who liked to gamble and could afford the formidable stakes. Hilary Hudson Cummings was a charter member. It was her favorite place to be, home. Her gambling wasn't limited to the club. She would wager money on anything, cock fights, outrigger canoe races, sporting events, the next volcanic eruption. Everyone had hobbies, she had told herself more than once. Her hobby took intelligence and money, but she always covered her bets, and winning was euphoria. Three weeks ago she took home twenty thousand dollars after four hours. Not bad for an investment of one thousand dollars.

A smug look of satisfaction settled on her face. She worked hard for Hudson Enterprises. She deserved every cent she made. If Alana controlled the company, she'd try to push Hilary out, but Alana wouldn't get the chance. Hilary would get that land, controlling Hudson Enterprises and taking what was rightfully hers. Her breath quickened. She smiled and nodded her head at the tuxedoed waiter who offered her another glass of champagne before she hurried into one of the rooms off the main salon. She felt lucky tonight. Sinking onto a cranberry velvet chair she smiled at the croupier and waved a hand at the handsome Hawaiian man approaching her with a silver tray of multicolored chips.

"Ten thousand, Foster. I'll double it in an hour." She almost rubbed her hands together in glee. An hour later she grinned at the pile of chips in front of her. She had tripled her money. Her cheeks were rosey, her eyes sparkled like twin sapphires, and she radiated confidence. Hilary was floating on a rainbow. She was invincible, untouchable. She could stop now and take home thirty thousand dollars. Or she could continue. She tapped her toes and drummed her fingers on the table. She was on a winning streak. Sixty thousand would be wonderful.

Two hours later she rubbed her palm over the empty spot where her stack of chips had been. "What's the matter here! Tables must be fixed." She stumbled to her feet, narrowing her eyes and trying to focus on the blurred images around her. One of Simon's men tucked her arm through his and guided her out of the room, his grip firm and unyielding when she tried to return to the table.

"You've had some bad luck, Mrs. Cummings. You'll have another chance to try your luck some other evening."

"I should have stopped long ago," she grumbled, trying to pry his fingers from her arm. "I'm not going to create a scene." Her voice was bitter. He didn't release her until she was back in the limousine. Hilary's cheeks burned. Once she controlled

Hudson Enterprises she wouldn't be humiliated like this. She'd buy Zachary's. She'd show Simon. She'd show them all.

Melanie prowled around her favorite bar, an elegant little place in Waikiki that catered to the rich singles. She danced with several men on the crowded dance floor before one man caught her eye. Sauntering up to him, she leaned on the bar, the neckline of her jade dress gaping slightly. "Hi, Greg. Haven't seen you around lately."

"Been on the mainland for a month," he murmured, smiling at her over the rim of his imported beer. "Anything interesting happen while I was gone?"

"Phillip died." She watched his reaction.

He let out a low whistle. "Sorry about that."

"I'm not." She drained her glass. Fred had gone back to the club to pick up his wife and Melanie was still restless, the ache firmly in place.

"Let's dance." He took her arm and led her through the crowd.

The song was a slow ballad, couples were crushed together on the miniscule dance floor. Melanie circled his neck with her arms, pressing her body close to his. Charles hadn't called since the board meeting. Why did she keep thinking about him? He didn't care about her. She was convenient when he was in Hawaii. Maybe Greg was the answer. He might be able to block out the memory of Charles. Fred hadn't, but Greg was six inches taller than Charles, fifteen years younger than either man, had a terrific body, and was wealthy. She touched her lips to his chin. "Let's go."

He nodded and snaked through the crowd until they were outside. His arm around her shoulders, he said, "Your place or mine?"

"Mine." She stepped into the waiting limousine.

Greg gave his driver Melanie's address. "It's been a long time." He pulled her into his arms and kissed her before holding her slightly away. "Want to talk about it?"

"You mean why we haven't seen each other for so long?" she murmured, knowing very well what he was talking about.

"I mean your father."

"No." She didn't even want to *think* about the will. She sought his lips, trying to lose herself in the expertise of Greg's kiss.

By the time they entered Melanie's bedroom, they were pulling off their clothes between frenzied kisses.

His breath was ragged as his hands roamed over her body.

She demanded more.

His lips moved over her face and down the slope of her shoulders.

Melanie arched her body into his, her hands kneading the muscles in his back.

They fell into bed, a tangle of arms and legs. Greg pressed her back onto the satin sheets, his body touching hers from shoulder to hip. His hands cupped her buttocks, urging her closer.

Melanie caressed his skin with her tongue, trying to lose herself in the sensual game they were playing.

His hand slid between her thighs and she willingly opened her legs for him, pressing against his hand as he massaged her with skillful fingers.

She abandoned herself to the urgency of the moment, her hands stroking and caressing him, enjoying the texture of his body, reveling in the shudders that raked his body as her tongue made him wild with desire.

They joined in a passion as raw and elementary as time itself. The world dimmed for Melanie as they surged over the crest of a wave, diving and spiraling, turning and twisting, before riding the surf back to the calm tidal waters.

Wrapped in Greg's arms, her eyes closed, Melanie could almost believe Charles had been wiped out of her thoughts, but Melanie was always honest with herself. No amount of frantic lovemaking could erase Charles. He seemed to have permeated the core of her being.

When Melanie awakened, she turned her head, not surprised that the bed was empty. Greg never stayed the night. She looked up, saw her reflection over her head and grimaced. Greg was good, but he wasn't Charles. Damn!

Pushing herself out of bed, Melanie strode toward the open doors to her pool, dove in and swam for half an hour, her frustration not eased one bit.

She returned to the house and wrapped herself in a bath towel. She thought about Greg and Charles, and then pushed them both from her mind, her thoughts turning to her father's will. There had to be a way of assuring that Alana wouldn't inherit a cent. She wandered into her library and pulled down a book on psychology, turning to the section on mental competency.

Hilary stared out the window of her penthouse apartment, oblivious to the beauty of the azure sky and turquoise sea. Her blond hair was perfectly coiffed, her eyes as cool as ever, her tan suit impeccable, the bow of her blue blouse tied in a precise knot. Cool and composed on the outside, inwardly she seethed. The situation looked just as grim in the morning light as it did yesterday. The only difference being the headache that made her wince when she so much as blinked an eye. If Phillip wanted the final revenge on the women in his life, he had picked the ultimate weapons, power and money. He was a cunning man, and she knew that nothing was ever as it appeared to be concerning Phillip Hudson, but what was his ultimate goal? To pit his daughters against his wife? To humiliate them all? Making them beg his enemy for some rock and sand was sadistic! She rubbed her throbbing temples. One thing was certain, her father controlled everything and everyone, and he'd never let a little thing like death get in his way. Damn! She paced in front of the windows, one hand on her hip, the other tight against her side, her hand curled in a ball. Time . . . she needed time. Two months. Hilary stopped pacing and pressed her finger tips to her temples once again. It hurt to think. She took a deep breath.

Rubbing her neck, she thought about going to the yacht club for a bloody Mary, but decided against it. She didn't feel like answering probing questions or acting like nothing was wrong, or accepting any more insincere sympathies. Phillip's death had been a relief, but never in her wildest dreams did she think he would leave Hudson Enterprises in such an upheaval.

Hilary slumped down on the piano seat, playing a favorite Mozart melody while her thoughts churned like waves breaking among the rocks. Her life would be bleak indeed if she didn't get that land. Chandler had no money, and they counted on her income to maintain the lifestyle they enjoyed. The money and stock would only last for a few years. Alana would love to make life miserable for Hilary and Melanie. Her friends would desert her, people would laugh at the mess the Hudson sisters had gotten into. A shudder ran through her body. Humiliation. Complete and total. People gravitated toward power and money like iron to a magnet, and she'd have neither. Hell, she'd do without the power just to have the money. If Alana got control of the company and Phillip's personal estate, everything Hilary deserved, desired, and needed would vanish. Her hands crashed on the keyboard, the discordant sound echoing through the empty apartment.

Pushing herself away from the piano, she walked purposely

to the bar, stared at the array of bottles for a long moment, then with a slight shrug took a crystal glass, filled it half full of vodka and topped it off with tomato juice and spices. So what if it was only nine o'clock in the morning? One drink wouldn't hurt. If anyone deserved it, she did. Hilary took a long swallow before returning to her chair. Crossing her legs and staring at the tip of her white alligator shoe until it blurred, her thoughts returned again and again to the will and the devastating effect it would have on her life. Money meant power, status, and control. She craved all three as much as her father ever did. She had to have that land! Tilting her head back, she finished off the drink, got to her feet and headed back to the bar. There had to be a way of getting that land!

By the time Chandler got home, Hilary was beyond caring about the money or the land. One shoe was on the glass-topped table, her blouse was pulled out of her skirt, her hair fell over one cheek, and her eyes were glazed. "Hi, Shandler. How's it goin'?"

Chandler looked at his wife in disgust, a camera bag slung over one shoulder. "You've been drinking all day."

"Very good." She tried to clap her hands but missed. Shrugging, she groped for her glass.

Chandler shook his head slowly, before dropping his bag and putting the glass out of her reach. He picked up the empty bottle and squeezed his hand around it, sighing in resignation. Someone should have warned him about Hilary's vices. She thought of them as hobbies. He knew better. There were some things that one just shouldn't have to put up with, even for a sizable fortune. The drinking he could tolerate slightly more than the gambling. Once, he had accompanied Hilary to a cock fight in the mountains. She had been exhilarated by the action, the contest, the gambling. The blood made him sick. She had

275

insisted they stop on the way home and make love in the back seat of the car. He had never gone with her again. There were times when she disappeared for two or three days, but he never questioned her whereabouts. He didn't want to know. As long as she didn't interfere in his life, he left her alone. But today, he had to talk to her. He had stopped at the club on his way home and the rumors were buzzing like bees around a honeycomb. He had to find out the truth about Phillip's will. Hilary had come home late the night before, too drunk to be coherent.

"Hilary, you're drunk." He hoped he could get her to talk before she passed out.

"I jus had a lil." She struggled to get to her feet, groaned, covered her eyes with her hands and collapsed back into the chair. "An I had trouble before I took one itsy drink."

"How much did you lose at Zachary's?" he asked, knowing a weekend could not pass without her visiting the place at least once.

"Jus a lil." She sniffed. "Tha's not all."

"Your father's will," Chandler muttered, running his hand through his hair before kneeling next to her chair. When she didn't say anything, he finally asked. "What happened at the lawyer's yesterday?" When she was still silent for a few minutes, he shook her. "Hilary! What happened yesterday?"

She sniffed again. Taking a deep breath, she opened one eye. "I need coffee.'

Chandler got to his feet, pulling Hilary after him. "Yes, dear." He gritted his teeth. "Why don't you go take a shower, and I'll get some coffee for you." Chandler directed her down the hall toward the bedroom, giving her a slight push. "Would you like me to bring it to your room?"

"Here," she murmured her hand fluttering toward the room as she bounced against one wall and then the other.

Chandler watched her go, his face grim. It must be bad news. He headed toward the kitchen. He had stayed with Hilary because the Hudson name had helped establish his photography business and he anticipated millions of dollars when Phillip Hudson died. His business was bringing in good money now because of his association with the socially elite, but he wanted more, and he was willing to wait. Now it seemed the wait had been in vain. If the rumors were even partially correct, he had put up with Hilary's drinking and gambling along with her spoiled, obnoxious son for nothing.

After a cold shower, Hilary felt only slightly better as she slipped an aqua caftan over her head and white sandals on her feet. Her hair was pulled back into a knot at her nape, her makeup was freshened, and even if her head felt like the middle of Lunalilo Freeway during rush hour, she was in control.

Walking toward the living room, carefully putting one foot in front of the other, she gingerly accepted the cup of coffee Chandler held out to her. "Thank you, Chandler."

"Feeling better, mother?" The cynical voice from the door to the lanai made her wince. "Mitchell, I didn't know you were home."

"I got in while you were showering. Chandler told me you had been drinking." He dropped into a chair opposite her, his handsome features sullen, a beer in his hand. Brown hair was skillfully cut to look casual yet sophisticated. His round face and flat broad nose combined with full lips and dimpled chin to give him a perpetual little boy look. The petulent look in his brown eyes belied that impression. "What happened yesterday? Did Phillip donate the family fortune to charity?" He gave a harsh laugh. "Or did he leave it to his daughters and grandson?" His pink and black flowered shirt hung open to his waist, loosely tucked into black shorts.

Hilary rubbed her temples. "Your grandfather thought you

should be working instead of surfing. You're twenty-one. Perhaps we can get you into Hudson Enterprises now."

He stared at his bare feet, his face grim. "And have everyone know I got the job because my grandfather owned the place? No thanks."

"He's dead. Your last name is Jones. No one will know." Mitch had been eleven years old when Hilary married Chandler. Her son had resented her second husband since they first met. He had refused to take Chandler's name.

"I'll think about it," he muttered, draining his bottle. "So what did the old man do with the loot?"

"It's complicated." She paused, taking a deep breath before glancing at Chandler.

"Come on, Hilary, you might as well tell us." Chandler sat down in another chair, and crossed his legs, picking the lint off his trousers. "What happened?"

"It was awful," Hilary said with a sigh, cradling the cup of coffee in her hands. It was painful to think about. Hadn't she spent the day trying to escape when there was no escape? "Phillip was a ruthless, cruel man." She suppressed a shudder. "I never thought he'd carry his power to the grave." Taking a deep breath she said, "If one of us produces the title to the land daddy had been trying to buy from Raine Bradburn within sixty days, that person gets ninety percent of his stock and ninety percent of his estate."

"That leaves the other sister ten percent of the stock and Phillip's estate." Chandler shrugged. "We could live on that, couldn't we?"

"You don't understand. It isn't just the two of us." Her voice was laced with disgust and scorn. "Alana is part of it. The losers would each get five percent."

Chandler let out a low whistle as his eyebrows shot up. "Five percent? That's all?"

Her head pounded when she nodded. "And if none of us can

278

pry that land from Raine Bradburn, the three of us split the ten percent." A hand fluttered in the direction of the table and then she grasped the cup again.

Mitchell's gaze was intense as he said, "Did he mention me in his will?"

A lump formed in her throat. "Not a word."

Chandler looked at her for a moment before saying slowly, "What happens to the ninety percent if no one gets that land?"

Hilary closed her eyes. "Phillip's stock is liquidated, everything is sold and the money goes to build and maintain a super yacht for Hudson executives and clients." A bitter laugh escaped her lips. "Isn't that just like Phillip? He couldn't do something nice, he had to do something that would destroy us."

Mitchell rubbed his jaw. "What are your chances of getting the title to that land?"

"About the same chance of snow on Waikiki. We'd have better odds trying to bring Phillip back from the dead. He tried every way he knew how to get that land, but he never could." She gave the men a rueful look. "How would I even get a second glance from a man like Raine Bradburn? When I see him at the club, he never even looks at me, he looks *through* me."

"If you explained the situation to him, maybe he would be willing to sell for a piece of Hudson Enterprises," Chandler suggested.

Hilary sipped her coffee, silent for a moment. "That's what some of the board members wanted to do, but Phillip wouldn't hear of it."

"That sounds like your father," Chandler muttered, pulling on the cuff of his shirt until it was exactly an inch below the sleeve of his blue blazer.

"If he wouldn't sell to Phillip, I can't imagine him selling to me." She put the cup on the coffee table, picking up her shoe and putting it on the floor. She sat back and folded her hands in her lap. "Even Alana got upset and not much gets through that ice-cold professional veneer." A fleeting smile crossed her face.

"What chance does she have of reaching Bradburn?" Mitchell slouched in the chair, his arms crossed over his chest.

"The same as mine, zero," Hilary said, laughing harshly. "Oh, she thought she was going to inherit everything since she was Phillip's wife, but he saw through her scheme. If Melanie or I get that land, she's out of the company. We'll see to that. If a miracle happens and she manages to get that land, she will have enough stock to make her the majority shareholder of an international company along with fifty million dollars in personal assets. The stock alone is worth over a hundred million."

Chandler choked, his eyebrows skyrocketing. "That much?" he managed to say.

"I haven't been involved in the finances of the company and Phillip's personal accounts without knowing what he's worth." Twin flags of anger stained her pale face. "How could he do it to us? Melanie and I are his children. We deserve to inherit everything. Instead he pits us against *her* in his cruel game."

"Maybe he really wants the two of you to have it, but he's making you work for it," Chandler said, stroking his chin with a perfectly manicured hand.

Hilary's thumb began to work on her finger, lines creasing her smooth forehead. "He said something like that at the reading of the will." At Chandler's quizzical look, she said, "He had a video made to show us. Isn't that just like him? I think he was crazy."

"Too bad you can't prove it." Mitchell gave her a hopeful look.

"It would take too much time, and probably wouldn't solve anything." Hilary closed her eyes. "It's impossible."

Chandler gave her a thoughtful look. "Five percent of his

personal estate is two and a half million. We could live on that for quite a while."

"It's nothing compared to controlling the company and getting my hands on his entire fortune!" she retorted.

"So how can we make sure you get the land and our family gets the money?" Chandler said slowly, looking at his fingertips splayed across his thigh.

"I don't know." She shook her head then pushed herself to her feet and wandered over to the window, looking at the breakers rolling into shore, rubbing her forehead to ease the pounding. "I want that company, if only to prove that Phillip can't have his way all the time. Oh, I know Melanie has a better chance of getting it than I do. She uses sex as a weapon. She gets whatever she wants." Her voice was grim. "Alana might resort to using her body, too ... lord knows she didn't hesitate where father was concerned. He consulted me about major decisions until *she* took over. But I'll get it. Somehow, I'll get it," she gritted between her teeth. "I'm going to have the final revenge, no matter what the cost." Her fists were clenched in her lap as she looked first at Mitchell and then Chandler. "You'll both help me, won't you?"

Chandler looked uneasy. "It depends what you're planning to do."

Mitchell gave the older man a cold look. "Naturally, I'll help you, Mother. I'll do anything to get my hands on the Hudson fortune."

Chandler wandered out onto the lanai, leaning on the railing. Two and a half million and some stock wouldn't last long with Hilary's habits. The old bastard didn't even mention his grandson. He couldn't believe he had stayed with Hilary all these years for such a small share of Phillip Hudson's fortune. He would have to start looking around for a better deal. There were plenty of wealthy women on the island. Many of them were lonely. He would bale out of this marriage, but first he would assure his own future.

He turned around and looked at Hilary. Life with her was bad enough, but such a life without endless money would be hell.

Chapter Twenty

Melanie paced around her office, the silk of her pale green shirtdress swirling around her knees. The gold hoops in her ears danced as she tossed her head. She had tried to talk to Raine at the club, but he had rebuffed her efforts, telling her to make an appointment during business hours. She couldn't wait that long.

Her phone buzzed, making her jump. "Hello!"

"Is this Melanie Hudson?"

She recognized the wary voice at once. "Yes, Arty." She sat down. "Do you have anything to report?"

"Nothing you could use. The subject has been going to work and then home every night. She spent most of the weekend at the office." He paused. 'Maybe she's having an affair with someone in the building."

"I doubt it, but I'll check it out." Melanie made a note to herself. "Anything else?"

"Why doesn't she live at the Hudson estate? Why does she live in an apartment?"

"Good question." Melanie made another note. "Why don't you work on that. Maybe it's something I can use." She leaned back in her chair. "Doesn't she go anywhere else?"

"A couple of business luncheons and a cocktail party. That's it."

"We don't have much time," Melanie reminded him. "Stay with it, and find out why she's not living on the estate."

"Right. I'll talk to you tomorrow."

Melanie put the receiver down and frowned. All she had were more questions, no answers. There had to be something on Alana. No one was that good.

She stared at the telephone. She wanted to talk to Charles. Had to talk to him. He had such a calming influence on her and right now, she was too agitated to sit still. Maybe Charles could give her some ideas, not that she had told him everything. No one knew.

Melanie picked up the receiver and put it down three times before calling Charles. His secretary answered the phone. "I'd like to speak to Charles Reese, please." Her palms were sweaty.

"I'm sorry. He's in Europe this week. May I take a message?"

Melanie lacked the nerve to ask if it was business or pleasure. "No. I'll call again." She slammed the receiver down. She was desperate to hear his voice and he was in Europe!

She was frustrated and angry.

She slumped into her chair, jabbing a button on her intercom. "Come in here for a few minutes."

When Chad appeared, she stood and walked toward him. "Lock the door."

He did as she asked. Their eyes met. He cleared his throat. "Melanie, please don't take this wrong, but did you hire me for anything other than servicing you?"

She stared at him. She wasn't in a mood to explain herself, but perhaps it was a good time to see if Chad had any information she could use. He might hear a lot more office gossip than she would. "Of course. You were tops in your class at Harvard. That was the primary reason I wanted you. The sex came later." She watched him visibly relax. "Why? Don't you like it?"

"Sure I do. But I was hoping you'd notice my work as well."

Melanie stepped toward him, lifting her hand to his cheek. Her voice was soft. She understood his dilemma. She had often had the same concerns. "I have noticed, Chad. You've come up with some very good ideas to promote the new condos on the Big Island. Jeff Morino is impressed." She smiled. "Does that make you feel better."

He nodded, a sheepish look on his face. "I didn't even want to mention it, but—"

"Don't worry." She slid her hands under his jacket and pushed it off of his shoulders.

"Thanks." His hand moved to the zipper of her dress, slowly releasing it. When it dropped from her body, his lips touched her shoulder.

She threw her head back, giving him free access to the sensitive cord in her neck. Closing her eyes, she murmured, "Chad, have you heard any gossip about Alana Hudson?"

He traced her mouth with his tongue. "A little."

She loosened his tie and unbuttoned his shirt. "What have you heard."

He slipped her camisole over her head, then bent to remove the rest of her clothing. "A few people seem to think she's having an affair."

Melanie finished undressing him. "With whom?"

Chad pulled her close, making her feel his desire. "Robert Somers, Ben Adams, Raine Bradburn."

"All three?" she whispered, her lips against his throat.

"Depends on who you talk to." He lowered her to the leather couch, his mouth moving hungrily over her taut breasts.

"Anything else?" she murmured, running her hands through his hair.

His thumbs stroked her nipples.

She licked his.

Chad groaned.

Melanie reversed their positions. Straddling him, she ran her fingers through the thick mat of hair on his chest. She tried to forget everything but the sensation of the moment.

Chad pulled her head down and captured her lips, his tongue invading her mouth, hot and hungry.

She arched toward him, digging her nails into his shoulders.

He joined their bodies in an urgent rhythm, driving them toward a fiery climax.

Melanie went eagerly, straining for the release that failed to come. She urged him on, twisting and turning, seeking the ultimate moment of freedom, but it didn't happen. Chad lay spent and she rested on his chest, wishing Charles had never touched her.

Hilary made an appointment to see Raine Bradburn on Tuesday, surprised she was able to get in to see him so quickly, but then he had to know about Phillip Hudson's will. Sondra Williams couldn't wait to tell her that she had seen Alana with Raine Bradburn on Friday. Alana would probably sell herself to get that land and control Hudson Enterprises.

Hilary snapped her briefcase shut, her features grim. Smoothing her black linen suit jacket over her hips, she squared her shoulders. The conservative cut of her suit and severe lines of her red blouse would show Bradburn that she meant business. The perfectly matched strand of pearls around her neck and on her ears would convey her breeding and wealth. He'd have to take her seriously. Impressed, he'd sell the land to her. Determination hardened her classic features. She would see Alana destroyed and gain control of Hudson Enterprises herself if it was the last thing she did. Mitchell deserved an inheritance and when she controlled Hudson Enterprises, Mitchell would take his rightful place at her side, no matter what Chandler or anyone else thought. She glanced at the diamond watch on her wrist. She'd make Raine Bradburn an offer he couldn't refuse.

Entering his office building, she was impressed. Gleaming chrome and glass combined with plants and warm earth tones to make an otherwise harsh building seem warm and inviting. The lobby had a three story fountain in the center, surrounded by tropical plants and flowers. All the floors circled the lobby, a smoked glass elevator silently moving between floors. Mauve and rose love seats and chairs were grouped into small conversation areas on oyster white carpeting. Large ceramic vases filled with fresh flowers stood on a glass-topped table in every grouping. Several areas were occupied as Hilary walked toward the guard desk. No surly guard here like Phillip employed. Instead, a beautiful woman in a trim uniform greeted Hilary with a pleasant smile, directing her to the glass elevator after she signed in. Raine Bradburn's business was first class.

Stepping off the elevator on the top floor, she approached the receptionist, gave her name and sat on the edge of a grey suede chair. She thought of all the angles he might come up with to refuse to sell the land, but she was certain he would ultimately agree to her offer. The deal she had put together was irresistible.

When she was finally ushered into his office, her palms were damp and her stomach tied in knots. He had kept her waiting for half an hour. She needed a drink. One look at his face told her this was going to be a challenge. "Hello, Mr. Bradburn." She held out her right hand. "Thank you for taking the time to see me."

"Hello, Hilary." He waved a hand toward a chair after an abrupt handshake. "Let's get right down to business, shall we? The only reason a Hudson would come to see me is because he or she wants something." He leaned back in his massive black leather chair. "And the only reason you would condescend to talk to me is because you want my land so you can control Hudson Enterprises. Now what's your offer going to be?''

His direct approach shocked Hilary. She was silent for a moment, digesting his words. Alana must've made him an offer, but he hadn't sold the land yet or he wouldn't ask what her offer would be. That was encouraging. Had Melanie also been in contact with him? Hilary hated being at a disadvantage. "What have the others offered?" she finally asked, gripping her brief case with both hands.

"What are you offering?" he countered, crossing his arms over his chest.

Hilary cleared her throat. She really needed a drink. "Hudson Enterprises needs the land you own on Maui to build our resort complex. I know that you wouldn't sell to my father." She paused. "What about a trade? The land you own on Maui for the land you need from us on the Big Island? We would both profit from the exchange. We could build our resort complex and your ranch would have direct access to the main highway rather than having to go around our land."

Raine was silent for a moment, rubbing his jaw with the knuckles on one hand. "Are you authorized to make that kind of deal? Doesn't the board have to agree to a sale like that?"

Hilary wished his face would register some reaction so she knew if he was considering her offer. She snapped opened her briefcase and pushed a folder of papers toward him. "If you agree to the exchange, I'm certain the board would go along with me." She shut her brief case and put it on the floor. "All you have to do is sign on the bottom and I'll take care of the rest. How can you go wrong? It's a good deal for both of us."

Raine opened the folder and glanced through the sheaf of paper, finally closing it and tossing it onto his cluttered desk. "Except that I only get a piece of land, while you get controlling interest of Hudson Enterprises and the bulk of your father's estate. It seems to me that you get much more in the deal than I do." He pierced her with the intensity of his gaze.

She shifted her weight, moving to sit on the very edge of the chair, her legs pressed tightly together, her hands clasped. She frowned, gathering her thoughts before speaking. She hadn't been prepared for his abrupt questions and his almost hostile attitude. "Well, I suppose we could add some financial inducements."

"I want controlling interest in Hudson Enterprises!" The harsh tone of voice made her cringe.

"What do you want another company for when you're so successful? You don't need Hudson Enterprises." She lost her composure as her eyes hardened to ice, her mouth compressed. How could he even think that his land was worth controlling interest in a major corporation. "Don't be a fool, Bradburn! This is a deal you can't pass up!"

Raine looked at her with contempt. "No one calls me a fool, Hilary. Seems to me you need this deal a hell of a lot more than I do. Perhaps your gambling isn't the innocent diversion you like people to think it is."

Hilary's mouth snapped shut, color flooding her face at his barbed attack on her personal life. "Who's been telling you such lies about me? Visiting Zachary's is entertainment. A hobby. It's no different than sailing or running in a marathon." She glared at him. It wasn't any of his business what she did, and it galled her to justify herself to him. "You're right I want Hudson Enterprises, but I want it because I'm entitled to it. I am Phillip Hudson's daughter." She raised her chin and looked down her nose at him.

His voice mocked her as he leaned forward to pick up a dagger carved of koa wood. He rubbed a finger along the blade, his eyes like flint. "I want to control it so I can merge it with my company. There will be no more Hudson Enterprises."

She frowned and swallowed past the lump in her throat, her eyes on the dagger. She raised her eyes to meet his. Raine was as ruthless as her father. "Why?"

He dropped the knife and picked up a gold pencil from his desk, tapping it lightly on the folder she had given him. "I want more than this for my land. I don't need the money, I want the Hudson name wiped out of the business world. I have all the chips, Hilary. The odds are in my favor. I'm the only sure winner.'

She was silent for a moment, then picked up her briefcase, her shoulders slumping in defeat. It was hopeless trying to deal with a man like Raine Bradburn. It was like trying to reason with her father. "So your answer is no."

"See if you can come up with a better offer, Mrs. Cummings. Go back to your board of directors. Tell them I want to be CEO of Hudson Enterprises in exchange for that parcel of land." He paused and threw the pencil on the desk, leaning forward, his hands clasped over the folder. He regarded her for long moments before speaking. His voice was low and mocking as he said, "How about a wager, Hilary? What's your percent if someone else gets the land?" He didn't wait for an answer. "Five percent, right? And if you get my land you control the company. How about a bet? Something simple, like picking the winner of the Wyatt Cup. Your choice. If that boat wins, you buy my land and gain control of Hudson Enterprises. If I win that race, I get all your shares of stock in the company and you're out of a job."

Hilary's eyes widened. He had reached her most vulnerable area and he knew it. How did he know so much? She thought about that race. He had won for the last three years. Several others came close, but never quite caught him. If his boat was sabotaged, she might just do it. "I have everything to lose, but you can only win."

He laughed. "I wonder if Hudson knew how much I'd enjoy

his will!'' She cringed at the taunt in his voice. "Think about it, Hilary. The ultimate wager. Everything on the line. Exciting, don't you think?''

Hilary thought she couldn't hate anyone more than she hated Alana, but Raine Bradburn had just made the top of her list. Getting to her feet, she glared at him. "My father was right in despising you. You're an evil man, preying on people's weaknesses.'' She whirled around and headed for the door.

"I learned from a pro. Phillip Hudson.'' His grating reply stopped her.

Her hand on the knob, she said without turning around, "You'll be sorry, Raine Bradburn.''

"Not as sorry as you'll be if you turn down my wager and I lose that race. Hudson Enterprises could have been yours. You'll never forgive yourself for turning down the ultimate bet.''

She slammed the door behind her but not before she heard his deep laughter. Of all the horrible, disgusting, demeaning things. His taunts made her blood boil. Betting everything on a yacht race! She stalked out of the building and climbed into the limousine without glancing at Leonard. A sly smile crossed her face. Maybe between her and Mitchell they could insure that Raine Bradburn couldn't win the race, and whomever she picked would win. Losing everything didn't even enter her mind.

Raine read the offer Hilary had made to him. If Phillip Hudson hadn't been involved, he would readily trade the land on Maui for direct access to the main road on the Big Island. But Phillip was involved, and he had made damn sure Raine was involved as well. Hilary had put together a very impressive proposal. If she would forget she was a Hudson she could succeed in the business world, but her attitude prevented it.

He thought about Alana. She wanted the land, too. Melanie was the only one who hadn't made an offer yet. She had tried to approach him at the club, but he wasn't about to talk business with so many eager listeners around.

In one respect, he hated being the focus of the attention for the three women, but on the other hand, it was nice to be the one in control. No matter what happened with the land, he would be the winner.

Raine frowned. Except where Alana was concerned. The disposition of the land would assure that there was no future between them. There would be too many doubts, too many unanswered questions.

The question foremost in his mind worried him more than he wanted to admit. Had Alana killed Phillip? She had millions of dollars at stake. People had been killed for much less. And there was her pride. Phillip had wounded it when he beat her up.

He turned back to the proposal, all his questions still unanswered.

Hilary waited impatiently for Mitch and Chandler, eager to tell them about the offer Raine Bradburn had made to her. She paced the length of the living room, casting longing looks at the crystal decanters behind the bar. She would drink later. She had to concentrate. Her determination wavered. What if Raine's offer was a joke? What if he was only teasing, taunting, playing on her weakness? Would he turn down an exchange of the Hudson property on the Big Island for the small parcel he owned on Maui? Hilary collapsed on the sofa, burying her head in her hands. He was right, damn him, he held all the cards. He could play one woman off against the other until he got what he wanted. Hudson Enterprises. She shivered and pushed herself to her feet. The bar beckoned, glassware shining and twinkling, There was so much at stake. She wanted Phillip's millions and his stock. Five million was nothing compared to what she could have. Power. Control. Prestige. It was worth any price. She stepped behind the bar, running one hand along the etched monogram. One drink. She would just have one drink. Her hand shook. One drink would steady her nerves. She reached for the bottle and took a glass. She could control her drinking. A grim smile touched her face as she poured the amber liquid into the glass. Scotch. Smooth and straight. She tossed her head back and drained the glass, sighing as the liquid burned a trail to her stomach. Better. One more would be even better.

By the time Chandler found her, the decanter was empty. "Hi, honey," she muttered, waving a glass in his direction. "Wana drink?"

"How many have you had?" he asked, taking the glass from her limp hand.

"Not enough," she muttered, pushing herself to her feet and weaving toward the bar. When she reached for another bottle, he grabbed her wrist.

"You've had enough." He filled a glass with soda and handed it to her. "What happened today when you went to see Bradburn?"

She glared at him and slammed the glass on the bar. "Gimme a drink an I'll tell you." They confronted each other until Chandler shrugged and turned toward the bar.

"Try to get the whole story out before you pass out," he muttered in disgust, filling a glass and handing it to her.

She took a long drink before placing it carefully on the bar, squinting at the contents, speaking slowly and distinctly. "He countered my offer."

Chandler raised his brows. "What was his offer?"

"Wyatt Cup." She frowned. "If he wins the race, he gets my interest in Hudson Enterprises. If the boat I pick wins, I get his land."

Chandler let out a low whistle. "The man knows how to hit where it hurts. Either we're broke or you get everything. Did you accept?"

" 'Course not!" She rubbed her eyes. "Too mad to think straight. Don't know if he's serious. He laughed at me!" The laughter had been like a knife in her heart. She hadn't had enough to drink to make the pain go away. Getting to her feet, she swayed before heading back to the bar. "How am I going to find out if he's serious?"

"You mean you'd actually risk losing a sure two and a half million on a yacht race?" he asked, shaking his head in disgust. "You're worse off than I thought."

"You just don't want me to lose 'cause you'd have to support us," she sneered, liquor sloshing over the side of the glass as she poured it. Even Chandler was against her. Nobody cared about her. No one loved her. A tear trickled down her cheek. She'd show 'em all.

Mitch sauntered into the room, looking at his mother and then Chandler. "What's going on?"

"Your mother saw Bradburn today. He wanted to put his land and her shares of stock up as prizes for the Wyatt Cup. Your mother would have to pick the winner." Chandler poured himself a glass of sparkling water.

"And if she loses?"

"We have nothing." Chandler looked at his wife in disgust.

Mitch looked at his mother incredulously. "I can't believe you'd even consider such a wager. Bradburn might lose a little piece of land, but you could lose everything."

"I could win. Set for life." She tried to focus on Mitch as he stood on the other side of the bar. "We could cheat."

Mitch looked at her with contempt, slamming the glass on the bar. "That's the stupidest idea you've ever had. What would we do? Drill a hole in the bottom of his boat? Turn on the engine of the one you picked to win? There's no guarantee that he'd make good on the wager, especially if you rigged it. And I, for one, would not want to be around when he found out you cheated. I wouldn't mess with him."

"We could win!" She swiped at her wet cheeks, slashes of black mascara making her look like a warrior. Mitch never backed away from anything. She couldn't believe he wouldn't want to help her now. Chandler and Mitch were both against her.

Mitch's words mocked her as he wandered to the patio doors and walked outside. "I'd settle for a few million and some stock. You're sick if you even consider it."

Chandler stood in front of her. "Raine Bradburn knew exactly what he was doing when he offered that deal to you. He knows the Hudson family better than they know themselves. He'd never offer a deal like that if he didn't know he could win." He paused. "The word around town is that he's after Hudson Enterprises at any cost. Phillip and Raine were two of the most powerful men in the islands. Now one of them is dead. Do you really think someone like Raine Bradburn is going to settle for five percent of the company when he could control the whole thing?"

"But I would own it," she protested, his words not penetrating her fuzzy mind.

Chandler grabbed her shoulders and shook her. "Be realistic. Did you ever think that he might let your boat win so that you would control the company? And then he would control you?"

Hilary squinted at him. "What are you talking 'bout?"

He spoke as if to a child. "He knows gambling is an addiction for you, and you'd take a chance on this."

"Half the island knows I like to take a chance now and

then." Hilary didn't like Chandler talking to her like this, but she didn't have the strength to stop him. Was her gambling really so well known?

"If Bradburn knows you'd seriously consider this kind of proposition, he knows a lot more about you," he muttered. "That means he has access to a lot of information. You think you would control the company, but he would do it through you. Hell, he'd probably want you to own the company. He would be able to take it over easily enough if you did."

Hilary was stung by his attack, reinforcing her belief that no one really cared about her. She'd have to do it herself.

Mitch stared out over the water. He turned around and sauntered back into the living room. "Maybe you should talk to Melanie and see if she would agree to a joint effort to get that land. She might succeed in a way you can't."

"What's that supposed to mean?" Hilary could see the glitter in his eyes even through the haze that settled around her like a shroud. Not much would hurt her now.

He looked at her with disdain. "You're about as sexy as a grey day, while Mel is one of the hottest women in the islands."

"Bradburn wouldn't give up his land for sex." Hilary shook her head. "No."

"She's got a great body."

"What d'you know 'bout Melanie's body?" Hilary demanded, glad she had finished another drink.

"A little imagination goes a long way," he taunted. Mitchell dropped into a chair and crossed his arms over his chest. He let out a long sigh. "I used to hang around the club just to watch her sun bathe."

"That's your aunt you're lusting for!"

He shrugged. "If anyone can get to him, she will."

"Who?" Hilary blinked, unable to remember what they were talking about. Was it Melanie or Raine Bradburn?

"Raine Bradburn." Chandler shook his head in disgust, getting to his feet and turning toward the steps to his room. "It's useless talking to you."

His retreating back swam before her eyes. Hilary leaned back, closing her eyes, welcoming the darkening fog. Soon, soon, she wouldn't have to think. Everything faded. Joyous oblivion. Her mouth went slack, her features relaxed.

Chapter Twenty-one

Melanie slammed the front door, and threw her purse in the direction of the red velvet settee, her footsteps sharp on the marble floor. She didn't even stop to admire the lifesize male and female nude figures entwined in the fountain in the middle of the foyer. She stomped up the stairs to her suite, her steps muffled by the plush white carpeting. She couldn't even get an appointment with Raine Bradburn until the following week! Phillip's will was the most outrageous, cruel, pain he had ever inflicted on his family, and he had done many hurtful things in his lifetime. The only good thing Phillip did was put Alana in the same position as his daughters. Her mouth thinned. If Alana succeeded in getting that land, she'd regret it.

Melanie collapsed on a corner of the king-sized bed. Her hand absently rubbed the black geometric print satin spread. Her mother hadn't deserved the hell Phillip had put her through. Marriage to the bastard was bad enough, but then demanding a divorce to marry a woman young enough to be his daughter. That was the final humiliation. It had caused her death.

She pushed herself to her feet and unbuttoned her blouse, tossing it on the floor. She stripped off her remaining clothes and stalked toward the bathroom. Doubts assailed her. Feeling vulnerable and insecure, she trembled. Her mother was gone and Charles was in Europe. She had no one to turn to.

She twisted the gold faucets, pinning her hair on top of her head as the water reached the temperature she wanted. She stepped into the sunken tub, closing her eyes and letting the jets of water soothe her weary body. So Phillip wanted to play dirty, even in death. So what else was new? Phillip Hudson hadn't built his fortune by being a nice guy.

Melanie reclined, her head against the cushioned head rest, letting the water calm her nerves. It was an hour before she soaped her body. She had laughed off the unethical, illegal, and immoral actions of Phillip Hudson, rationalizing and justifying his means to the end. Until her mother died. He had crushed the only woman who really loved him. Melanie had no illusions about Alana. She loved Phillip's money and power. The delicate fragrance of lemon made Melanie inhale deeply before rinsing silky bubbles from her body. It was impossible not to think about her life and how it could drastically change in the next couple of months. There was no way she could maintain her present lifestyle with less money. That didn't bother her overly much. There were plenty of men on the island who would maintain her comfortable lifestyle. Her hands traced lush curves. She wasn't as stupid as people thought. She knew how to use her assets. She could adjust. It wouldn't be the end of the world. Even the thought of Hilary in control of the company wasn't terribly painful.

Melanie grabbed a thick towel from the heated bar. The sky light gave a soft glow to the cream ceramic tile. Tropical plants grew lush and green around the miniature waterfall in the corner. Water overflowed from the small pool into the large tub, big enough for six people when Melanie was in the mood for company. Melanie contemplated her body reflected from the bank of mirrors surrounding the room. She had a few years before she'd have to head for Rio and a little preventative surgery. She leaned forward, carefully examining her face. A couple of lines around her eyes and on her forehead. Better call Ariel and get some cream. She sighed as she toweled herself. Phillip had caused her mother's death, and Alana had been instrumental in his demand for a divorce. That was enough to make her want to kill for the joy of revenge. She wanted his shares of Hudson stock so she could take the whole damn thing and sell it for five cents if she wanted to. *That* made the hunt worthwhile. Maybe it would ease the hurt. She rubbed her long arms and legs vigorously. Her emerald eyes hardened, her jaw set. He might try to dictate the rules of the game and manipulate the people around him, but he was dead, and she was very much alive and determined to avenge her mother's death. He would never succeed in death what he failed to do in life. Oh, Phillip was clever, there was no doubt about that, but he wasn't around to change the rules now. A sly look hardened her features. He never knew what really went on in Melanie's mind. He couldn't have guessed the cunning determination of the daughter he considered a nymphomaniac. He only thought he had won.

Melanie tossed the towel over the rack and unpinned her hair, running her fingers through the copper tangles. She had never given Phillip the letter her mother had written the night she died, and now she wondered if silence had been the wisest thing. She splashed on cooling cologne before padding back into the bedroom. Not that it mattered. In her heart, she believed her father had killed her mother as surely as if he had plunged a knife into her heart. He would prove his dissatisfaction with having daughters instead of sons . . . they would never be Hudson's. It would be his ultimate revenge for the dirty trick nature had played on him, using the Hudson fortune to damn his daughters. Melanie threw back her head and laughed for the first time that day.

A sensuous smile curved her lips. If Raine wouldn't see her at the office until next week, she'd just have to make a house call. The thought of Raine Bradburn's magnificent body quickened her pulse. It would be a pleasure seducing him and getting his land. The trap would be easy to set. She would be the bait to lure him and bring him to his knees with desire. Maybe Raine was the man to make her forget Charles. No one else had been able to.

She would be thirty-three in a few months. Ironically, her birthday was the day after Phillip's deadline. After she had the money and the stock, she'd celebrate. Tossing her mane of red hair, she tilted her head to one side, running her hands over her silken skin. Her breasts were full and firm, her waist small, her stomach flat, and her legs trim and tan. She closed her eyes. Raine Bradburn would be the finest trophy in her collection. Green eyes glittered dangerously when she finally opened them. She knew what people thought of her, but she didn't care. They didn't know why she seduced so many men. Only she knew the real reason, and even that wasn't much fun anymore. She flipped her hair over her shoulder and sauntered out of the room, heading for her dressing room.

Pulling a multicolored silk caftan from a hanger, she slipped it over her head, enjoying the sensuous material. She took a deep breath and walked out onto the balcony off her bedroom, leaning on the wrought iron rail. There was no time to waste. Alana and Hilary would be planning their strategy. Melanie frowned. She'd have to get Raine when he least expected it. He would be wary of any advance from a Hudson, but his hatred of Phillip made the hunt more exciting. Sex with Phillip's enemy excited her.

Raine would be racing this weekend. By Sunday evening he would be tired, relaxed and in the most receptive mood for her proposition. His guard would be down. It would be easy to seduce him then. Almost too easy. She rubbed her arms with her hands. Maybe he'd protest a little. That would only increase her pleasure when she won. Melanie sauntered down the steps, her skirt swirling softly around her knees, a satisfied smile on her face. Her first priority was getting onto the grounds of his estate. She knew a man who could help her with that. The rest would be easy, and not very distasteful, either. Raine Bradburn was the most eligible bachelor in the islands, and his reputation as a lover was unrivaled. Perhaps they could teach each other something . . . interesting.

Late Sunday afternoon Melanie found it easier than she anticipated getting onto Raine's estate. She didn't question why it was so easy, just accepting it as her due as she drove her Rolls up the winding drive. After checking her makeup and hair, she slipped out of the car. She wore a figure hugging silk sundress that matched the color of her eyes. The deep slash of the V neck and backless style left little to the imagination, just enough to cause an erotic shock when she unbuttoned it. She sauntered up the drive, her spike heels making her hips sway in invitation, ready to give Raine Bradburn the surprise of his life.

She was the one surprised when the oak door opened and the butler said, "Mr. Bradburn is waiting for you in the living room. This way please." He turned and walked through the large foyer not looking to see if she followed.

Melanie was speechless, quickly hiding the frown on her forehead. How did Raine know she was here? She knew it had been too easy. She might have to change her approach. She followed the ramrod straight back, looking around as she went. Raine Bradburn had good taste. The art work alone was worth a fortune. Her eyes focused on the man leaning against the wet bar. She licked her lips in anticipation. Excitement glowed in her eyes. What a specimen of manhood. Her gaze hungrily devoured him from the top of his dark head, across the broad shoulders to his flat stomach and lean hips in kahki shorts. His legs, lean and tanned, were crossed at the ankles. Yes, this would be fun.

"Hello, Raine," she said, her throaty voice breathless as she struck a pose in the doorway.

"Hello, Mrs. . . ." he paused, one dark brow quirking. "Is it still Shaunessay?"

She ignored the sarcasm in his voice. "I'm a Hudson again, but please, call me Melanie." The blue of his polo shirt matched his eyes. Gorgeous. She ran her tongue over her top lip and strolled into the room, her eyes never leaving Raine's face. She had to know exactly what he was thinking, but his face was expressionless, his eyes shuttered. She couldn't even tell if there was a spark of desire at the sight of her. She swallowed the frustration and impatience. A man like Raine Bradburn wouldn't be rushed.

"Would you like something to drink?" His question was polite, but she had the uneasy feeling that he didn't care if she said yes or no.

"Gin and tonic," she said, wandering around the living room, running her hand over the back of the blue and coral sofa. She thought of curling up in a provocative position in one of the coral wing chairs, but the green of her dress would clash. She chose the arm of the sofa, leaning back on one hand, crossing her legs to expose tanned thigh. Looking at him through her lashes, she murmured, "I suppose you're wondering why I'm here."

Raine handed her a glass, sat in a chair across from her, and stretched out his legs in front of him. He barely glanced at her. "You want to buy my land so you can control Hudson Enterprises and get all that Hudson money. You're going to make me an offer I can't refuse." He sounded bored.

Melanie thought fast. She'd have to change her tactics

slightly. Alana or Hilary must've already gotten to him. She gave him a wry look. "Good news travels fast."

He checked his watch and yawned. "So tell me, what's your offer?"

Melanie could have hit him for being so rude. He could at least look interested in what she had to say. She pushed herself off the arm of the sofa and moved to sit directly across from Raine. "You hated my father as much he hated you." She took a sip of her drink, running her tongue over her lips. "Now that he's dead, wouldn't you consider selling?"

His voice was dry again. "You haven't made me an offer."

She leaned back, staring thoughtfully into her glass, swirling the liquid, feeling the warmth from the drink begin to seep into her body. She leaned forward, giving him an excellent view of her cleavage. "I could give you more than just money."

"A social disease, perhaps?" he countered, the blue of his eyes icy.

Melanie felt her face flush, something that hadn't happened in years. She was supposed to be in control of the situation, but instead she felt frustration and an anger beginning to burn inside of her. "That's a hell of a thing to say to a lady."

"You're no lady, and we both know it." He rested one ankle on the other knee, his body looking relaxed, almost lazy, but Melanie knew better as he pinned her with a cold stare. "Get on with it, Melanie. What are you offering me for my land?"

She drummed her fingernails against the side of her glass, talking as if to herself. "I understand why you hated my father." God, even at the club for a simple scrub race, you'd think you were in contention for the America's Cup." Her eyes narrowed. "You were enemies for almost twenty years.

305

Don't you think it's time to put that rivalry and hatred to rest?"

"Kind of ironic that the first race your father was ahead of me this season was the one where he died." His gaze was still shuttered.

What was he thinking?

"The thrill of victory must have been too much for his heart," Raine said, cynicism lacing his voice.

"He didn't have a heart," Melanie said, draining her glass.

Raine shrugged. "That may have been, but you still haven't offered me anything." He paused, his gaze raking her body. "Nothing worthwhile."

She smothered the angry retort on her lips. He was baiting her, trying to get her to lose control. Her chin tilted upward. "Everyone has a price. Even you." A seductive smile crossed her face. She had noticed his gaze lingering on the deep V of her dress. He wasn't as immune to her as he wanted her to think.

"Depends on what you're selling." He took a sip of his drink watching Melanie all the time.

She had his interest now and was determined to keep it. "We could share Hudson Enterprises, Raine. You sell that little piece of land to me, and I control the corporation with Phillip's shares of stock." She leaned forward to put her drink on the huge glass-topped ship's wheel, giving him an even better view of her golden chest. "I'd be willing to let you have five percent of Hudson Enterprises ..." she paused. "And one hundred percent of me." She stood, circled the table, and stood directly in front of him. "I'd make it worth your while." One manicured hand went to her neck, slipping a button from the button hole. Her dress fell in a green pool around her ankles. She watched him intently, but there wasn't even a flicker of his lashes. She ran her hands over her breasts, supporting their weight in her hands as she flicked the nipples into hardened peaks. "I'm worth a lot more than rock and sand," she murmured. "You wouldn't be sorry."

His gaze lingered on her hands and then he lifted his head and met her heavy lidded eyes with a mocking look in his eyes. "Those green eyes and that copper hair are a lethal combination, Melanie. But how do I know you won't dump me just like all the others after you get what you want?"

"You and I are a lot alike," she murmured, wetting her lips and slipping one of her hands over her waist and down between her thighs. "We both have a reputation for being insatiable lovers ..." Her voice was husky, her fingers stroking the copper curls between her legs, while the other hand continued to caress her breast. "Come on, Raine, honey, you know you want to touch me, kiss me. Do it and make us both happy."

"A free sample so I know what I'm getting?" His voice was cold and hard.

It took her a few seconds to focus on his words and the contempt in his voice, but she wasn't ready to give up. There wasn't a man alive she couldn't control with sex.

"Nothing is free, Raine," she murmured, leaning forward, her hands on his shoulders, her breasts inches from his face. Triumph touched her face when his eyes widened and then narrowed. She knew she had won when he got to his feet and scooped her into his arms. She curled her arms around his neck. "I guarantee you'll never forget this." She closed her eyes and nibbled on his ear, her hands buried in his dark hair. When she felt the sun on her body she opened her eyes just before Raine released her and let her drop. She screamed as warm water covered her head. When she surfaced, she sputtered and pushed the hair from her face. "Is this your idea of a joke?" she demanded, treading water and wiping at her face, wrinkling her nose in disgust at the black streaks on her fingers. "My

307

hair is a mess, my makeup is running!" She glared up at him. "You have a hell of a sense of humor!"

"It's not meant to be funny." He stood over her, his hands on his hips. "You needed to be cooled off." As she swam to the side, he reached into a cabinet and pulled out a large towel. "When I want a woman, *I* am the aggressor, not the other way around."

"That's archaic!" She pulled herself out of the water.

Raine tossed the towel at her, his eyes like chips of ice. "When you're ready to talk business ... if you really want to talk, come back into the living room."

She gave an indignant snort. "You're as ruthless and cruel as my father ever was! You should have been great friends instead of enemies!" She wrapped the towel around her sarong style and padded back into the living room, picking up her dress. "Where's a bathroom?" she demanded.

Raine reached for his drink, settling back on the sofa, his face implacable. "You took it off in here. Might as well put it back on."

She glared at him, clasping her dress in one hand and the towel in the other. In all her encounters with men, none had humiliated her like Raine had in just a few minutes with a few well chosen words. He'd pay for this, she vowed. She dropped the towel and pulled her dress back on, fuming silently. How was she supposed to talk business with her hair dripping on her shoulders and her mascara smeared all over her face? She faced him with as much dignity as possible. "I have to have that land."

He put his drink down and crossed his arms over his chest. "Why not just give it up and get on with your life?"

"I have to control Hudson Enterprises," she muttered. "It's a matter of pride." She paused, her eyes narrowing. "And revenge."

"Powerful motivators," Raine said, pushing himself to his feet and heading back to the bar. He handed her a fresh drink.

Melanie accepted the drink, taking several swallows before putting it down and rubbing the back of her neck. No one could ever understand the depth of her hatred and bitterness, and she wasn't about to tell Raine Bradburn, opening herself to more hurt. "There are some things a person has to do."

He leaned one hip against the end of the sofa. "You're not a business woman. What will you do if you're elected CEO?"

Melanie knew she couldn't bluff him, but partial honesty might appeal to him. Taking a deep breath she said, "My mother deliberately drove off that cliff. It was no accident."

"You're sure?" He cocked his head, looking at her intently.

She had his undivided attention now, and she was going to use it. "My mother left a note before she left the house. My father had demanded a divorce. She just couldn't face it." Contempt laced her voice. "He wanted to marry that slut, but first he had to get my mother out of the way. He was going to discard her like an old bed sheet."

"Did she know that for sure?" Raine asked, a slight frown puckering his brow.

Melanie had her head bowed and didn't see the look on his face. "No, but the way he married Alana so quickly after mother's death certainly proves it." She picked up her drink and drained the glass.

"What does control of Hudson Enterprises have to do with all this?" Raine got to his feet and stood with his back to her, looking out the windows.

"I want that company to destroy it," she said, her voice low, her hands clasped in her lap.

Raine was silent for a moment, leaning against the door frame, one hand in the pocket of his shorts. "You'll be cutting off your supply of money, too."

"The profits will do nicely. A few investments and I'll live happily ever after." She met his gaze and lifted her chin. She wished she could find a way to wipe that arrogant look from his face. "Other men find me very attractive. I'm sure I won't have any trouble finding someone to keep me company."

"I'm sure." His voice was dry.

"We would have been great in bed," she murmured, regret in her voice as she imagined him as her lover.

"Probably terrific," he said, mockery in his eyes. "But I don't mix business with pleasure."

Melanie's brows flew up, her heart beating faster as she took a step toward him. "You mean if we weren't involved in this business, you might be interested in me personally?"

Raine straightened, his hands on his hips. "No, Melanie. Going to bed with Phillip Hudson's daughter would be like going to bed with the devil."

"But we'd have a hell of a good time," she murmured, her voice husky as she smiled at him, taking another step toward him.

"You're trying to seduce the wrong man." His eyes were cold, his face grim. "Don't waste your time."

She didn't like being rebuffed, not one little bit. A thought struck her. "What about Alana? I know you've seen her. You even went sailing together. She was married to the bastard!"

"I'll think about your offer, Melanie." He strode over to a chair and picked up her purse, handing it to her and guiding her toward the door. Obviously he wasn't about to discuss his relationship with Alana. "But my counter offer is controlling interest in Hudson Enterprises."

"How could I guarantee that?" she demanded, resisting his efforts to get her out of his house.

"If you're as smart as I think you are, you'll find a way." He opened the oak door and stood aside.

She was startled for a moment. Could he see beyond the facade she kept firmly in place? She recovered quickly. "I'd think you'd jump at the chance to destroy the company," she argued, standing in the open door way.

"I don't know for sure that you really intend to do that." His eyes narrowed, his mouth thinned. "You're a Hudson. I have no reason to trust you."

"I'll be back," she muttered, meeting his gaze with a determined glint in her eyes.

"Don't take too long," he mocked. "There are two other women who are just as anxious to get that land as you are."

She threaded trembling fingers through her hair. There was so little time and so much to do. She opened her purse and searched for her keys. He had her at such a disadvantage she couldn't even find her damn car keys. Her hair was a mess, her makeup ruined, and her ego shattered. Raine Bradburn topped her hate list. "I'll top any offer either Alana or Hilary make."

"Easy to say, difficult to do." He bent over and plucked the keys from her purse and dropped them into her outstretched hand.

She glared at him. "Good bye, Mr. Bradburn. I'd like to say it's been a pleasure ..." she let her voice trail off. Whirling around, her resolve for retaliation strengthened as his laughter followed her down the long walk.

She climbed into the car and slammed the door shut, blocking out his laughter and the image of a man in complete control. She refused to look in the mirror. Gunning the motor she got out of his estate as fast as possible. She had to think. What was the worst that could happen? Phillip would win and she'd end up with a few million in cash and some shares of stock.

The majority share holders would probably try to get her off the board, but they'd have a fight doing it.

Damn! Phillip was dead, but he still controlled and manipulated so many people. She wondered if he realized the power he gave Raine with the stipulation in his will. Probably. He knew Bradburn was ruthless. She shuddered, then squared her shoulders. He had humiliated her. He'd pay.

A wicked look crossed her face. A nice murder or two would solve everything. She chuckled to herself, pushing a damp strand of hair from her cheek. Self pity wasn't her style. Somehow she'd find a way to get out of this.

Melanie turned into her driveway, slamming on the breaks when she reached the front door. Hurrying into her house, she prayed no one saw her. Once she was in her room, she stripped off her dress and tossed it into the waste basket. She'd never wear it again.

Showering and drying her hair, she slipped on a red sun dress and walked out onto her lanai. She tossed her head back, watching the feathery clouds spread across the sky. Phillip loved a good fight.

Too bad he couldn't have found a suitable son-in-law to take over. Things might have been different. Melanie threw back her head and laughed, watching the birds scatter at the noise. Chandler was a lazy aristocrat, his mind on photography, not business. She leaned on the rail and sighed deeply. She hadn't done very well in the husband department either. Jonathan was more interested in boats than he was in business. Nathan wanted the money, oh, yes, but he didn't want to work for it. Phillip thought Nathan might work out until he caught him embezzling money. No, definitely not Nathan. A wry look crossed her face. Kevin had definite possibilities. He was bright, enthusiastic, had a good mind for business, and was creative. Too bad he was hooked on cocaine or he might have convinced Philip that he could run the company. She sighed.

She had an uncanny ability to pick losers. Raine Bradburn was no loser. Just the thought of the man sent a chill skittering up and down her spine. Tangling with a man like Bradburn was like walking into a cage with a leopard and hoping to beat him at his own game. Too bad he had humiliated her. They would have made a stunning couple. And he might have erased the ache Charles caused.

Chapter Twenty-two

Alana walked into her closet, searching for just the right dress, but nothing seemed right as she discarded outfit after outfit. She didn't want to go to this charity dinner-dance and auction, but since Phillip had been one of the sponsors of the event, she had to represent him.

Sometimes she felt as if she'd spend the rest of her life representing Phillip's interests ... unless she didn't get Raine's land. She hadn't asked anyone to accompany her, she'd rather go alone, but it was difficult knowing what to wear. Elegant, but subdued. She finally pulled a black sheath from a hanger and slipped it over her head, smoothing it over her hips. The simple sheath became an elegantly sexy dress as it hugged her curves, the scooped neckline exposing ivory skin. Her back was bare, the silky material draped to her waist. The straight skirt was slit to midthigh. Alana pirouetted in front of the mirror, trying to decide if it was too provocative for a widow to wear to a formal event. She liked the dress, it felt good, and she wore it.

Diamond stud earrings and a Cartier teardrop diamond necklace set off the black of the dress.

She waited for the company limousine, clutching her black

velvet purse. Would Raine be there? Would he even speak to her? Did she even want him to? Alana wasn't sure what she wanted anymore and gave up trying to figure it out as the long black car pulled up.

The ballroom of Hudson Enterprises' most luxurious hotel was filled with women in designer gowns and sparkling jewels and men in elegant tuxedos. The crystal chandeliers cast a soft glow on the guests as they mingled discussing the best stocks to buy and the newest restaurant to try.

Alana glanced at the tables. Crystal wine glasses, fine bone china, and sterling cutlery rested on snowy white cloths. Her gaze was drawn to the colorful floral arrangements in the center of each round table. Candles flickered in the centerpieces. Sea shells holding engraved place cards were at each table. Alana crossed to the registration table.

"Hello, Alana." Suzanne Munroe gave her a cool smile. Suzanne was the daughter of an oil baron from Texas. She was married to a prominent surgeon and for the last twenty years considered herself to be the arbiter of good taste. She had been vocal in her condemnation of Phillip's hasty marriage. Suzanne wore a stunning jeweled off the shoulder white dress. Her black hair was arranged in an elaborate style on top of her head, and a fortune in rubies and diamonds adorned her ears, neck, wrists, and fingers.

"Hello, Suzanne."

The older woman handed Alana a paddle with a number on it. "This is your bidding paddle. Please use it frequently. We're trying to break last year's record of one hundred and fifty thousand dollars." She showed Alana where she would be sitting and dismissed her without another glance.

Alana wandered into the ballroom. The skin on the back of

her neck tingled. She turned around, her gaze held by Raine's mocking one.

She took a deep breath, drinking in the sight of him, her eyes the color of spring violets. His double-breasted tuxedo covered a finely tucked white shirt. His bow tie and cumberbund were red. He looked self assured, slightly arrogant, and devastingly male. No man had a right to look that handsome, she thought as a slow burning fire lapped at her nerves. Cobalt eyes returned the inspection as Raine's gaze lazily traveled from her ebony hair to her creamy shoulders, lingering on the swell of her breasts before continuing a sensuous journey over her hips, thighs and calves before returning to her face.

Alana held her breath, the noise of the other guests receding into the background. He hadn't touched her physically, and yet she felt as if he had caressed her. Her body came alive under his intense scrutiny as she felt the pull of his magnetism. She wanted to bury herself in his embrace, forgetting Phillip's will. The thought of wild passionate love with this man made her tremble. The intensity of her feelings scared her, while the desire in his eye excited her.

"Hello, Alana." Raine's eyes glittered.

"Hello." She racked her brain for something to say while her heart hammered against her ribs. "How did you do in the race today?" she finally asked.

He shrugged, his gaze never leaving her face. "First to finish, first in division, first overall." His expression showed his interest in something other than a yacht race.

His nearness made it difficult to think. "Not bad against the competition you had. I'm impressed." It was more than the race that impressed her. The clean, lime scent of his cologne filled her head and the desire in the depth of his eyes made her weak.

"I'm impressed as well." His hand touched her bare back,

317

sending a tremor down her spine. "I believe we're seated at the same table."

Alana's eyes widened. "We are?"

"I arranged it," he murmured, guiding her toward a table. His fingers ran lightly down her back. "This dress is going to make it difficult for me to think about anything except what's under it."

Alana tried to ignore the tingling sensation that radiated from his touch. "It's a simple dinner dress," she murmured, looking over her shoulder at him. "It's none of your business what's underneath it."

He held out her chair, bending over to whisper in her ear, "I know exactly what's underneath, Alana. My knowledge is of the most intimate nature." He straightened, smiling at the three other couples approaching their table. "You're safe for now," he said as he slipped into the seat next to her.

Alana greeted the others while wanting to wipe the self-assured look from Raine's face. One couple were both doctors Alana knew, the husband of the second couple worked for Raine and his wife was in real estate, and the third couple both taught at the university. The women wore sequins and jewels, the men tuxedos.

When Raine introduced Alana to his vice president and his wife, Alana cringed when the woman's eyebrows disappeared into her bouffant hairdo.

"I was sorry to hear about your husband," the bearded professor murmured. "It must be very difficult for you to try to fill his place."

"No one could replace Phillip." She looked at Raine through lowered lashes. "What classes do you teach?" she asked the woman next to him.

While the woman launched into a discussion of her classes, Alana exchanged a wry look with Raine.

As dinner was served, Alana leaned toward Raine. "People

think we came to this together," she hissed. "The gossip is going to be terrible."

"The island is already buzzing about Hudson's will. We just happened to be seated at the same table." He shrugged broad shoulders, his eyes twinkling. "Relax. There's nothing you can do about it now."

Alana couldn't relax knowing the whispers and glances were aimed at her. It didn't help to have Raine being so solicitous.

During the main course, Raine glanced at her. "How is your filet?"

"Perfect."

"Good." There was a satisfied look on his face.

Alana was wary. "What difference does it make to you how the meat tastes in a Hudson hotel?"

"Because the meat comes from one of my ranches." He chuckled at her incredulous expression.

She shook her head. "Phillip would never allow it."

"Phillip never knew it."

Her gaze narrowed. "I don't believe it."

"I admit, I had to bury the connections in a string of holding companies, but ultimately, Bradburn International owns the suppliers of beef and produce to all the Hudson hotels."

Alana had to laugh. "That is the most outrageous thing I've ever heard. You must've been hysterical every time a check came from Hudson Enterprises."

He grinned. "That's about it."

Melanie looked over Greg's shoulder and saw Alana and Raine sitting at a table not far away. Were they here together? Melanie couldn't imagine Alana being seen in public with another man so soon after Phillip's death. What were they up to? Melanie sat back, the green of her strapless silk dress matching the color of her eyes. Elaborate gold and jade earrings almost touched her bare shoulders. Her hair was piled on top of her head, exposing the creamy column of her neck. She toyed with the large chunk of jade around her neck. This was the second time she had seen them together. It had to be more than a coincidence. She would have to talk to Arty in the morning. She hoped they were having an affair, because it would make her job so much easier. She could get rid of Alana and persuade Raine to sell the land to her.

"Melanie, you haven't heard a word I've said," Greg muttered.

She turned a dazzling smile on her escort as Raine looked their way. She would show Raine Bradburn what a fool he had been. Greg was young, handsome, and wealthy. Melanie leaned toward Greg. "I'm sorry, honey." She patted his arm. "I was just thinking about some of the auction items. I'd really like to have that Corvette."

He put an arm around her shoulders, nuzzling her neck. "Maybe we can make a deal."

"Hmmmmm." She smiled at him meeting Raine's mocking gaze. "What did you have in mind?"

"A weekend on Kauai." His lips touched her cheek.

"In exchange for a Corvette?" She turned to look at him, laughter in her eyes.

"A very long weekend."

Melanie thought about it. She really wanted that silver car. It would be nice to drive something different. "When?"

"Name the date." Greg sat back, a look of satisfaction settling on his face.

Melanie thought fast. There was a special board meeting coming up. She would show Charles he wasn't the only man in her life. She gave the dates to Greg.

"Fine." His hand stroked her bare shoulder. "You'll look wonderful speeding through Honolulu with that car."

Melanie sat back and relaxed. The evening wasn't a total

loss. She would prove to Raine that he had made a mistake by turning down her offer, Charles would find out that she wasn't waiting around for him, and she would have a shiny new car to drive. Not to mention a weekend with Greg.

Hilary jabbed Chandler in the ribs. "Is that Alana with Raine Bradburn across the room?"

Chandler glanced around the room. "Where?"

"At the table next to the Millers." Her eyes narrowed. "What the hell are they doing here together?"

"Hilary, keep your voice down." Chandler shifted in his chair.

Hilary's mouth snapped shut. Her blue silk organza off-the-shoulder dress matched the blue in her eyes and the sapphires in her ears and around her neck. "Do you think they came together?"

Chandler shrugged, straightening his cuff and the diamond cufflink. "Alana is too smart for that. Phillip was a major patron of this event. She's probably here representing him. It's just a coincidence."

"It's too much of a coincidence," Hillary muttered, reaching for her martini. "Do you think he's sold the land to her?" The thought made her stomach tighten.

"You would have heard about it if he had." Chandler sipped his Perrier. "Bradburn isn't going to sell quickly while he can play with the three women in Phillip's life." His gaze was thoughtful. "I wonder what his price is."

"I don't know," Hilary said with a sigh, taking another sip of her drink. "I wish I did. I thought I was giving him an excellent deal and he laughed in my face." She rubbed her temple. "He's right about one thing. He doesn't need to sell that land at all, while the three of us need it desperately."

"Don't give up, Hilary. There must be something he wants."

"Controlling interest in Hudson Enterprises." She finished her drink, looking for a waiter so she could order another one.

Chandler took the glass from her hand. "I'll get it for you." He stood, straightened his jacket, and sauntered toward the bar.

Hilary watched him go and then turned back to Alana and Raine. Her face hardened as she watched them, their heads close together. If Alana was having an affair with Raine, Hilary would never have a chance at getting that land. What did the woman have that turned strong, powerful men into fools?

Chandler strolled toward the bar, Hilary's empty glass in his hand. He had no idea what was between Raine Bradburn and Alana Hudson, but he knew it meant Hilary's chances for getting his land were slim. It was time to think of his own security.

Whitney Jameson was standing near the bar. She was fortyish, with a tall, athletic frame. Her brown hair was cut very short, emphasizing her high cheekbones and oval face. Huge brown eyes were fringed with the longest natural lashes Chandler had ever seen. Her lemon silk brocade sheath gave her an exotic, sultry look that took his breath away. Whitney had inherited millions from her father's shipping company and she was between husbands.

Chandler approached her. "Hello, Whitney."

"Chandler." She nodded at him and noticed the empty glass in his hand. "Hilary couldn't wait, hmm?"

He shrugged. He didn't want to talk about Hilary. "Whitney, would you consider posing for me? You've got such beautiful bone structure."

One dark brow lifted. "Why haven't you asked me before?"

Chandler decided to play it cool. Whitney was a sophisticated woman of the world. "I guess I was too afraid you'd laugh at me." He didn't add that she had been married at the time.

322

"I'm flattered, Chandler." She looked at him with renewed interest. "Would you make me look glamourous?"

"You are glamourous. I want to capture your beauty on film." He also wanted to have some insurance if Hilary didn't get the lion's share of her father's money.

Whitney preened. "When would you like to photograph me?"

"At your convenience." He gazed into her eyes, sending a subtle message to her.

She responded as he had hoped she would. "Call me Monday morning. We'll set up a time." She paused. "Will this be at your studio?"

He concentrated on her features, lifting her chin with one lean finger. "I think both the studio and in your home." He lowered his voice. "You won't be sorry."

"I'm looking forward to it."

Chandler smiled and went to the bar. If everything went as he planned, Whitney Jameson would be his insurance policy. He might even get a second one. A man couldn't be too careful.

By the time the auction began, Alana was almost enjoying herself. Looking through the program, she saw several items she wanted to bid on, but when Raine began outbidding her on the items she was interested in, she turned to glare at him. "You just paid a thousand dollars for a tennis racquet worth two hundred! What did you do that for?"

"You were willing to pay seven hundred," he countered.

"That's because I wanted it," she muttered, snapping her program open to the next page.

"Maybe I'll let you buy it from me if you're a good girl," he teased, his arm draped over the back of her chair. He leaned closer. "I might even give it to you if you're really good."

"I might be terrific, but you'll never know," she muttered

under her breath before smiling sweetly. "I hope you enjoy your new racquet."

"Not as much as I'd enjoy you." He returned her smile with a mocking one of his own.

Alana tried to shift away from him. There was only one more item she wanted to bid on, so she watched in amazement as Raine spent thousands of dollars on articles worth a fraction of what he was paying.

He leaned over. "It's deductible. Don't worry."

"I don't care how you spend your money." She turned away from him.

The earrings she wanted were the last item for sale. They were large square cut amethysts of deep purple surrounded with diamonds. The bidding opened at five thousand dollars. Alana's bidding paddle went up. She was here because of Phillip, so she decided he could pay for the earrings.

Alana stayed in the bidding until the price hit fifteen thousand. Raine continued to bid until he finally got them for twenty thousand. An odd tug of jealousy made her wonder what lucky woman would get Raine's generous gift.

"Those earrings were only worth fifteen thousand," she whispered.

"It's for a good cause." He leaned back, smiling at her. "And I needed a special gift for a special lady. How could I lose?"

Alana was silent. Maybe he couldn't lose, but if she stayed around him, she could be the big loser. Quickly getting to her feet, she excused herself and headed for the powder room. She had done her part, put in an appearance, and now she wanted to leave.

Alana had stepped out onto the street, ready to ask the valet to get a cab, when Raine's Lamborghini stopped at the curb.

Before she could move, Raine had stepped from the shadows, gripped her elbow, and guided her toward his car.

Too stunned to protest, she settled next to him, then stared at him. "What do you think you're doing?"

"I thought it might be nice to take a walk along the beach."

"You might have asked me." She should be upset, but was secretly pleased to be with him.

"You would have said no." They drove in silence until he parked his car on a deserted stretch of beach. "Come on. Let's walk." He opened the door and took her hand, pulling her toward him. He bent over and slipped off her shoes, kicked his off and tossed them into the car before leading her toward the water's edge. A full moon cast a silver path over the ocean as gentle waves lapped the shore. The trade winds ruffled their hair and caressed their skin.

The sand was cool beneath her feet, the soft rhythm of the surf relaxing. Her voice was so soft, Raine had to strain to hear it. "It's beautiful out here."

"You're beautiful." He took her hand and walked further down the beach.

"Did you really plan for us to sit together tonight?" She stopped walking and turned to him. The moonlight softened his features to silver and ebony.

"Would it bother you if I said yes?" He put his hands on her shoulders and cupped her face.

"No, I guess not. I had a good time in spite of the stares and whispers."

His thumbs traced the outline of her lips. "Better get used to them. When people see us together, they're bound to speculate on what's going on."

"Why should they see us together?" Did he think she would be his mistress in exchange for the land?

"You ask too many questions." He paused, his gaze locking with hers. "I have more important things on my mind."

"Like what?" she murmured, reaching up and running a finger along the line of his jaw.

"Like kissing you." His lips touched her temple and forehead. His hands went to her hair, pulling out the pins and dropping them into his pocket. His fingers combed through the silky curtain, as the breeze swirled it around her shoulders. "Like taking you into my arms like this and making you forget everything but me." He wrapped his arms around her, kissing her hungrily. She was quick to respond as her mouth opened to his probing like a thirsty flower drinks the morning dew. His hand roamed over her bare back, creating a trail of fire the trade winds fanned into flames.

Alana leaned into him, desperate for the feel of his body next to hers, imprinting her body on his. She melted from the heat of his desire, but the clothing between them frustrated her. She started to slip his jacket from his shoulders, but he stopped her.

"Wait." Raine reached into his pocket and pulled out a small box. "These are for you."

She opened the box, surprised to see the amethyst and diamond earrings she had wanted. "I can't accept them," she murmured, regret in her voice.

"They were made for you." He pulled them from the box and replaced the earrings she wore with the new ones. "No strings, Alana." He kissed her and all thought of objecting drained from her mind and body.

Raine's jacket fell to the sand. Alana reached up to loosen his tie and tossed it aside as well, a smile lighting her eyes. One button at a time she loosened the studs of his shirt, dropping kisses as she progressed. "You're such a study in opposites," she whispered. "You're so strong, your muscles are like steel, and yet the skin covering them is as smooth and warm as the ocean." She pushed the shirt from his shoulders, rubbing the palms of her hands over his chest. The springy chest hairs caught between her fingers, and she heard the sharp intake of his breath as she kissed first one and then the other male nipple.

"And you are a captivating tormentor." He lifted her hair and kissed the sensitive skin at her nape. His lips touched her shoulder as his hands found the button at her neck and the short zipper at her waist. His lips nudged it from her shoulders and Alana wiggled impatiently as it fell in a dark pool around her feet. The warm night air did nothing to cool the fires burning inside of her, but rather fanned them until she thought she would burn up with desire. Raine's lips touched the sensitive skin at her inner elbow, her wrist, the palms of her hands. She leaned toward him, but he held her away, his tongue leaving moist circles around her breasts, teasing and tormenting until she couldn't stand it.

Raine eased her down onto the silky sand, slipping his hand under her lace panties and pulling them off. Alana lay still as Raine towered over her, the moonlight making her skin look like antique ivory. She heard the soft rustle of his clothes, and then he was kneeling over her, one hand tracing the path of the moonbeams.

"You are so beautiful, so beautiful." His touch was gentle as his voice shook.

Alana's eyes clouded with desire, her voice husky with need. "Don't talk, Raine. Kiss me." She moved restlessly as he continued to caress her.

"Do you want me to kiss you here?" he asked, touching his lips to first one taut peak and then the other.

"Oh, yes, yes!" She couldn't lie still under his sensual onslaught.

"And do you want me to kiss you here?" His voice was deep, rolling over her and adding to her pleasure as his mouth trailed a moist path to her soft stomach.

327

"Oh, God, yes," she sighed, arching her body to meet his mouth.

He moved lower. Instinctively she spread her thighs, willing him to ease the ache that coiled inside of her, the desperate need and desire that could only be satisfied by him. "And what about this?" he asked, breathing hard as first he brushed the soft mound of dark hair with his finger before tracing the path with his lips.

A low groan came from deep in her throat. Her hands gripped his shoulders as she moved under him.

He stopped abruptly, kneeling over her, his hands on either side of her head. "Do you want me, Alana?"

"Oh, yes." Her breasts ached for his touch, her legs were ready to wrap around him, uniting them in their mutual need. His desire was as great as hers. She started to run one hand down his body. He stopped her hand.

"No more denying, Alana. No more pretending." His eyes glittered in the darkness, boring into her soul.

She met his gaze with a heated one of her own. "I want you more than I've ever wanted a man before in my life. Please, Raine."

"God help me, Alana, but I need you and only you," he said so softly she wasn't certain she had even heard it. He entered her with great shuddering thrusts, sending them into oblivion, two shooting stars entwined as one.

It wasn't until later as they floated back to earth that Alana even remembered where they were. Nothing mattered but the moment. She was cradled in Raine's arms and nothing could touch her.

He nuzzled her neck, his hand stroking her arm. "How about a moonlight swim?"

She pretended shock. "We don't have any suits."

His breath was warm as he chuckled and ran a knowing hand from shoulder to hip. "We have all we need."

"Okay." She outlined his mouth with her tongue, pushing against him and jumping to her feet. "Last one in cooks breakfast." She felt light as air, as joyous as a free flying kite, younger than a new born babe. She ran toward the ocean. Tonight was hers.

She splashed into the surf, her body glowing in the moonlight like an ancient goddess of the sea. She didn't hear Raine mutter to himself, "What am I going to do with you, Alana? What the hell am I going to do with the damn land!"

Chapter Twenty-three

Raine dropped his frame onto the multistriped lounge beside the sparkling water of his pool. Twenty laps hadn't begun to ease the tension in the pit of his stomach. He tossed back a whiskey and slammed the glass onto the pebblelike frosted surface of the glass table next to him. Alcohol couldn't numb the sense of loss. Damn! Of all the women in the world, why the hell did Alana Hudson have to be the one to infiltrate his mind, his body, his very soul. He leaned back and stared sightlessly over the dark ocean, knowing sleep would evade him again tonight. He wanted her beside him, now, tomorrow, perhaps forever. He slammed his right fist into the palm of his left hand. Stupid. That's what he was. Just plain stupid. A woman had never gotten under his skin before. Why did it have to be the widow of his worst enemy?

Raine rubbed a hand wearily over his eyes, wishing he could give his brain a rest, welcoming even a short respite from this dilemma. That damned piece of rock stood between him and the woman who had penetrated his defenses. He had enjoyed holding that piece of land over Phillip Hudson's head, but when the older man died, its importance had taken on monumental proportions. Hilary was desperate enough to almost risk gambling away the company, and Melanie was willing to use her body and any other means to get it. How much of her story was true? Had Phillip Hudson demanded a divorce causing his wife to drive off a cliff? It wouldn't come as a great surprise. He let out a long sigh. And then there was Alana. She was the most capable of the three women to run the company, and after the hell Phillip put her through, she deserved every penny of his fortune. Raine wanted a personal relationship with her, but that land was a wall a mile high between them. If he sold it to her, he would never know if she was his lover because of gratitude for the land or some deeper emotion. If he didn't sell to her, he was throwing her into the lion's den with her stepdaughters. There was always an outside chance the directors of Hudson Enterprises would elect Alana permanently as CEO or president, but he had his doubts. Phillip had wanted the land because Raine owned it, trying to force Raine to bend to his will, proving which man was the most powerful, but Alana had helped plan the beautiful complex. It would be a jewel in the crown of the islands. He wanted to see her succeed. Of course, there was always the chance that if Hudson Enterprises didn't get the land and Alana was out of a job, she'd come work for him. He groaned. Sure. Then *she'd* never know if he had deliberately withheld the land just so she'd have to work for him, or she'd think she'd have to be his lover to keep her job. With her pride she'd probably disappear from the islands rather than put herself in that position. Even if she agreed to work for him, she'd always wonder if he had hired her because of his interest in her. She'd never be certain that when he was no longer interested, he'd fire her. She didn't trust men very much right now, and he understood her reasoning, but it sure made for a no-win situation.

Getting to his feet, he rested his hands on his hips, grim determination etched on his hard features. He wanted Alana and he wanted her now. He wanted her nestled next to his body at night, he wanted to wake up with her beside him, make love with her, talk to her, laugh with her. He'd never get to sleep if he kept thinking of porcelain skin and ebony hair, her eyes the color of violets when she was happy, the color of amethyst when aroused, or the color of delicate orchids when she was upset. Maybe a run would help clear his mind. He padded into his bedroom, glancing at his bed, but when images of Alana plagued his mind, he muttered under his breath and reached for his running shoes. Maybe he should just kidnap her and sail away to Tahiti or Australia. Grumbling at this unexpected whimsical side of his nature, he pulled on his running shoes and stomped out the door.

The first call Chandler made Monday morning was to Whitney Jameson. "Good morning, Whitney."

"Chandler! I wondered if you'd remember."

"I couldn't forget you." Or your money, he thought as he doodled on the paper on his desk. "When would you like to come into the studio?"

"I don't know." She paused. "I don't have anything to wear. What would you suggest?"

The purring in her voice was unmistakable. He wanted to suggest she wear nothing at all, but that would come later. He hoped. "The dress you wore the other night was lovely. Dark colors would photograph well."

"Could you come by the house and help me choose something to wear?"

Chandler smiled. This was easier than he thought it would be. He had been wasting his time waiting for Hilary to inherit her father's millions. "How about one o'clock today?" He had the afternoon free.

"Fine." She paused. "We could set up an appointment after we meet this afternoon."

Chandler sat back after hanging up the receiver, a wide smile on his face. It was time to get back into an active social life. The prostitutes were okay, but an affair was much more exciting, especially with a wealthy woman.

Raine was in a surly mood as he stalked into his office. He had run ten miles, done another twenty laps, and still sleep evaded him. Not having a solution to his problem frustrated him. He was used to assessing a situation, taking calculated risks, making decisions, and winning.

"Good morning," Rebecca said with a smile, following him into his office. Slight in stature and the same age as her boss, she had worked for him for fifteen years, starting out when the business consisted of just the two of them. She was not intimidated by his testy mood.

"Good morning," he snarled as he slammed his briefcase onto his cluttered desk, sending papers flying in every direction.

"How about a cup of coffee? You look like you could use it." She walked to a wall of bookcases and pushed a button. A door slid open, revealing a counter with a coffee pot and a small refrigerator. "You really shouldn't stay out all night, Raine. You're not twenty-one anymore." Her tone was light and teasing as she made coffee.

Not in the mood for teasing, he gave her a dark look, raking a hand through rumbled hair. "You're my secretary, not my mother."

She clicked her tongue and shook her head. "My, my. We're in a good mood today. Haven't seen you this grouchy since you lost out on Boat of the Year by one point."

He glared at her, opening his brief case, feeling like he had been tossed from a wave along the Bonzai Pipeline. "Just give me the coffee."

She returned with a mug of steaming liquid, raising her eyebrows, a knowing look on her face. "A woman has finally gotten to you. Who is it? Anyone I might know?" She seemed pleased by the idea as she bent to pick up the papers that had drifted to the floor.

"Don't look so damned happy about it," he growled taking the cup and easing into his leather chair, wondering if he was really that transparent.

"It's about time you found a woman who didn't fall all over you trying to please you." She put the papers back on his desk and handed him a stack of phone messages. "You've always been able to love 'em and leave 'em. How does it feel to be frustrated?"

"It feels like hell." He sipped the liquid and sorted through the messages, dumping some into the waste basket and setting others aside. He sat back, his gaze narrowing on Rebecca's face. His voice was thoughtful. "So you think it's a woman and I've met my match, do you?"

"Obviously," she said with a smile, handing him a letter to sign. "So who is it? You know I won't say a word."

He knew she wouldn't, and he had to tell someone. "Alana Hudson."

Rebecca gasped. "Phillip Hudson's widow? You're not serious!"

"I'm afraid I am." He leaned back and looked at her. "Crazy, isn't it?"

"That's an understatement." She sat down on the edge of the chair, looking at him curiously. "From everything I've heard about Alana Hudson, aside from the nasty gossip about marrying Phillip Hudson, she's one exceptional lady. It would take someone special to get your attention."

He signed the letter and handed it back to her, a wary look in his eyes. "Just exactly what have you heard?"

"All of it?" she asked, raising her brows, a smile tugging the corners of her lips. "Or just the good stuff?"

"Rebecca, you can be replaced," he muttered, taking another sip of coffee. She was one woman he could talk to and not worry that his words were going to appear in print the next day. She was the soul of discretion, knew what was happening on the island before most people did, and was happily married to a police detective with two lively teenagers.

"I know hundreds of women who would line up for my job," she returned easily, handing him a file on one of their projects. "Of course, they'd be more interested in Raine Bradburn's personal life than in typing his letters."

He grunted in reply. As he scanned the papers he said, "You still haven't told me what you know about Alana Hudson."

She gave him a knowing look, then tapped her pencil on her chin. "No one seems to know anything about her family. She never mentions mother, father, brothers or sisters. Lots of speculation about that, but no facts. She worked her way to the top of Hudson Enterprises. Started out in the marketing and advertising division, moved on to corporate headquarters, and when she hit the new projects division she caught the eye of the big man himself." She paused. "I think he was her mentor before he became her lover, not the other way around." Rebecca frowned. "She seems like a well-grounded, classy lady. Why would someone like that pick up with scum like Phillip Hudson?"

"You're prejudice," he told her, putting the file down and concentrating on the woman sitting across from him. She was one of his best sources of information. "Have you heard anything new about what's going on at Hudson Enterprises?"

She shook her head. "No more than you already know. That piece of land you own is certainly causing a lot of problems. Those three women were never friendly, but Phillip Hudson has made them enemies. No one seems to have drawn the first blood. I wonder if Phillip realized the power he was giving to you when he made that will. You could make any one of them rich and powerful if you sell the land to them. If not . . ." she shrugged. "Three unhappy women."

Rained nodded in agreement. He had wondered more than once why Phillip would put him in this position. Had he guessed at Raine's interest in his wife? He didn't think so, but then, Phillip had his own set of spies. "Why would I want to make any of them happy?"

"Why indeed," she murmured, her voice dry. "I can think of one woman in that trio that you'd like to make happy, and it's not Hilary or Melanie."

"If only it were that easy." Raine leaned back in his chair and drained his cup. "It would be a lot easier if Alana needed *me* more than she needed that land. It would be even better if she didn't need that damn land, and if she weren't the widow of Phillip Hudson."

"But she needs that land to keep her position in the company, and she is the widow of Phillip Hudson, so it's no use wishing otherwise." Rebecca handed Raine another folder. "Here's the file on the electronics firm you're interested in. Ben said it looks good. Do you want him to close the deal?"

Raine was silent as he took the folder and skimmed the contents. California. Maybe he should finish negotiations himself. A little time and space could do wonders to get his thinking back in order. He was a practical, self-contained man, used to being in control of everything, including his emotions. Some time in California might be just what he needed. New faces, new ideas, new women. "Set up a meeting as soon as possible," he finally said, his mind made up. "And then book a flight for Ben and me." He leaned back, closing his eyes. "I'll close the deal myself."

"I'll see to everything, boss."

When she closed the door behind her, Raine ran his hands over tired eyes. He was weary, bone-tired. This stupid land was one problem he had no solution for. Oh, it was almost fun watching Hilary and Melanie vie for his attention and thinking of creative ways to get the land on Maui, but Alana was another matter. That little piece of land might as well be Moana Loa standing between them. Damn that Phillip Hudson!

Raine got to his feet and stared out the expanse of windows, watching sailboats skim over the blue water. What did he care as long as he got Alana into his bed? Maybe it would be even better if he held onto that land until after the deadline. Alana would probably be out of a job. She'd need him. He could have her on any terms he wanted. And yet, somehow, that still wasn't good enough.

He turned from the window and settled into his chair. He had work to do. He returned to the folder in front of him, willing himself to concentrate on the work to be done before going to California.

Chandler had never been to Whitney's estate on Koko Head, but from the moment he entered the elaborate wrought iron gates, he was enthralled. The house and grounds appealed to his aesthetic taste. He parked his white BMW sedan and strolled up the walk skirting the pond stocked with huge gold fish and lilies. He made his way toward the entrance portico of heavy wooden columns and lava rock. Whitney waited in the foyer, striking in white against an antique Hawaiian tapa cloth.

"Hello, Chandler." She held out her hand to him.

"Hello, Whitney." He took her hand in his and raised it to his lips, his gaze meeting hers.

"Would you like something to drink?" She turned to walk into the living room.

Chandler followed, his gaze taking in the white plaster walls, the wicker furniture, koa wood tables, and Oriental rugs on hardwood floors. The neutral colors were splashed with vibrant colors of fresh flowers in huge pottery vases and tropical greenery. "Iced tea would be fine." He wandered around the room, impressed with the artifacts of other cultures.

Whitney handed him a glass and led the way outside. A swimming pool and tennis court were visible from the banyon-shaded courtyard. The gentle trickle of water draining into a lava rock pond gave Chandler the feeling of peace and tranquility. He settled onto a cushioned rattan chair. "Your home is lovely," he murmured.

"Thank you." She sipped her tea. "You said you'd help me find something suitable to wear."

"Anything would look good on you." Chandler decided to take a chance. "You'd look equally as stunning in nothing at all." He watched her reaction carefully. If she drew back, he knew all they would do is work, but if she agreed, he knew she was interested in him.

Whitney sat back, a slight flush to her cheeks. "Do you want me to pose in the nude?"

"It's been done before." He smiled at her. "My work is tastefully done."

"I know. Helen showed me the portrait you did of her for her husband's birthday. I hardly recognized her. You did a fantastic job."

"Will you consider it?"

She smiled at him. "Definitely." Getting to her feet, she said, "Would you like to see the gowns I've picked out?"

Chandler nodded and followed her through the cool interior of the house to her suite. A fan softly whirled from the peak of the high beamed ceiling. White walls were decorated with paintings of Hawaiian royalty and carved koa wood statues of ancient gods. The sitting room had overstuffed chintz chairs in a lemon and white stripe. A gilt fireplace dominated one wall.

Whitney continued on into the bedroom. Chandler followed. She waved a hand toward a settee covered in creamy damask. "I'll be right back."

Chandler waited. He was in her bedroom already. Whitney wasn't shy. She must be attracted to him.

Reappearing in a filmy black negligee, she posed in the doorway. "How's this?"

Chandler felt a stirring in his loins. The light from her dressing room outlined every lovely curve of her body. Her nipples peeked through the sheer fabric. "It's lovely."

She walked toward him. "Will we be alone in the studio?"

"If it makes you feel more comfortable." His gaze rested on her breasts.

"I think it would be nicer. Just the two of us." She stood before him, smiling down at him, her fingers toying with the satin belt.

He reached up and ran his finger down the lacey edge over the gentle swell of her breast. "Just the two of us," he repeated. His fingers covered hers as he slowly released the belt, the front of her gown separating.

Whitney stood as Chandler's mouth closed over one taut peak and then the other, his hands stroking her waist and hips. He pulled her closer, the satin of her skin feeding his desire. His mouth moved lower, hovering over her flat stomach and then to the mound between her legs.

Whitney groaned and pulled Chandler to his feet, wrapping her arms around his neck and plunging her tongue into his mouth. She pulled off his shirt and helped him with his slacks. Her gown was on the floor.

Naked, they collapsed on her bed. She teased him with her breasts, rubbing them across his chest. Whitney pressed kisses along his shoulder, exploring his body as he longed to do to her.

Chandler captured her mouth again, pushing her back onto the pillows, his body poised over hers. He covered her body with kisses until she was quivering with desire.

She pulled him into her, her legs wrapped around him as she

arched toward him, her hands gripping his buttocks. They rocked together in a heated embrace, gutteral sounds coming from both of them. They strained toward a searing climax, writhing and turning, their bodies slick with perspiration.

It was a long time before Chandler could breath normally. He hadn't felt so wonderful in years.

Whitney was the first to speak. "Well, I was wrong."

Chandler turned to look at her, his softly stroking hand stopping. "What?"

"I was wrong," she said, her eyes still closed.

"About what?" His heart sank. The sex hadn't been good enough for her to want him to be her lover. She was used to more sophisticated men. Chandler hadn't cheated on Hilary often enough to get that experience, although now, he wished he had. Making love to Hilary was like making love to a corpse.

"I thought you were gay."

Chandler threw back his head and laughed. "Gay? What gave you that idea?"

"Hilary always looks so . . . frustrated. And you are so prim . . . and proper. Distinguished, but oh, so, proper." Whitney opened her eyes. "I couldn't believe it when you came on to me the other night."

"I didn't! I really do want to photograph you," he protested. He had to change his image if women thought he was gay.

"And you didn't even think of taking me to bed?" she questioned, her voice mocking.

"The thought did enter my mind," he admitted, running a hand over her breasts.

"Good, because the thought has been in my mind for a long time." She turned to him. "Would you like to start photographing me tonight? In the moonlight?"

"It would be my pleasure." He pulled her into his arms.

* * *

Hilary slammed the receiver down. Where was Chandler? His receptionist said he had left for the day. At noon? What was he doing? He hadn't mentioned a word to her about taking the afternoon off. He wasn't at the club either. She had tried there. Was he with another woman? Hilary discounted the idea immediately. Chandler didn't like sex any more than she did.

Mitch stretched out on the beach, his hands behind his head, his eyes closed. He had been incredibly hurt when his grandfather hadn't even mentioned his only grandchild in his will. What did the old man have against him? Just because he refused to work as a janitor in the family business wasn't enough of a reason to cut him out of his inheritance.

He thought about his mother's suggestion. With her connections she could get him a decent job. He'd better take her up on the offer while she still worked there. If Alana got the land, his mother would be out the door ... unless she had enough stock to stay on the board. He wished he knew.

Mitch sat up and watched a group of his friends organize a volleyball game. Most of them had jobs, some as waiters and busboys so they could surf all day and work after the sun set. It might be nice to make some money. And there were some good looking chicks working for Hudson Enterprises.

He scrambled to his feet. If he got a good job he could move out of the apartment. Get his own place. Have parties.

Two girls in skimpy bikinis walked past, smiling at him.

There might be some advantages to having a job.

Chapter Twenty-four

Detective Daniel Maxwell climbed out of his white sedan and punched a button on the intercom imbedded in the stone pillar at the entrance to the Hudson estate. He ran a hand through his dark hair and rubbed the tense muscles between his broad shoulders. Black eyes were hidden by dark glasses, his rugged features grim. His short sleeved white cotton shirt stuck to his back like fly paper, and his tan chinos were wrinkled and limp. He'd make a great impression on Alana Hudson, if he ever caught up with her. She hadn't been at work, and he hoped she'd be at home. If he had to chase this lady all over the island he'd never get to his son's baseball game. It was four o'clock in the afternoon and he was exhausted. Paperwork was stacked a foot deep on his desk at the station, and this case promised to be a real winner. Any time the police had to investigate a prominent person on the islands, things had a way of getting confused and blown out of proportion, politics and influence had hindered more than one of his investigations. His ancestors had an easier way of handling wayward people . . . run them off the cliffs or dump them into a volcano. Sure cut down on the paperwork. The buzz of the intercom startled him. "This is

Detective Maxwell from the Honolulu Police. I would like to talk to Mrs. Alana Hudson."

There was a short pause and then a masculine voice said, "One moment, please." Disapproval was evident in the voice.

Dan leaned against the cool stones while he waited to be admitted.

"You may proceed," the faceless voice intoned. "I will open the gates."

"Thanks," Dan muttered, making a face at the control box. He turned around and eased his six foot frame back into the hot car. He drove up the twising driveway slowly, taking in the well kept gardens and manicured lawns. It wasn't the first time he had been to the Hudson estate, but his other visits concerned what Phillip had done, not what had been done to Phillip.

A white-jacketed butler opened the door and looking down his nose at Dan, led the detective through the massive foyer and into the living room.

Alana Hudson stood, a polite smile on her face, her right arm outstretched. "Detective Maxwell? I'm Alana Hudson. Please come in." She tilted her head to one side, curiosity in her eyes. "What can I do for you?"

It took Dan one look into those violet eyes to see why Phillip Hudson had tied this woman to him by marriage. The delicate purple flowers of her silk caftan matched her eyes. Her hair was tied back from her face, making her look young and vulnerable, but there was a set to her chin, a look in her eyes that bespoke strength and determination. Photographs didn't do her justice, nor did they record that throaty voice, or let you inhale the delicate fragrance that surrounded her. Alana Hudson was a classy lady. He cleared his throat as she led the way into the living room. "I'm afraid I have to ask you some questions about your husband's death."

Alana looked at the butler hovering in the doorway. "Please

bring some iced tea." She looked at Dan. "Or would you prefer something stronger?"

He shook his head. "Tea would be fine."

Alana motioned him toward a chair and then sat across from him. "What kind of questions?" A frown marred her features.

He scanned the room with a practiced eye. It hadn't changed. Gaudy displays of wealth abounded. The elegance of Alana Hudson seemed oddly out of place in the cluttered room. Dan pulled out his notebook and a pen, flipping through several pages. "Your husband had heart trouble." He paused, looking at her for conformation.

Alana met his gaze, leaning back in her chair, tucking her legs underneath her. "He had a heart attack a few years ago. Why?"

Dan wondered how she was going to take this newest development in the Hudson case. The investigation had begun as a routine matter, but it hadn't taken long before it was anything but routine. "Was he taking any kind of medications for his heart?" Dan tapped his pen against the paper, leaning forward.

She shrugged, Dan observing her reactions to his questions. He couldn't let her beauty get in the way of his job. "Three or four." Her forehead creased. "Why?"

The butler returned with a silver tray, placing it on the table in front of Alana. "Will there be anything else?" he asked, polite but remote.

Alana shook her head, leaning forward to drop ice cubes into two tall frosted glasses and then pouring in the tea. "Lemon or sugar?" One dark brow quirked.

Dan shook his head, taking a glass from her hand. "I need to know what medications he was taking at the time of his death." He'd have to tell her sooner or later, but he put it off, reluctant to be the one to break the news. If what they suspected was true, all hell would break loose.

Alana lifted the glass to her lips and after taking a sip, said,

"Detective Maxwell, I'll be happy to cooperate with you, but I want to know what's behind these questions. Either you can tell me now, or you can leave." Her gaze was open, her voice firm.

Dan admired her spunk. Most people just answered the questions. She was aware there was some kind of investigation. He could see it in her eyes. "Mrs. Hudson, we have reason to believe that your husband's death wasn't from natural causes."

"You think someone killed Phillip?" She shook her head in disbelief, both hands around the glass. "He died of a heart attack. I was there. We were on a boat. How could anyone kill him?" She looked at Dan with a penetrating gaze.

Dan sat for a moment, taking a drink of tea and observing Alana. It was obvious that she was intelligent as well as beautiful. Surprise had flickered across her face, but not shock. Dan made a note in his book. "I need to know what medications he was taking."

"I don't know the names, but the bottles are still in his bathroom." She placed her glass on the table and pushed herself to her feet, her hands in the slash pockets of her caftan. "Would you like me to get them for you?"

Dan stood beside her, bending to place his glass next to hers. "I'll go with you."

Alana gave him a long, assessing look before saying, "As you wish."

Dan followed her up the steps and down a long corridor to a closed door. "I haven't gone through all of his personal things yet." She took a deep breath and opened the door. "I feel like I'm invading his privacy," she said in a small voice.

Dan looked at her in surprise. Why would a wife say a think like that about her husband? He looked around the room. It was dark and overpowering. Beige walls, brown carpeting, a king sized bed with a brown and black quilt, brown drapes, and a brown leather sofa and wing backed chair opposite it. A thoroughly depressing room. Had Alana slept with her husband in this dreary room?

"This was my husband's room," she explained. "He had an office through that door." She pointed to the far end of the room. "His dressing room and bathroom are through here."

Dan followed her into Phillip's bathroom spying the medication bottles on the marble counter in the bathroom. When Alana reached for them, he said, "I'll get them." He took out a plastic bag and dropped the bottles into the bag without touching them. He looked at the labels. "Is this all he took?"

Alana frowned, wrapping her arms around herself. "He always kept nitroglycerin tablets with him for chest pain."

Dan could see that she felt uncomfortable in this room. Why? "Did he use it the day he died?"

"Sure." She paused, looking around the room. "It feels like Phillip is going to materialize at any moment." She shuddered and walked out of the room.

Dan followed, scribbling notes as he went. "Mrs. Hudson, did your husband use digoxin in tablet or liquid form?"

She pointed to one of the bottles in his hand. "See for yourself. There are still tablets in the bottle."

He looked down and then back at Alana. "Did your husband seem ... ill or complain about anything before this attack?"

Alana was silent for a moment, a thoughtful look on her face before heading toward the living room. She picked up her iced tea, wandering around the room. "Just exactly what do you think happened to Phillip?" She turned to face him, her caftan flaring out before settling back into place.

Dan put the bottles into the pocket of his pants and leaned back. "You'd better sit down, Mrs. Hudson."

Alana sat on the edge of a chair, her hands wrapped around her glass. "Tell me everything." Her voice was calm but firm.

Dan hunched his shoulders, leaning his elbows on his knees, his notebook dangling from one hand. "Mrs. Hudson, the results of the autopsy indicate that your husband died from an overdose of digoxin. Traces of liquid digoxin were found in his body. If your husband only used the tablet form, it means someone knew he took the drug, and by giving him the liquid, they could kill him and make it look like a heart attack." His gaze never waivered from her face as he watched her reaction to his news. Her face paled, her eyes were dark and wide.

"Murdered?" Her voice broke on the single word. A shudder raked her body.

"It's a possibility," he answered, his curiosity growing. He opened his notebook again and repeated a previous question, "Did he seem ill before the attack?"

Alana was quiet for a moment and then said slowly, "He complained of nausea, but I thought it was because of the rough seas."

"Anything else?" Dan wrote her answers down, wondering if she was a good actress or if she had killed him. Nothing like millions of dollars and a corporation to give a person a motive for murder. The idea that Alana would harm anyone left a bitter taste in his mouth.

She frowned. "Before the race began he complained about being dizzy and seeing yellow halos around everything." She looked bewildered, putting the glass down and lifting her hands in a helpless gesture. "That's all I can think of. Phillip was a very competitive man. He wanted to win that race, putting all his energy into sailing as fast as possible. It's so difficult to believe he could have died from something other than a heart attack."

"That's exactly what someone wanted us to assume." Dan noticed she called him by his first name but didn't make reference to him as her husband. What kind of relationship had they had? "Can you think of anyone who might want to see your husband dead? Anyone who could have slipped him the drug?"

348

Alana gave a short laugh, meeting and holding his gaze, a cynical twist to her lips. "If you interview everyone who wanted Phillip Hudson dead, you'll be an old man before you're finished. There were a lot of people who could have given him the drug."

He noted the bitterness in her voice, the disillusionment in her eyes. "Let's start with that list. Who could have given him the drug?" He tapped his pen on his notebook. "In fruit juice, coffee or booze probably." He flipped back through his notes. "Liquid digoxin is green, so it couldn't be slipped into clear liquid."

Alana was quiet for a moment, twisting a diamond and amethyst ring on her right hand. "He had an argument in the bar with Raine Bradburn before the start of the race. His daughters were there. So was I." She pursed her lips. "That makes me a suspect, doesn't it?" Her gaze met his, fear and anger making her eyes glitter. "I was closest to him. You think I killed him, don't you?"

This interview wasn't going as Dan had planned. She was correct about one thing. He had come here convinced that she had the most to gain by Hudson's death, but now he wasn't so sure. She couldn't be that good of an actress, and his gut told him she couldn't kill anyone, but her motive and opportunity were overwhelming. An intelligent woman like Alana Hudson could find a pharmacist willing to help her kill her husband. He had seen the fear in her eyes when they entered Phillip's rooms. Her motive might have been more than money. It might have been self-preservation. "Mrs. Hudson, I'm just collecting information. Phillip Hudson was a powerful man. We can't very well look the other way if there's the slightest chance that he was murdered."

"I understand, but if I'm a suspect, and it certainly seems like I am, you'll have to get your information from someone else." Alana got to her feet.

Dan stood and followed her out of the living room. Whoever had killed Phillip Hudson knew what he or she was doing. It was going to be hell trying to interview people of Phillip's class. Knowing Phillip's business practices, the list could be pages long. "Thank you for your time, Mrs. Hudson. I'll be in touch."

"I'm sure. Good-bye, Detective Maxwell." Her voice was cool as she led him toward the door. "The gates will open automatically."

When she closed the door, he stood outside for a moment. What had been going on behind these doors before Phillip Hudson died? He sighed and walked toward his car. Tomorrow he would interview Phillip Hudson's daughters, Hilary, the ice queen, and Melanie, the siren. There was also Raine, who happened to be a good friend of his, his wife's employer. The feud between Hudson and Bradburn was legendary. This was going to be a bitch of a case.

Alana slumped in a chair, burying her head in her hands. So Phillip had been murdered. His death was no accident, and she was a prime suspect. As his wife of six months she had everything to gain from his death. Thank God no one knew about their plans for a divorce. With that premarital agreement she had signed, and then a divorce, she had even more reason to kill him. Only Raine knew about those plans, and she was certain he would never tell anyone. Raine. He could have killed Phillip. Their mutual hatred was well known. He had been beaten up by Phillip's men and he wanted Phillip's wife. With Phillip out of the way, Raine could seduce his wife and try to control his company. He could be just as cold and ruthless as Phillip. Could he commit murder?

* * *

Dan tried to get comfortable in one of Hilary's modern chairs, but he found it impossible. The chairs were as hard and unyielding as they looked. His gaze took in the harsh lines of the room, the lack of color and warmth, and wondered if Hilary Hudson Cummings was going to be as unwelcoming and cold as the room. Dan mentally went over the questions he was going to ask Hilary while he waited for her to make an appearance. When she finally walked into the room, he knew this was going to be more difficult than the interview with Alana Hudson.

She approached him with a determined step, her blue silk designer dress matching the frosty look in her eyes. The dress had a high collar, long sleeves, and fell below her knees. Her hair was smoothed back from her face and confined in a French twist. Her jewelry was elegant but subdued. Everything about her was controlled.

She held out her hand and said, "Detective Maxwell? I'm Hilary Cummings. I understand you wish to ask me a few questions about my father's death." She motioned toward a chair, taking a favored position across from him. Her back was to the windows, making it difficult to note subtle changes in her expression.

Dan took another chair angled toward the one she chose. She sat like a queen holding court, her head high, her back stiff, her eyes remote. "Thank you for agreeing to see me, Mrs. Cummings. Your busy social schedule must have made it difficult to fit this interview in on such short notice."

"I work for Hudson Enterprises, Detective Maxwell." Her voice was frigid. "I do not spend my days going from one social function to the next." Her resentment was almost a tangible thing.

Dan stifled a sigh. It was not a good beginning. Pulling out his notebook, he flipped through several pages before saying, "You were with your father in the days preceeding his death and on the day he died. Do you remember anything out of the ordinary happening?"

Hilary was silent for a long time, her face inscrutable. "He was upset at the board meeting. He took several nitro pills. remember that. It wasn't really so unusual, he was always ranting and raving at those meetings." She paused, a frown forming on her forehead. "He wanted some land Raine Bradburn owned. It has holding up an important project. Bradburn refused to sell. It was definitely a sore spot with my father, but wasn't out of the ordinary." She looked bored with the conversation.

Dan hoped he could prick that confidence. "What kind of relationship did you have with your father?"

Hatred flared in her eyes before she could hide it. "He was like most executives, too busy to build a relationship with his children. Until Alana came on the scene, he used to consult with me about special projects. We had a good working relationship until she wormed her way into his life." Her voice was brittle, her mouth thin.

There was little time to feel satisfied. Dan knew he had to press his point. "Was your father's interest in her the reason for her being a vice president of the company?"

"She slept her way to the top," Hilary snapped, her eyes flashing. "She knew exactly what she was doing when she became lovers with the president of the corporation."

Dan noted the rapid rise and fall of her chest, the flush creeping into her face, her hands clenched in her lap. Underneath that ice was tremendous rage. "How did you feel about him marrying a woman younger than you after your mother's death?" She managed to control her fury with great difficulty. He watched the internal struggle with interest.

"He wasn't the first old man to be duped by a young, sexy woman who was after his money," she spat out, her eyes narrowed, the flush spreading over her face.

"So your stepmother was after your father's money?" he asked, leaning forward, intent on every nuance of her voice.

"Alana thought she was going to inherit everything. It

352

wouldn't surprise me if she killed my father to get his money. But he fooled her!" Her eyes glittered with satisfaction, her finger rubbed against her thumb. "Melanie and I have just as good of a chance of buying that land from Bradburn as she does. Whoever gets it, inherits everything. I intend to get that land." Her chin lifted and Dan didn't doubt that she'd do anything to get that land and Phillip's money.

Dan scribbled a few notes in his notebook, rubbing his chin with his thumb. He looked up. "You think your father was killed?"

The color drained from her face. She grabbed the arms of the chair. "I didn't say that! I said it wouldn't surprise me if Alana had done it to get his money. But he died of a heart attack." She paused, looking uncertain for the first time. "Didn't he?"

Dan tapped his notebook on his knee, wondering at her initial reaction to his question. She had revealed only what she wanted to reveal. So far she had made a good case against her stepmother, but hadn't said anything he didn't already know. "Phillip's heart stopped beating, but it wasn't because of natural causes. He died of a drug overdose."

Hilary was in control of her emotions again. She looked down her nose at him. "My father would never intentionally take his life."

Dan crossed his legs. "I didn't say he did. Someone slipped him a lethal dose of one of his drugs on the day of the race. The medication and stress killed him."

Hilary stared at the detective. "Murdered? My father was murdered?"

Dan didn't answer her question, but watched her reaction. It was well choreographed for effect as Hilary jumped to her feet and crossed to the windows, turning her back on him. It was another moment before she whirled around, the light from the windows behind her, shadowing her face. "She did it. That bitch did it. She killed my father just so she could have the whole company." Hilary stood like an avenging angel, one arm raised over her head, her hand in a fist. "Thank God, my father knew by the end what a conniving tramp she was."

"She has as much chance of getting that land and meeting the terms of Phillip's will as you and your sister," he pointed out. "If Phillip felt the way you say he did, why didn't he cut her out of the will completely?" He wondered what kind of answer she'd have to that. She seemed to have answers to everything else.

"Probably didn't have time," she muttered, pacing around the room. "They were only married for six months."

"Long enough for him to change the will if he wanted to." Dan stretched out his legs, crossing them at the ankles.

"He was a busy man," she countered. "It takes a lot of time to run a major corporation. He hadn't planned on dying six months after he married her." Her face hardened, a fierce look in her eyes as she stood in front of him. "I'll make sure she doesn't get that land from Raine Bradburn. I'll see her dumped onto the street before she gets one cent of Hudson money." Her hands curled into fists, her mouth a thin line.

"What about you, Mrs. Cummings?" He tilted his head back and looked at her with a piercing gaze. "I've talked to a few of the directors. Your father humiliated you more than once in front of all of them." He paused. "That must've made you angry."

"Angry?" She laughed, sitting down across from him. "I was furious, especially when he began to ignore me and turn to Alana for business consultations. My father was a tyrant. It was no secret. He manipulated people, using his money and power for his own benefit, and woe to anyone who stood in his way." She leaned back, her expression mocking. "If you're looking for motives to murder him, you'll be interviewing half the peo-

354

ple on this island and even more on the mainland. My father was hated by a lot of people."

"Including his daughters?" Dan wondered if she knew how much information she was giving to him. There was a cunning look in her eye. She knew exactly what she was doing. Cold and calculating, just like Phillip Hudson.

"I did not hate my father enough to kill him, if that's what you're saying." She lifted her chin a notch, just the right amount of indignation in her voice.

Dan tried to scratch the tough veneer she used for protection. "You've owed half the bookies on the island at one time or another." He flipped back through his notebook.

"How did you find that out?" she demanded, leaning forward, her hand reaching out to grab his book, but not quick enough. Her hand curled in her lap. "Gambling is a hobby. Everyone has hobbies, and I never bet more than I can afford to lose."

"Never?" Skepticism laced his voice. Hilary had a reputation for high stakes gambling.

"No." Her words were uttered between clenched teeth. "I don't owe anyone anything."

Dan would check on that. "Were you with your father before the race?"

Hilary looked confused, rubbing her cheek with a finger. "Sure. I was at the club and wished him luck."

He leaned back, crossing his arms. "You could have slipped the lethal dose of medication into his drink."

"So could a lot of people. My father enjoyed throwing his power around. He ordered a lot of people to do silly, menial tasks, just to make them grovel at his feet, to see how much power he really had," she snarled, her lip curling. "My father was a bastard. I'm glad he's dead!" Her voice was filled with venom, hatred in her eyes.

"Hilary, I think you've said enough," came a deep voice

from the doorway. Chandler strode into the room, moving to stand behind his wife's chair, his hands on her shoulders. "I don't know who you are, but you've upset my wife. I think you'd better go."

Dan got to his feet and flipped his notebook closed, towering over Chandler and Hilary. "Thank you for talking to me, Mrs. Cummings."

"The next time she'll have her lawyer present," Chandler warned, his voice defiant.

Dan lifted one eyebrow. "Why do you think she'll need a lawyer?"

Chandler colored, his confidence slipping under Dan's mocking gaze. "Well, I certainly don't want my wife implicated in anything . . . scandalous."

"No, of course not," Dan said, his voice ironic. His gaze moved from one to the other before he turned around and walked out of the room.

Hilary looked up at Chandler. The news hadn't been much of a shock. "The police think Phillip was murdered."

Chandler let out a low whistle as he sat down on the couch. "And you're a suspect?"

"Along with half the island." Hilary got to her feet, heading for the bar. How long would it be before they caught the killer? "I'm glad he's dead." She poured wine into a tall, slim glass. After her last hangover, she had decided to switch to wine. Not that she couldn't stop drinking completely if she wanted to, she just didn't want to. "He deserved to die for making so many people so unhappy."

"Have you had any luck with Bradburn?"

"I haven't even talked to him. His secretary said he's out of town for a few days. He just doesn't want to see me." She sipped her wine. "Where were you all afternoon?"

Chandler crossed his legs and looked at the toe of his loafer. "I had some free time and went to the other side of the island. There were some scenes I wanted to experiment with."

Hilary looked at him for a long moment. Before she could speak, Mitchell burst into the room.

"I'm ready for that job, Mother. Will you arrange an interview for me tomorrow?" His shirt was open and his sunglasses hung around his neck. His hair was wind tossed and his face bronze.

Hilary's features softened. She was thrilled that he finally wanted to work. "Of course. Is there anything you're really interested in?"

He was silent for a moment. "Public relations. Marketing."

"I'll see what's available."

Chandler crossed his arms. "The police were here."

Mitch pulled a beer from the bar and opened it. "Why?"

"They think your grandfather was murdered."

Hilary thought he almost sounded bored.

Mitch looked from Chandler to his mother. "Wow. Who knocked him off?"

Hilary glared at her son. "I'm a suspect!"

Mitch took a long pull of his beer and sauntered back into the living room, dropping onto the couch. "So. Did you do it?"

Hilary jumped to her feet, her fists clenched at her sides. "Of course not! That's a terrible thing to say to your mother!"

Mitch shrugged. "The old guy deserved whatever he got. You don't expect me to be surprised, do you? There are a lot of people who are glad he's dead. I'm one of them."

Hilary collapsed onto a chair. "I am, too," she admitted in a soft voice.

Chapter Twenty-five

On his way to interview Melanie Hudson Adams Steinberg Shawnessey, Dan Maxwell thought a lot about Hilary Cummings and her reactions to his questions. Her emotions only surfaced when Alana was mentioned, her hatred evident. She hadn't been too surprised to learn her father might have been murdered either. He had heard enough about Chandler Cummings to know that his preference for prostitutes would prevent him from melting that block of ice Hilary wore like a shield. So why did a woman with her money and looks stay married to a man like that?

He pushed the buzzer and heard the chime inside. The outside of the house was two stories high, white stucco with a red tile roof, rows of arched windows along both levels, and the medieval look of black wrought iron swirling around the doors and windows. The door opened and a tiny woman appeared. A single grey braid hung down her back. Her shoulders were hunched in the loose fitting black cotton dress. Faded blue eyes were sunken in a weathered face. "What you want?" she demanded, a scowl on her face.

"I'm Detective Maxwell and I'd like to talk to Melanie Shawnessey."

Dan was surprised at the fierce look in the old woman's eyes. "Miss Melanie is a Hudson. No more Shawnessey. He bad." Her face brightened just a little. "He gone." She opened the door and pointed to a spot in the middle of the foyer. "You stay here. I go see if she can talk." The woman shuffled from the room, leaving Dan slightly bemused.

Dan looked around the foyer. The focal point of the entry were two lifesize bronze figurines entwined in an erotic pose, water splashing around them, a skylight bathing them in sunshine.

The old woman returned and as they walked through the living room, his eyes widened further. Red, black and silver gave the room a dramatic look. On the wall above a red lacquered Oriental trunk Japanese etchings were in stark contrast to the black metallic wall covering. Another wall was all mirrors. The third wall was dominated by an artist's rendering of the fire goddess, Pele, emerging from an erupting volcano. Huge overstuffed red and black leather loveseats, couches, and chairs were grouped in intimate settings on silver-grey carpeting. Free form glass tables displayed priceless sterling figurines. Melanie had a flare for the dramatic, her home a stunning display of bold decorating. He slowly followed the old woman through the living room and then outside onto the patio. The patio surrounded a huge oval pool, a cabana at the far end, a whirlpool to the left, red and white striped wrought iron lounges and chairs scattered about, and wet bar close to the house. Melanie Hudson was stretched out on a lounge on her stomach, her firery hair pulled into a loose knot on top of her head, a string bikini barely covering her tanned, smooth buttocks. Dan couldn't see a top.

She propped herself up on one elbow, teasing Dan with a shadowed view of one breast. She looked him over from head to toe. Dan now knew what it felt like to be visually undressed. He cleared his throat, feeling the sweat trickle down his back, making his tan sport shirt stick to his body. "Mrs. Shawnessey? I'm Detective Maxwell and I'd like to ask you a few questions about your father's death."

"My name is Melanie Hudson." Her voice was languid, her eyelids heavy. "Ask away." She settled back down, her head resting on her arms, her eyes closed.

Dan had trouble finding a spot to focus on where he could concentrate on the questions he had to ask. He finally took a chair in the shade of a red striped umbrella, pulled out his notebook and concentrated on that. "Did you notice anything different about your father at the board meeting or before the race the day he died?"

She was silent for so long he wondered if she had gone to sleep, but she finally shook her head slightly and muttered, "He was just as arrogant and obnoxious as usual. He was barking at everyone because he couldn't get some land from Raine Bradburn."

Dan couldn't resist looking at Melanie, traveling down the length of her well oiled body. She was magnificent.

"Like what you see?" she asked in a throaty voice, opening one eye.

He didn't answer her question. "The land needed for Aloha Shores?"

"You've got it." She wiggled deeper into the lounge, the string of her bikini leaving nothing to Dan's imagination.

He forced himself to return to business. "Did you serve him coffee or make him a drink?"

She propped herself up on one elbow again, turning slightly, giving Dan a better view of tanned breast. She frowned, then said, her voice tinged with bitterness, "He was always ordering people to do things for him. He had to keep proving he had control, power."

"And you hated it?" Dan's gaze rested on the swell of that breast shadowed by her arm.

361

"He degraded everyone." Melanie put her hands next to her shoulders and lifted her upper body off the lounge.

Dan held his breath. She wouldn't. He was a stranger. A police officer. He was a man.

She arched then turned over onto her back, a satisfied smile crossing her face, her arms stretched over her head, one knee slightly bent. It was a classic pose.

Dan was grateful for the sunglasses as he clutched his pen in one hand and his notebook in the other. He thought he had seen everything in his fifteen years on the force, but this boggled his mind. Melanie Hudson, daughter of one of the most powerful men in the islands, lay before him, her perfect breasts golden brown, her stomach flat, her hips rounded. The miniscule triangle of cloth was irrelevant. Melanie Hudson had a body most men fantasized about all their lives and she knew it.

She shaded her eyes with one hand and looked at Dan. "So why are you here, Detective Maxwell?"

"Your father was murdered, Ms. Hudson."

"And I'm one of the suspects." She glanced at him and closed her eyes.

"Where were you the day of the race when he died?" He tapped his notebook on his knee.

She reached for the tanning lotion and sprayed it all over her body. "I was at the club and wished him luck." She moved her hands seductively over her shoulders and arms. "Actually, I didn't get to talk to him much. We were at the bar when he began to argue with Raine Bradburn. I didn't stick around." Her hands moved over her breasts and down over her stomach.

Dan tried not to watch her hands. "Your sister was there?"

"Yes." Her hands moved to the bikini bottom and she slipped her fingers under the string.

Dan held his breath as she ran a finger under the string, toying with the tie at the side. When her hands moved lower spreading lotion over her thighs and calves, he let out the breath. "How did you feel about your father's death?" He looked at his notebook and tried to write, wondering if he would be able to decipher his notes when he got back to the office.

"Ecstatic. Is that what you wanted to hear?" Mockery in her voice, her lips lifted in a sensuous smile as she swung her legs over the side of the lounge and faced Dan, her body gleaming.

"Only if you really felt that way." Dan was glad his sunglasses hid his gaze traveling the length of Melanie's body when she stood, stretched, and sauntered to the edge of the pool.

"He killed my mother. Isn't that reason enough to be happy he got what he deserved?" She spoke in a deadly calm voice before diving into the water.

Dan watched as she disappeared into the water, her image shadowy and blurred. His lips thinned. She was deliberately trying to distract him. Why? Melanie Hudson used her body like her father used his money and power to control and manipulate people. He thought back on his interview with Hilary Cummings. In her own way, she had used him, too. How many of the reactions he had seen were real and how many were staged just for his benefit? He berated himself for letting the glamour and wealth get in the way of his investigation. Alana Hudson had seemed the most honest, but perhaps she was only the most cunning.

Melanie swam several lengths of the pool, putting on a performance guaranteed to make a man's blood flow like hot lava. A few minutes ago, Dan would have been tempted, but now her antics left him unmoved. When she emerged from the water, her body glistened in the hot sun. Her bikini bottom was gone, the tanned surface of her body unbroken by any lines. A smile of satisfaction touched her lips as she reached up and smoothed the hair from her face. She stood on the top step, her hands splayed on her hips, her body posed for optimum affect. "Any more questions?" Her voice was husky.

"Just a few." He leaned back in his chair. "You said your father killed your mother. Do you have proof of that?"

Melanie turned and dove back into the water, returning again and tossing her head. "Yes." She walked up the steps and pointed toward the lounge. "Get my towel for me, will you?"

Dan tossed it to her as she crossed the patio. She wrapped it around her body like a sarong.

"My mother left a note the night she died. Phillip had demanded a divorce. Obviously Alana wanted him to marry her. My mother couldn't cope with the shock. She'd be an outcast among her peers. She knew her friends would gravitate toward the person with the money and power. That was Phillip. She did the only thing she could to save face ... she drove his Porsche off a cliff." Melanie paced back and forth and then stood in front of Dan. "Even if he didn't actually push her off, my father was responsible for my mother's death. I'm glad he's dead" She paused. "The world is better off without him."

"Who paid for all this?" Dan asked, a hand encompassing the house, lawn, and gardens.

"Phillip Hudson," she answered with a toss of her head.

"Yet you hated the man who bought all this for you?" He rested one hip against the wet bar, his hands folded across his chest.

She threw back her head and laughed, moving behind the bar. "I haven't been a very good hostess, have I? Would you like something to drink?" She leaned forward on her elbows. "Or eat?"

"A glass of water would be fine," he answered, watching as she bent over and opened the refrigerator.

"Perrier?" She reached for a glass and dropped ice into it.

"Fine." He sat on one of the stools, looking at her over the rim of his glass as she mixed a martini for herself.

"I have a good job at Hudson Enterprises. And ... well, there are ways of getting what I want."

Dan shook his head. "From Phillip Hudson? He didn't seem like the kind of man you could force to do anything."

Her eyes took on a cunning look. "He's not the only wealthy man in the islands. Phillip has paid for his sins, Alana will, too.

"How is she going to pay?" he asked, surprised at her answers.

"By losing everything when I get Bradburn's land." She looked at him with a clear gaze.

Dan had misjudged Melanie badly. She wasn't the bubble headed sybarite he had thought she was.

A shuttered look crossed her face for a moment before a seductive smile touched her face. "It's so hot out here. Wouldn't you like to continue this conversation inside?" Her tongue touched her top lip.

"I think my wife might object," Dan said, his voice dry as he took another drink. She was adept at avoiding direct answers to the questions she didn't feel like answering. He wouldn't get any new information from her.

"You mean she's not ... understanding?" Melanie purred walking around the bar and standing a foot away from him.

Dan was silent for a moment, wondering what was in her past that made her throw herself at men. Was this her way of getting back at a father who ignored her? Was she the female counterpart to the macho man whose self-worth was based on sex? If so, why? He'd have to start digging for that information, but he'd never get it from her. He put his glass down. "Do you have any idea who might have wanted your father dead?"

"Half the world, I'd suspect," she murmured. She ran her fingers through her hair. "We've done enough talking, don't you think? You're not going to learn anything more from me."

Dan looked at her for a moment before speaking. She had told him exactly what she wanted him to know. "Thank you for your time. You've been very helpful."

Melanie chuckled. "Glad to help."

He walked to the table, picked up his notebook and pen and slid them into his pocket. "I'll call if I need any additional information."

"You do that," she murmured, pushing a button on the bar. "See the detective out." Melanie turned her back and returned to her lounge.

He sighed, and retraced his steps through her house and back to his car. Melanie Hudson didn't like to be thwarted anymore than her father did.

Now he had to question Raine Bradburn, an appointment he didn't look forward to at all. Raine had been a close friend for a long time, and Dan already knew he had more than one motive for killing Phillip Hudson. Hell, there were so many people who had motives that he was thankful it had to be an inside job. There was no way an outsider could have slipped Hudson the digoxin.

Melanie watched Detective Maxwell leave and then padded into her bedroom. So the police thought Phillip Hudson had been murdered. Not much of a surprise to anyone who knew him. She dropped the towel and turned on the shower.

Alana had to be the prime suspect. She would have had the most to gain until Phillip's will had been revealed, and she hadn't known anything about that. Any relationship between Raine and Alana was important now. Melanie had to find out how involved it was. If she could discredit Alana, and prove to Raine that she killed Phillip, he would have to be so grateful that Melanie had saved him from the little gold digger, that he would sell Melanie his land.

She smiled as she stepped under the water. Arty had a big job to do.

* * *

Raine Bradburn smiled in welcome as Dan Maxwell came into the room. "Dan! It's good to see you. Been too long." He noted Dan's slight frown, the uneasy look in his eyes. Dan had a problem, and Raine guessed it had to do with him.

"Don't I know it." Dan held out his hand to his friend. He looked around the living room. "House hasn't changed much." He nodded at the seascape dominating one wall. "New painting."

Raine followed his gaze and nodded in satisfaction. It was his favorite. "A relatively new artist. She's going to make a name for herself."

"And you're giving her an extra push. I suppose you got the painting as a personal gift for being ... a patron of the arts?" Dan teased Raine as he walked over to the bar.

"Paid cash for it, Dan. I know it's hard to believe, but not every woman finds me irresistible." His mocking tone of voice was light. "A beer?"

Dan shook his head, his back to Raine, looking at the painting.

Raine frowned then pulled a beer from the refrigerator for himself, and poured Dan a large glass of iced tea. He returned to the room, handing the glass to Dan. When Dan had called, Raine had suggested they go for a sail, but Dan declined. Dan loved to sail and only business would prevent him from saying yes to an afternoon on the water.

Dan sat down, resting his elbows on his thighs, the glass of tea clasped between his hands. "Raine, I've got to ask you some questions about Phillip Hudson." He paused. "I understand you had an argument the day he died."

Raine was silent for a moment. He was surprised at the question. Maybe Hudson hadn't died from a heart attack. Hudson had more enemies than there were boats in the Ali Wai Yacht Harbor, and he topped the list. "We were at the bar after the skipper's meeting and he made some snide remark. I didn't like it and we exchanged a few words. That's all."

"And before that?" Dan took a sip of his tea, watching Raine carefully.

Raine got to his feet and walked to stand in front of the painting, taking a long pull on his beer. "Yeah. I saw him the day before the race. I own a piece of land he wanted to buy. I wouldn't sell it to him. He had me beat up a couple of weeks before the race to intimidate me, but I still wouldn't sell, so he cornered me at the club the day before the race and offered me something he didn't think I would refuse in exchange for that land."

Dan put his glass on the table, taking out his notebook and pen. "What was it?"

Raine turned around, his features grim. "His wife."

Dan let out a low whistle, his eyes widening. "I knew Phillip Hudson was slime, but I didn't think he'd stoop to that. Alana Hudson is a beautiful, young woman. I thought he was insanely jealous of her." He scribbled as he talked.

"He was." Raine's features were taut as he remembered Alana bruises, physical evidence of Hudson's jealousy. He wondered again if Hudson had noticed the attraction between his wife and his enemy at the restaurant and played on that attraction. Alana must be a suspect, too. She certainly had the motive. Had she killed Phillip? The thought chilled him. "Now you know how much Hudson wanted my land. He was possessive and jealous as hell, but he offered her ... services to me to sweeten the pot." Raine's voice was filled with contempt. He emptied his bottle and walked toward the bar.

Dan rubbed his chin with his hand. "Did she know about the deal?"

He knew Alana well enough to know that she would have killed the bastard if he had suggested it. Another motive. He leaned his elbows on the bar. "If he had suggested it, she would never agree to something like that."

Dan nodded his head, tossed his pen onto the table and leaned back in his chair. "Did you accept his gracious offer?"

Raine gave a snort of disgust. "I told the bastard to go to hell."

"You hated him." Dan's voice was weary.

"Enough to see him dead, but you already knew that." Raine grabbed another beer and dropped back into his chair, guessing what Dan was about to tell him. "I didn't kill him. He died of a heart attack while I was on another boat."

"He was murdered, Raine." Dan sighed and reached for his tea. "The autopsy showed high levels of digoxin. Someone slipped him a lethal dose the day of the race."

Raine shook his head, laughing. "So someone beat the old bastard at his own game. He thought he was so smart and someone was smarter! It does my heart good to know that someone knocked the old guy off. It's so much better than dying of natural causes."

"Except that you are one of the suspects," Dan voiced Raine's thoughts, his voice quiet. "You had the motive."

Raine raised his eyebrows, his gaze boring into Dan's eyes. "You don't believe that, do you?"

Dan sighed and leaned forward, raking a hand through his hair. "No, personally, I don't, but my personal feelings don't mean anything in this investigation." He put his glass down and reached for his notebook. "Phillip Hudson offered you his wife as part of the deal for that land. I've talked to a couple of people who suspected you of having an affair with Alana Hudson. That's motive enough for murder. Add that to your hatred of the man, the fact that he had you beat up, and that makes you, along with several others, a prime suspect."

Raine gave Dan a level look. "I had a motive, perhaps, but what about opportunity?"

"You were at the bar together the day before the race and just before boarding your boat. You could have slipped the drug into his drink." Dan rubbed his forehead, looking at his notes.

"Where would I have gotten this drug?" Raine's voice was dry. He didn't blame his friend for his questions. It was his job, but Raine wasn't going to make it easy for him. Another thing Dan had said niggled his mind. Who would have suggested to Dan they were having an affair? He should be so lucky.

"It could have been Alana Hudson herself." Dan got to his feet and wandered around the room, all the while watching Raine.

"It could, but it wasn't." Raine rubbed the back of his neck. His voice was wry. "I admit an attraction to her, but she's too straight to have an affair while married."

Dan jammed his hands into his pockets. He crossed the room, standing in front of Raine, a scowl on his face. "She's not married anymore." He took a deep breath. "So why did she come to you after Hudson beat her up?"

Raine's gave Dan a dark look. "How did you find out about that?" When Dan remained silent and dropped into the chair across from him, Raine muttered, "Your sources only gave you part of the story. She didn't come to *me*, she was washed up on the beach. If she had landed further down the beach the Smiths would have found her. A little further down the line and she would have been splattered on the rocks! Hell, she was too bruised and battered to let anyone touch her." He clenched his fists. He still felt like killing Hudson for what he did, even knowing the man was dead. "A beautiful woman like that beaten up by a bastard like Hudson."

Dan got to his feet and walked to the windows, staring sightlessly at the panaroamic view of the ocean. "*After* Hudson died, did you have an affair with his widow?"

"Affair is not the right word," Raine said, choosing his words carefully. "The timing just hasn't been right for us."

Dan turned to look at Raine. "I do believe you've met your match, my friend."

"You may be right," Raine growled, leaning back and crossing his arms over his chest, his features hard. "That doesn't mean I have to like it or give in to it."

"True." Dan crossed the room and patted him on the shoulder. "But then, neither does she."

Raine grunted. "She hasn't. She's a stubborn lady. Won't even consent to an affair. She's so ... self-contained, has a depth of character that's scary, is strong, intelligent, controlled, and yet, she's ... vulnerable." Raine shrugged. "She's one complex person."

Dan raised an eyebrow at the regret evident in Raine's voce. "But then you wouldn't be interested in her if she wasn't a challenge. Why do you suppose she married Phillip Hudson in the first place?"

"Who knows? She said she loved him, but it was the biggest mistake she ever made."

"Hudson made one hell of a will. Three women fighting for their lives." Dan picked up his notebook again.

"You can't believe what they've offered me for that bit of rock and sand." Raine shook his head.

"I'd believe anything after interviewing Melanie and Hilary." Dan paused. "Everyone has a motive for killing Phillip Hudson. It's going to be one hell of a case." He groaned. "I hate these society murders. So many motives and so much influence." He turned to Raine, reluctance in his voice. "You're still a suspect, no matter what I think."

Raine shrugged, his face impassive. "So be it. I didn't kill him, but I'm glad he's dead." He paused. "For more than one reason."

Dan groaned, rubbing tired eyes. "Don't tell me that. I have more than enough reasons already. I'll be talking to you again."

"Sure." Raine walked him to the door. "Just do me one favor. Be gentle with Alana. She's been through enough."

Dan gave him a knowing look. "I'll try."

Dan was more confused than ever as he scanned his notes. So many motives, so much opportunity. How was he ever going to sort it all out?

Chapter Twenty-six

Alana joined the other board members at the long teak table. It still seemed strange meeting without Phillip. Charles had taken over as temporary chairman and was calling the meeting to order.

"We've got to make some decisions," he said. "The stock is fluctuating with every new rumor about Phillip's will. The shareholders are getting nervous. The switchboard can't keep up with the calls." He looked down the length of the table, his gaze moving among the three women. "Have any of you had any luck with Bradburn?"

Alana shook her head, her blue silk wrap dress conservative and sexy at the same time. Her jewelry consisted of gold hoop earrings and a thin gold chain around her neck. The board would be shocked if she told them about Raine's proposition. "He isn't in any hurry to sell. He wants stock and control. His demands are outrageous."

Hilary's voice was clipped as she straightened the cuff of her navy linen suit. "I made him a generous proposal, offering a trade of the land on Maui for the parcel we own on the Big Island. Like Alana said. He wants controlling interest in Hudson Enterprises. He won't even listen to anything else."

Alana regarded Hilary for a long moment. After Dan Maxwell's visit she wondered if Hilary had killed Phillip, but uppermost in her mind was the thought that Raine might have murdered him. He had the opportunity, and plenty of motive. Perhaps she was even part of that motive. A shudder raked her body.

Melanie spoke up, her voice cool. "He refused to listen to reason. I wonder if father knew how much power he was giving to Raine when he made up that will." She fingered the bold, multicolored, hand painted silk scarf tied loosely around her neck. It was in striking contrast to her white suit.

Dan spoke up. "This murder investigation isn't helping at all. I've talked to the police about being discrete, but reporters are everywhere. They've been interviewing the security guards and cleaning personnel. Not a day goes by without some reference in the media about the death of Phillip Hudson."

"What can we do?" Ben asked. "The police seem to think he was murdered. We can't very well cover it up."

"We can ask our employees to refer all questions to Jeff," Melanie said. "As head of public relations, he is the official spokesman. We could threaten them with dismissal if they don't comply."

"Good idea," Charles said with a smile.

Melanie didn't return his smile.

"Could we go to court on harrassment charges against the police?" Hilary asked. "I resent being questioned about my father's death."

"I didn't like the questions the police asked either," Charles muttered. "They make you feel guilty even when you aren't."

There was a thoughtful look in Hilary's eyes. "Has everyone on the board been questioned?" When they all nodded, she said, "We've got to calm the shareholders. Since Charles is temporary chairman until the will is settled, maybe he could issue a statement."

374

"We'll have to do a lot of positive PR work," Melanie said, looking at Charles.

Alana watched the expression on Charles' face when he looked at Melanie. Was he involved with Melanie?

Jeff Marino spoke up. "I can issue a statement to the press. We can have employee meetings and tell them about funneling everything through me. I think closed meetings will be better than a memo. Memos have a way of getting in the wrong hands, and you can't deny they were written."

Alana nodded her head. "Let's do a media blitz on the opening of our condominium complex on the Big Island. We could do a campaign on the plans for our expansion into the Japanese and Australian markets, too."

"How about the dude ranch?" Hilary said, leaning forward. "We have the land for that project."

"But if we invest it now, Aloha Shores can't be built even if we get that land from Raine." Alana looked at the other directors, seeing their doubtful looks. No one really believed they would ever get the deed to Raine's land.

Charles rubbed the top of his head. "How about a motion."

Melanie spoke up. "I move we have the meetings, do a media blitz, and really have a classy grand opening on the Big Island."

"Second." Jeff added.

"Discussion?" Charles asked. No one spoke. "Those in favor?"

All hands except Hilary's went up.

"Passed." He turned to Jeff. "Set up the meetings immediately. Set the opening for two weeks. Get our ad agency on the other ideas."

"What about the dude ranch?" Hilary's voice was sharp.

"Let's wait on that," Charles said. "Let's see if this works first. If not, we can try something else. Who knows? Maybe this will be settled and we can get back to normal."

Melanie wrinkled her nose. "With Phillip gone, nothing will be the same." She paused, pushing her hair behind one ear. "What will it do to the price of stock if they prove Phillip was murdered?"

"Not much as long as we can prove we're still progressing and things are running smoothly," Ben muttered.

"But are we progressing?" Alana probed. In the short time she had been CEO she was frustrated by the feeling of being on hold instead of moving forward. "We're going to have to make a decision on Aloha Shores and a takeover bid on a communications company soon."

Charles looked down the table. "I know this is inconvenient for the rest of you from the mainland and other countries, but how about if we meet right after the opening of the new resort. We can evaluate the situation and go from there."

"Excellent idea!" David Jones said. "If the media campaign is successful, we might be able to ease off until after the deadline for Phillip's will. Maybe Phillip's death will be resolved as well."

Melanie sat up straight. "With Phillip's stock tied up until the will is settled, who has the majority of stock?"

Ben looked at the figures in front of him. "You, Hilary, and Alana all have the same amount. There's been a lot of trading action since Phillip's death. Several firms are buying Hudson stock for a private party, but we haven't been able to discover the identity of that person. Why?"

"I wonder if we had enough authority to call a special shareholders meeting." Melanie's gaze flicked over Alana. "Perhaps elect new directors."

"Not now," Dan said. "If we did that we would be asking for trouble."

"Not necessarily." Charles tapped a finger on the report in front of him. "It might calm them down. They would see that

376

we're capable of handling this corporation without Phillip Hudson."

Alana groaned. A shareholders meeting would be a disaster right now. "Let's not make any decision until after the opening."

"An excellent idea," Hilary said, her voice cold. A nasty smile curved her mouth. "Perhaps by exposing the killer, we'll save ourselves the trouble of a special meeting." Her gaze rested on Alana's startled features.

Alana had no time to gather her thoughts before Melanie spoke.

"What was your motive, Alana?" Melanie asked, tipping her head to one side. "Money? Power? Raine Bradburn?"

Charles raised his gavel. "Enough. Does anyone want to bring the question to a vote?"

Hilary nodded. "I move we call a special shareholders meeting right after the opening of the new resort."

"Second." Melanie spoke quickly.

Charles took a deep breath. "Any discussion?" After a moment of silence he said, "Those in favor, raise your hands." Four hands went up.

"Opposed." Four hands went up. "Tied." Charles grimaced. "I'll break the tie by voting against a special meeting."

Alana let out a long sigh, surprised that he had voted against Melanie and Hilary. Maybe she was imagining something going on between Melanie and Charles.

The meeting was adjourned, but before Alana could escape, Melanie cornered her. "You think you're the perfect grieving widow, but we both know better, don't we?"

"I don't know what you're talking about." Alana tried to step around Melanie, but Melanie blocked her way.

"I saw you and Raine leave the party. Are you having an affair with him so he'll sell you the land?" Melanie's eyes narrowed.

Alana remained silent. How could she answer Melanie's accusations when she wasn't sure of the answers herself.

"Had I known that my father was going to marry you so soon, I'd have made certain he knew the truth about you." Melanie's voice was deadly calm, an eerie look on her face that sent a chill down Alana's spine. "My father demanded a divorce from my mother, and it crushed her. She didn't have an accident. She deliberately drove off that cliff and I have the evidence to prove it. That makes you indirectly responsible for her death. I hope that weighs heavily on your conscience ... if you have one."

Alana was too shocked to speak.

Hilary joined them, looking from Melanie to Alana. "We all want Hudson Enterprises and Phillip's fortune. I won't even begin to talk about who deserves it. We won't get anywhere if we begin on that." She took a deep breath. "We all want to break Phillip's will and his insistence that we get that damned land in order to inherit anything. Asinine thinking." She shook her head. "I think we need to come up with an alternate plan in case none of us gets that land." She paused. "Let's face it. Raine Bradburn isn't about to sell. He's enjoying this farce." She looked at the other women. "Do either of you have any realistic ideas on what to do so that we get more than five percent of the whole thing?"

Melanie was silent for a moment and then said, "What about seducing that old lawyer Daddy hired?"

"If figures that you'd come up with an idea involving sex," Hilary said, her face grim.

"Well, it might work better on him than it did on Raine Bradburn."

Alana's stomach knotted and climbed into her throat. The thought of Raine and Melanie together made her sick.

"What did you do?" Hilary muttered, one brow lifting, mild interest in her eyes.

"I mean, I offered." Melanie's eyes were wide with disbelief. "I can't believe he turned me down. I was terrific. That guy must be made of stone." She frowned slightly. "He must be gay."

Alana was surprised at the rush of pleasure that coursed through her. Melanie had tried to seduce Raine but he had rejected her. She thought of the passion she had shared with Raine. If he was gay, she was King Kamehameha.

Hilary's voice broke into her thoughts. "Let's assume he won't sell his land. That leaves us sharing a pitance while a boat gets the lion's share of the money, and someone else takes charge of the corporation."

"Someone will have to be elected chairman of the board, and there will be a CEO and president. There's always the possibility that one of us might be elected to one of those positions." Alana's voice was quiet.

Melanie's voice held distain. "You need stock to carry that kind of clout, stock we won't have. They'll elect a man to all three positions and you know it. They're not going to give a woman that power permanently. You're only in the position temporarily because you're Phillip's widow. It looks good to the public."

"True," Hilary muttered, and Alana had to agree. "But I think I know a way we can all profit and get around the terms of the will." She paused, looking from one curious face to the next. She leaned forward, her voice low. "We start selling off the profitable divisions of Hudson Enterprises and divide the profits. At the same time we sell Phillip's personal property. The artwork alone will bring in a few million." She looked at them with a satisfied smile on her face. "When we go back to Sims, there won't be any property to sell to support a boat, and the stock will be worthless without the profitable divisions."

Alana and Melanie stared at her for several seconds. "That's a great idea, Hilary!" Melanie chuckled. "What an ironic twist.

We get the money from the estate and the sale of the divisions, while the stock takes a dive! Perfect!"

"How do you intend to sell off entire divisions of the company and split the profits without board approval?" Alana asked, wondering at Hilary's audacity and tempted by the plan in spite of herself.

Hilary's expression was thoughtful. "That would be tricky, but I think we could pull it off with some creative bookkeeping. No one would know until it would be too late."

"Isn't that illegal?" Melanie asked. "We could go to jail instead of the Riviera."

"Not if we work it right. There are all kinds of people who would pay to get their hands on our profitable companies."

"Did you read the addendum to Phillip's will?" When they both looked at Alana blankly, she explained, "The last three pages attached to the copy of Phillip's will?" When they shook their heads, she said, "Phillip must have considered the possibility of selling off property before the deadline. There is a list of everything of value in his estate, complete with identification numbers. It's impossible to sell an ashtray." She took a deep breath. "Because he had controlling interest in Hudson Enterprises, all of his stock is frozen until the will is finalized. The day-to-day operations of the company can continue, but you couldn't sell a desk or pencil until the will is settled."

"Damn." Melanie crossed her arms. "He sure didn't trust anyone, did he?"

"Obviously," Alana replied, her voice dry.

"There must be something we could do," Hilary muttered.

"Raine Bradburn's land is still the key." Alana nodded to both of them. "If you'll excuse me, I have work to do." She brushed past them and walked out of the board room on shaking legs.

* * *

Melanie sat alone in the board room, staring down the length of the table, wondering how to proceed. Both Raine and Alana had to wonder if the other murdered Phillip, Raine because he hated Phillip and Alana because she wanted all his money for herself.

And then there was Charles. He was here for the weekend and it was the same weekend she had promised Greg she'd go to Kauai. When she had made the promise, she had meant to show Charles she didn't care about him, but after seeing him today, she wasn't sure she could pull it off.

The door opened and Charles entered.

Melanie's face lit up and then she scowled. She didn't want to see him when she was so confused. "What are you doing here?"

"Looking for you." He closed the door and approached her.

"You've found me." she crossed her arms over her chest, her gaze wary.

"Why are you mad at me?" he asked, pulling out the chair next to her and sitting down. "Because I broke the tie vote to hold a special shareholders meeting?"

"That's only part of the problem. I thought you were on my side. Why did you vote against me?"

"I didn't vote against *you*. I voted against the proposal for a special meeting, and if you think with your head instead of your emotions, you'll realize it was the right thing to do."

She glared at him without answering.

"Melanie," he said softly, "if there was a special meeting and people started throwing accusations around and electing new directors, our stock would plummet. That stock is valuable right now. Would you really want to risk losing a great deal of money just to see your stepmother off the board?"

She hated it when he was right. She changed the subject, getting to what was really bothering her. "Do you think you can come to Hawaii every few months and think I'll be waiting for you to take me to bed?"

He sighed and shook his head. "I wish it could be different. Did you miss me?" he asked, his eyes twinkling, taking her hand in his and kissing each fingertip.

"I won't be your occasional mistress." She found it so difficult to be angry with him when his tongue was making erotic circles in the palm of her hand.

He ran a hand up her thigh. "You're wearing the garter belt I gave you." His hand moved higher. "And nothing else." His fingers began to tease her. "How can you say you don't want me and then wear something guaranteed to turn me on?"

"I hadn't planned on you finding out," she muttered, shifting in her seat, welcoming his ministrations.

"Do you want me to make love to you?" He smiled at her.

"Here? In the board room?" She had fantasized about that often enough.

"Why not?" He squeezed her inner thigh and moved closer.

"Aren't you going to lock the door?" she murmured, her pulse quickening.

He shook his head, slowly untying the scarf around her neck. He unbuttoned her suit jacket, a teasing smile on his lips. "Melanie Hudson! No bra either. It's a good thing I didn't think about this before the meeting." He cupped each golden globe in his hands, rubbing the tips with his thumbs. "We would have been finished in record time."

Pulling Melanie to her feet, he lifted her until she sat on the table. Charles leaned forward, his face earnest. "I'm going to ask my wife . . ."

Melanie silenced him with her fingers over his lips. "Don't tell me anything about your wife." A knowing look entered her eyes. "I've heard it all, Charles. I couldn't bear to have you lie to me."

"I'll only tell you the truth." His tongue outlined each taut peak. "I missed, you Melanie." He eased her skirt up around her waist. "I thought about calling you, but it just wouldn't be the same as being with you."

Melanie buried her fingers in his hair, urging him closer. He held the weight of her breasts in his hands, kissing and stroking her until she thought she couldn't stand it anymore. Her head went back as she braced herself on the table with her arms.

Charles gently pushed her thighs apart and caressed her feet and ankles, then her calves and thighs. He traced the line of her garter belt with one finger and then his tongue.

Melanie writhed. He was doing it to her again and she couldn't help herself. She lifted her hips and arched into his hand. He nuzzled the mound of soft curly hair and then his lips began their magic. Melanie was lost. She shuddered and groaned, lost in a sensual oblivion only Charles could create. She groaned, her breathing hard, her eyes heavy with desire.

Charles slipped out of his pants and closed the slight gap between them.

When he entered her, Melanie let out a long heartfelt sigh, wrapping her legs around his waist and urging him closer. Her hands clutched his back. Their mouths met and fused. All the frustrations and tensions of the last few weeks fled. Melanie felt as if she were being catapulted into space, tumbling and turning, unable to tell which way was up or down. They soared and twirled before floating back to earth.

It was a long while before either could speak. Melanie rested her forehead against Charles' temple. "Melanie, I have to fly back to New York in the morning."

She heard the real regret in his voice and was glad. "Spend the night with me," she murmured. She would tell Greg she couldn't leave until the morning.

"How about the afternoon, too?" he teased, his tongue in her ear.

"Think we can get out of here fast enough?" She wiggled away from him and hopped off the table.

"If not, there's a hotel a couple blocks away." He planted a kiss on each breast and then her mouth, sending desire spiraling through her.

"We'd better hurry." Her voice was husky as she grabbed her clothes and pulled them on in record time.

Hilary sat at her desk, trying to decide how she could channel funds from the corporation into numbered Swiss bank accounts. It wouldn't be easy, but if she could create some dummy companies for subcontracting work, she might be able to pull it off. It was worth a try. She had given up hope of getting that land from Raine Bradburn.

There was a knock at her door. Mitch burst in.

Her eyes were bright with pride. He wore a new three piece grey pinstriped suit with a snowy shirt and red tie. He looked superb. "How's the first day on the job?"

"Okay. I'm starting out as an errand boy, but I think public relations is the place for me." He put one hand in his pocket. "They've got the best looking chicks in the building."

"Mitch, you're here to work."

"All work and no play . . ." He blew her a kiss and slipped out the door.

Hilary shook her head. Oh, to be young, without a care in the world. She couldn't remember ever feeling like that. She reached for the telephone. Maybe Chandler would like to go out with her tonight. She dialed the studio number. There was no answer. Where was he? He said he had to work all afternoon.

She put him out of her mind. There were some interesting basketball games this weekend. She could place a few bets before going to Zachary's. She looked at her checkbook. She'd have to transfer more money from the savings account. Simon insisted on being paid on time.

Alana thought of the long weekend ahead. She had agreed to play in Cindy Adams charity tennis tournament and now regretted it. She didn't feel like playing tennis all weekend. She had stacks of work to do.

Melanie's words came back to her. Was she indirectly responsible for Betty's death? Phillip had never talked about it and she had avoided asking too many questions. It wasn't something she wanted to think about.

She turned her thoughts to Hilary's plan. She had been tempted. Was there any way to legally secure her position in the company without Raine's land? She would have to check into it.

Bone tired, she stuffed papers into her briefcase and snapped it shut. It was time to go home. She wished she were going home to Raine.

Chandler posed Whitney in front of her fireplace, the golden tones of her chiffon negligee blending with the background. He adjusted the tilt of her chin and returned to his camera.

"Whitney, darling, could you give me a more sensual look?" He focused the camera.

Whitney pouted. "How can I do that when you're so far away?"

He chuckled, walking over to her and bending down to sit beside her. He was aware of everything about her from the graceful curve of her neck to the gentle slope of her breast. His hand touched her cheek and he bent to kiss her. His fingers wandered over her shoulder, slipping her gown down and exposing her breast to his gaze. His tongue flicked over the rosy peak.

Whitney closed her eyes and sighed.

"That's perfect," he said, his voice thick. He scrambled to his feet and looked into the camera. "Whitney, I want you to make love to me through the camera. Can you do that?"

"For you, Chandler, anything." She ran her tongue over her pink lips, her lids heavy. Sunlight filtered through the windows, bathing her in a soft glow. Whitney was reclined against a pile of white satin pillows. She hooked the strap of her gown in her finger and pulled it slowly down until both breasts were exposed, the camera clicking while Chandler murmured encouragement.

"Beautiful," he whispered, his voice ragged. "Caress your breasts, pretend they're my hands."

Whitney arched toward the camera, her hands holding the weight of her breasts in her hands, her fingers circling their taut tips. "Oh, Chandler, I want you."

"Soon, sweetheart, soon." He repositioned the camera and approached her. Hovering over her body, he reached out and kissed her, probing the interiors of her mouth before moving down to the soft mounds he loved to touch. He ran his hands down her sides, pushing the gown further. "Show me how much you want me," he said, backing off and returning to the camera.

Whitney sighed, her hands moving over her body where Chandler had touched her.

He swore under his breath when he ran out of film. Quickly changing cameras, he crooned, "You're beautiful, Whitney. Show me how beautiful you are."

She sat up for a moment, her gown around her waist. Easing it down her legs, she laid back, her eyes slightly glazed. Her hands continued their slow, erotic movement.

"Lower, Whitney, darling. Where do you want me to touch you, kiss you?"

She groaned, parting her legs, one hand between her thighs while the other clutched a breast. "I can't stand it," she muttered. "Chandler, come here."

He set the camera aside and approached her, stripping off his clothes on the way. He dropped to his knees, pressing a kiss to her eager mouth.

Her arms wrapped around his neck.

His tongue traced the outline of her lips.

Her hands travelled over the contours of his body, restlessly, eagerly.

He pressed his body into hers.

She welcomed him.

Their mouths met in a kiss that lasted forever as their bodies reached a fever pitch, reaching for the sweet moment of release.

Chandler rolled to the side, taking Whitney in his arms. When he could breathe, he murmured, "We're never going to get many pictures if we end up like this."

"Who cares," she said with a sigh, cuddling closer to him.

Chandler almost agreed with her, but these rolls of film were important to him. They were his insurance policy if Hilary lost the Hudson fortune. Whitney was a wealthy woman. If she decided to dump him, he'd show her some of the photos he had. They weren't the type of thing she'd like to see in a magazine. Either way he would win. If she wouldn't pay for them, he'd sell them. There were plenty of magazines who would pay for nude photographs of well known women.

It had been so easy. And rewarding. Why hadn't he thought of it before? How many other women could he persuade to pose for him?

His thoughts returned to Whitney. He didn't care how many photos he took of her. He liked the fringe benefits best of all.

Chapter Twenty-seven

Melanie slung her tennis racket over her shoulder and walked into the tennis club after entrusting her new car to the valet. Her short white skirt barely covered her lacey panties, while her halter top allowed for maximum sunning with a minimum of coverage.

The club had a high, beamed ceiling with white walls and a slate floor. Green and white canvas chairs were grouped around bamboo and glass tables. A bar overlooked the courts. The pro shop was to the right and the weight room, sauna, and locker rooms were to the left. An open air dining room was adjacent to the bar.

Melanie hoped she had a decent partner. It was the luck of the draw for this mixed doubles charity event, and if she drew a low-level player, she would just have to sprain her ankle and withdraw from the tournament. She wasn't going to get out on a tennis court and make a fool of herself in front of hundreds of spectators! She didn't know how she had let Cindy Adams talk her into entering in the first place.

She saw Raine Bradburn leaning against the bar. He looked better than a lot of pros in his tennis whites. She approached him. "Hi, Raine. Cindy talked you into playing, I see."

He nodded. "Have you seen the pairings yet?"

"Nope. I'm afraid to look."

"It can't be that bad. At least you know Muffy Henderson can't be your partner."

She stared at him with a wide smile on her face. "Is she your partner?"

He shook his head. "Thank God!"

Melanie leaned an elbow on the bar. After calmly thinking about it, she knew she had made a mistake trying to get Raine's land by seducing him. She was embarrassed by the scene she had created, and if she wanted any credibility with him, she would have to apologize. Especially if she ever wanted him to believe her stories about Alana. "Raine, about the other day . . ."

"It's forgotten, Melanie." He signaled to the bartender. "Would you like something to drink?"

"Lemonade for now." She took a deep breath. "I wish you'd let me apologize. I feel stupid enough about what happened."

"Apology accepted. Desperate people do desperate things." He gave her order to the bartender.

"Thanks." She rubbed a spot on the bar with her finger. "About the land—"

"I won't discuss it here." His voice was clipped.

"Could I make an appointment with you at your office? I have a firm offer for you and I'd like to discuss it with you."

He looked at her for a long moment then nodded. "Call my secretary. Set up a time. I'll let her know you'll be calling."

"Thanks." She picked up her glass. "Good luck."

Turning, she walked toward the crowd gathered around the pairings posted on the bulletin board. Her change of tactics had worked. She held little hope of coming up with a plan he would accept, but the doubts she could put in his mind would be worth the effort.

"Who is Joseph Morgan?" she muttered under her breath looking at the gayly decorated board.

"A new member," the woman next to her whispered with a sigh. "And he is gorgeous. You sure were lucky." She wrinkled her nose. "I get Monty Wentworth."

Melanie sympathized with her. Monty was in his sixties, fifty pounds overweight, and had a fiery temper. He held the club record for broken rackets in one season. He also donated more money than anyone else to this charity event, so everyone put up with his tantrums.

Melanie scanned the rest of the pairings, surprised to see Alana's name. Cindy must've talked her into playing as well. Then she saw the name of her partner and her eyes widened. Did Cindy have any idea what she was doing? She should have found another partner for Alana. Alana Hudson and Raine Bradburn playing tennis together would fill the stands! This might be an interesting day after all. Watching them together might give her a better idea of how to approach Raine with the "rumors."

Wandering back into the bar, she saw Greg and walked over to him. "My condolences."

He was hunched over the bar, a bloody Mary between his hands. "Thanks. Muffy Henderson will be quite a sight in her tennis tent."

Melanie giggled. "I drew a new member, Joseph Morgan. Do you know anything about him?"

"Never heard of him." Greg took a healthy drink from his glass. "I figure Muffy will last one set and then melt into a huge puddle of fat right on center court."

"Take me to the dance tonight and I'll console you," she murmured in his ear. She wanted to see if Raine and Alana would appear together.

He grinned at her. "That's a deal. I haven't seen you since

391

that weekend in Kauai." He sighed. "Neither of us were in the mood."

"That's what friends are for," she said quietly, rubbing his back.

"But we make great lovers," he protested, his voice low.

"When we're both in the mood."

He lifted his glass to her. "Here's to the mood. After making a spectacle out of myself with Muffy, I'll need my ego stroked."

"Is that all you'll need stroked?" she teased.

He made a clicking sound with his tongue. "Looks like we're in the mood already. How about a quick visit to the storage area behind the weight room?"

"It's probably occupied," she muttered. The little room was noted for illicit interludes.

She headed for the ladies locker room. Greg was everything a woman could want, so why couldn't she feel more for Greg and less for Charles?

Raine watched Melanie walk away. He had no illusions about her change in attitude. She was up to something. Melanie was Phillip Hudson's daughter and she knew exactly what she was doing.

These charity events were a pain in the ass, but in his position, it would look bad if he didn't do his part. He'd rather write out a check and be left alone, but Cindy Adams had talked him into it. Or rather, knowing that Alana had agreed to play had made him agree to participate. It had taken a substantial donation to assure Alana would be his partner.

He had stationed himself at the bar so he could see everyone as they came in and registered. He waited for Alana. He felt sorry for Muffy's partner. She looked like a short, white tank as she waddled up the steps, short of breath already.

Then he saw Alana. Her short pleated skirt left her long, slim legs bare. Thin straps held the bodice in place, her curves thrust against the thin material. A single braid down her back held her hair in place. He felt his body tense. He wanted her as much as ever.

Alana was furious when she discovered she and Raine were to be partners. This was either someone's idea of a joke or Raine's money at work. "How much did it take to bribe Cindy?" she demanded after stalking over to Raine.

Raine leaned one elbow on the bar. "Why not? I hate these silly tournaments. With you as my partner I assured myself of a pleasant time, especially when you play the net." His gaze skimmed over her bare legs. "Very pleasant."

Alana's mouth snapped shut. "Raine, be reasonable. Think of the speculation. All those people watching us, knowing the situation. We'll be the subject of all kinds of gossip."

"But it'll be for a good cause." He chuckled. "Don't take it so seriously. Lighten up. Let them gossip." He paused, lowering his voice. "Don't you want to play with me?" She couldn't miss the innuendo in his voice.

"Play with you, Raine? Right now I'd like to strangle you!" She turned and stalked off toward the locker room.

Hilary sat in the stands, bored. She didn't play tennis. She hated to run around and get sweaty, but she had come to watch Mitch. His first match wasn't for another hour, and she thought it was silly to sit in the sun and watch adults hitting a little ball back and forth. She thought about going into the bar, but chose not to. It felt like a giant ball was bouncing around in her head. A night at Zachary's had cost her more than a good night's sleep. She had lost twenty-five thousand dollars in two hours.

"Chandler, would you get me something cold to drink?" She

turned to her husband, wincing at the pain. "Maybe some lemonade."

"Sure." He got to his feet, his white slacks uncreased, his red shirt unwrinkled.

Hilary watched him go, a frown puckering her brow. He had been more remote than usual lately. Was he concerned about the will? He hadn't said anything. He had been so busy with work that they hadn't talked about it. She shrugged, her attention drawn to the players walking onto the middle court. Her mouth gaped open. She heard the murmurs around her. Raine and Alana were partners! The luck of the draw? No way! Who had set it up? Raine or Alana.

Hilary leaned forward, her gaze focused on the stunning couple. If she watched closely, maybe she could get a better insight into the situation, find Raine's weak spot so she could take advantage of it.

Alana looked from Raine to the couple warming up on the other side of the net. "Think we have a chance?"

"As long as I can concentrate on the game." He hit the ball cross court.

"You'd better. I want to win. Wanda beat me in the singles tournament a couple of months ago. I want revenge."

Raine glanced at Alana. "Nice attitude," he muttered.

"I'm competitive." She hit a backhand that skimmed the net.

"Too bad we're not playing Muffy Henderson and her partner." A smile touched his lips. "You're distracting."

She bounced a ball and looked at him over her shoulder. "Would you prefer I wore sweats?"

"Honey, you could wear sack cloth and look gorgeous."

Alana shook her head and said with a sigh, "Let's just play the game."

By the third set Alana was exhausted. Perspiration dampened

her hair. Her tennis dress clung to her damp skin. She felt lightheaded and lethargic, her stomach queasy. When they changed sides, she wiped her face with a towel. Usually she could play doubles all afternoon without a second thought.

"Are you all right?" Raine asked, propping his sunglasses on top of his head.

"Just a little warm. I usually don't have to work so hard to win." She shook her head. "I can't believe you missed that overhead shot."

"You were in my line of vision," he grumbled, pushing his sunglasses back in place.

Alana had to smile to herself as Raine finished out the third set with grim determination. His concentration had returned with a vengeance. They won easily.

As they walked off the court Raine gripped her arm. "Alana, we have to talk."

She shook her head, toweling her neck and face. She needed something cold to drink. "There's nothing to say. And we never end up talking."

"Making love is a form of communication," he said in a low voice.

"I don't wish to communicate with you." She tried to pull away.

"Like hell you don't." He looked around and pulled her behind the bleachers. He took her into his arms, his lips seeking hers in a kiss that left them both breathless. "Now, tell me you don't want to communicate with me."

It was useless to lie. "About the land—"

"I'm not talking about the land and you know it." He ground out the words as he pushed her away from him.

She was tired of arguing with him. "I'll meet you here at three for our next match." She turned and fled to the safety of the locker room, his kiss still burning on her lips.

* * *

Hilary wondered what had happened to Alana and Raine. They had walked off the court together, but now she didn't see them.

It had been difficult listening to the gossip floating around the stands as Raine and Alana played. The speculations ranged from the two of them plotting to murder Phillip and get his company and money to a hot new feud between Alana and the man she suspected of murdering her husband.

Hilary smiled suddenly. That was it! If she could make Alana think that Raine had killed Phillip, she would never let him near enough to her to even negotiate for that land. By the time Alana knew the truth, it would be too late to meet the terms of Phillip's will, and Hilary would have another chance at it.

She scanned the crowd looking for Chandler. It was hot and she was thirsty. He had left half an hour ago. She was sick of waiting. If he wasn't back in ten minutes, she'd get her own drink, and it wouldn't be lemonade!

Chandler sauntered through the crowd, stopping to talk to several golfing buddies. He was heading for the auxiliary bar when he saw Tammy White. She was about Whitney's age, was tall, had a round face and bad complexion. She was also married to an eighty year old man worth millions. He decided to give it a try. He had nothing to lose and everything to gain.

"Hi, Tammy."

She returned his dazzling smile with a shy one. "Hello, Chandler. How's business?"

"Great." He paused to look at her closely. "You know, Tammy, you have really good bone structure. I'd like to photograph you."

She blinked in surprise. "You would?" She put her hands to her face. "But I look terrible."

He waved her weak excuse away. "We'll retouch the negatives and you'll look gorgeous." She wasn't as aggressive as Whitney, but he saw her interest. "We could do some poses that your husband would love." He lowered his voice. "You would really be doing me a big favor."

"Could you really make me look beautiful?" she asked, her voice hopeful.

"Gorgeous." His voice was filled with assurance.

"I'll call you Monday and set up an appointment." He smiled at her eagerness.

"That would be terrific. I'll look forward to seeing you." He walked away with a wide grin. It was so easy. He couldn't believe it.

Alana and Raine won the next round. By their third match, she was completely drained. Raine realized it, and he covered for her. They won in the third set and won the tournament.

She was surprised when Raine hugged her and kissed her in the middle of the court. Sweat was dripping from his forehead and his shirt was plastered to his body. He still looked and felt good to her.

"We did it!" He smiled down at her before releasing her and walking to shake hands with their opponents.

Alana slowly followed him wondering how she could get out of attending the banquet that evening.

Raine was wiping his face by the time she crossed to the sidelines. His features softened. "Go home and take a nap, Alana. I'll pick you up at seven."

She shook her head. "I'm coming alone."

"No." He jammed his racket into his bag. "We won together

and we'll come to the banquet together." He paused. "You owe it to me."

Her eyebrows lifted. "How do you figure that?"

"I covered for you in that last set. The least you can do is keep me company during a boring banquet." His grin was boyishly endearing.

She nodded reluctantly. She was too tired to argue.

Later after a nap and a long, leisurely bath, Alana felt revived. She almost looked forward to the evening.

She slipped a shimmering violet dress over her head, the fine fabric clinging to her curves. Thin straps started from the center of the bodice and flared out over her shoulders, forming a delicate web on her bare back before ending at her waist. She held Raine's earrings in the palm of her hand. They were perfect with the dress. She put them on as the intercom buzzed.

Raine straightened the jacket of his white tuxedo and sipped his scotch, his gaze riveted on the woman sitting next to him at the table. Alana was breathtakingly beautiful. His gaze lingered on the curves he knew so well and wanted to touch again. She was wearing his earrings.

"You look wonderful," he said in a low voice. "I was a little concerned about you this afternoon."

"So was I," she admitted, taking a deep breath. "We do have to talk."

"Later." He touched one earring, ignoring the stares and whispers. "I'm glad you're wearing these."

"Doesn't it bother you when people talk about us?" she asked softly.

"Not really." He moved closer to her, inhaling her intoxicating scent, his arm draped over the back of her chair. His fingers brushed her bare back. He controlled the urge to kiss her creamy shoulder. "You were without an escort and we played together today. Nothing special about that."

She gave him a wry look for an answer.

Melanie saw Alana and Raine walk in together and frowned. She had to prevent Alana from getting that land from Raine. If Arty didn't get any real information this week, she'd have to invent something. Time was getting short, and she was worried about Alana's success. She turned to Greg. "What do you know about Raine Bradburn?"

He shrugged. "He likes beautiful women. He's ruthless in business. He's an excellent sailor. He can buy and sell half the island. What more do you want?"

She knew all of that. She needed more.

As the trophies were awarded, Alana began to tense. What would Raine do when they had to step to the front and accept their awards? She glanced at him through lowered lashes. He looked relaxed and pleased with himself. It worried her.

When their names were announced, they walked toward Cindy. She handed Alana and Raine their trophies, then said with a giggle, "It's traditional for the winning couple to kiss."

People started laughing and clapping. Alana gaze locked with Raine's.

He pulled her close, his mouth covering hers in a searing kiss.

Alana forgot everything as he sent her senses spinning, her body quickening with desire.

When he finally lifted his head, the clapping increased. Desire turned to embarrassment. How dare he kiss her like that in front of so many people. There was bound to be some comment made about it in the paper.

"Does this mean the Hudson-Bradburn feud is over?" someone shouted.

Raine saw the sparks in her eyes and took a deep breath. "Not a chance," he told them with a wicked grin, taking Alana's hand and leading her back through the crowd to their table.

After the banquet Raine insisted on driving Alana home.

They drove in silence until they reached her apartment building. "Thanks for a delightful evening. I can't wait to read about it in the paper." She fumbled with the handle, giving Raine time to get out and open the door for her.

"I'll see you to the door."

"And that's all," she told him in a firm voice.

He rubbed a weary hand over his face. "Can't you just relax?"

With Raine around? Not a chance. Alana gave herself a stern lecture on the elevator. Sex was not the answer to her problems. Raine was one of her problem. She had to stand up to him.

She pulled her key from her purse. "I'm safely at my door now. Thank you and good night." She turned her back to him and inserted the key. She tried to slip through the doorway and close the door before he could enter, but he was too strong for her.

He was in before she knew it. He took her into his arms, his lips descending slowly. "Say the word, Alana, and I'll leave."

She held her breath. She wanted to tell him to go, but the words wouldn't come out. "Stay," she finally breathed, her lips seeking his.

They met and clung together as if they had been apart for months. Neither of them could let go as passion burned between them. Alana acknowledged to herself that she wanted him more than she had ever wanted Phillip.

She welcomed him, her mouth opening for his thrusting tongue, demanding her own exploration as well.

He covered her cheeks, eyes, forehead with feverish kisses. "It's like I've never touched you before," he muttered.

"I know." She tried to take a breath, burying her head against his neck. Her arms slipped under his jacket and around his waist. He smelled so good, like fresh limes. His muscles were taut under her fingers. She pressed her body closer to his.

He groaned and sought her mouth once again, leaving her breathless with drugging kisses.

Alana slipped his jacket off his shoulders, impatient with the clothing separating their bodies. She tugged at his shirt, pulling it from his slacks. Her hands craved his warm strength. "I've missed you."

"It hasn't been that long." He strung kisses along her shoulder.

"It seems like forever." She unbuttoned his shirt, nuzzling his chest.

"Where the hell is the zipper on this dress?" he muttered, his breathing ragged.

She laughed softly and stepped away from him. She released the straps in the front and slowly unzipped the side zipper. The dress fell into a violet pool around her feet. She stepped out of it and taking Raine's hand pulled him toward the bedroom.

They stopped in the living room and he shrugged out of his shirt. He lifted her breasts in his hands and lovingly kissed each one.

In the hallway, he pulled her hose and panties off, stopping to caress her thighs and hips.

She fumbled with his belt and zipper, finally easing his slacks over his hips. Her hands traced the rock hard muscles of his thighs.

He lifted her into his arms and placed her gently in the middle of her bed. His gaze followed the path of his hands, reverently tracing her feminine curves. "Just as silky as I remembered."

She tried to pull him closer, but he resisted. "Not yet, Alana. Let me love you." His tongue dipped into the hollow at the base of her throat, then trailed down the slope of her breast until his mouth fastened on the tip of one rosy breast, tugging gently until Alana groaned.

Her body arched toward him and he obliged by easy himself over her, her body opening to his with a thirsting desire. She urged him closer, her hands feverishly roaming over his back, her nails digging into his flesh as he carried her to the brink of desire and then lifted her higher.

Their limbs entwined, they called out each other's names, emotion spiralling them into a galaxy of exquisite sensation. She floated back to earth in his arms, safe and content.

Chapter Twenty-eight

Melanie sparkled with anticipation as the airport came into view. She pushed a button. "Stop at the lei stalls."

"Yes, ma'am."

She scrambled out of the car and hurried toward the first stall, picking out a plumeria and an orchid lei. She grabbed a men's leaf lei for good measure and after paying for them, returned to the car, a wide smile on her face. Charles was coming to Hawaii for four days and there wasn't even a board meeting.

She waited impatiently, smoothing the skirt of her aqua shirt dress. As the plane lumbered toward the gate, she toyed with one of the pearl buttons that ran the length of her dress. The fragrance of the leis in her hand increased her excitement.

Charles was one of the first passengers off the plane. Her face lit up and she ran to meet him, kissing him hungrily after putting each lei over his head.

"I've missed you," she murmured, tucking her arm through his as they walked toward the baggage conveyor.

"Not as much as I've missed you," he said, pulling her into a doorway and pressing his body into hers. His tongue thrust into her mouth, greedily drinking as if he were parched.

She returned his ardor, her arms wrapped around his neck. When they parted, Melanie rested her forehead against his. "We'd better get out of here. I can't wait much longer."

He nodded and grabbing her hand, they practically ran to claim his luggage. He had one small bag. "I didn't think I'd need much."

"You won't need anything at all," she murmured, nuzzling his ear. "We're going to lock the door for four days. No one home but you and me."

"Sounds terrific." He pulled her into another doorway, his kiss making her knees weak.

Once they were in the limousine, Melanie fell into his arms. His hand slid under her dress, stroking her thigh.

"It'll take half an hour to get to my house," she murmured against his lips.

"Tell Leonard to take the long way home."

She giggled and did as he said while Charles started with the bottom button of her dress. He slowly opened her dress as if he were opening a present. His mouth followed the path of the buttons up her silky thighs. "Melanie, darling. If I had known you weren't wearing anything under that dress, I would have taken you the moment I saw you."

She closed her eyes and smiled. "I thought it might be a nice surprise." A coil of fire began in her hips and slowly spread throughout her body.

He reached the button at her hips, urging her thighs apart.

His touch increased her need for more. She moved restlessly.

He released another button, his lips circling her navel. He moved higher until her breasts were free. He slipped her dress off, glorying in her body. His lips teased her golden breasts, never quite touching the throbbing peaks until she moaned and pressed his head against her.

Melanie quivered with anticipation, the heat building in her body. She shifted her weight, pushing Charles back against the leather seat. She unbuttoned his shirt, her mouth tasting and touching him, urgent in her need for him. She had to feel him inside of her before the ache could begin to fade. She rubbed his chest with the palm of her hand. Her hand moved lower as she unbuckled his belt and flicked open his pants. She quickly pulled them off, running her hand over the source of his desire.

His hands caressed her, the twin peaks the objects of his kisses. Her breasts strained toward him, burgeoning under his touch. He tugged at them with his teeth until she gasped, eager for more.

Her hands raked over his body, pushing his shirt from his shoulders, excited beyond her wildest dreams. She didn't understand it. She didn't even try. Being with Charles was like coming home.

His lips tantalized her as they trailed over her stomach and hips. He pulled her down on top of him and then in one swift movement had shifted her onto her back.

Her nails scraped his nipples, her hands tangled in the wiry hair on his chest.

Charles' mouth sought hers, their tongues duelling as their bodies pressed closer together.

Melanie had never felt such a dizzying passion, driven to the brink by insatiable desire. She pulled him into her, her legs wrapped tightly around his back as if she would never let him go. They moved together in a renewed urgency.

"Melanie," he rasped, his breathing labored. "Oh, Melanie!"

She showered kisses on his shoulder and neck as time stood still. She was wrapped in a passion and desire so overwhelming, she couldn't begin to comprehend it. She cried out his name as they climaxed together, lost in a sensuous frenzy.

In the hazy afterglow, their bodies still locked together, Melanie whispered, "Aloha." The fragrance of the crushed leis filled the car.

"I hope that means 'hello' and not 'good-bye.'" He shifted his weight, his fingertips pushing a strand of hair from her cheek.

"Ask me again in four days," she said with a touch of sadness.

"Hey! We're together, aren't we? Let's not worry about saying good-bye."

Alana hadn't seen or heard from Raine in a week. Could the passion they had shared been a dream? Her mind was filled with doubts as she dressed for a benefit concert on Saturday night. Would he be there? If he was planning to attend, he could have invited her to go with him. But she didn't really want to go with him. It was too unsettling. Her thoughts turned to the continuing investigation into Phillip's death.

Raine was still a prime suspect and so was she, but she knew *she* didn't do it. She wasn't so positive about Raine. Now that Phillip was dead, Raine was the one who seemed to benefit the most. Hadn't she told him she couldn't have an affair as long as she was married? And at the time of Phillip's death, Raine didn't know that they were planning on a divorce. She didn't want to think he was capable of murder, but she had seen that ruthless look on his face too many times to discount it. She pushed the worrisome thoughts from her mind. She had to get ready for the concert.

She didn't even want to go tonight, but she was on the fine arts board sponsoring the event. Her presence was expected. She wore a slim, strapless white beaded dress with a matching bolero jacket. A choker of five strands of matched pearls circled her neck, a large pearl surrounded by diamonds at the base of her throat. Matching pearl and diamond earrings completed her outfit.

When Alana saw Raine in the box seats directly across from

her at the concert, her heart skipped a beat. He was devastatingly handsome and his smile did funny things to her pulse. The seat next to him was empty. Was he here alone? Why?

She returned his smile with a frosty look and tried to concentrate on the program, but every time she glanced at him, he was staring at her. She breathed a sigh or relief when the lights went down and the concert began, but she could still feel the intensity of his gaze.

She remained seated during intermission, her program in shreds. Raine remained across from her, but as soon as the second half began, his box was empty.

The silver sequins in her figure-hugging gown glittered when she made a move to leave, but he was already beside her.

His hand clamped down on her arm. "You'll cause a scene if you leave now," he whispered.

She stopped struggling. "What are you doing here?" she hissed.

"Listening to Mozart." His voice was low and teasing.

"That's not what I meant and you know it," she muttered, glancing at him in the muted light. Mozart filled the air. The music made it difficult to stay angry.

Alana took a deep breath. "If people see us together, it'll only start more rumors. It was difficult enough trying to explain that picture in the paper from the banquet last week." She was still upset that he hadn't called all week.

Raine was silent for a moment and then took her hand and pulled her to her feet. "Then we'll have to make sure they don't see us."

Before she could protest, she was following him down the dimly lit hallway, down the carpeted steps, and out the front door.

"I'll take you home." He started walking down the street.

"What if I don't want to go home." Her nerves were stretched to the breaking point as she held back.

407

"Then I'll take you to my house," he said, his voice mocking.

"I'll call the police."

"Before you do that, there's something I just have to do." He pulled her into the shadows of a building and then into his arms, his lips demanding and getting a response from her.

Breathless, she looked up at him in a daze. "I wish you wouldn't do that."

He kissed her again, his lips tracing the outline of her trembling mouth. "Then don't look so damned kissable," he growled, sending her reeling with another devastating kiss.

His car was parked in the valet lot. Alana stared at him. "Why didn't you have the valet get your car?"

"Because I could hardly kiss you under the bright lights, could I?" He touched the tip of her nose and opened the door of his car with a flourish.

Alana was bemused, looking around after a few minutes. "This is the way to your house."

"Smart lady," Raine said.

"You never asked me if I wanted to go to your house." She crossed her arms over her chest.

"You said you didn't want to go home," he returned, glancing at her with a teasing grin.

"I did not."

"Don't be so stubborn," he chided.

"Why can't you leave me alone?" He had entered the gates and stopped outside his home.

"I don't know," he murmured. He helped her out of the car, his gaze raking over her flushed face and stubborn chin, down her heaving chest, and further to the toes of her shoes peeking out from the hem of her dress.

"So use some of that famous steely control," she retorted.

"Believe me, I would if I could." He pinned her with the heat of his gaze.

"Why didn't you call all week?" she asked in a small voice.

He dropped his hands onto her shoulders. "I thought you'd hang up on me," he admitted, a rueful look on his face. His hands moved to either side of her face, lifting it so she had to look into his eyes. "We'll have a drink. If you want to go home afterward, I'll take you."

She wished he wouldn't touch her. He made it difficult to think clearly. "Promise?"

"Promise." He opened the door and escorted her into the living room.

"Just one drink and then I'm going home." Her voice lacked conviction and they both knew it. She saw devilment lurking in the depths of his blue eyes as he handed her a drink. What was he up to now? She slipped off her jacket and tossed it onto a chair.

"Don't worry. I didn't slip anything into it." He grinned at her and settled down next to her, his arm around her bare shoulders, his fingers touching her neck. "I'm glad to see you're through wearing black."

She shrugged, trying hard to remain indifferent to his touch. The scent of his aftershave was clean and inviting. "It seems senseless with this fighting over Phillip's will. It seems more a mockery than anything else."

"And you're tired of pretending a love for a man you hated."

"Something like that." She wanted to melt into his arms and forget the harsh realities of the world, but that was out of the question. It would muddy already turbulent waters.

He nibbled on her ear. "You don't have to pretend around me." His voice was husky, the touch of his lips on her ear creating a desire for more.

"Just trying to preserve my sanity," she murmured, barely resisting the urge to wrap her arms around his neck.

"So we'll be crazy together." He blew softly into her ear while one hand caressed the side of her breast.

She wiggled and tried to move her head away. It was difficult to keep her mind focused on release when her body was yearning for his touch. Mind over matter. The problem was the matter was strong and warm and inviting and her mind wanted to succomb to the very masculine matter. She made one last desperate try. "You promised you'd take me home after one drink." Her breath was coming in short gasps as she leaned into him.

"Only if you wanted to go." His warm breath tickled her neck and spread flames already licking at her nerves. He took the glass from her lifeless hands and pulled her into his arms. "Do you want to go home?" His lips were warm on her neck.

"No," she murmured, tipping her head to give him better access, her hands moving to his shoulders, enjoying the feel of strength beneath her fingers.

He cupped her breast, the sequins getting in his way. "This is like a suit of armour," he grumbled.

"Some knight you are." Her hands moved to his neck, her fingers playing with his hair.

"I could be if you'd let me." One lean finger touched her chin, forcing her to look into his eyes.

The desire she saw came as no surprise. Her body was responding to his touch more quickly than she thought possible.

His hand moved lower to the slit in her dress, easing underneath and caressing the length of her thigh. "I knew there had to be a way inside of this."

"There's a zipper." Her voice was little more than a husky whisper.

"Are you inviting me?" His lips teased hers, his voice ragged. He pulled the combs from her hair and ran his fingers through it. His hands circled her waist.

"Yes." She turned in his arms and wrapped her arms around his neck, smiling up at him. She pressed her body against his. "Are we alone?"

"What did you have in mind?" he asked, returning her smile, his hands spanning her waist.

"A swim in your pool. It's such a lovely night." She reached up and touched the corner of his mouth with her tongue. His skin was slightly salty, firm, and so desirable.

"Swimming is the last thing on my mind." His voice was gruff as he ran his hands down her spine.

"You might like it." Her tongue traced the outline of his firm lips. She felt his hands tightened and she signed. Why fight her own needs?

"We're alone." His hands cupped her buttocks. "So, you want to swim?"

"A moonlight swim." She closed her eyes and threw her head back.

"Perfect." Raine's lips touched hers.

She stepped away from him, pulled down the zipper hidden on the side of her dress and smiled at the passion she saw in his gaze as her dress lay in a glittering pool around her ankles. She had an innocent look on her face as she stepped out of her remaining clothes. "Any extra suits around?"

He bent his head and flicked each breast with his tongue.

Alana stood before him, her hands on his shoulders, her body shadowed in the soft light. Raine's hands traced a path from her waist over her hip and down her thigh to her calf and ankle. "Beautiful," he murmured, his voice husky. One finger traced the triangle of silky hair between her thighs. His tongue circled her navel, his hands caressing her hips and thighs.

His touch excited her more than she had thought possible. Slowly, Raine got to his feet, meeting her eager mouth with a crushing kiss that left them both breathless.

Alana shifted restlessly, wanting to touch the warmth of his skin. "You have too many clothes on." She fumbled with his jacket, bow tie, and buttons on his shirt, running her hands over his chest. She loved the feel of him, the hard muscles

411

under the smooth skin covered with crisp chest hair. She moved her hand to his belt, but was quickly frustrated when she couldn't remove it fast enough.

A low chuckle came from Raine. "In a hurry?" He stripped off the rest of his clothes and took a step back.

Alana drank in the sight of him, her eyes hungrily devouring him as if she hadn't eaten in a week. She grinned at his arousal. "Looks like I'm not the only one in a hurry." She closed the gap between them, running her hands over his back and then between their bodies, gripping him with her hand.

Raine shuddered. "Not fair."

"All's fair," she returned, her voice little more than a husky murmur.

"Witch." He covered her mouth with his, plunging his tongue into her mouth, exploring and drinking as if he couldn't quench his thirst.

Neither of them could wait any longer as the passion between them was overwhelming. Raine pulled Alana with him onto the floor, covering her body with his as she opened her legs and wrapped them around him. Time ceased as fiery passion consumed them, the white heat searing them as they clutched each other, Raine thrusting deeper and deeper, Alana welcoming him. They exploded with a climax that left them both panting, their bodies covered with a sheen of moisture.

Afterwards, they went for a swim.

As the water covered them in a warm, sensuous blanket, their bodies touched from shoulder to thigh. Coming up for air, they were both breathless. Alana wiped the water from Raine's face, wrapping her legs around his waist. "As long as you brought me out here, you might as well hold me up."

"My pleasure." He loosened her hold on him, supporting her back as she stretched out, floating on her back.

"It's beautiful out here." Alana looked up at the sky, the stars looking like glitter scattered on velvet.

"Beautiful," Raine agreed, running a hand over her legs and stomach to the curve of her breasts and back again. He lifted her slightly out of the water as she arched her back, running one finger around a rosy nipple before enclosing it with his mouth. His teeth gently pulled on one crest and then the other. "Satin." His voice was husky as a hand slide between her thighs, his fingers stroking until Alana squirmed. "Silk." His lips covered her mouth. The warmth of the water was nothing compared to the heat of their bodies as Alana righted herself and then wrapped her legs around Raine.

Her mouth sought his, her tongue exploring his mouth, desire flickering through her body. Her hands roamed over his back and shoulders, finally burying in the damp hair at his nape. She sank lower into the water, feeling him enter her. Her grip tightened as she covered his face with kisses, her senses reeling. Their lips met, their bodies joined from hip to shoulder.

Raine shuddered and Alana felt the passion build between them until she thought she would explode. The release was euphoric, like free falling through the sky, turning and tumbling before floating back to earth.

They were gasping for breath.

"Whoah . . . we're going to drown if we keep this up," Raine finally said.

She nestled against his chest, stringing kisses up the strong cord in his neck. "I'm comfortable." She wiggled against him.

"I'm not," he said. He climbed the steps, Alana still firmly clasped around his waist.

"What a way to go," she murmured, her head on his shoulder.

Raine didn't stop until they reached the master suite. Alana was carried into the master bath, and bypassing the huge sunken tub, Raine turned on the shower, the water cascading over both of them.

He released her and she slowly slid down his body, her arms still wrapped around his waist. He kissed the tip of her nose and turned her around. "I think it's time to cool you off." He reached for the soap and began to lather her body.

"That's not the way to cool me off," she murmured, leaning back against him, her eyes closed. "But don't stop."

He ran his hands over every inch of her body until she was tingling with renewed desire.

Turning around, Alana grabbed the soap. "My turn." She loved the feel of him, from the taut skin over his broad shoulders, down the mat of hair over his chest, and down the firm columns of his sturdy legs. Raine was a marvelous specimen of manhood, so different from Phillip. The thought of Phillip made her frown. Had Raine hated Phillip enough to murder him? He had said he could kill Phillip for beating her.

"Hey, what's the frown for?" he asked softly, massaging her shoulders.

She shook her head and smiled. "I was just thinking." Thoughts of Phillip disappeared as Raine kissed her, pressing her body close to his.

"About what?" He turned off the water and grabbed a fluffy towel from the heated bar.

"I forgot," she said with a sign as he gently wrapped her in a towel.

Much later they finally wandered into the kitchen to find something to eat.

The following Monday morning Hilary waited for Alana to reach the elevator before she approached her. They stepped into it together, and Hilary flicked a glance over Alana's white suit and pink blouse. There was a new radiance about Alana. Hilary wondered if it had been Raine Bradburn who had put the glow in her cheeks.

"Good morning, Alana." Hilary shifted her briefcase, and put one hand in the pocket of her navy linen skirt after straightening her pale blue blouse.

"Morning, Hilary."

"Who do you suppose murdered my father?" she asked, keeping her voice low and impartial as her fingers curled in her pocket.

"I don't know, but I'm sure the police will find the person responsible." Alana turned slightly away from her.

"They said someone put a lethal dose of one of his medications in a drink." Hilary watched Alana closely. "I saw Raine fiddling with Phillip's drink when they were fighting in the bar. He certainly hated my father."

Hilary was satisfied when Alana paled and her mouth thinned.

"There were a lot of people in the bar. Anyone could have doctored his drink. The police don't even know if that's when it happened."

"But it's a possibility." The elevator door opened on Hilary's floor and she stepped out, a smile on her face.

Alana sat in Raine's office, feeling like she was in enemy territory, surprised at his phone call earlier in the day. He said he wanted to discuss the land, in his office at four o'clock. It was almost four-thirty and the land hadn't been mentioned yet.

"Raine, what about the land?"

"I've got a proposal." He tapped a paper in front of him. Before he could continue his intercom buzzed. He jabbed the button. "What is it?"

"Ralph Mortimer is here. He says it's urgent."

Raine raked his hand through his hair, glancing at Alana. "Go ahead," she murmured. "I'll wait."

"Show him into the conference room. I'll see him there."

He released the button. "Sorry about that." He stood up. "I'll be right back."

Ten minutes later she shifted her weight. She was restless. Getting to her feet, she walked around his desk. It wouldn't hurt to read the proposal. Just as she was reaching for it, she glanced at the credenza behind his desk. A sheaf of papers with her name on top caught her eye. She picked up the papers and scanned them. It couldn't be. She tried to read the report but tears blurred the words.

"Alana? What's the matter?" Raine stood in the doorway. He took a step into the room.

"You bastard!" She whirled around, the papers in her hand. She stomped across the room and shook them in his face. "You had me investigated! How could you? What were you looking for? Contageous diseases? Murder in my past? Other lovers?" She tossed the papers at his chest.

He made no move to grab them, frowning. "Alana—"

"Investigated! I told you how I felt about Phillip doing the same damn thing to me!"

Raine was silent for a long moment. He closed the door and leaned against it, his gaze never leaving her face. "I had that investigation started after that first luncheon meeting with Phillip. I knew how he operated, and I figured he'd offer you as an added incentive to sweeten the deal for my land." When he paused, she walked to the windows, her back to him, her arms folded across her chest.

"Phillip was insanely jealous and possessive. He never would have offered his wife to his enemy." A chill raked her body. The thought nauseated her.

Raine took a deep breath. "The night before he died, we met. He offered . . . your services to me in exchange for that land, Alana."

"Oh, God, no!" She buried her face in her hands, her shoulders shaking.

Raine crossed the room, guiding her to a chair and gently pushing her into it. He stood to get a glass of whiskey from a hidden bar and returned to kneel beside her. "Drink this."

She sobbed, gulped, and sipped it before handing it back to him. Tears streaked down her cheeks.

Rained reached out to touch her but dropped his hand when she flinched. "Phillip offered. I told him to go to hell!"

"Sure! And then when he was dead you decided to collect! And Phillip didn't even get the damned land!" She wiped at the tears with the back of her hand. "What kind of evil game are you playing? Do you want to destroy my soul because you hated Phillip?"

"Alana, it's not like that and you know it. Damn it. I told you that investigation was started long before we got involved." He got to his feet, prowling around the room, raking a hand through his hair. "I needed to know what kind of person you were."

"And what did you find out?" Her voice was clipped.

He moved to stand beside her, watching her carefully. "I didn't find out very much," he admitted. "You are exactly what you appear to be. A young woman on the way up the corporate ladder. Until Hudson became your mentor." He paused. "Was he your lover or mentor when you became vice president?"

"Why don't you ask your investigator?" she muttered, wrapping her arms around her shaking body.

A thoughtful look settled on his face. "Funny thing though. Your early life is so sketchy. The agency couldn't find out much about your childhood."

She turned on him, lashing out at him in her hurt and anger. "What's the matter? Couldn't they find out when I took my first step? Got my first tooth? Lost my virginity? Snared my first rich husband?" Her lip curled as she looked at him with disgust. "Want all the gory details or just the highlights?"

He shook his head. "Alana, I'm sorry. I never meant for you to know."

"I'm sure you didn't." She rubbed her arms, willing herself not to cry again, not to break down completely, not to let him know how deeply he had wounded her.

He stood in front of her, watching her with an intensity that would have frightened her under other circumstances. "Who's Jeremy?"

Alana's head snapped back, a dangerous glitter in her eyes. "Why?"

He shifted his weight and looked anywhere but in her eyes. "Ah, well, you, ah, had his name and birthday written on your calendar."

"On my calendar at home!" She stared at him. "You went through my personal things?"

"I noticed it when I was there once." He finally met her gaze. "I'm not going to apologize for it. I wanted to know more about you. You never share anything about your personal life."

"You haven't said much either," she countered. Her stomach tightened and she felt cold, her emotions frozen. "You had me investigated, and you went through private things in my home. I thought I could trust you, but this proves that I can't trust anyone but myself." Her gaze was remote as she withdrew from him.

"You won't try to understand my side, will you?"

"There's nothing to understand. The report said it all." She wouldn't look at him.

"You won't listen." Raine's voice was weary.

"No." Alana walked toward the door, not looking back.

Before she could leave, he was there, taking her wrist in his grasp. "This isn't the end, Alana."

She met his determined gaze with a stony one of her own. "I never want to see you again."

"And my land?" he said, his dark eyes glittering.

"You and your land can join Phillip in hell!" She wrenched her wrist from his grasp and stalked out of the building.

Chapter Twenty-nine

Melanie slammed the car door and walked up the incline muttering all the way, her hair blowing in her face, her dress plastered against her body. She would have preferred a less windy, warmer meeting place. Gale force winds were always blowing at the Pali Lookout. She scanned the sightseers lined up along the railing like birds at an arcade. Melanie swore under her breath. He promised to be here on time, but he was late again. She took her place along the railing, idly watching a group of Japanese tourists snapping pictures of each other and the view below. Sheer cliffs surrounded the lookout, but it was a clear day, making Mokolii Island visible on the horizon. Spread out below were lush pastures, farms, rolling hills, and civilization in the form of a golf course, cemetery, villages, and towns. Kaneohe Bay looked like a giant aqua mirror from Melanie's vantage point. She tapped her foot and looked at her watch. She'd give him another five minutes, but that was all. She wished she were a man, then she wouldn't have to depend on someone else to do what she herself was capable of doing. She leaned forward on her hands, looking at the steep drop to the rocks below. What had her mother felt the night she drove off the cliff? She had been drinking. Melanie could tell that much from the note her mother had left behind. Her mother had been desperate and lonely, any strength she possessed being drained by Phillip's bullying. Melanie was mesmerized by the long drop. How long did it take to reach the bottom? A few seconds, probably. Did it hurt much or did a person die instantly? What thoughts would go through your head while you were flying through the air? They said a person's life flashed through their minds just before death. She didn't want to remember all the men who had passed through her life. She only wanted to remember Charles. He had been gone a week and she missed him terribly, but now she had other things to think about. Other plans to make.

"Hi, Ms. Hudson. How ya doin?" Arty approached and slipped in the narrow opening between Melanie and a tourist.

"Did you do it?" she demanded between clenched teeth.

He looked around before saying in a low voice, "Yeah. I told you I would. Getting the key from the manager was a big help. How did you get a master key from him?"

She smiled in satisfaction. "Men will do almost anything for me." Digging into her purse, she took out an envelope and her eyes narrowed. "You're sure no one saw you."

"Positive. Look, lady. I'm a pro." He looked around again, waiting to speak until a couple next to Melanie moved away. "I took the bottle and planted it in his locker. The hardest part was being inconspicuous. I'm not exactly the yachting type."

Her gaze raked the fat man dressed in a garish print shirt, plaid shorts, red hat, black socks, and tennis shoes. She tilted her head, curious in spite of herself. Arty would stand out in the conservative atmosphere of the club like a rooster in a hen house. "How did you get into the club?"

"Through the back door with the beer truck. The rest was easy." His chins wiggled when he laughed. "I did just what you wanted." He held out his hand. "Now I want my dough."

She held on to the envelope. "Have you been following Alana?"

He nodded. "Boring. Work and home. Home and work. A few parties thrown in. She never goes with anyone." He paused, looking sheepish. "I did lose her at a concert the other night. She went in alone and I had plenty of time before the finish, so I went for some shaved ice. She never came out at the end. Must've left early."

"You ninny! She might have slipped out with a man!"

"I haven't seen her with anyone." He shrugged. "You want me to keep following her?"

She nodded. "Give me the master key to the club, too. I have to get it back."

He handed her the key and she gave him the envelope. A dangerous glitter hardened her eyes, her face menacing. "Do you know what Kamehameha did to warriors who opposed him?"

The man shrugged, stuffing the envelope into the pocket of his shirt. "Naw. What?"

"He forced them off that cliff." She pointed to the highest cliff, her voice cold and hard.

The man looked up and gulped, awe on his face. "Good thing they don't do it anymore."

"Right," she murmured, turning her head so the wind blew the hair out of her eyes. She pinned him with her gaze. "Don't let Alana out of your sight!" She hated Alana almost as much as she had hated Phillip. And Raine Bradburn was at the top of her hate list. No one rejected her without paying for it. Even Charles couldn't erase the burning humiliation. Even if she had asked for his scorn, he didn't have to laugh. That was the worst part.

Melanie turned her thoughts back to the man at her side. "Alana has to have a lover, and it just might be Raine Bradburn. I have to know." The setup would be perfect.

"Okay, okay." He put up a hand. "Don't get your underwear in a knot." He frowned. "What if she doesn't have a lover?"

"She will." Melanie's voice was dry. She hoped this job would be done soon. The sooner Alana was out, the better Melanie would feel. And she would see that arrogant look wiped off Raine Bradburn's face as well.

She looked at Arty with disgust. Why did he have to look so tacky? She hadn't had much choice in the matter. There were few people she could trust to get this job done, and this toad had come highly recommended. "Make sure you finish this job right and don't tell anyone."

"I've done what you've asked. You think I'm a fool?" He grunted. "Dames. Who can figure 'em out." He turned to go. "I'll contact you tomorrow."

Melanie watched him disappear into the parking lot. Everything was falling into place. She smiled complacently, relaxing as she turned to go back to her car. Raine Bradburn and Alana would get what they deserved. Now she had to phone police headquarters to tip them off about searching the lockers at the club and keep her appointment with Raine. It wouldn't do to have Raine find the bottle before the police did. She chuckled to herself, imagining the look on Raine's face when she made him an offer he couldn't refuse.

Raine stood as Melanie entered his office. He sized her up as she crossed the room. Her black suit was stylish, her black and white striped blouse tasteful. Her hair swept back from her face. Her ivory jewelry was discrete. She looked the epitome of professionalism. Raine was on his guard.

"What's your offer today, Melanie?" He leaned back in his chair as she sat across from him.

"Did you know that my father had told Alana she would

inherit everything if he died?" She crossed her legs and smoothed her skirt.

"Why would I care about that?" His gaze darkened. He cared more than he wanted to admit.

"Don't you think that would be an excellent motive for murder?"

It was exactly what he thought, but it was something he preferred to push from his mind. "That's for the police to decide." His voice was clipped. He leaned forward, his hands clasped on his desk. "Did you come here to gossip or to make an offer?"

She uncrossed her legs and slowly pulled her briefcase onto her lap. "I saw Alana with Harry Walters the other day. Isn't he looking for a new executive vice president? Maybe she's realized her days at Hudson Enterprises are almost over." She paused as she pulled out a folder. "What do you think?"

"I think you like to gossip." He reached for the folder. "Is this your latest offer?" His expression gave away none of his inner turmoil.

She nodded toward the sheaf of papers. "I made a mistake the last time. I underestimated you. I won't make that mistake again." Her voice was calm and businesslike. She crossed her legs again, her hands folded in her lap. "I don't really care who runs Hudson Enterprises once I get my share of the stock and Phillip's estate. Once I have them in my possession, I'm willing to sell you all Phillip's stock at half the market value. It'll cost you millions, but you'll double your investment. Once you own it, I don't care if you tear it up and toss it away." She paused, looking at her manicured hand. "Just to prove I'm serious, I'm willing to turn over the stock I already own in exchange for the deed to your land."

Raine opened the folder and scanned the contents, startled at the offer. Melanie was serious. She was willing to sell controlling interest in her father's company to him. Just the exchange of her stock for his land was worth more than half the island. His face was shuttered. "I'll consider your offer."

"The deadline isn't far away. I assume you'll give me the time to tender another offer if this one isn't suitable?" She was aloof and businesslike. Raine knew she was up to something.

"Of course." He sat back, regarding her intently. "You're doing this without board approval."

"It isn't something they control." she gave him a bored look. "It's my stock I'm bartering with, and if I control Hudson Enterprises, I can sell all my stock." She paused. "It's no one's business what I do with my stock." She stood up. "Thank you for your time." She held out her hand, shook his, and picking up her briefcase, left his office.

Raine was dumbfounded. Melanie's offer exceeded anything he could have imagined. He had said he wanted to control Hudson Enterprises, and now he had the opportunity to do so. Maybe. Melanie was too cunning not to have some ulterior motive. He'd have his legal staff check the documents. If she was in fact offering him the Hudson corporation, what was he going to do with it?

His thoughts turned to Alana. Was she already looking for another job? Had she given up on getting his land? She had told him as much. Maybe it would be better this way. He could control Hudson's corporation, put his own men in charge until he was ready to absorb it, and Alana Hudson would be no more than a pleasant memory.

Who was he trying to kid? Alana meant much more than that to him. The nagging doubt was still there, though. If Hudson had told her she was going to inherit everything if he died, and then when they divorced, she knew she would have nothing ... it was too damned convenient that he had died just days before the divorce proceedings would begin.

* * *

Hilary looked across the desk at Raine Bradburn. Her stomach was in knots and her palms were sweaty. He had to accept this offer. She didn't know what else she could give him to induce him to sell his land to her. She had to have more than five percent of her father's estate. Her savings account was getting dangerously low. She needed the money. She straightened the sleeve of her grey silk jacket and smoothed her black blouse.

She pushed a folder toward him, clearing her throat. "I'll turn over all my stock to you for the land. I've inherited some from my mother. It's all listed on the second page." He nodded and she continued. "In addition, once I control the corporation, I'm willing to sell you all of Phillip's stock for ten cents on the dollar. I'll also give you ten percent of his personal estate . . . in cash. No one will know about it except for you and me." She took a deep breath. "I've listed his personal worth. Your share would be close to ten million dollars." He had to accept this offer. He would have ten million dollars in cash, stock worth millions for a fraction of the price, and controlling interest in Hudson Enterprises.

"It's an interesting offer." His gaze was enegmatic.

"Interesting?" Her voice rose and she fought to remain calm. "It's everything you wanted, plus the cash. All for a piece of land you can't even develop."

"I'll consider it along with the other offers." He closed the folder.

"And you'll give me time to make a counter offer?" Desperation clogged her throat.

"Yes." He stood and escorted her to the door.

She stopped with her fingers clutching the handle. "Did you know that Alana's secretary has a brother who is a pharmacist? Quite a coincidence, don't you think, since she needed someone to get the lethal medicine for my father?"

With that she lifted her chin and walked out of his office.

* * *

Raine looked from one offer to the other. The Hudson sisters certainly wanted their father's company. Both their offers were spectacular. They had offered more than he wanted. He liked Hilary's twist of ten million in cash. He wondered if Phillip knew just how intelligent both his daughters really were.

He thought about Hilary's last comment. Whoever killed Phillip needed help getting the medication to slip into his drink. It wouldn't have been very difficult for Alana to get the medicine from a relative of her secretary.

On the other hand, maybe Hilary and Melanie were playing some sort of game. But what? They were offering him their father's company. What did they care if Alana worked for him or if she was out of a job?

He studied the documents carefully before calling his top lawyer.

Dan Maxwell returned to his office and looked over the notes he had taken while at Hudson Enterprises. So many people had so many motives. He grabbed a cup of coffee and eased himself into his chair. Hilary Hudson Cummings had a gambling habit that ran into the thousands every week. Phillip didn't pay for her vices. She thought she would inherit millions. Melanie Hudson thought her father was responsible for her mother's death. Had she killed him to avenge her mother's death? Alana Hudson had a motive, too. His cousin's daughter worked in the Hudson mansion two days a week cleaning. She had told Dan about the fight and how Phillip Hudson had beaten his wife and threatened to divorce her. Alana Hudson would have been out of a job as well as out of money if a man as powerful as Phillip Hudson had kicked her out of his life. He tapped a pencil on his desk. Alana Hudson had turned up at Raine's home. Coincidence or planned? The same girl worked at Raine's three days a week, her story verifying Raine's account of what happened. And then there was Raine. He hated Phillip ever since his own father's death. He blamed Phillip for that. And Dan knew Raine was attracted to Alana.

Dan frowned and rubbed a hand across his face. Raine and Alana. If Raine was fooling around with Phillip's wife, and if they thought she would inherit everything if the old man died, what better reason to knock him off? Dan leaned forward his elbows on the desk and propped up his chin with his fists. Great. Just great. His gut instinct said they both had too much integrity for murder, but if they were having an affair, gut instinct wasn't going to hold up in court.

"Hey, Dan! Why so glum?" Another detective sat in the chair next to Dan's desk. He pulled out a cigarette, propping it between firm lips before lighting it.

"You wouldn't believe how involved the murder of Phillip Hudson is getting, T.J." He leaned back and rubbed a knot of muscles in his neck.

"I just finished testifying in the Abbott case." His face split in a wide grin. Unruly, curly brown hair fell across his forehead as brown eyes twinkled with surpressed laughter. Bushy brows wiggled. "You should have seen old man Abbott. After the third prostitute got on the stand, he was finished."

"One more for our side." Dan sighed, his voice dry. "I could have used your help the last couple of days. These society murders make me jumpy. You're much more comfortable with them than I am." He filled T.J. in on the interviews he had conducted.

"I sure wish I could have seen Melanie Hudson nude. The woman has a body that will not stop!" He rolled his eyes.

Dan laughed, feeling better already. T.J. did that to him. He was the best partner Dan could have ever had. "The captain got an anonymous tip about searching the lockers at the yacht club, so I've got to get a search warrant."

The other man let out a low whistle. "A lot of powerful people belong there. They won't take very kindly to having us come in and search the place."

"I know. Hopefully, it'll only be a few lockers and just a formality." He paused. "I hope." He leaned forward, his hands clasped, looking around before lowering his voice. "One of the prime suspects is Raine Bradburn."

"Your old college chum?" T.J. shook his head. "You're crazy, man. This case sounds like a case of dynamite. One of the suspects is a friend of yours and powerful in his own right, and there is a bevy of suspects and motives. You should have dumped this back in the lieutenant's lap."

There was nothing T.J. could say that Dan hadn't said to himself a hundred times. "I know, but I never thought Raine would have the opportunity and motive."

The other man cocked his head. "What's his motive besides hating a scumball like Hudson?"

Dan took a deep breath. "Hudson's wife."

"Ouch!" T.J. paused. "You could still withdraw from the case."

"No. I want to see this through to the end. I just hope it's not the ending that I think it's going to be." Dan picked up his notebook. "Come on. We'd better get the paperwork going on the search warrant."

T.J. stubbed out his cigarette. "I haven't had time to sail in a month."

Dan glanced over at his friend. "Must be nice to be independently wealthy," he teased.

"Yeah. Sure am glad my old man didn't make me work for the family fortune."

Dan laughed. "You getting lazy in your old age?" T.J. Harris had just turned thirty-five and was the hardest working cop on the police force. His father had owned pineapple fields and sugar cane fields at the peak of the industry, selling everything off when he found out he had cancer and investing the profits wisely, knowing that T.J. had neither the time nor the inclination to spend his life in the business world. T.J. moved easily between the worlds of the wealthy people he grew up with, the middle class cops who were his friends, and the dark world of crime he had to work in. Somehow he maintained his sense of humor and common sense through it all. Dan valued his friendship and his insight into difficult problems. This was definitely one such case.

"I'm almost ready to retire," T.J. answered cheerfully. "Then where would you be for a partner?"

"I'm going out the same time you do," Dan answered, clapping him on the back. Dan was suddenly serious. "I have a feeling I'm not going to like what we're going to find." Dan pushed open a door and headed into the hall.

T.J. stopped at a vending machine, digging in his pockets for change. "Hey, Dan, have you got some money?"

Dan shook his head and chuckled. "You could buy and sell the whole department ten times over and you don't have money for the damned coffee machine!" He fished in his pocket and produced the needed money for two cups of coffee. "You owe me a steak dinner by now."

"As soon as this case is closed, you've got it, man." Coffee in hand, they sauntered down the hall, neither of them looking forward to the ordeal ahead.

Chandler looked at Hilary, his voice incredulous. "You what? You offered him ten million dollars in cash, your stock, and all your father's stock for ten cents on the dollar?" He stormed around the room, all gentleness and kindness gone. "How could you do something so stupid?"

"It was not stupid." Hilary poured herself a tumbler of whiskey. "It's probably the smartest move I've ever made."

"Would you care to explain that?" Chandler stood on the other side of the bar, his arms crossed over his chest. He couldn't believe Hilary would actually give everything to Raine for that damned land.

"I'll try to tell you in terms you might understand," she said, her voice and manner condescending. "I know exactly what I'm doing. Neither Alana nor Melanie would have thought of such a daring plan. First of all, the ten million is just ten percent of my father's personal fortune. That leaves me with ninety million." She took a long drink from her glass. "I don't know about you, but that could keep me happy for a long time." She sauntered out from behind the bar and headed for the patio. "Secondly, I don't think you realize how much stock Phillip had to have in order to control the corporation. We're not talking a couple thousand shares. We're talking about hundreds of thousands. Hudson stock is doing very well. It's a lot more money than five percent." She looked at him over her shoulder. "Now do you think it was a dumb idea?"

Chandler shrugged. "Ninety million."

"Give or take a few million. My father was a very wealthy man."

His gaze was speculative. When she was sober, she was a smart woman. He watched her drain her glass and return to the bar. She was on her way to another drunken evening. "Bradburn would be a fool to turn down an offer like that."

"That's what I think." She refilled her glass. "He didn't give anything away though. I expected him to raise his eyebrows or smile or something, but he didn't blink an eye." She was thoughtful. "You don't suppose Melanie or Alana made the same offer, do you?"

Chandler shook his head. "Not likely. It's such a crazy idea, it just might work." He smiled at her and put his arm around her shoulder. When she stiffened, he dropped it. "I'm going back to the studio tonight," he told her, tucking his red and blue striped shirt carefully into white duck pants.

She frowned. "Why?"

"I've got some dark room work to do." He looked at the bottle in her hand. "You've got company. You won't even miss me."

Hilary shrugged. "I'll see you in the morning."

Melanie sat behind her desk, looking at Chad. "I can't believe I actually did it!" She had just told him about the offer she made to Raine.

"It was a great idea, if I do say so myself." He loosened his tie and unbuttoned the top button of his shirt.

"Brilliant. How did you ever think of it?" She rubbed the back of her neck.

"It wasn't easy," he muttered. "I decided to appeal to his greed and obsession with owning Hudson Enterprises."

"I wonder if it will work." She fingered the collar of her blouse.

"He'd be crazy not to accept it." He took off his jacket and tossed it over the other chair.

"Unless Hilary or Alana made a similar offer." She stood and began to unbutton her blouse.

"Neither of them can match your style." He unbuckled his pants.

"You say the nicest things." She unzipped her skirt.

"What will you do with your life when Bradburn owns Hudson Enterprises?" He took off the rest of his clothes and moved around the corner of the desk.

"Retire to some nice tropical island, sip exotic drinks, and make love all day long." She perched on the edge of her desk, wrapping her legs around Chad's waist.

"I'd love to be your assistant." He blew in her ear.

"I'll consider it." She ran her tongue over his shoulder.

"Any position. Any time." His thumbs rubbed the dusky pink peaks of her breasts.

"You already do that quite well." Her hands grasped his buttocks.

"It's a pleasure." He slowly entered her, felt her tense and then relax as he began to stroke her, his hands wandering over her lush body.

Melanie clung to him, her mouth seeking his. The thought of besting both Alana and Raine was an aphrodisiac. She soared, she floated, she twisted and twirled. Frenzied desire made her frantic as she held him close, climaxing time after time until Chad was spent.

When she could breathe again, she leaned her hands back on her desk, her legs still wrapped around Chad. Her head was thrown back, her eyes closed, her breasts still taut. "One more time, Chad. One more time."

Chapter Thirty

Alana went for a run just as the sun began its climb into the sky. It had been almost a month since she had seen Raine to talk to him, and she had developed a severe case of insomnia. But she did her best thinking when she was running, and right now, she needed to come up with a brilliant idea to get Raine to sell his land to her. At least they would have to talk, and maybe they could sort out the other things as well.

She ran along the beach, joining early morning fishermen, other joggers, people walking their pets, and a variety of athletic young men heading for the beach with their surf boards under their arms. Hawaii awoke with the sun, and she was a part of it.

Her mind cleared of everything except the land. She wouldn't consider her fears that Raine was her husband's killer or about the file she had found on his desk. She wouldn't think about Melanie or Hilary getting Raine's land and controlling interest in the corporation.

As she ran an idea began to formulate in her mind. Perhaps there was a way to get his land without getting involved personally. She still hadn't gotten over the shock of seeing that file on his desk. Just when she was beginning to think they had a future together. Her plan was simple. Offer Raine the stock she had in her possession as collateral for the rest of the stock. She would give him half of Phillip's stock in exchange for the land. He would become the majority stockholder, but she would retain enough stock so she was assured a position on the board. If he decided to absorb the corporation into his own company, she could force a hostile takeover. There were several people who had approached her about a takeover. She could help them if Raine wanted to destroy the company. It wouldn't hurt to have Phillip's millions behind her either. Raine would have to agree to it. He stood to make millions of dollars. He'd be a fool to turn it down, and Alana knew he was no fool.

She returned to her apartment, hot, sweaty, and feeling better than she had in weeks.

One major problem remained. She had to call him.

It was dawn when Melanie pulled into the lookout over the Halona Blow Hole. She walked along the restraining barrier. The skid marks were long gone, the barrier repaired. No outward signs remained of her mother's accident. She looked over the edge, watching the waves crash into the rocks, a plume of water spurting out of the lava tunnel, pushed high into the air by the force of the water. All external evidence had been washed away. Except inside of her. Her mother was gone, and now her father was dead.

"Raine will be so grateful to me that he'll practically give me the land," she murmured to herself, mesmerized by the pounding waves. "Even without the inducement of controlling interest in the corporation. It's an ideal plan." There was just one piece of the puzzle missing.

Another car screeched to a halt. Melanie glanced at the stocky man struggling to climb out of the compact car. He was panting by the time he reached her side. "What's up?"

"Have you seen Alana and Raine Bradburn together?"

He shook his head. "She hasn't seen any man except at work."

Melanie pulled out a bulky envelope. "I don't care if you have to hire additional help. Watch both of them twenty-four hours a day and as soon as you see them together, let me know immediately."

He took the envelope and nodded. "No problem."

"It better not be," she muttered. They had to be found together or the set up wouldn't work. What if her suspicions were unfounded? All her careful planning would be wasted. If Arty didn't find them together in the next couple of days, she would have to engineer a meeting. It was vital to her plan.

Hilary looked at her bank balance and frowned. She had lost another twenty-five thousand at Zachary's. She was going to need money soon. Getting that land would certainly solve her problems. She spoke in the intercom. "Get Raine Bradburn for me." She released the button and sat back. He had to make a decision soon, and she knew he would decide in her favor.

Her secretary buzzed. "Mr. Bradburn can't be disturbed."

Hilary frowned. "Call again and set up an appointment to see him as soon as possible."

Hilary was settling down to work when Mitch burst into her office. "I've got a little problem."

She sighed. "What is it?" She had been afraid to ask too many questions about his work. He didn't want people to know he was related to Phillip Hudson ... until he was in trouble.

"I, ah, well, see, this cute little secretary and I got caught in the copy room." He shifted his weight from one foot to the other, not meeting her gaze.

"What did they catch you doing?" As if she didn't know.

"Well, she had her skirt up around her waist and I, ah, got

caught with my pants down, if you know what I mean." He jammed his hands into his pockets. "Mr. Marino is threatening to have us both fired. Can you talk to him?"

Hilary rocked back in her chair. She could help him, but she had been helping him all his life. Maybe he should get fired. It might help him gain a sense of responsibility. Or it could send him right back to the beach. "I'll see what I can do, but, Mitch, you've got to be more ... discreet."

"Like Chandler?" he said, his voice thick with sarcasm.

Hilary blanched. "Chandler has never been unfaithful to me."

"You can't be that blind." He shook his head, his confidence restored. "Mother, have you seen some of the photography he's done lately? It's almost pornographic! You don't get that kind of look from a girl just by clicking the camera."

Hilary covered her ears. "I don't want to hear another word. I'll see what I can do for you. Now leave me alone."

Mitch turned and sauntered out of her office, saying "Thanks, Mother," as he closed the door.

Hilary buried her face in her hands. Chandler unfaithful. She just couldn't believe it. He was so reluctant to have sex with her, she had had her doubts about his manhood. He was always so formal, so proper. What kind of photographs was he taking? She didn't want to confront him about Mitch's suspicions, and that's all they were, suspicions. She'd watch and wait. Two failed marriages would mean she really was frigid. Mitch was an adult. She would have no one to call her own. The thought made her reach for the bottle she kept in her bottom drawer ... just for emergencies.

Alana stared at her calendar, her elbows on her desk, her chin resting on the palms of her hands. It was funny how your entire life could be condensed into such a minute time frame.

It had been a month since she had seen Raine. Two weeks, just fourteen days, left to fulfill the terms of the will or be forced to start her life all over again. She was too tired to even think about lunch. Her future would have to wait until she could get some sleep. She pushed herself to her feet, swayed slightly, and clutched her desk, waiting for the light-headedness and nausea to pass. Her ulcer was kicking up again, not surprising when she considered the stress in her life and her poor eating habits. She should have eaten breakfast, but she wasn't hungry. Come to think of it, she hadn't eaten at all yesterday. Every time she thought of Raine, she lost what little appetite she had. Crossing to the hidden refrigerator, she opened it and pulled out a container of yogurt. Grabbing a spoon, she crossed the room, looking out the window as she took a spoonful of yogurt. The last four weeks had seemed like a lifetime. She couldn't decide if she was more angry with Raine for betraying her or with herself for letting down her guard and trusting him. She understood why he had had her investigated in the beginning, but why continue it? The date of the last entry had been the week previous. She was miserable without him, but she'd never be able to trust him again either. She had the offer she wanted to make, but didn't have the nerve to call him. Her body ached to be held in his arms again, but her heart was locked in a steel box and only she had the key. She hoped she had learned a lesson from Phillip and Raine. If she didn't, she was not as smart as she thought. Maybe she just had an uncanny ability to pick the wrong men. That thought did little to drag her self-esteem off the ocean floor.

Alana put down her unfinished yogurt. The problem was that she *had* to think about him if she wanted to run Hudson Enterprises. Settling into her chair, she scanned the figures in front of her. It was an excellent deal for Raine, and she wouldn't suffer either. She reached for the telephone and snatched her hand away three times. She sat back, playing with the pearl stud in her ear. She would never know if she didn't give it a try. Before she could change her mind again, she pressed the button on her intercom. "Leilani, get me Raine Bradburn at Bradburn International. I want to talk to him."

Now that she had made up her mind, Alana wanted to make her final offer and then get on with her life. If he didn't accept, she'd have to update her resume and start looking for another job. She refused to work with Hilary and Melanie. Even if Raine didn't sell, they could combine their shares of stock and cause havoc ... if they were smart enough to join forces. She didn't want to be around if they did.

If Raine accepted her offer, she'd breathe a sigh of relief, thank him, and pray she could forget him. She picked up the yogurt, stirred it, and set it down. Would Raine talk to her? She hadn't heard a word from him in a month. He had probably found someone else to warm his bed. Her heart twisted. Images of Raine and another woman entwined as she had been with him made her break out in a cold sweat. She jumped at the sound of the buzzer on her desk. She took a deep breath before answering. "Yes, Leilani?"

"I have Mr. Bradburn on the line."

"Thank you." Alana paused. She had to be calm. Business-like. The fluttering in her stomach had to stop. She closed her eyes for one moment before she punched the blinking button. "Hello, Raine." She clutched the receiver.

"Hello, Alana."

A tremor ran the length of her body. How she had missed the sound of his voice. Was he glad she had called? Was he bored? Did he care? "Thank you for taking my call."

"Did you doubt that I would?" The dryness of his voice was unmistakable.

She wished she could see the expression in his eyes. They would tell her so much more than his voice, but then, maybe it was better this way. If she saw him, she would have to fight the urge to press her body against his, feel his lips against hers. She kept her voice as steady as possible. "We didn't part on very friendly terms a month ago."

"It was you who made the break." His voice hardened.

She didn't want to discuss their personal life over the telephone. In fact, she didn't want to discuss it at all. "This is a business call." She gripped the phone.

"Why am I not surprised," he mocked.

She closed her eyes and took a deep breath. "Raine, I have a business proposition to present to you for the land." She was talking too fast, but just hearing his voice again brought back too many memories. When there was silence on the other end, she cleared her voice. "Will you at least listen to my offer?"

"If you want me to consider your plan, you'll have to tell me in person. I won't even consider it over the telephone." The hard, implacable tone of his voice told her he meant what he said. It was useless to argue.

"When and where." She pulled her calendar closer.

"A friend of mine is opening a new restaurant. I promised I'd be there tonight. I'll pick you up at eight."

"I'll meet you somewhere," she quickly answered, panic in her voice. "For lunch."

"Dinner tonight and I pick you up or forget it." The implacable tone was back. "It'll be strictly business. Trust me."

She'd give anything to tell him to go to hell and he knew it. But she couldn't . . . not while he had the land she needed.

"I'll see you at eight." She hung up the phone. Dread and anticipation fought an internal battle. She just wouldn't think about it. She couldn't stop thinking about it. He had said strictly business. Trust him. Could she trust him ever again?

Raine leaned back in his chair and closed his eyes. He had asked Alana to trust him, and yet, did he trust her? Phillip

Hudson had been murdered, and Alana had the opportunity and a hell of a motive. It would have been so easy for her to slip a drug into his coffee or a drink. Phillip had beaten her, humiliated her. A divorce would have meant no job, no money, no power, no status. Could Alana really have given all that up and just walked out? He wasn't sure and it was eating at him. She certainly wanted his land enough to have dinner with him even though she didn't want to see him again. Melanie and Hilary might have been right. Maybe Alana had killed Phillip.

He opened his eyes and stared out over the ocean. Was it possible to care about a woman and still not trust her? He rubbed his neck and stretched. Alana just couldn't be the killer. He sighed. Was he too close to look at the situation clearly? And yet, whom could he confide in? Dan? Not a chance. Rachel? She was married to Dan. She'd tell him immediately. There was no one else. He would just have to work it through by himself.

Tonight he'd see just how desperate she really was.

By seven-thirty that evening discarded dresses covered every available space in Alana's bedroom. With time running out, she opted for a simple sleeveless hot pink brocade sheath. Not too plain, not too fancy, modest, yet fashionable. She failed to notice that when she walked, the slit on the side exposed most of her thigh, and the mandarin collar emphasized her graceful neck. Her hair was pulled into a severe knot at her nape, accentuating her high cheek bones and her fragile features. It was impossible to completely hide the deep circles under her eyes, but she gave it a valiant effort. Adding a gold and diamond necklace and her Cartier earrings, she felt ready to face Raine, unaware that the combination of self-contained strength and vulnerability lurking in her violet eyes made her infinitely desirable. When she heard the intercom buzz, her stomach lurched.

She opened the door, one hand clenching her beaded purse. "Hello, Raine."

His gaze swept over her from head to toe and back again.

Her gaze touched his features. There were new lines of strain around his mouth and eyes, a bleak look in his eyes.

He held out his hand to her, and she put hers in it. "I never thought I'd say this to any woman, but I've missed you, Alana."

For a heartrending moment, she allowed him to see the depth of her anguish, the hurt, loneliness, and longing. Then her gaze became shuttered, once again withdrawing into herself. "I wish it could be different, but I can't make love to a man I don't trust."

"You made love to Phillip Hudson and you didn't trust him," he said, his voice harsh, his hands gripping her shoulders.

"He was my husband, and I did trust him in the beginning." She took a step backward, and he released her.

"And when you confronted him about having you followed, he beat you up." He took her elbow and guided her toward the door. "But I'm not Phillip."

"I know." They were silent in the ride down the elevator. Alana let him lead her toward his car. "I think that's why it hurts so much, Raine. I expected better from you."

Raine was silent until they were both seated in his car, then he turned to her. "I intend to regain your trust, Alana."

She met his gaze with a cynical one of her own, wondering why she had agreed to this meeting. She should have known they couldn't keep it strictly business. Is that why she had agreed? Was there a part of her that continued to hope?

When they arrived at the restaurant, Alana forgot her anger for a moment as she looked around with interest. A waterfall two stores high dominated the room, but instead of it being noisy, it had been so fashioned to be as soothing as the lapping of waves on the beach. Orchids and bougainvillea clung to the rocks and tree branches. Huge gold fish swam in the waters around the base of the waterfall. Along the outer edges were small tables of bamboo and glass where people waiting to eat or just enjoying the scenery could have a drink and relax. Soft Hawaiian music played in the background as a young Polynesian woman came forward with leis of plumeria and put one around Alana's neck and then around Raine's, kissing them on each cheek. "Aloha. Welcome."

A tall, good looking Hawaiian man came forward, greeting Raine warmly. Raine introduced Alana to him. He owned the restaurant and Alana guessed from their conversation that Raine had helped him finance it.

He personally escorted them to an elevator. Alana froze. Melanie was walking in their direction. She clutched Raine's arm, trying to figure out a way to avoid Melanie and her date, but it was too late.

Melanie saw them, her eyes darting from Alana to Raine. "Hello," she murmured, a smile on her lips. "Are you here for dinner? The food is excellent."

"It's a business dinner." Alana colored at the knowing look in Melanie's eyes.

"Certainly." Melanie looked at Raine. "Have you made any decisions about my proposal?"

"I'm considering it, Melanie." His face was expressionless. "I'm also considering an excellent offer from Hilary. She's offering me ten million in cash, plus other inducements." He looked from one startled face to the other. "Now I'm waiting to hear what Alana's willing to offer. Then I'll make my decision."

Melanie was thoughtful. "Ten million. If that's her best offer, I'll double it." She smiled at Raine, then looked at Alana. "Have a nice dinner.' She walked away without a backward glance.

"Is she serious?" Alana whispered as they rode the tiny elevator.

"I'm afraid so," Raine muttered, frowning.

The elevator could hold no more than two people, and Alana was acutely aware of the man next to her, temporarily forgetting Melanie. She inhaled that unique blend of his aftershave, the soft linen of his suit brushing her arm. She felt his breath touch her temple, and longed to lean against his strong chest and let the rest of the world pass them by. All too soon the little thatched roof elevator glided to a halt and they were greeted by another beautiful young Hawaiian woman. She bowed and led them to a private booth. The booths were situated so that a couple had complete privacy from other diners, but they could look in one direction and see the waterfall and look the other and see the lights of the city below, stretched out like ribbons of twinkling diamonds. As Alana slipped onto her chair and Raine sat next to her, she knew this was going to be a difficult evening. It would be impossible to discuss business in a romantic setting such as this. She wondered why she had never heard of this restaurant or been to it.

Raine seemed to read her thoughts. "I thought this would be a good place to discuss business since you insisted on a public place. It just opened a month ago, so it helps business as well."

She regarded him for a moment. "And your part in it?"

"I financed it, and have an interest in it, yes." He nodded as a young man in an old fashioned sailor uniform approached their table. "A friend approached me with the idea and I liked it. I'll get a good return on my money, and I'm assured of a table whenever I want one. How could I go wrong?"

When the man took their drink order, Alana said, "Are you ready to talk business? I'd like to know what Hilary and Melanie have offered you."

"Before drinks and dinner? Alana, you know me better than that," he chided.

She knew him too well, she thought to herself. That was the problem. After a drink and an intimate dinner, the last thing they would discuss would be business, but the short conversation with Melanie had piqued her curiosity.

Raine leaned over and covered her hand with his. "Relax, Alana. We'll talk about the land later. I'm not going to do anything you don't want me to."

"That's exactly what I'm afraid of," she said with a sigh, leaning back and closing her eyes so she missed the fire in Raine's eyes.

He touched the pulse at her wrist and sat back, a satisfied look on his face. His gaze caressed her face, touching each feature as if he were burning it into his brain so he'd never forget. His gaze wandered lower, smiling as her body responded to the heat in his eyes. Her fingers drummed the table.

He held up his glass. "Here's to us, Alana. It's destiny or fate or a curse of the ancient gods. But our lives seem to be intertwined."

He put his glass down and took her hand, his thumb caressing her palm. "What are we going to do about it?"

Taking a deep breath, she finally met his gaze. "I shouldn't even have to answer that, Raine." The pain in her heart showed in her eyes. "When you had me investigated, you took my trust and crushed it like yesterday's flower blossoms."

"Alana, you don't understand." He frowned as he ran a hand through his hair. "This is a different situation for me, too. I've never felt this way about a woman before. They used me, and I used them. I never cared that they looked at my money more than they did me. None of them bothered to look beneath the surface, and I preferred it that way." He paused, the words coming slowly, almost against his will. "You were married to the man I hated most in this world. I won't go into the reasons,

446

but believe me, they were valid. If that weren't bad enough, he's been murdered, and his will makes my land the prize for three determined women." His gaze was troubled as he looked at her. "Now, put yourself in my place. Wouldn't you wonder if this woman really wanted you or your land? If I sell it to you, I'll never know if you care about me or just what the land can do for you. If I don't sell the land to you, you'll blame me for letting you down. If I sell the land to you, you'll be a wealthy woman and you won't need me. If I don't sell, I won't be able to live with myself for causing you so much misery, and I know you're too proud to ever accept any help from me."

Alana leaned back, surprised that he had shared so much of his inner turmoil with her. They were both suffering, and for what? Some damned rock and sand. She cursed Phillip and the will. "You could sell it to Melanie or Hilary."

Laughter lit up his face. "It would serve Phillip right for what they've got in mind." He sipped his drink, his gaze never leaving her face.

"So. What are you going to do?" Alana toyed with her drink. He was right, and she knew it but didn't want to admit it. The land might as well be a mountain between them. Phillip's death didn't make matters easier either. She just couldn't forget that Raine had a powerful motive for seeing Phillip dead. And he had the opportunity.

"I don't know. I've got fourteen days to decide." He took a long drink. "Got any good ideas?"

Alana took a deep breath. This was the time to present her plan. "Maybe." She pulled a sheet of paper out of her purse and handed it to him. "You would sell me your land. When I inherit Phillip's stock and estate, I'd give you half his stock, no strings attached. You could sell it, use it as leverage in a buy out, whatever you wanted to do." She paused. "Melanie said she'd give you twenty million in cash. I'll make it twenty-five. You would make a lot of money with no effort on your part."

She wished his expression wasn't so shuttered. "The crucial point here is that you would have to trust me to carry through on it after you turn over your land to me."

He leaned back, his arm draped over the back of his chair, and she knew what he was going to say. "You don't trust me," he countered. "Why should I trust you?"

"I've never given you reason not to trust me." She sat back as the waiter brought their food. She inhaled the delicate aroma of the mahi mahi. She picked at her food, looking at Raine through her lashes as he cut into his steak. Would he ever answer? "Well?" she finally said, unable to wait any longer.

"How many shares of Hudson stock do you have?"

His question startled her. "If no one gets the land, I'll inherit five percent of Phillip's shares. I have about two percent that I've acquired on my own. Why?"

"You sign over all your shares of stock when I sell you my land. When I get my stock, you get your stock back." He glanced up at her, an odd expression in his eyes. "Fair?"

She shook her head, taking a small bite of her fish. "My stock is worth more than your land. How do I know that you won't keep it?"

"You don't. And you don't know if I already own Hudson stock. Your stock could put me in control or force a hostile takeover. If you give me half of Phillip's stock, we'll be about equal. Your five percent would give one of us control." His dark eyes held her captive. "You would have to trust me."

Alana blanched. Trust. Such a little word with such a magnitude of meaning. Raine had done his homework. Now, she wondered if he was the one who had been buying Hudson stock. He had so many companies in his corporation, it would be difficult tracing ownership of the stock. "Wouldn't you consider my offer?"

"Will you consider mine?" His voice was soft, his gaze intense.

"I'll think about it," was the best she could offer. She had to think and Raine's nearness made that impossible.

"And I'll think about yours." He pointed at her plate. "Now eat. You've lost weight." His eyes narrowed on the shadows under her eyes. "Aren't you feeling well?"

She gave a little shrug, her appetite gone. "My ulcer."

"Have you seen a doctor about it?" She saw genuine concern on his face.

"There hasn't been enough time." And she hadn't felt like eating for the past month, but she wasn't going to tell him that. He knew too much about her already.

Chapter Thirty-one

Dan Maxwell rubbed the knot of muscles between his shoulders. The Hudson case got more complicated by the day. He should have taken himself off the case as soon as he knew Raine was implicated. Now the chief was on his back to solve the murder. Important people had their murders solved more quickly than the ordinary person, he thought with uncharacteristic bitterness. He sifted through the papers on his desk and thumbed through the notes he had taken. If Raine did mastermind the crime, he had to have help. Someone had to get the digoxin. Had Hilary or Melanie helped him? Unlikely. Raine wouldn't team up with Phillip's daughters for a game of volleyball, let alone murder. Alana? Possibly. Dan didn't have proof they were involved in an affair, but they had been seen together. A love triangle had been the motive for more murders than he cared to count, and when one added the millions of dollars at stake, it was an excellent motive.

Even if she weren't having an affair with Raine, Alana had the motive and opportunity to kill her husband. If his facts were right, she would have been without money or a job if she and Phillip divorced. She had the opportunity, too. She also had the closest access to a pharmacist.

Dan leaned back in his chair and stretched his hands over his head. Melanie Hudson knew a lot about this case and all the people involved. He didn't discount the idea that she was involved somehow. Oh, she appeared to be a bimbo who had nothing on her mind but sex, but he'd bet his next paycheck Melanie Hudson wasn't as dumb as she appeared.

Hilary needed money. He could buy groceries for five years with the money she lost in a weekend. Was that motive enough to kill her father? It was if she thought she would inherit her share of his estate and if a man like Simon Chong demanded payment. He had ways of convincing people to pay their debts. He glanced at his watch. Time to go home.

His phone rang, and he reached to pick it up. "Detective Maxwell."

"Maxwell?" The voice was scratchy and muffled, difficult to understand.

He frowned. There was something familiar about that voice. "Can I help you?"

"I can help you." There was silence for a moment. "Go to The Rain Forest restaurant. You'll find the motive for Phillip Hudson's death." The line went dead.

Dan looked at the silent receiver for a moment, his shoulders sagging. He had a good idea what he'd find at the restaurant and he was reluctant to go, but he had a job to do, and that meant following up on phone calls such as this. His forehead puckered. That voice. Even though the person disguised it, it was familiar. Where had he heard it before? T.J. came sauntering into the room.

"I just got an anonymous tip about the Hudson case," Dan told him. "We have to go to The Rain Forest restaurant."

While Dan had been talking to family members, T.J. had been talking to board members and business associates. T.J. slumped into the chair next to Dan's desk. He stretched out his long legs and rubbed calloused hands over his face. "It's been a long day, Dan. What are we supposed to find at the restaurant?"

Dan grunted. "The motive for Hudson's death. Damn. That voice was familiar. Who's trying to frame Raine?"

"That's who you think we'll find?" T.J. ran a hand through his sandy hair, ruffling the curls even more. He rubbed weary brown eyes. The grooves from his nose to his mouth were pronounced. He pulled a cigarette from the pack in his pocket. "Got any ideas who's there with him?"

"Yeah, and I don't like it." Dan tapped the paper on his desk. "If I'm right, we'll find Raine and Alana at The Rain Forest."

"Someone is going to a lot of trouble to set them up," T.J. muttered, stubbing out his cigarette.

"The question is who wants to see Raine Bradburn pay for a crime he didn't commit?" Dan headed down the steps toward the door.

"We discover that and we've solved the case," T.J. answered, following close behind.

The two men were silent on the ride up the mountain to the restaurant. When they pulled into the parking lot, they saw Raine's distinctive silver Lamborghini parked in the lot.

"Want to go inside?" T.J. asked, checking his gun and replacing it.

"No. Let's wait out here and see what happens." They pulled into an empty space where they could see Raine's car, and then settled down to wait. The evening breeze felt cool after the heat of the day. Insects chirped and the trees rustled as night settled over the island like a protective cloak. Dan knew he could go in and probably arrest Raine on the spot. There was enough evidence, but he just wouldn't do that to his friend. If he was in there with Alana Hudson, then Dan knew he would have to arrest him and get a warrant to search Alana's apartment, house, and car. Would they find another empty drug bottle, just like the one they found in Raine's locker at the yacht club? Somehow, he knew they would.

They didn't have to wait long. Raine walked out of the restaurant with his arm around Alana Hudson. They stopped next to his car and kissed for a very long time. Dan's heart sank. "Get headquarters, T.J." He shook his head. "We're going to have to search Alana Hudson's house, apartment, and car."

"You want to arrest him now?" T.J. asked, watching his partner closely.

Dan took a deep breath. "If I wait any longer, the chief will have my head." He listened absently as T.J. called in to the station and then opened his car door. This would be the hardest thing he had ever done in his life.

Dan walked over to Raine's car. "Raine, we have to talk to you." He pointed to his car. "T.J. is with me."

Raine looked at Dan for a long moment, his arm tightening around Alana. "It's about Hudson, isn't it?"

Dan nodded.

Raine released Alana and leaned against the side of his car, his arms folded. Raine's face was shadowed in the dim light of the parking lot. "How did you know we were at this restaurant?"

"We got a tip that we'd find the motive for Hudson's murder." Dan looked from Raine to Alana. "You must admit that it looks suspicious when Hudson's sworn enemy and his widow are having an intimate dinner and then kiss in the parking lot. Your picture was in the paper together over a month ago."

"You think I killed Hudson because I wanted his wife?" Raine shook his head slowly, his voice hard. "You should know me better than that, Daniel."

"The evidence points to you and Mrs. Hudson." T.J. took a step forward, his voice low.

"Damn it, T.J. Dan, you and I have been buddies for years!

You don't really think I'd do something that stupid!" Raine never moved as his voice lashed out into the night air.

T.J. took another step forward, waving a hand toward Alana. "It doesn't make any difference what we think. It's the evidence, Raine. What better motives than passion and greed? With Hudson dead, his wife inherits millions and you get rid of the competition . . . businesswise and personally. And you get a beautiful woman."

"Now wait a minute," Alana muttered, stepping between the men. "Why the hell would he want Phillip's money when he's got more than enough of his own? And if you had done all your homework, you would know that I won't inherit much if I don't meet the terms of the will. And no woman is worth killing for!" She waved a hand toward Raine. "Go ahead. Ask him! Do you really think a man who can snap his fingers and have ten women lined up, ready and willing, would kill for one woman!"

"It depends on the lady," T.J. said, admiration in his eyes.

Raine stood up, his hands thrust into his pockets, looking from T.J. to Dan, his gaze steady. "What do you think, Dan?"

Dan took a deep breath. "It's not what I think that counts here, Raine. It's the evidence." He paused, choosing his words carefully. "We searched the lockers at the yacht club yesterday. We found a bottle with traces of liquid digoxin in a duffel bag in your locker."

"How convenient. Again on a tip?" Raine asked, his voice dry. "How could I have slipped him something like that?" Raine cocked his head to one side and watched Dan.

"You were seen with him the night before he died. You argued with him at the bar at the yacht club before the race. You could have done it both times." He paused. "Or you might have had an accomplice who had access."

"Me." Alana's one word was clipped.

Raine regarded his friends for a moment then reached inside his car and pulled out his telephone, punching numbers into it.

"Rick, sorry to bother you this late, but you'd better meet me down at police headquarters." Raine looked from Dan to T.J., his voice dry. "I'm going to be booked for the murder of Phillip Hudson." He hung up the phone and looked at the two men. "You can read me my rights while we drive. It'll save time." He paused, his voice hard. "Are you arresting Alana, too?"

"Not at this time," Dan said, a weary slump to his shoulders.

Raine pressed the car keys into Alana's damp palm. He lowered his voice. "Take the car to your place. I'll call you later." He touched a finger to her chin and made her look up at him. "You okay?"

She nodded, her eyes glistening in the moonlight. "You didn't do it ... did you?"

He flinched from the question in her voice and walked toward the police car.

T.J. began reading as they headed down the mountain, Dan silent and grim, his hands in a white knuckle grip on the steering wheel.

Melanie curled up in the middle of her bed, listening to the late news, a smile on her face as they flashed the news. The police had arrested Raine for Phillip's murder. They had to do it. She had handed them enough evidence for any jury to convict him. It had been a stroke of luck seeing Alana and Raine tonight. It gave her plenty of time to call Detective Maxwell. And she had been able to find out what Hilary had offered for the land. Of course, so did Alana, but the information wouldn't do her any good.

Her telephone buzzed and Melanie picked up the receiver, disappointed when it wasn't Charles. "Hello, Hilary."

"Did you hear the news? Raine Bradburn was arrested for Father's murder."

"I heard." Melanie looked at her newly painted fingernails.

How much should she tell Hilary? When Hilary was drunk, she talked. Melanie was surprised to hear her sister's voice sober at this time of the night.

"I thought they might get Alana, too."

Melanie sighed, wondering why they hadn't. "So did I. Maybe they'll arrest her tomorrow."

Hilary was silent for a moment before saying, "Do you think this will have any influence on Raine selling his land to one of us?"

"Only if he thinks we framed him." Melanie closed her eyes and smiled to herself. Her plan was working perfectly. The last piece had been put into place. She couldn't lose.

"Why would he think that?" Hilary demanded.

"Because I framed him," Melanie said with pride in her voice. "I won't go into details, but I did it. I had some help, but I'm the one who thought of it."

"Melanie!" Horror was in her voice. "Why would you do that?"

"All in good time, Hilary. You'll find out soon enough." Melanie sat up and opened her eyes. "I heard that you offered Raine ten million in cash as an added inducement to accept your offer on that land." She paused. "I doubled it."

Hilary groaned. "Melanie, maybe we could work together on this."

"Why share the estate when I can have the whole thing?" she retorted.

"Why not? Right now, we're both losing money," Hilary muttered.

"I plan on having it all," Melanie said with a purr in her voice before hanging up on her sister.

Hilary stared at the telephone, wondering if she had heard correctly. Melanie had planned to frame Raine for the murder of their father. Why? Melanie didn't want to work together to get Raine's land either. That meant she thought she would get it herself. Was it possible?

Hilary grabbed a pillow and hugged it to her chest. It was after eleven o'clock and Chandler still wasn't home. He never worked this late. At least Hilary didn't think he did. She was usually asleep or passed out when he came home. Not tonight. She was sober and she meant to stay that way.

She heard the click in the lock and saw Chandler before he saw her. "It's about time you got home," she muttered. "Where have you been?"

Startled to see her, he looked at his watch, then back at her. "I've been working."

"I tried the studio. Your answering service took the call." She tossed the pillow aside.

"I never answer the phone after business hours. You know that." He crossed to the bar. "Do you want a drink?"

"No! I want to know where you were." She crossed her arms over her chest.

"I told you. Would you like to come down tomorrow and see the work I did tonight?" He poured some rum and cola into a glass.

Hilary grunted. He could show her anything and she wouldn't know when he had done it. She got to her feet, standing close to him. She couldn't smell any perfume. He didn't look messed up, but he was having a drink. Chandler never drank. Mitch must've been wrong. Chandler was drinking, not out with a woman. "Have you heard what happened?" she said, resting her hands on his chest. She felt him tense and then slowly relax.

He shook his head.

She rubbed her hands up and down the front of his shirt. "Raine Bradburn has been arrested for the murder of my father."

458

He grabbed her hands to stop the movement. "Are you sure?"

"I heard it on the news." She tilted her chin up, touching his chin with her lips. He needed a shave.

Chandler pursed his lips. "I wonder what that will do to your chances of getting his land."

"I talked to Melanie. Somehow she found out I had offered him ten million in cash. She doubled it." Hilary sighed, wrapping her arms around Chandler. "I suppose I could go to twenty-five."

"If you get the chance." He rested his hands on her shoulders. "Raine Bradburn will be furious. He probably won't sell at any price."

Hilary laid her head on his shoulder. "Let's not worry about it tonight." She closed her eyes. "Make love to me, Chandler."

"Now?" He pushed her gently away.

"Yes." She looked up at him.

He rubbed his eyes. "I'm tired. It's been a long day. Maybe tomorrow."

"Don't you want me?" She couldn't believe she was begging.

"It's not that. I'm just tired." He touched his lips to her forehead. "I'll see you in the morning."

She stood and watched him walk away. She had offered and he had turned her down. That had to mean something. She walked toward the bar. This had been a terrible night. She poured some whiskey into a glass. Was Raine guilty of murder? Melanie said she had framed him. Why would she do that ... unless she killed Phillip. It was a preposterous thought. Melanie wouldn't kill anyone, and she wasn't smart enough to plan all this out. No, it couldn't be her sister.

Hilary drained the glass and poured another one. She had to talk to Jeff Moreno and persuade him to give Mitch another chance. She knew she would help him. He knew it, too.

She drank in the dark, finished the bottle, and staggered off to bed. Alone.

Alana read the headlines in the paper the next day while police officers searched through her belongings. They had completed Phillip's house and her apartment, and were downstairs going through her car. Her eyes widened and she paled. RAINE BRADBURN ARRESTED FOR MURDER OF PHILLIP HUDSON! It had been on the news last night as well. She had finally taken her phone off the hook after the tenth phone call. People couldn't wait to tell her the news. She hadn't slept at all, waiting for Raine to call, pacing from room to room, unable to sit still.

She'd never forget the look on his face when she had asked him if he had done it, when she voiced her doubts. She still wasn't certain that he was innocent! Frustration mounted as she read with growing horror. Oh, God, the implication was there in print. The police thought the two of them had killed Phillip. She forced herself to focus on the article. It didn't say he had been released on bail. Where was he? What were they looking for now to tie Alana to Phillip's murder? Fear clawed at her heart. She read further. Her name wasn't mentioned, but it didn't have to be. The writing was clever enough to implicate her without actually naming her. She looked at the byline. Dudley. Did he know about the real relationship between her and Raine? She couldn't swallow past the lump in her throat. Her heart was beating a wild primitive beat. What was she going to do? Her stomach churned and as she stood a wave of nausea washed over her. She ran into the bathroom, emerging white faced and limp several minutes later.

She took a deep breath and putting one foot in front of the other, slowly, consciously, she made her way into the kitchen, opened the refrigerator, poured herself a glass of milk and ate three soda crackers. The cool liquid and crackers helped soothe her stomach, but did little for her shaking hands and watery knees.

She walked out onto her deck, her arms crossed as if she could protect herself from what was happening. She hadn't been able to bear seeing the police sift through her possessions. She didn't care about Phillip's house, but here in her apartment she had come close to falling apart. It was the ultimate humiliation. A thought burned through her mind. If Raine was innocent, and she wanted to believe that he was, someone else had planted that bottle in Raine's things at the club. They could have done the same thing to her. She had to think, logically, clearly. It had to be Melanie or Hilary or both of them. Alana paced back and forth, the heat of the sun failing to register. Hilary and Melanie. Could one of them pull this off by herself? Which one would be most likely? Hilary was the most vindictive, calculating woman Alana had ever seen. With her penchant for gambling, she had more to lose if she didn't get Raine's land. But what purpose would it serve to have him arrested? She tried to put herself in Hilary's place. She snapped her fingers. Of course! Raine's arrested; Hilary somehow comes to his rescue; and he's so grateful, he sells her the land. Alana thought back to the days before Phillip died. Hilary had plenty of opportunity to slip a drug to Phillip. But when Phillip's will made it necessary to get Raine's land, she had a complication. When Raine didn't accept her offer, she found a better way to get even and get the money.

But what about Melanie? She hated her father and accused him of being the force behind her mother's death. Was that motive enough to kill Phillip? It was if she thought she was also going to inherit her share of his estate. Why would she frame Raine? He had rejected her obvious seduction, but was that enough reason to frame him for murder? Whoever had put this together knew what they were doing. She didn't think Melanie was that cunning.

Alana walked and walked. It had to be Hilary. Unless it really was Raine, but he wouldn't have left the evidence in his locker. He was too smart for that. She turned her thoughts back to Hilary. She could have planted that bottle. Once she had the land, she'd admit to putting it there to frame Raine and get rid of Alana. She'd plead guilty to some obscure charge, get a good lawyer with all the money she'd inherit, and get a suspended sentence. It made sense.

Alana stalked back inside. "Are you finished with my car?" she demanded. Determination made her forget the humiliation of the search.

"Yes, ma'am." An officer handed her the keys.

"Did you find anything?" She glared at him.

"No, we didn't."

She took the keys and headed out the door, meeting Dan at the door. "If you need me, Detective Maxwell, I'm going to visit my stepdaughters." She glared at him. "I refuse to stand around waiting to be framed for a crime I didn't commit!" She stalked out of the apartment building and headed for her car, ignoring his warning not to do anything stupid.

Alana had no definite plan in mind, but felt she had to confront Hilary. She had the most to gain and the least to lose. Using her car phone, she telephoned the office. Hilary wasn't expected in until noon.

When Alana pulled up in front of Hilary's apartment building, she waved the doorman away. "I won't be that long." She hurried inside, got the elevator and punched the button for the top floor, tapping her foot as if to hurry it along.

Chandler opened the door, his eyes widening when he saw Alana. "What brings you here?"

"I came to see your wife." Alana's face was grim.

Chandler stood aside. "She's having breakfast." He watched

as Alana hurried up the marble steps and strode toward the dining room, then followed behind her.

Hilary looked up, a piece of toast freezing between the plate and her mouth. "What are you doing here?" Her voice was hard.

"Hilary, I know you did it." She looked at Hilary with disdain.

"Have you finally snapped?" Hilary asked, satisfaction lighting her eyes. She carefully wiped her mouth and then took a sip of coffee.

"What are you talking about?" Chandler demanded, his hands on his hips.

"Murder." Alana leaned on the table with both hands.

Twin flags of color on Hilary's cheeks and trembling hands gave away her agitation. "Now I know you've flipped." She looked down her nose at Alana. " Would you like the name of a good therapist?"

"No, but you may need a good lawyer," she retorted. "Raine Bradburn has been arrested for Phillip's murder and the police suspect me as an accomplice. The only other people who had the opportunity to slip Phillip the drug were you and your sister. Melanie doesn't have enough brains to think this thing through. That leaves you! You drugged your father!"

Hilary's laughter echoed around the room, her cat jumping into her lap. Hilary stroked the cat, breaking off a piece of toast for the animal. "Be serious, Alana. Sure I hate you. I always will. You wormed your way into my father's life and into his business. But if I wanted to kill anyone, believe me, it would have been you!" Hilary got to her feet, the cat jumping to the floor. Hilary walked around the table to confront Alana.

"So now you're going to frame me along with Raine for the murder of your father. You'll never get his land."

"I wish I had thought of framing you," Hilary muttered, her eyes an icy blue. "It would have been tempting." She paused, a look of disdain on her face. "Why would I want to frame Raine Bradburn?"

"The land! You clear him in exchange for the land, and you've got everything. You get the lion's share of the stock and the estate. You see that I get fired, and you're home free." Alana's gaze locked with Hilary's. "I have to admit, it's clever, but you screwed up. I won't give up without a fight." Her hands were on her hips, her eyes flicking from Hilary to Chandler. "Did the two of you do it together?" she demanded.

"That's absurd," Chandler retorted. "There was no reason for us to kill Phillip or frame Bradburn."

She regarded him through narrowed eyes before turning back to Hilary. "When you made your second offer to Raine, what did he say?"

"He said he would consider it." Hilary paused, looking at her fingernails. "Maybe he's looking for more than money." She glanced up at Alana, her face hardening. "After all, if you slept with my father to get on the board and be his wife, maybe you'd sleep with a man like Raine Bradburn for that land." She looked at Alana with disgust and contempt.

It suddenly struck Alana that if Hilary didn't know that she and Raine had been seeing each other, she couldn't have tipped off the police about their dinner last night. But Melanie had seen them together! Melanie, who was as evil as her father, but in a more cunning way.

"Thanks, Hilary. I'll return the favor some day." Alana whirled around and hurried out of the apartment.

Hilary looked at Chandler. "Do you have any idea what she was talking about?"

Chandler shook his head.

Mitch wandered into the room, sitting down and pouring a cup of coffee. "What was Alana doing here?"

"She accused your mother of framing Bradburn for Phillip's murder." Chandler stretched and yawned. "She sure was fired up."

"Why did she leave in such a hurry?" Mitch sipped his coffee.

Hilary shrugged. "She thanked me and ran off." She leaned back in her chair. "I wonder if Melanie did kill Father. She said last night that she framed Raine. And she was proud of it. What do you suppose she's up to?"

Chandler sighed. "She's trying to get Raine's land and throw suspicion off of herself." He got to his feet. "I've got to get to work."

Hilary watched him go and then looked at Mitch. "I'll talk to Jeff today. I'm sure I can get him to give you another chance, but please, don't get into any more trouble."

"No problem." He sauntered out of the room, his hands in the pockets of his pants. He was whistling under his breath.

Hilary took her coffee cup to the bar, pouring a little whiskey into the dark liquid.

Chapter Thirty-two

Alana tried to call Dan Maxwell from her car phone, but he wasn't at his desk. She left a message and dropped the phone into place. There was a shrewd person underneath that sexy exterior.

Alana pulled to a stop outside Melanie's house, hurrying up the steps. She punched the buzzer and tapped her foot waiting for someone to answer the door.

Melanie ... a woman capable of murdering her own father. Alana began to have second thoughts about confronting her alone. If she was capable of everything Alana suspected, she was dangerous. Perhaps she should wait for Dan Maxwell.

Suddenly the door opened.

Melanie herself stood there in the doorway.

"Where's Lela?" Alana asked.

"Sick." Melanie shrugged, a bored look on her face. "What are you doing here?"

"I'd like to talk to you." Alana's gaze skimmed over Melanie. Melanie wore an aqua skirt and matching silk blouse. Her tumble of red curls were tied back with an aqua and red print silk scarf.

Melanie looked pointedly at her watch. "You'll have to make it fast. I've got an appointment in an hour."

"Believe me, I'll make it as fast as possible." She followed Melanie into the house. Alana had been in Melanie's home once before when she had hosted a dinner for the directors of Hudson Enterprises. Alana's look encompassed the bold color scheme. It wasn't her idea of warmth and comfort. When Melanie led Alana into the kitchen, Alana's gaze swept the sunny room. The kitchen was modern in decor, the counters and cupboards were chalk white, the floor imported tile of white, brown, and beige. Copper kettles hung from the dropped ceiling around a central cooking island. Huge sliding doors opened onto a courtyard containing a small white table, two dainty chairs, and a profusion of flowers.

Melanie stepped around the island, turning to face Alana. Her eyes were wide, a hint of challenge in her voice as she said, "I was having some coffee. Want some?"

The simple words sent a chill down Alana's spine. "Yes, thank you." She moved into the room, watching Melanie's every move.

Melanie handed her a cup of coffee and waved a hand toward the breakfast bar. "Help yourself to cream or sugar."

Alana leaned against the counter, cradling the hot coffee between her hands. "Raine Bradburn is in jail."

"I heard about it last night on the news." Melanie perched on the edge of a stool next to the counter, sipping her coffee, looking bored. "So what?"

"Then you know that he was arrested for Phillip's murder." Alana's gaze never left Melanie's face.

A satisfied look touched Melanie's face for just a moment before she shrugged, putting her coffee down. "What's so surprising about that? Someone killed Phillip. We both know that. Why not Raine?" Melanie lifted the top off a gold box and took out a cigarette.

"There were others who had as much motive as Raine," Alana pointed out, putting her cup down and crossing her arms over her chest.

"True, but, according to the paper, the evidence points to Raine." She snapped a gold lighter and lit her cigarette, the smoke blurring her image for a moment.

"And if he was framed?" Alana's gaze narrowed as she watched Melanie carefully.

"Who would want to do a thing like that?" Melanie murmured, gazing back at Alana with wide eyes, taking another drag on her cigarette.

Alana wasn't fooled. There was triumph in those green eyes. "Someone who wants revenge." She paused, her voice low. "Someone who needs Raine's land."

Melanie stood and wandered toward the window, silent for a moment before turning to look at Alana. "That description fits you very well," she said, her voice filled with contempt.

"He rejected your offer for his land," Alana said, her palms on the counter, leaning forward.

"He said he would consider it. Twenty million in cash plus controlling interest in the corporation. How can he refuse?" Melanie said, a smug look on her face.

Alana was startled by Melanie's offer. Was she really willing to give Raine controlling interest in her father's company? "But I didn't hate Phillip enough to kill him. You did." At the glitter in Melanie's eyes, Alana knew she had struck a nerve. She pressed further. "You were very vocal about blaming Phillip for your mother's death."

Melanie stiffened, a palor under her tan making her face look almost yellow in the bright light of the kitchen. "That has nothing to do with this. We're discussing Raine's land." She paused. "What about Hilary? She made him an offer, too. She could have framed him, then planned to clear his name and persuaded him to accept her offer."

Alana straightened and walked around the counter. "That's exactly what I thought at first, but Hilary couldn't have framed Raine."

A belligerent look settled on Melanie's face. "Why not?" Her fists rested on her hips.

Alana watched Melanie closely. "On the news and in the article in the paper it said the police received an anonymous tip leading them to an empty bottle of liquid digoxin in Raine's locker at the club. Not many people have access to the lockers."

"That doesn't prove a thing." Melanie tossed her head.

"I saw you often enough with the club manager. It would have been easy for you to get the master key from him."

Melanie stubbed out her cigarette. "You don't know that for sure."

Alana took a step closer. "Last night when the police arrested Raine they said they received another tip, telling them they could find the motive for Phillip's murder at The Rain Forest restaurant."

Melanie waved a hand through the air. "What does that have to do with me?"

Alana was silent for a long moment. "I went to see Hilary before coming over here. I confronted her, but there was one important piece of information that she didn't know. You did."

Melanie brushed past Alana and picked up her coffee cup, filling it again, her hands shaking slightly. "What's this vital information?" Melanie gave Alana a mocking look.

"We met you in the restaurant, remember? You're the only one who could have called the police."

Melanie was absolutely still for a long moment, her face grim. "You have no proof."

Alana took a step toward Melanie, her fists clenched at her sides, the adrenaline flowing, alert to Melanie's every move. "You did it, Melanie. You murdered your father, and then framed Raine Bradburn for it."

470

Melanie threw back her head and laughed, an eerie sound echoing through the room. "No one would ever believe you." She tilted her head and pouted, her voice a mocking drawl. "I'm too dumb. Just ask anyone." An evil gleam lit her eyes. "They'll tell you. Hilary is the smart one. Not me."

"But you did it," Alana breathed, certain of Melanie's guilt. "You killed your own father. Why?"

Melanie's face contorted in anger as she slammed her cup down. "You want to know the truth? I'll tell you, because it won't make any difference now." Her eyes narrowed, her lips thinned. "He deserved to die." She leaned against the counter, facing Alana, her hands behind her. "He never took me seriously. He never had time for me." Melanie's face was filled with rage. "As soon as I was old enough, I slept with anyone I could find, making sure Phillip knew about every one of them. I adored my father but he couldn't be bothered. I showed him!"

Alana stood frozen, trying to assimilate what Melanie had said. "I'm sorry," she finally whispered. "But his indifference wasn't reason enough to kill him and frame Raine."

"I had plenty of reason to kill him." Melanie's face was grim. "He killed my mother. The night she drove off that cliff, he demanded a divorce." Her voice was venomous. "She left a note. She said she couldn't go on without him. The humiliation would be too much for her. Can you imagine that? You'd think she would have been grateful she was finally getting rid of him, but for some reason known only to her, she saw it as the ultimate disgrace. She took his favorite car and a bottle of booze and drove off that cliff. She was the only person who really loved me, and he killed her with his selfish disregard for her feelings." Her chin jutted forward. "It's your fault, too. You wanted to marry the bastard, and he was stupid enough to think that's what he wanted, too." She shook her head in disgust. "What is it that you have that makes an intelligent man so stupid?"

Alana was frightened by the cunning, evil look that radiated from those green eyes. "I didn't know your father had asked for a divorce that night. I never said I wanted to marry him."

"Not asked, *demanded.* There's a difference. I'll show you." She whirled around and stalked out of the room, leaving Alana no choice but to follow. After everything Melanie had said, she wondered what her next move should be. She should run while she had the chance, but she needed proof of Melanie's guilt. Melanie would never turn herself into the police voluntarily, and if Alana left and told the police what Melanie had told her, they'd never believe her.

Why hadn't she questioned Phillip about his wife's death more closely? He hadn't given her time to think about his wife in his hurry to sweep her off her feet and marry her. Raine's words came back to her. Phillip had offered her sexual services as part of the deal for Raine's land. Had Phillip thought of other 'deals' he could clinch with his beautiful young wife as part of the package. He had been possessive and jealous, but in all probability it was because he didn't want her to have any affairs he himself didn't profit from. The thought made her blood run cold.

Alana followed Melanie to a small room off the living room. Alana glanced around quickly. It was a well organized office. Another surprise. Melanie had her back to Alana as she opened a drawer. For a moment, Alana froze. Did she have a gun? When Melanie turned around, Alana relaxed slightly as Melanie handed her a sheet of paper.

"Look for yourself." Melanie rattled the paper, her voice harsh. "See what Phillip did to my mother." She thrust the sheet of paper into Alana's hands and then turned her back to Alana.

Alana read the note, written by an anguished woman, tormented by the fear of humiliation and loneliness. "I'm sorry about your mother, but I had no idea . . ."

472

"Forget it." Melanie's voice was harsh. She whirled around. "No one can hurt her anymore." Her hands were clenched at her sides.

Alana stiffened when she saw the rage on Melanie's face. "Why did you frame Raine Bradburn for your father's death?" It was the one piece of the puzzle that didn't fit.

"I included you in the frame, only they haven't found the evidence yet," she said. "You were the reason my mother died. I've planned all along to kill you just like I did my father." She picked up a silver letter opener, the blade gleaming as Melanie tapped it against her palm.

Alana took a step backward, fear threading its way through her mind and body. She had to get out. "I didn't know."

"I don't give a damn!" Melanie's voice was brittle as it rose with each word.

Alana backed away, letting the note slip from her hand. Melanie raised her arm and Alana saw the glint of a blade. She grabbed a lamp from the edge of the desk and threw it at Melanie, but the other woman easily sidestepped it, lunging for Alana.

Alana ran for the door, but Melanie was quick, jumping at Alana. Pain seared her arm before she knocked the letter opener out of Melanie's hand. Adrenaline pumped through her. Escape. She stumbled into the foyer, clutching her throbbing arm.

Melanie blocked her exit, a vicious smile on her face. "You're trapped, Alana. Who's the dumb one, now?" An eerie laugh echoed through the foyer.

Running into the living room, Alana felt lightheaded. She forced herself to concentrate on getting out of Melanie's house. Her leg caught the leg of a table, sending her sprawling onto the floor.

Melanie grabbed a blood red vase, raising it over her head, her body looming over Alana. "You can't get away from me!"

Alana rolled as the vase crashed to the floor. "They'll find you, Melanie," she managed to say, scrambling to her feet, working her way toward the glass doors and freedom. She tossed pillows, priceless porcelain, a wooden cigarette box, magazines, anything to distract Melanie, but the other woman laughed at her efforts.

"You'll be dead." Melanie picked up a crystal ashtray, her pursuit relentless.

Alana grabbed a lamp as she rushed toward the glass doors. She heaved the lamp at Melanie. Melanie jumped forward. The lamp grazed Melanie's shoulder. "Damn you!" she screamed, holding her shoulder with one hand, her eyes wild.

The blood on Alana's hands made them slippery and she fumbled with the lock on the doors. Out of the corner of her eye she saw the ashtray flying toward her. Falling to her knees, the crystal hit the door and shattered into thousands of glittering pieces.

Alana dragged herself to her feet, the glass shards grinding into her knees and the palms of her hands. Melanie grabbed a handful of Alana's hair and yanked her backward. Stumbling into Melanie, Alana jabbed the elbow of her good arm into Melanie's stomach.

"Bitch!" Melanie shouted, doubling over.

Alana staggered into the dining room. She swayed and almost fell before regaining her balance. Her arm throbbed, blood oozed from her knees and palms, and she was scared. "You won't get away with this." Her breath came in quick gulps as she looked over her shoulder.

"Yes, I will." Melanie was right behind her.

With a final effort Alana fled into the kitchen. The glass door opened easily and she stumbled outside, the glare of the sun blinding her for a moment. Melanie took a flying leap and tackled her, sending her crashing to the slate patio floor, the breath knocked out of her.

Melanie grabbed Alana's arms, but Alana recovered, gathering her remaining strength and rolling over to knock Melanie off balance. Scrambling to her feet, she had gone three steps when Melanie grabbed her hair again, jerking her to a stop.

Alana reached back, clawing at Melanie's face. "Damn you, Alana."

"Leave me alone!" Alana muttered, breathless as she continued to scratch and claw at Melanie. Melanie had the advantage with her hand wrapped around Alana's hair.

Melanie tripped Alana, sending her to her knees. Her knee pressed into Alana's back, dropping her to the ground. Alana tried to move, but Melanie grabbed her arms. She felt Melanie wrap something around her wrists and pull tightly. Melanie's silk scarf. She was exhausted and defeated as Melanie pulled her to her feet and whirled her around. The triumphant look on Melanie's face sent a shaft of white hot fear through Alana.

"Who's going to believe dumb old Melanie could possible think through a crime like this." She raised a hand and slapped Alana across the face. "I've wanted to do that for a long time" she murmured with satisfaction as Alana gave her an icy glare. "You can't escape now." She laughed again, her face inches from Alana's, venom in her voice. "You'll be sorry you ever heard the Hudson name."

Melanie pushed Alana back toward the house. "I hadn't planned on you being quite so smart. Your talents are wasted in business." She shoved Alana ahead of her through the house, stopping in the foyer.

Alana cleared her mind of everything but escaping certain death. She had to think, outsmart Melanie. Her hands were numb as she tried to loosen her bindings. "Why do you want all Phillip's money? You could live on the five percent."

Melanie forced Alana into her office, shoving her into a chair. Melanie opened a drawer and pulled out a small revolver, the metal gleaming in the palm of her hand. She smiled at the look of horror on Alana's face. "This is my insurance policy." A wicked light entered her eyes. "You want to know why I want it all? So I can destroy it! I won't be happy until Hudson Enterprises is in ashes, just like Phillip Hudson himself!" She slipped the gun into her pocket and grabbed Alana's arm, wrenching her out of the chair. "Where would you like to die? My swimming pool?" She shook her head. "Your apartment?" She tugged on Alana's hair. "Answer me, damn it!"

"You're crazy, Melanie!" Alana looked at her captor with scorn. Her head jerked from the blow of Melanie's hand. Alana might be a prisoner, but she wasn't dead yet.

Melanie grinned. "Of course! The perfect irony. I know exactly where you're going to die." She grabbed Alana and dragged her outside.

Alana struggled, but Melanie's iron grip made it futile. How could she escape and where was Melanie taking her?

When Melanie dumped her on the driveway and started the car, Alana was sure that she'd run her over. Her eyes closed, she tried rolling out of the way, blocking out the roar of the engine. The car screeched to a halt, and Alana forced her eyes open. The tires were inches from her head. Sweat poured from her body, her heart pounded painfully, and the blood rushed through her head, her breath coming in quick gasps.

Melanie got out, looming over her, her hands on her hips, her head thrown back in laughter. "I'm not going to make it that quick and easy." She dragged Alana around the side of the car, pushing her onto the passenger seat. Alana tried to free her hands, but the bindings were too tight. Her heart was in her throat when Melanie put the gun in her lap. "If you even think about screaming for help, I'll blow your head off."

Alana didn't doubt the threat was real. Melanie was going to kill her, just as she had killed her father.

Melanie headed up through the mountains. Alana knew where they were, but didn't know why. Melanie slammed on the brakes.

"Why are we here?" Alana asked, still struggling to free her hands.

"Why, this is where you're going to die!" She opened the door, looked around, and then hauled Alana out. "This is the cliff my mother chose for her death. Don't you think it's fitting that you should die in the same place?"

Alana's eyes widened. "You're going to push me off the cliff?"

Melanie shrugged. "Actually, I had hoped you'd jump. I suppose that's asking too much."

"You really are crazy." Alana couldn't believe Melanie meant what she said until she looked into the other woman's eyes. Melanie meant exactly what she said.

"You think so?" Melanie gave her that knowing little smile. "Perfect defense, don't you think? Unable to stand trial. Incompetent." She bent over and picked up the gun off the seat of the car. "How long do you think they'd put me in a nice, plush, private sanitarium? Six months? A year?" She touched the short barrel of the revolver to Alana's temple. "I'd be out, free and clear, and you're dead." A low guttoral laugh parted her lips.

"Melanie, don't do it. You might have had good reason to kill Phillip, but you don't have any reason to kill me. You'll never get away with it. No one would believe I would jump off this cliff." Alana was desperate. She was on an isolated mountain cliff with a mad woman who had a gun, intent on killing her. Alana looked around, her eyes wild. The only escape was the car and she couldn't drive with her hands tied behind her back. The scarf was beginning to loosen. She needed time.

"Of course they will. When I explain it to them." Melanie put the barrel of the gun under Alana's chin, forcing her to look into Melanie's glittering eyes. "You killed Phillip Hudson for the money. You wanted to marry Raine, but you were so distraught at the thought of your lover in jail and arrested for the murder you committed, that you resorted to suicide." She

477

grinned in triumph at Alana's frantic eyes. "You thought you were so smart. Ha! I'll admit I framed Raine, but only to prove you were the murderer." She licked her lips in satisfaction. "I'll be the one to clear his name, and he'll be so grateful that he didn't fall into your trap, he'll give me the land. He'll believe me, Alana. You know he will! You had the motive and the opportunity.

I'll destroy Hudson Enterprises and everything associated with it. It's perfect. I even get rid of you!"

Chapter Thirty-three

Raine looked up at the cloudless sky, squinting in the bright sunlight. He hooked his jacket over his thumb and flung it over his shoulder. It had been a hell of a long night and he was tired, but he had to find Alana and talk to her. The look on her face when Dan had confronted them in the parking lot had haunted him all night. To the casual observer she would have appeared calm and controlled, but Raine knew her better than that. Raine ran a hand through tossled hair. He wanted to erase the pain from her eyes and her heart. Dan had told him this morning that another empty bottle of liquid digoxin had been discovered in Alana's locker at the club. Someone was out to ruin them both.

Dan pulled up to the curb, his voice curt. "Get in, Raine."

Raine leaned his arms on the open window of the unmarked squad car. He frowned, growling, "Where are you taking me now? Back to the station?"

Dan shook his head. "I think I know who set you up and Alana is in danger."

T.J. pointed to the back door. "Get in or we'll leave you here. There's not much time."

Raine climbed into the back seat, leaning forward, his arms

on the back of the front seat, holding on as Dan pushed the accelerator to the floor and T.J. put the flashing red light on the roof and turned on the siren.

"What the hell is going on?" Raine demanded, a sinking feeling in the pit of his stomach. He knew T.J. and Dan too well. They were the calmest detective team he had ever seen. Tension filled the car as Dan wove the car in and out of traffic, never slowing down.

"We had a tail on Alana," T.J. said, turning slightly as Dan rounded a corner on two wheels. "We figured whoever was framing you, wanted her, too. With you in jail, she was vulnerable. Early this morning, as soon as we finished searching her car, she hurried over to Hilary Cummings' house." He looked at his notebook. "She was there for about fifteen minutes, and when she left, she was one determined lady, rushing over to Melanie Hudson's estate. Melanie tore out of there about an hour later." He paused, rubbing his temple, looking from Dan to Raine and back to Dan.

Dan gritted his teeth. "You might as well tell him the rest."

He rubbed his jaw. "When Alana didn't come out, they investigated. There had been quite a struggle, blood all over the place."

Raine paled. "Alana! Is she hurt? What happened to her?"

"We don't know," Dan answered, his voice tight. "Her car was there, but she wasn't. We're assuming Melanie has her."

"Where?" Raine demanded. "Where could she be going?"

"She headed for the mountains." T.J. snapped his notebook shut. "Dan thinks she might be headed for Halona Lookout where the first Mrs. Hudson drove off the cliff. That's where we're going to start looking. We've got squads checking some of the other lookouts."

Raine slumped back in his seat. He knew that Alana's life was in danger. "Can't you go any faster?" he muttered.

"Not unless we all want to end up in the bottom of that gorge," Dan replied, taking a hairpin turn on two wheels.

"What the hell was Alana doing at Hilary's and then at Melanie's?" Raine leaned forward, his elbows on his knees.

"I think she was going to try to prove your innocence." T.J.'s voice was dry as he pulled out his gun and checked it.

"How could she do something so stupid?"

"Her only thought was probably for you," Dan answered. "I wonder what she discovered that we didn't know."

"Phillip Hudson's killer," Raine said curtly.

Dan had turned off the siren a few miles back and now pulled to a stop. The three men got out. Dan pointed to the sign marking the scenic spot. "That's where she'll be if she's here."

Raine felt his heart stop and then thud painfully against his chest. His eyes were hard as flint as he looked at Dan, his voice hard. "What the hell are we doing standing around here for? Let's go get her!"

Dan pulled out his gun. "T.J., you cover the far end, and I'll work my way in on this side." He looked at his watch. "Five minutes and we rush her."

"What about me?" Raine asked. "You're not leaving me out of this."

"Come with me." Dan's voice was quick and decisive.

When they reached a vantage point where they could see the women, Raine's heart was in his mouth. Tension coiled in him like a tight spring, ready to explode. Melanie was dragging Alana toward the edge of the cliff, Alana struggling all the way. The sun reflected off the gun in Melanie's hand.

Dan glanced at Raine. "We don't have time to wait for T.J. I'm going to go out there and distract Melanie. As soon as you see a chance, you dive for Alana." Raine gave a quick nod, crouching low.

"Stop, Melanie!" Dan ran forward, his gun raised.

"Don't come any closer," Melanie shouted, her voice shrill,

one hand clutching Alana by the hair, the gun held to her temple with the other as she dragged Alana over the guard rail. "You come any closer, and I'll shoot her before I push her off."

"You'll go with her," Dan warned, not moving.

"No." She shook her head, a silly grin on her face. "I can fly. I push her and she breaks like Humpty Dumpty while I fly like Tinkerbell." She paused, her eyes narrowing. "I'll bet you don't think I can fly." She took another step closer. "I'll show you!"

"Don't believe her!" The desperation in Alana's voice tore at Raine's heart. "She said she'd pretend to be insane so she wouldn't have to go to prison. Don't believe her!"

Raine couldn't wait any longer. He jumped from the shadows, keeping as much distance as possible between Dan and himself. At least if Melanie took a shot at one of them, the other would be able to get her. The wind whipped at his hair, the sun hot on his face. His worst nightmare had never been as horrifying as this. "Let Alana go!" he shouted, drawing Melanie's attention.

She whirled around, waving the gun in the air. "What are you doing out of jail?" Her voice was brittle. "Don't come any closer!" She waved the gun at him and then Dan. "Stay away. I'll kill her just like I killed Phillip!"

He took a deep breath and smiled at Melanie. "If you kill her, you'll go to jail and you won't get my land. How can you destroy Hudson Enterprises without my land?"

Dan never took his eyes off Melanie and Alana, whispering to Raine, "Keep her talking." He signaled to T.J.

"You do want my land, don't you, Melanie?" He took a small step.

"You don't want to sell it to me," Melanie muttered, looking at Raine and shifting her weight, pulling Alana closer to the edge.

He tried to make his voice as calm as possible while inside he wanted to rush to Alana's side. Her face, knees, and arm were stained with blood, but her eyes were alert, wide with fear. "You must've misunderstood me. I said I would consider your offer. Your offer was brilliant. It was the best one I received."

"See, Melanie," Alana said, her eyes holding onto Raine like a lifeline. "He'll sell to you, not me. You'll have everything."

Melanie yanked Alana's hair and snarled, "Damn right I will. If I don't get that land, neither do you."

Dan took a step. "Stay back," Melanie warned. "I have to get rid of her." She moved another step closer to the edge, waving the gun through the air. Her eyes widened. "I know! Raine, you could be Peter Pan and I'll be Tinkerbell, and we can fly away together."

"I can't fly, Melanie." Raine tried to think of anything he could to distract her. T.J. emerged from the other side of the parking lot.

"You could teach me," T.J. said, making Melanie turn again.

While T.J. distracted her, Dan and Raine stepped closer. Raine watched Alana carefully. Although she was terrified, she seemed alert and controlled.

"Who are you?" Melanie demanded, shoving Alana to the very edge of the cliff. She almost lost her footing, loose stones crumbling and disappearing from sight.

Raine caught his breath, his eyes on Alana. One more move and Alana would follow the stones. He crept forward.

"Who are you!" she snapped, stamping one foot and waving the gun around.

"I've always admired you. You're the most beautiful woman I've ever seen." He didn't take his eyes off of her as Dan moved. "I've seen your picture in the paper, and I've seen you around town. I've always wanted to meet you."

Melanie preened under his compliments. "Well, I wish you

would have said something sooner. You're very good looking."
She batted her eyes. "What's your name?"

"T.J. Harris."

"What does the T.J. stand for?" she asked, openly curious
as she shifted her weight, her grip on Alana's head relaxing
slightly.

"Promise not to tell anyone?" he asked as Dan and Raine
inched toward Melanie.

"I promise." She giggled.

"Thomas Jefferson," he said.

Melanie threw back her head and laughed, shooting the gun
into the air. No one moved as the sound bounced off the walls
of the mountains. "I'd change my name." She sobered suddenly. "I changed my name lots of times, but I'll always be a
Hudson. Depressing thought, isn't it?" She gripped Alana's
arm, the gun at her temple. "Aren't you depressed that you're
going to die a Hudson?"

"Does this mean you don't want my land?" Raine asked,
praying that Melanie wouldn't pull the trigger.

Melanie looked at him and then back at T.J.. "I don't know."
She shook her head. "I can't decide which will give me the
most pleasure, killing Alana or destroying the company." Her
eyes were wide. "Can I have both?"

"You can't destroy the company if you're in prison." Raine
tried not to think of Alana so dangerously close to the edge.
Dan was just a few steps away from Melanie now. A flash of
red and green behind Alana alerted Raine. He met Alana's gaze
and the instant communication made him tense. He was ready;
his body coiled, his arms outstretched, his hands curved.

"Just let me get rid of her," Melanie said, her voice harsh
as she moved to push Alana over the side.

Alana screamed, "Now!" She jabbed Melanie in the side, the
gun going off and grazing Alana's temple as she stumbled forward, away from the edge.

Dan tackled Melanie and T.J. helped drag her back from the cliff.

"Damn you! You've ruined everything!" Melanie shrieked. She struggled with the men, biting and scratching. "She deserves to die! She killed my mother. How dare you put those handcuffs on me!" She kicked Dan in the shins. "My lawyer will have me out in minutes! I'll sue!" She screamed at T.J. "You tricked me!" She raised her arms and drove an elbow into his ribs. "You'll both be fired for this!" She stomped on Dan's foot.

Dan and T.J. carried her struggling and screaming obscenities toward the police car.

Raine gathered Alana into his arms. "Thank God, you're alive." He touched her temple, frowning when she winced. He lowered her to the ground, taking out a clean handkerchief and pressing it to the wound. "We've got to get you to a hospital."

"I'm okay." She closed her eyes for a moment and then opened them.

Raine saw the glaze of pain in her eyes, wishing he could take the pain away. "You are one very brave, very stupid woman." He wanted to crush her to his chest, tell her everything that had gone though his mind in the last twelve hours. He wanted to take her home with him and cherish her for the rest of his life. Alana stirred emotions he never knew he had.

Raine stood, Alana in his arms. "You're safe now, Alana. Nothing's going to hurt you."

Dan came back, looked at her and frowned. "We'd better get her to the hospital."

Raine nodded. "But not in the same car as Melanie."

Dan grimaced and shook his head. "I called for a backup squad. They'll be here any minute."

"No one ever gets the best of me!" Melanie screamed from the car.

Another squad pulled into the parking lot.

Dan looked at Raine. "You want to go to the hospital with her?"

Raine looked at Alana and then at Dan. "Try and stop me."

"You'll have to come down to the station to answer some questions and fill out a few forms before you're officially released." Dan looked apologetic. "You know I didn't want to arrest you."

"I know. We all have a job to do." Raine frowned. "What's going to happen to Melanie?"

Dan shrugged and looked over his shoulder. "I don't know. We'll have to get a warrant and search her house. I sure wish we could find the pharmacist who gave her the medication. It would strengthen our case. Right now, we just have her confession and a case of attempted murder." His lips thinned.

"But she killed Phillip! She admitted she did it!" Alana shook her head. "She can't go free." She closed her eyes. "She can't." Alana sighed as Raine eased her into the car, holding her as if she were a fragile piece of glass. "I won't break, Raine," she muttered, snuggling closer.

"If I didn't know that before, you sure proved it today." He cradled her close to his heart, a troubled look on his face. She needed him, whether she admitted it or not. He had seen it in her eyes, felt it as she clung to him for strength and comfort. The time she had spent on the edge of the cliff, hanging between life and death, would be etched in both their minds forever. Her head rested on Raine's chest. He cared for her, and she cared for him. Did they care enough to really trust each other, putting the past behind them, and starting out fresh?

When Alana awoke, she was startled at first to find she was in a hospital. Memories washed over her like a dam breaking. She sat up, her head pounding with the sudden movement. She touched her temple. A bandage covered the wound. Her head felt like the Lunalilo Freeway at rush hour. She collapsed back on the pillow. Slowly she raised her arms, but one was stiff. That was bandaged as well. Her palms were crisscrossed with scratches. She felt her face with her fingers. She must look a sight. A nurse came into the room and smiled down at her when Alana opened her eyes.

"How are you feeling, Mrs. Hudson?" She put her finger on Alana's wrist and looked at her watch.

"My head feels like it's going to blow up, and I ache in places I didn't know could ache, but it's nothing I can't live with."

"Good." She adjusted the blood pressure cuff. "The headache is from the wound to your temple. I'll see what the doctor ordered for you to ease the pain." She smiled again. "Are you ready for lunch?"

Alana looked startled. "What day is it?"

"Sunday." She took Alana's hand. "Squeeze my hand as hard as you can." She took the other hand. "You've slept through breakfast." She recorded the information on Alana's chart. "Mr. Bradburn stayed with you yesterday and has been calling every hour today."

Just then a doctor came in. Alana frowned. She had never seen him before in her life. "Who are you?"

"Collin Bentley, Raine Bradburn's physician. Raine called me yesterday. He didn't know if you had a doctor and asked me to take care of you."

Alana looked at him carefully as he scanned her chart. He looked to be in his mid-thirties, had blond hair, tiger eyes, and looked like a male model. His broad smile made her feel better immediately. She returned the smile. If he was Raine's doctor, he had to be the best. "We'll give you something to ease the pain."

"It's not necessary." Alana raised one arm, and flexed her fingers. "I'll be fine."

"You don't like medications?"

She shook her head with a rueful smile. "I think I've had an ulcer and haven't had enough nerve to go to a doctor. I hate pills." She sighed. "I suppose as long as I'm here, I should have that checked out."

He chuckled. "Mrs. Hudson, your 'ulcer' will go away in about seven months." His tiger eyes twinkled.

Alana gave him an odd look. "What's that supposed to mean?"

"You don't have an ulcer. You're pregnant."

"Pregnant?" She sat up, the color draining from her face, before she collapsed back on the pillows. She couldn't be. Oh, no. Oh, God. Pregnant. "No." She shook her head. A horrifying thought occurred. "How long?"

"I'd guess about two months."

Alana closed her eyes and wished Melanie had tossed her over the cliff.

"I know your husband has been dead for a few weeks, but at least you'll have his child." The words were meant to be consoling, but they chilled Alana. If she was two months pregnant, this baby could be Phillip's. Or it could be Raine's. She thought she had an ulcer and it was a baby!

She looked him square in the eye. "This is confidential information, isn't it?"

He looked startled. "Of course, but in a few weeks it won't be." He paused. "Are you thinking of aborting the pregnancy?"

Alana rubbed the sheet between her fingers. "I don't know. This comes as a shock." She took a deep breath, looked at the nurse and said, "Could I talk to you alone?"

He nodded and dismissed the nurse, pulling up a chair and sitting down. "What would you like to talk about?"

She struggled to find the right words. "How much did Raine tell you about me?"

A knowing light entered his eyes. "Quite a lot." He paused, speaking slowly. "The baby might be his."

"Yes." Alana closed her eyes. "Dr. Bentley, if I'm two months pregnant, this baby could be Phillip Hudson's. Or it could be Raine's."

"There are tests that will tell you the paternity of the baby." His voice was dry.

She opened her eyes, meeting his gaze with a mocking one. "With my luck, both men will have the same blood types. You know Raine. Can you imagine what his reaction would be to something like this? He'd figure I had trapped him as no other woman ever had. No thanks, I don't want to know now. I might think of getting rid of it, and then I'd have to live with the knowledge that I wasn't any better than Phillip." She shook her head. "Talk about a no-win situation. I seem to have more than my share lately.'

He gave her a thoughtful look. "Don't underestimate Raine. He cares a great deal for you. Maybe you should tell him and let him make the decision."

She laughed. "You may know Raine, but you don't know me. I'm too independent to let someone else make my decisions. I have to know what I want to do before I'd even think of telling Raine. He'd try to bully me into doing something I'm not willing to do."

"Like marriage?" he said with a grin.

"He just might come up with that idea," Alana said, her voice dry. She picked at the sheet. "I don't suppose you take care of expectant mothers."

"No, but my partner does, and I think you'd like her a lot. You're two of a kind." Had she detected a note of frustration? Good. No man that handsome deserved to have everything. "Would you like me to set up an appointment for you?"

"I suppose." Her voice was dry as she said, "Thanks for the good news, doctor."

"It is good news, Mrs. Hudson." He stood up and replaced the chair, standing next to her bed.

"Please call me Alana." She paused. "You won't tell Raine, will you?"

He shook his head. "The tests are confidential, and so is this conversation. I'd like to be your friend, though. I think you could use one."

"That is the understatement of the year." She rubbed her eyes. "I'm exhausted."

"Considering everything you've been though, you deserve to sleep for a week. I'll be in to see you in the morning. If everything checks out, you can go home."

"Thanks." She closed her eyes, but as soon as the room was silent, she opened her eyes, staring at the ceiling. Pregnant. One hand rested lightly on her stomach. She had always wanted a child of her own, and she wasn't getting any younger. This could be her last chance. She could support a child as a single parent. A frown marred her forehead. But if it had the Hudson genes, she was in trouble. She thought of Phillip's ruthless nature, his selfishness, his cold heart. She prayed this wasn't his child. Raine. She pictured Raine as a child, sturdy legs, dark hair and laughing eyes, proud and strong, a handsome child. When Raine found out she was pregnant, she knew he would feel obligated to care for her and the child. She didn't want him under those conditions. What if it was Phillip's child? Raine hated Phillip. He'd hate Phillip's child as well. One thing she knew for certain, she would have to know exactly what she was going to do before Raine discovered the pregnancy. He was too adept at getting his own way. He mustn't detect even the slightest hesitation in her decision.

There was a light knock on the door and Raine entered. He smiled down at her. "How are you feeling?"

"Like Moana Loa blew up in my head," she muttered.

He bent down and touched her lips with his. "If you only

knew how glad I am that you're alive." He reached out and traced her features with one finger. "When Melanie held that gun to your head, and I saw the fear in your eyes, I felt as if my heart was being ripped out of my body."

Alana lifted her face and met his gaze. "I was petrified, but knew I couldn't panic. I thought she was going to push me over the edge, and I wasn't about to go without a fight. Thank goodness all of you arrived when you did."

He sat on the edge of the bed. "I hope you didn't mind my doctor taking care of you."

She teased him with a smile. "A hunk like that? Are you kidding? He'd make any woman's heart beat a little faster."

"Hey! If I had known you were going to fall for Collin, I would have asked for some grizzled old bear of a medic."

"Thanks." She wished she could share her news with him. Under other circumstances it would have been the most wonderful moment of their lives.

"The doctor said you'd be able to leave in the morning, but you won't be able to stay by yourself. You're coming home with me for a few days."

She opened her mouth to argue, but he layed two fingers across her mouth. "No arguments. You've been through enough. Let me take care of you until you're on your feet again."

"What else did he say?" she asked, her voice wary.

"Just that you should rest for a few days." He shrugged. "What else should he say?" He paused, his gaze narrowing on her pale cheeks. "Is there anything else?"

She shook her head and let out a long sigh. "I just want to sleep." She yawned, touching his hand with her lips. "I should go home."

"You will be going home. With me."

She was too tired to argue. She closed her eyes. "What's going to happen to Melanie?"

"She's in a hospital being evaluated right now." He smoothed the hair from her forehead.

"Hope they put her away forever." Her voice was soft.

"I do too." His voice began to fade. "I'll be back, Alana. I'll take care of you. No one will hurt you again."

She wished it were true, but knew that he had the power to hurt her more than Melanie ever could.

Chapter Thirty-four

Alana sat in the shade, letting the trade winds soothe her aching body. Outwardly she looked tranquil, while inside her thoughts tumbled about. There was too much to think about, too many decisions to make, and so little time. At least she was out of the hospital. Raine had been so thoughtful and kind, that she wanted to cry. She wanted to tell him about the baby, but couldn't. She wanted to melt into his arms and let him make the decisions, but resisted that as well. She was exhausted from the effort.

She looked around her little deck. This apartment was fine for adults, but it wouldn't be the best setting for a child. She thought about the home Thomas and Jeremy shared. Maybe she could move in with them. An hour drive back and forth to work would be worth the effort if she knew the baby was being taken care of by someone who would love it, and Thomas loved children. Jeremy was a product of his efforts and his love. Sighing, she got to her feet and braced herself against the railing. She had to put these decisions in a priority. The first one had a deadline of ten days. Phillip's will. Knowing that she was pregnant made it even more important that she obtain Raine's land and take over at Hudson Enterprises. She had to provide for the future of this child whether it was Phillip's or Raine's. And when Raine found out about the pregnancy? She didn't even want to consider that.

She turned her head when the intercom buzzed.

Crossing the room, she pushed the button. "There are two men from the police department here to see you." Frank's voice was gruff. "Should I send them up?"

Alana smiled at Frank's protective voice. "Yes."

When Dan Maxwell and T.J. entered, Alana approached them, her hand outstretched. "Hello, Dan. I think we should be on a first name basis after everything that happened." She shook his hand and turned to the other man, her brows raised in question.

"T.J. Harris." He took her hand and clasped it in a firm grip. "It's good to see you walking around."

She smiled into his warm brown eyes. "Ah, Thomas Jefferson Harris," she teased, remembering how he had talked to Melanie. "Believe me, it's good to be alive." A shudder raked her body. "I don't ever want to go through something like that again."

"Could you answer some questions for us?" Dan took out his notebook and pen.

"Certainly." She waved them toward the chairs while she curled up in a corner of the sofa. "What do you want to know?"

"Why did you confront Melanie Hudson in the first place?" Dan asked, easing himself into the chair.

Alana was silent for a moment. "When you arrested Raine, I knew someone had set him up, but I thought it was Hilary." She looked at her hands clasped in her lap, then back at Dan. "I went to Hilary's house and confronted her. Her husband, Chandler, was there, too. I accused her of the tip sending you to the restaurant to confront Raine and me, but she didn't know that, well, ah, Raine and I were seeing each other. I knew then that it wasn't her."

"So you assumed it had to be Melanie?" T.J. asked, leaning one arm on the arm of the chair and rubbing the side of his nose.

"She's the only one I could think of at the time who might have had access to the lockers at the club. She had dated the club manager. Raine and I saw her at the restaurant the night he was arrested." She rubbed the back of her neck and got to her feet, wandering around the room.

"She admitted she had you followed by a private investigator. She was certain you would get Raine's land and that would have ruined her scheme." Dan paused. "Why didn't you call us?" Dan asked her, writing in his notebook and then watching her wander around the room.

"Didn't think about it until it was too late," she said with a long sigh. "I was so angry that she'd do something like that, I wasn't thinking very clearly. I did call when I was on my way to Melanie's, but you weren't at your desk."

"What happened when you confronted Melanie?" T.J. asked, his voice soft as he leaned forward.

"We had an argument." She gave a short laugh. "More like a battle. Her house must have looked terrible. She slashed me with a letter opener." Alana touched her bandaged arm. "I tried to get away, but the harder I tried, the worse it got. She managed to tackle me and tie my hands with a silk scarf she had worn in her hair." Alana paused. "She's a lot stronger than I would have given her credit for, and she's a whole lot smarter than anyone would have guessed."

"She dragged you out to her car?" Dan asked, shaking his head.

"She almost ran me over first." She shuddered. "That's the most frightening feeling of all, knowing someone wants to kill you, but not being able to do anything about it. And then when she had me on the edge of the cliff . . ." Alana looked from one man to the other. "I sure am glad you got there in time."

"So are we." Dan sat back. "Did she talk about Phillip Hudson's death at all?"

"She said she was glad he was dead. He deserved to die." Alana frowned. "She said I had helped kill her mother because I broke up her parents marriage. Evidently her mother left a note saying she was going to kill herself because Phillip had demanded a divorce and she couldn't stand the humiliation. Melanie must've loved her mother very much."

"My guess is that Melanie planned to kill you all along." Dan sighed. "Framing Raine was convenient to make it look like suicide. She could have you dead and maybe get Raine's land in the deal."

"And she made her father pay for driving her mother to suicide." T.J. nodded his head. "You're right, she wasn't as dumb as everyone thought."

Alana stood and paced back and forth in front of the windows. "What's going to happen now?"

T.J. and Dan looked at each other. Dan answered, his words carefully chosen. "We have enough evidence to charge her with first degree murder and attempted murder. After we arrested her, we searched her house and found the suicide note from her mother. We also found the name of a pharmacist in her desk. When we talked to him, he said Melanie had told him that her grandmother was in town, didn't have a doctor, and ran out of medication. He gave her the medicine. He'll have his license revoked, but it doesn't look like he knew anything about her plans. Melanie was in such a frenzied state, she was taken to a mental health facility for evaluation."

Alana looked at him for a long moment. "She told me she'd fake mental illness if she was caught. She said she needed a little vacation, and after six months or so in a luxury sanitarium, she'd be released. Is that true?"

"Possibly. It depends on whether or not the judge believes she's really incompetent. She killed Phillip Hudson, tried to frame Raine for the murder, tried to kill you, and won't spend one day in jail for any of it if she convinces the judge she's sick." T.J.'s voice was hard, his frustration visible.

"Could she really be out again in six months?" Alana trembled. She didn't want to think of another confrontation with Melanie.

"If she doesn't stand trial, she'll be there as long as she convinces them she's incompetent. When she's ready, she'll be released." Dan closed his notebook and stood up. "We'll do everything we can to see that she's convicted."

T.J. stood in front of Alana and put her hand on her shoulder. "She won't be around to bother you for a long time."

"I hope not." Alana had enough to think about without worrying about Melanie. "Do you think she did this by herself?"

T.J. and Dan exchanged a knowing glance. "No," Dan finally said. "We found the pharmacist, but how did she know about liquid digoxin, and that it could kill and look like a heart attack?"

"We may never know," T.J. said in a quiet voice.

Alana saw the two men to the door and closed it softly.

She turned and walked into her living room, sitting down heavily.

Looking over the papers, she finally took a deep breath and punched out the numbers to Raine's private line. When she heard his gruff hello, she almost hung up, but gripping the receiver, she said, "Hello, Raine."

"Why didn't you call me when you were ready to leave the hospital?" he demanded. "You were supposed to come to my house."

"You spent enough time hovering over me. I'm sure your work is piling up just like mine. I'm fine. Really. A little stiff and wobbly, but okay."

"Are you at the office?" he muttered.

"No," she told him. "I'm working at home."

He was only slightly mollified. "Don't overdo it."

Alana wondered how protective he'd be if he knew about the baby. "I won't." She cleared her throat. "Raine, I need to talk to you about the land."

"Can't you forget that damned land?" He ground out the words. "You were almost killed two days ago by a maniac. Can't you just relax?"

"No, I can't." Her voice shook with anger. "You have nothing to lose by forgetting about that land. I have everything to lose!"

"You wouldn't lose me." His voice was quiet.

"Raine, I don't have you," she answered him, suddenly sad. "Please, could we talk about the land one more time?"

There was a long silence and then he said, "One more time. Tonight. I'll come to your place." He paused. "Are you at your apartment or Phillip's house?"

"My apartment." Her voice was dry. "As long as you've set up the day and place, would you like to suggest the time, too?"

"Sure. I should be out of here by seven." He chuckled. "I kinda like having that land as a bargaining chip. If I sold it to you, what hold would I have over you?"

If you only knew, she thought to herself with a grim smile. "None," she replied sharper than she intended. "And if you don't sell me the land, you still don't have a hold over me."

"Always the independent lady." His voice was soft and seductive. "Two days ago, you weren't so independent."

"That's mean, Raine Bradburn." She remembered how good it felt to lean on his strength. "I'll see you at seven."

She quietly replaced the receiver. She buried her head in her hands. Raine Bradburn always got what he wanted. If only she could be certain she was pregnant with his child. . . .

* * *

Raine arrived at seven-thirty. Alana recognized the fatigue around his eyes, the deepened grooves around his mouth. "A bad day?" she asked, handing him a drink.

He grunted and slipped off his suit coat before taking the drink. "The worst. A barge sunk in a storm off Japan. Lost a whole shipment of transistors."

"Ouch." She watched quietly as he loosened his tie and unbuttoned the top button of his shirt.

"I didn't have time to go home and change. Sorry." He leaned his head back and closed his eyes.

"You haven't slept much in the last couple of days, have you?" Alana asked, a knowing look in her eyes.

"Not much." He didn't open his eyes.

"And you stayed at the hospital all night."

He grunted.

"Thank you." She watched as he sat up and leaned forward, his arms on his knees, swirling the ice in his glass.

He raised his eyes and locked her in the heat of his gaze. Alana almost broke under the intensity of it. She got to her feet and wandered to the bar, taking a bottle of white wine and then putting it back when she remembered the baby. She took a soft drink instead. "Raine, it won't work between us. We're both too independent and too strong. We'd fight all the time."

"But think of the fun of making up." He had moved behind her. He put his glass on the bar and put his arms around her, pulling her back against his chest. He rested his cheek on her hair. "We're good together." His palms rested on her stomach.

Alana closed her eyes and let herself sag against him for a moment. It would be so wonderful to be able to tell him about the baby, to be together, to share it. She loved him. She admitted it. She had never loved another man like she loved Raine Bradburn, and because she loved him, she couldn't tell him about the child. Not now. Steeling herself to the warmth and security of his embrace, she moved away from him. "Raine, we need to talk about that land."

"Ah, yes," Raine said wryly, "the land. How could I have forgotten? But what's the problem? I'll sell the land to you."

She blinked several times, wondering if her mind was playing tricks on her. She groped for a chair and collapsed into it.

"You will?" Her voice was little more than a whisper.

He raked a hand through his hair, a wry smile on his lips. "I don't understand it completely myself, but if we're to ever have a chance at a future together, the land can't be there between us."

"You're taking a big risk," she observed.

"I've taken risks before . . ." He wandered around the room. "It's a calculated risk," he said, turning to look at her, his hands in his pockets. "There are a few conditions."

Her heart sank. "What conditions?"

He stood in front of her, then leaned down, his hands on the arms of the chair again, his gaze boring into her, stripping her defenses and examining her very soul. He seemed pleased with what he discovered. "First of all, I'll sell the land to you, personally, not to Hudson Enterprises, and I'll make sure that you can't turn it over to the corporation. Is that agreeable?"

She nodded. The resort could be built. The will said nothing about the land being owned by Hudson Enterprises. It just said one of the three women had to have the deed. "Is that all?" She couldn't believe Raine would part with that property so easily.

"Aren't you even going to ask the price?" he taunted, his warm breath fanning her cheek.

She took a deep breath, steeling herself against the temptation to run her hands up his strong chest and brush the lock of hair that fell over his forehead. "What's the price?"

"After you meet the terms of the will, you'll sell me half of

Phillip's stock for half the market value, and I want a guaranteed seat on the board of directors." His voice was smooth, as if he were asking for a drink of water.

Alana's eyes widened. If he had half of Phillip's stock, the shares she already owned would make her the majority stockholder, but if Raine was the man behind the recent activity in Hudson stock, Phillip's stock might make him the majority stockholder. She would have to trust him not to destroy the corporation. Could she? "That's a big price to pay for one piece of land."

"You get Hudson's personal estate. What's it worth? Seventy-five or a hundred million? Plus, you'll get the money from the sale of his stock."

He had thought of everything. "If you had that much stock, you could vote yourself a seat on the board when there's a vacancy."

His voice was dry as he straightened, looking down at her with a knowing look. "There are three vacant seats right now. I want one of them."

"How did you know that?" she demanded, frowning up at him, wondering if there was anything he didn't know. The baby. He didn't know about the baby. That was still her secret.

He pulled her to her feet, his hands maintaining their grip on hers. "I told you a long time ago I know everything that goes on at Hudson Enterprises."

"So why take a place on the board if you already know what's going on?" She tried to concentrate on business, but he made it so difficult when he stood so close to her. How could she think about stocks and directors when his mouth hovered over hers, his warm breath on her temple made her heart beat faster, and the touch of his hands on hers sent a curl of desire though her body?

The heat of his gaze intensified those feelings until she was breathless. "Our personal relationship may be on hold, but I don't intend to sit back and wait for you to come to your senses. By being on the board, you'll never be able to put me out of your mind."

"That's unfair, Raine." Alana gulped, her eyes wide, swaying toward him.

"I never said I'd play fair." His gaze roamed over her face, noting the tilt to her chin, the rapid movement of her chest. One finger traced the lines of her face, the edge of her jaw, then moved over her shoulder and down over her soft curves. "There's too much of me that wants you any way I can get you, Alana." He bent down and touched her eager lips.

Without conscious thought she responded to him, opening her mouth to his thrusting tongue.

When he finally pulled away from her, his breathing was ragged.

She rested her forehead on his chest. "Have you been buying Hudson stock?" She had to ask.

"Why?"

"If you have, this stock will make you the majority shareholder."

"You'll have to trust me, Alana." His gaze was shuttered.

She took a deep breath. "You'll have to trust me, too, to sell you that stock after I have the land."

"Yes."

She searched his face. "Alright. I'll agree to your conditions. I'll have a contract drawn up in the morning."

"No contracts. This is between the two of us. It's a matter of trust." He gently kneaded her shoulders. "Agreed?"

"Agreed."

"And what about tonight, Alana?" His voice was a caress as his hands played havoc on her spine. "Do you want me to leave?"

She touched a finger to his lips. "Don't talk anymore, Raine. Kiss me."

Later, Alana sighed with contentment. She looked at Raine. He had fallen asleep. She loved him and she couldn't have him. Why did it have to be this way? How long would it be before he knew she was pregnant? She sighed. The entire island would know soon enough. It would make great headlines. Phillip Hudson's widow having a baby. The great countdown would begin. And Raine? She could only guess how he'd react, especially when he realized the child could be his or Phillip's.

Chapter Thirty-five

Alana stood before the board of directors of Hudson Enterprises with her future on the line and her heart in her throat. She straightened the jacket of her favorite white suit, mentally preparing herself for the task at hand. Taking a deep breath she looked down the table at the expectant faces. The only item on the agenda had been the Aloha Shores project. "I called this special meeting because Raine Bradburn has agreed to sell the parcel of land we need on Maui." She watched Hilary's expression turn from disbelief to outrage. Fury was close behind.

"That means you inherit the lion's share of father's estate!" Hilary shouted, jumping to her feet, shaking her fist. "I should have known you'd find a way to take advantage!"

"Phillip is the one who made up the terms of the will, not me," Alana reminded her, keeping her voice low, her cool voice. "Sit down, Hilary, and listen to the rest of what I have to say."

Hilary glared at her but slowly returned to her chair, her eyes filled with hatred.

Alana spoke again, her voice low and controlled. A wave of nausea swept over her, but she forced herself to remain calm. She could get sick later. "There are several stipulations."

Robert Somers frowned. "Can we live with them?"

"That's up to the board." She leaned forward, her palms on the table. "He will only sell it to me, not the corporation." She knew that would cause a stir and it did. Alana waited for the uproar to die down.

"What else does he want?" Ben Adams asked, tracing the company logo on the paper in front of him. "Bradburn would never let that land go so easily."

"You're right, Ben." Alana straightened, pushing her hands into the pockets of her skirt. "After I inherit Phillip's stock, I have to sell fifty percent of it to him for half the market value."

Murmurs moved around the table like the restlessness of palm trees before a storm. "Fifty percent of his stock!" Hilary erupted, banging her hand on the table. "My father wouldn't let him step in this building, and now he wants stock."

"Your father isn't alive," Robert pointed out, his voice hard. "Right now we're without the three top officers in the corporation because your father wouldn't share the power. We've got so much money invested in that resort already, we can't afford not to meet his conditions."

"Do you realize how many shares of stock that is?" Ben said, making notes on his paper. "If he's the one buying stock on the open market, it could make him the majority stockholder."

"Raine agreed to pay half the market price for all shares," Alana said. "And once it's in my possession, I can sell all of it if I want to," she reminded them.

"If Bradburn owns the corporation, it will be absorbed into his own company." Charles Reese's voice was firm. His square jaw jutted forward. "You're selling out to the enemy."

Alana's voice was dry as she said, "The enemy has a vital piece of land he's willing to sell for the first time." She watched him squirm, her gaze narrowed on him. "We can't build the complex without it." She thought of Phillip's methods as he tried to obtain the land. Physical violence and sex. Raine was being generous in his offer. "It's the first time he's even considered an offer from Hudson Enterprises. He could hang on to that land and watch us flounder," she pointed out.

"What did you have to do to get him to make that offer?" Hilary asked, her voice filled with bitterness. "Did you use the same tricks that worked so well with my father?"

Alana's eyes bore into her. She was sick and tired of having to defend her abilities. She'd be damned if she was going to cower or even explain her actions. Her eyes flashed, strength and determination in the set of her features. She might look fragile, but no one would mistake the steel in her voice. "That kind of remark has no place in this board room, Hilary, and you know it. If you can't confine your remarks to professional ones, you're free to leave." Hilary's mouth snapped shut as she lowered her gaze.

"If he sells that land to you," Robert said slowly, "then you have fulfilled the terms of Phillip's will."

"It's unfair!" Hilary pounded a fist on the table. "I'll appeal. That money will be tied up for years!"

"You'll tie up the company as well," Robert pointed out. "Phillip's personal estate and the company are tied together. If you take this to court, we'll stagnate and die. The stock would be worthless, and a great deal of money in his estate would be used for legal fees."

Hilary gave him a cold look. "Well, we all know what side you're one!"

Jeff Marino, director of public relations, tapped his pencil on the pad of paper in front of him. "We've put a lot of time and money into publicizing this project. If we have to scrap it, we're going to look incompetent. Anyone starts hearing rumblings of in-fighting and our stock takes a nose dive." He paused, looking from Alana to Hilary. "Let's face it, this fiasco of a will of Phillip's and Melanie's indictment for his murder isn't doing our image any good. The negative publicity has made our stock drop three points already. It's Alana's choice. She's right. Once she gets the stock she can do anything she wants to with it. Let's get on with business."

Ben looked at Alana. "Any more demands?"

Alana took a deep breath. "He wants a guarantee of a seat on the board."

"What?" said Hilary, on her feet. "If you go along with this, you're all stupider than I thought!" Her gaze locked with Alana's. "And as for you, dear stepmother, I'll make sure you pay for stealing my inheritance."

Dan looked at Hilary. "Are you through, Hilary, or would you like one of the security men to take you home?" The steel in his voice got through to her.

She lifted her chin. "I'm through." Her gaze raked over Alana. "For now. This isn't the end." She returned to her chair, her back ramrod straight.

Alana watched her with a feeling of forboding. Hilary was a force to be reckoned with. She looked down the table. "Well? Those are Raine Bradburn's conditions and the only ones under which he'll sell the land."

Robert looked at her for a long moment, choosing his words carefully. "You didn't have to bring most of this to a board vote. If he sold the land directly to you, you're the majority stock holder. You could have authorized the sale of your stock and used your shares to vote him onto the board."

Alana's gaze was clear as she said, "You're right. You all could have resigned in protest, throwing the company into even more turmoil. I also could have gotten that land, sold the company, and lived a very comfortable life." She paused, her gaze flicking over Hilary and Charles. "Despite what some people's opinions are, I do have personal integrity and good business sense. I want board approval because it's impossible to work with a board that isn't in agreement with major decisions like this. Railroad Raine Bradburn onto the board and we'd never accomplish anything. If he had a good idea, you'd automatically vote it down because it came from him, and if you wanted something, he'd fight you all the way." Her voice was dry. "We had enough of that with Phillip. Look what happened. We had to focus on a fight for one little piece of land instead of looking ahead at new projects. I don't want that to happen again." She paused again and looked down the table, meeting each board members eyes directly. "I'm not selling out to the enemy, and I'm not selling this company. I want this brought to a vote. If you vote this down, the company will survive, but no one inherit's Phillip's stock and once it's liquidated, we'll never be a major force in international business. If you vote for it, we move ahead and make Hudson Enterprises bigger and more profitable. It's up to you." She scanned the room again. "Are you ready to bring this to a vote?"

Robert's voice was strong as he said, "I move we accept Raine Bradburn's terms for sale of his land as a vote of confidence for Alana."

It was quickly seconded and voted on. The only negative votes were Hilary and two other board members, Charles Reese and David Jones.

"We'll have to have a special shareholder's meeting to fill the three vacant seats. We'll have to nominate two more people as well as Raine. If you have any recommendations for those positions, please let me know." She looked down the long table. "Are there any more questions or comments?" When there was silence, she said, "I think we've accomplished quite a bit this morning. Thank you for your vote of confidence. I see great things for this corporation if we work together."

"I move we adjourn," Hilary muttered. It was quickly seconded and voted on.

The room emptied quickly as directors from out of town were anxious to spend some time on the beach before heading back to colder climates. Others were just anxious to avoid any further confrontations. Charles was anxious to see Melanie.

A few minutes later Alana looked around the empty room and took a deep breath. The enormity of the responsibility confronting her made her light headed, but the challenges were exhilerating! She had the opportunity to prove she had earned her place on the board by hard work and good business sense.

Her hand touched her stomach. No matter who the father was, this was *her* baby, a chance to love and be loved in return.

After coming so close to death and adjusting to the new life growing inside of her, she was ready to face the future.